CHAPTER 1

A MURDER IN

The Crypt Keeper's Keys had a
the dank, claustrophobic tav
Arvum's most vilified and malicious
leaders to anti-Sagedom freedom fighters. It was rumoured that
many an unsavoury campaign had been drawn within the same
walls where assassins lingered to execute their bounties, and where
prostitutes lingered to execute their charm.

Centuries after the collapse of the Sagedom, the Crypt
Keeper's Keys had become more of a tourist attraction, now there
was seemingly less to oppose, and folk across the Arvum would
journey countless miles in pursuit of an overpriced drink, just
to sit in the booth where an ancient war criminal once plotted
against the government.

That's not to say that it didn't still lure in the familiar crowd
from decades long past, to stir trouble and conjure devious plans,
and tonight was no exception.

Storms were frequent on the east coast of the Arvum during
the spring and Rosensted was bracing under the wrath of intense
winds and heavy rain. With little else to do in such conditions,
it seemed that half the town and her mate were sheltering in the
Crypt, and getting merry to the backdrop of a lute-playing bard.

In a quiet nook, furthest from the music, Benjamin Denvillier,
whose attire was as handsome as his features, raised a toast to his
companions of the Covenant of Creation.

"What a backwards lot you all are," he slurred, beer foaming over the lip of his tankard, "but I'd be damned if I could find any better across the Arvum." He paused for a moment, then added, "Sages know I've tried!"

His subordinates laughed loudly, though the sound barely registered in the raucous tavern.

"With a little help along the way, our numbers are stronger than ever. Take my friend, our newest recruit, Horse Leg over there..." He gestured to a summer elf sitting uncomfortably at the table.

"It's Reishir," the summer elf replied in an annoyed tone.

Benjamin ignored him. "He joined us only a week ago, suffering a rotten leg and harbouring an immense hatred for the Sultan. Well, thanks to me and the Contact, he has an unrelenting hunger for revenge and a nice new leg!"

"Yes, a bloody horse's leg," Reishir muttered, taking a hearty swig of ale.

"Let's hope he doesn't crap like a horse!" called out Harlan, a young spring elf with a perfectly bald head.

This encouraged further laughter.

Reishir whipped out a sharp, narrow blade and held it in front of Harlan's neck. Harlan didn't so much as flinch.

"Quiet, squid, or I'll have your head."

"Now, now, Horse Leg, we all give and take in equal measure. Lower your sword," Benjamin said calmly, with an authority that could not be ignored.

Reishir remained for a moment before sheathing his sword.

When the energy had calmed, Benjamin continued. "The Contact has been most pleased with our disruptions to the canal and I can only commend you for your unwavering efforts. What was it you spoke to the Kelnish? *Sil'yhab forlein*? For them, indeed, the worst is yet to come. But, for us, I foresee a very

IN THE
HEART
OF A
SOULLESS
VESSEL

SIMON BATSMAN

CRANTHORPE
— MILLNER —
PUBLISHERS

First published by Cranthorpe Millner Publishers (2025)

ISBN 978-1-80378-271-3 (Paperback)

www.cranthorpemillner.com

Cranthorpe Millner Publishers

For Laurie.

As I write this, you are 6 days old, it is the middle of the night,
and you are fast asleep on my chest.

When you read this, you will be probably be at school so...
have you done your homework?

MARROW MYRE

THE FAR SEA

THE NEAR SEA

THE MYRE OF MAW

THE PARISH OF YORE

YORE VILLAGE

VALLEYS OF YORE

GREAT FOREST OF AULDEN

THE PARISH OF AULDEN

PORT WIDOW

WHISTLING LAKE

SWIRLEYBUCKET

THE PARISH OF ASERAE

ASERWELL

THE DIRE CLIFFS

FARWAY FOREST

FERRYMAN'S CROSSING

THE PARISH OF BEALE

RIVER RACKEN

HAMLISH HEATH

WYCHWOLD

THE INFANT MOUNTAINS

BEALE CAIRN

MOUNTAIN FOOT STABLES

ASERAE'S LIP

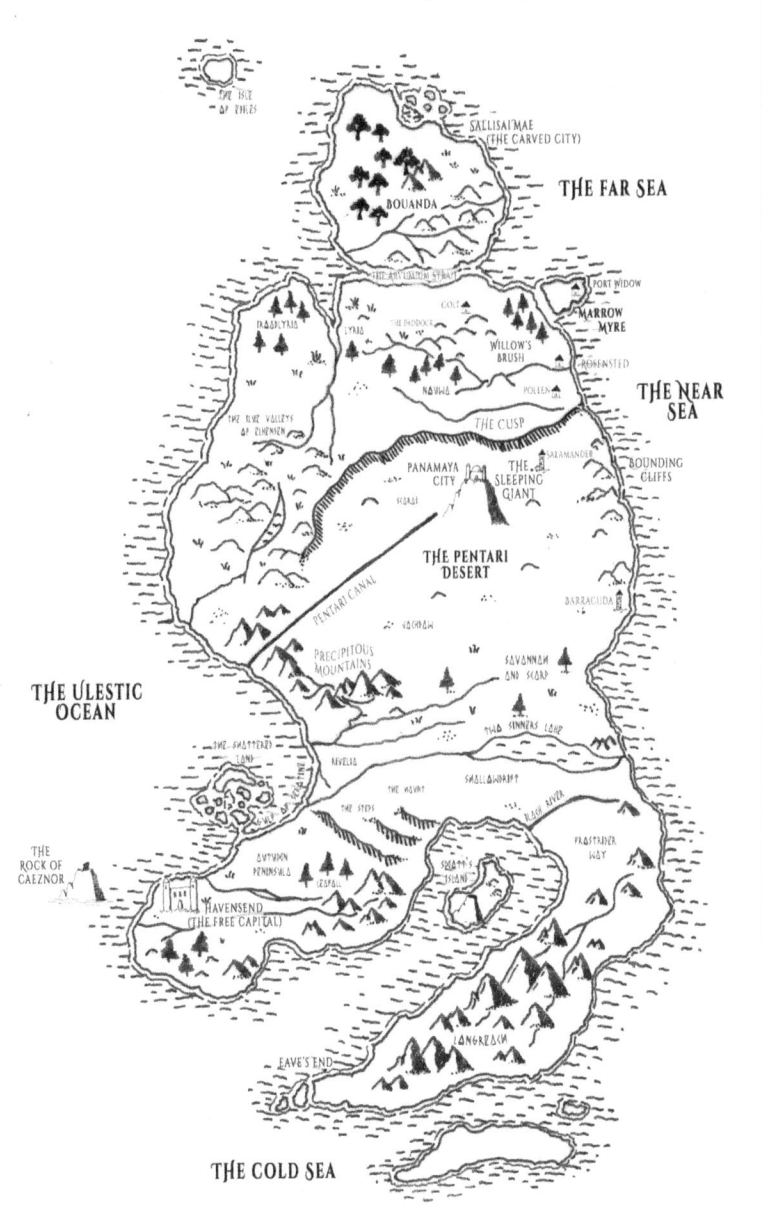

THE ARVUM

THE ISLE OF TREES

SALLISAI'MAE
(THE CARVED CITY)

THE FAR SEA

BOUANDA

THE ARVARIUM STRAIT

PORT WIDOW

MARROW MYRE

FIGGLYRIS

THE PADDOCK

LYRIA

GOLT

WILLOW'S BRUSH

ROKENSTED

THE NEAR SEA

NAVIIA

POLLEN GAT

THE BLUE VALLEYS OF CIMMERIA

THE CUSP

SALAMANDER

PANAMAYA CITY

THE SLEEPING GIANT

BOUNDING CLIFFS

SCARI

THE PENTARI DESERT

BARRACUDA

PENTARI CANAL

VACHHAW

THE ULESTIC OCEAN

PRECIPITOUS MOUNTAINS

SAVANNAH AND SCARP

TWO SINNERS LONG

THE SHATTERED LAND

NEVELIS

SHALLOWDRIFT

THE HOVEL

WOLF OF ARGENTINE

THE SEDS

BLACK RIVER

FROSTRIDER WAY

THE ROCK OF CAEZNOR

AUTUMN PENINSULA

SESPALL

SEBAT'S ISLAND

LONGREACH

HAVENSEND
(THE FREE CAPITAL)

EAVE'S END

THE COLD SEA

CHARACTERS OF THE ARVUM

Fjona Sarsen –*Sage in training*
Perciville Harper – *Sage who was alive 274 years ago when the Sagedom collapsed*

MARROW MYRE

Dharla Sarsen – *mother to Fjona*
Ascerat Sarsen – *father to Fjona*
Todie Farren – *cleric of Wychwold and Fjona's childhood friend*
Evelyn Tussel – *friend of Fjona and Todie*

PANAMAYA CITY

Ayermune Dhaller Sé – *Sultan of Panamaya City*
Oolia Khamun – *Steward to the Sultan*

THE ARCHIVUS

Kaikura Kendi – *Scholar at the Archivus and companion to her sandkat, Bobassa*
Daemund Newblood – *Warden of the Archivus*
Sialah Bouwer – *Proprietor of Intellect at the Archivus and Kaikura's mentor*
Isiah Fethen – *Proprietor of Intellect at the Archivus*
Lappili – *Curator at the Archivus*
Desmée – *Curator at the Archivus*

THE NOBLE GUARD OF THE SULTAN

Sigmund Kheller – *General of the Noble Guard*
Beric Lahsilli – *Captain of the West Division*
Lais Stone – *Corporal of the Fourth West Division*
Elian Sole, Callis Holden, Fayne, Cedarman and Lisbelle Bracker – *Rangers of the Fourth West Division*
Storm'Dune – *Ranger of the Captain's Division*

ROSENSTED

Benjamin Denvillier – *leader of the Covenant of Creation and brother to Lucinda*
Lucinda Denvillier – *assistant leader of the Covenant of Creation and sister to Benjamin*
Feldin – *Lucinda's ward*
Reishir (Horse-Leg) – *member of the Covenant of Creation*
Bosmar Fodd – *a friend of Perciville Harper*

THE ROCK OF CAEZNOR
Prior to the collapse of the Sagedom 274 years ago

Herak Siadonis – *Sagen Master and father to Santhé*
Santhé Siadonis – *powerful Sage who absorbed the Eight Afflictions*

UNKNOWN

Marseiha

lucrative future. Yes, there is much more work to do, but tonight, we must drink to those left behind, drink to what lies ahead of us, and drink to fortify the kinship that has brought us, this covenant, together."

As Benjamin raised his glass, his attention was swiftly stolen as the door to the tavern burst open and a forceful gust billowed inside. It was so strong that, for a moment, even the bard was distracted and performed a couple of dissonant chords before rediscovering his fingers.

Two hooded figures stepped into the quiet tavern, soaked through from the rain. Nearly every face turned to them.

The first figure pulled back her hood, a tangle of voluminous green hair cascading over her shoulders. "Don't stop on my account," she said with a silken voice.

"Lady Denvillier, please come through! Your brother awaits," said the kind, elderly proprietor of the tavern who was quick to greet her at the door.

"Thank you, Maurice," Lucinda replied. "Come, Feldin."

Feldin kept his hood on and followed Lucinda around to the rear of the Crypt.

"Lucinda, how nice it is that you could join us," Benjamin said, then kissed her on both cheeks. "Though I must admit, we were expecting you a little sooner."

"It was a job I simply could not rush," Lucinda replied coldly. She turned to address the bandits. Most of the men and at least two of the women were sitting up straight and adjusting their shirts to appear half presentable. "It is apparent that many of the Kelnish workers have fled the construction and their progress has been greatly inhibited. You must be very pleased, not least because my little assignment proved to be something of a success also." She gestured to Feldin. "Show them."

"Of course, my lady," Feldin croaked, extracting a small parcel

3

from deep within his cloak. With pale, scaly hands, he unwrapped the paper to reveal a sizeable copper key.

"Very fine work, Lucinda," Benjamin said, reaching out to take it.

Lucinda slapped his hand away. "I will hold on to this for the time being," she said firmly. "We wouldn't want it getting into the wrong hands, after all."

Benjamin turned a little red in the face. "True enough."

There was a moment's awkwardness until Reishir's new limb caught Lucinda's eye.

"I see we have a new member. Is this handi— sorry, *leg*-work of your notorious *Contact*?"

"No, actually. I stitched a horse's leg onto him myself!"

The bandits laughed again, their joviality cut short as Lucinda shot them a stern look.

"So your Contact was happy to help with *that* then?"

Benjamin shrugged. "Why the interrogation? Look, Horse Leg came to me with a problem and we solved it. Now, my dear, take a seat, order some wine and let's discuss your visit to the big city!"

As Lucinda settled beside them and the evening wore on, the members of the Covenant of Creation slowly deteriorated into a desperate state of drunkenness.

Much of the Crypt had quietened down and the bard had progressed to playing some gentler, slower songs to mirror the mood.

My seaward girl met my hometown wife,
Met my city mistress on a winter's night,
Met my lover's daughter and my Lady Right,
And that foxy whore; not so very tight.

Met my countess, duchess, sage and queen,
And that stableboy I shagged last spring,
Suffice to say she was not pleased,
When I came to bed with little seed.

There was a rumble of laughter from the remaining folk, who were slumped in chairs around the singer.

The Denvilliers and the bandits had stayed in the same booth for the entire evening and were a balanced mix of boisterous drunks and resting-one's-head-on-the-table drunks. Benjamin and Lucinda were, of course, the former. They muttered between themselves as was like them, particularly after a jug or two of wine.

"Father would be proud of us," Benjamin slurred.

"Mother would be ashamed," Lucinda retorted, then broke into giggles.

"Too long have we been *repassed*!" He just about managed to form the words.

"*Repassed*?"

"Re... *prassed*?"

"Repressed!" Lucinda realised.

"Yes, repress—" Her brother groaned, his eye twitching in the low light. "Soon, we'll be celebrated." He leaned in close to Lucinda and whispered, "The Contact says we're going to start quite the revolution!"

Lucinda smiled proudly and asked, "Tell me, how exactly do you intend to do that?"

For a moment, she thought her brother was going to reveal everything, but rather disappointingly, as always, Benjamin simply replied, "You know I can't tell you that..." before slumping back in his chair, thick red wine sloshing out of his jug and over the table. "After all—"

Benjamin suddenly gagged, his words cut short.

"Whatever is the matter?" his sister asked.

The conscious bandits turned their eyes to their leader and watched as a narrow slit appeared across Benjamin's neck, seemingly from nowhere.

His eyes widened with terrified realisation, and with dwindling strength he held his throat. Dark blood seeped between his fingers as he gasped helplessly for air.

Lucinda shot to her feet. "Benjamin!" she cried hysterically.

"Hel... p... me..." He managed to squeeze out the words, though his life was draining like the blood pooling around him.

All the bandits, even those who had been asleep, got to their feet and wielded their weapons: knives, swords and axes, though, as they surveyed the tavern, there was no sign of their assailant. In fact, the room was largely deserted and the remaining punters around the singer were oblivious to what had happened.

"What are you waiting for?" Lucinda screamed at them. "Find whoever did this!"

Nobody moved.

"Now!"

Commotion ensued as the bandits, Reishir and Feldin among them, dispersed around the empty tavern, weapons raised aggressively. The bard swiftly ended his set and disappeared through the door with his lute, while the stragglers suffered a bombardment of interrogations from the Covenant.

Maurice had ducked behind the bar and was fondling a stone charm for good luck while tables and chairs were thrown about, somewhat superfluously.

Meanwhile, in the booth, Lucinda knelt down next to her brother. Tears streamed down her pale cheeks.

"This was never supposed to happen. You're going to be okay," she said shakily.

But Benjamin knew only too well when his sister was lying.

CHAPTER 2

THE WISTFUL-EYED PIXIE

The moss-covered pebble rose several feet in the air, then hung there as if it were being held by string. It began to rotate steadily, then drifted smoothly towards a clay beaker placed precariously on a worm-eaten log. Gently, the rock floated downwards until it was only an arm's length above the beaker before suddenly losing control and plummeting into it, causing the beaker to tumble from the log and shatter on the hard trunk of a tree.

"For Aserae's sake!" Fjona cursed, whacking her Raw Wand against her leg in frustration.

"Better," Perciville said, using his staff to dematerialise the beaker, creating a new one on top of the log. "You're losing—"

"Focus, yes, I know," interrupted Fjona through gritted teeth. "Can we try something else?"

Perciville scowled at her. "Yeah, sure," he said in a voice rich with sarcasm, "let's just forget this basic teaching exercise and move on to something more complex, like conjuring a unicorn that will speak sweet nothings in your ear and bake bread in a—"

"Yes, yes, Harper, I get your point," Fjona said, rolling her eyes. "Let's try again..."

She took a deep breath, then lifted her wand and pointed it towards the pebble. After several days of relentless practice, Fjona still found the sensation of energy coursing through her body and into the wand to be extraordinary, even a little unsettling.

A pale, leafy light smoked out of the wand's tip, then seemed to fade into nothingness. Fjona could feel the energy latch on to the pebble like a fish caught on the line and she began to gently lift it off the ground.

As had happened countless times before, it drifted several feet up and bobbed towards the jar.

Fjona could feel a stray hair tickling her nose, but she didn't let that distract her. She refused to lose her concentration for even a heartbeat. This time, the mossy pebble descended into the mouth of the jar.

The moment it dropped, the jar erupted in a ball of fire.

"What the...?" Fjona turned to Perciville, her jaw wide open.

The sage was keeled over in laughter, clutching his staff.

"Very funny, Harper," Fjona said sourly.

"I couldn't resist! Look, anyway, you did it!"

"So does that mean we can finally leave Willow's Brush?"

"No..." Perciville replied.

"Well, why not? What are we waiting for?"

"I've told you."

"Not really. All you say is that we can't leave until I'm ready. Well I think I *am* ready. Besides, the Arvum is in danger and we're wasting time."

Perciville, clearly only half listening, conjured an electric shock to kill a black squirrel that was halfway up a tree. Picking it up by its limp tail, he said, "You do not decide when you are ready. In fact, I don't even decide when you are. Believe it or not, it is the Tree of Birth who decides, and only when it does will we be able to leave. Now, would you like some breakfast?"

Fjona stared at the dead squirrel. "You're kidding, right?"

Before she knew it, Perciville had conjured a fire with a spit and had used his staff to skin the small rodent. "This is all we have so unless you have a better idea...?"

"Than eating a bushy-tailed rat?"

The sage shrugged and proceeded to pierce the squirrel on the spit.

Wordlessly, Fjona dug into Perciville's satchel and extracted a knife.

"I saw some rabbits up above the creek yesterday. Big too."

"How is a rabbit any better than a squirrel?"

Fjona rolled her eyes again before heading for the woods.

"Be careful out there, Miss Sarsen. We've already seen what the pettywolves can do and they are way down the food chain."

"I think I'll be okay this time..." she replied, waving her Raw Wand and knife at her companion before disappearing into the woodland.

It was a crisp morning and the mossy dew was sparkling in the cold light that peered in through the canopy. Forest birds could be heard singing up in the branches and, somewhere in the distance, some sort of predatory animal was roaring its dominance. What predatory animal it was, however, Fjona could not discern.

"Perhaps a bear?" she wondered as she followed a brook that took her in the opposite direction. As she made her way up to the creek, Fjona was wrapped up in her thoughts. "What does he mean the Tree of Birth decides when I'm ready? I have a wand and I can already do the art of manipulation. What more can it want?"

She paused, then pointed her wand at the brook. With seemingly little effort, a fountain of water spiralled up out of the stream like a snake. It climbed to the length of her forearm and remained there until Fjona released it and it gently folded back into the waters.

"Not ready? Please!" she muttered, then determinedly continued walking.

The stream meandered along a rocky course, occasionally interrupted by small waterfalls and tributaries and, before too long, Fjona had walked to the top of the creek. The stream had widened into a river and was lined by steep cliffs on either side.

Sure enough, as she looked beyond the creek, Fjona could see the entrances to a busy network of burrows and, nuzzling around the bushes, a number of large rabbits. At least a dozen with richly coloured coats of dark browns, soft whites and black. They were foraging for berries and leaves with no care in the world, as if neither Fjona nor the pettywolves could cause them any harm. In fact, one or two of the rabbits were likely bigger than some of the pettywolves and no doubt as quick.

With the knife in hand, Fjona snuck up to the edge of the burrows and watched keenly from behind a tall, pointed rock. A grey rabbit, no more than a knife's throw, was picking redberries off of a thorny bush.

Fjona raised the knife, took aim. She narrowed her eyes and steeled herself. Then, just as she released her knife, a small golden figure popped up on the rock in front of her. Distracted by the intrusion, Fjona's knife sailed through the air and pronged into a tree – the family of rabbits dispersed in a clamour of paws, disappearing into the burrow.

"Thank you very much!" Fjona said frustratedly, collecting her knife, then searching about her for the miniature intruder.

Whatever it was, it was sitting on the rock giggling sweetly to itself. Bathed in a piercingly bright golden light, it was difficult for Fjona to make out exactly what she was looking at, but it looked like a tiny person, no bigger than her own head. On closer inspection, the golden figure had a pair of flimsy silken wings and wore a modest dress of cream-coloured leaves and vines. She had a pretty face and a warm, charming laugh.

"Who are you?" Fjona asked, startled as the glowing figure hopped up from her perch, then floated up to a high branch in a tree behind it. "Are you a fairy?"

No reaction.

"A nymph?"

Still nothing.

"How about a pixie? Are you a pixie?"

The golden figure leaped down from the branch with a tumult of laughter.

"So you are a pixie! Well, my name is Fjona, I'm new here," she said as the pixie hopped about her, inspecting her Raw Wand and tussling her hair. "You scared away my breakfast," Fjona added in a tone of mock reproach.

Unfortunately, the pixie didn't take the chiding well, for she promptly started to cry, then sombrely floated off towards the woods.

"Wait! I'm sorry, I didn't mean to upset you!" Fjona called, making chase. "Please, little pixie! Wait up!"

Not for the first time, Fjona found herself running through the bracken and branches of Willow's Brush, though it was somewhat refreshing not to be the one running away this time.

Up ahead, she could see the faint glow of the pixie hopping from one tree to another. The pixie was whining and sobbing as she navigated the branches and worked her way deeper into the forest.

"Please! I really am sorry!" Fjona cried out, though her apology was unheeded.

The morning dew was beginning to evaporate and a cold mist had formed a sparkling blanket as Fjona climbed a steep bank, taking her ever further from the creek.

"There you are! Look, I'm sorry little—" She cut herself off when she realised she was talking to a completely different pixie, with a disconcertingly mischievous look on her face. "Your friend, did they come down here?" Fjona asked. "I'm trying to apologise, you see. I think I hurt her feelings." She paused as she caught sight of her pixie further into the forest. "Never mind, I see her!"

As she began to run again, the new pixie accompanied her and led the way through the labyrinthine wood. Then another appeared from the undergrowth, and another from high up in the trees.

Before Fjona knew it, she was surrounded by the glow of dozens of golden pixies, bounding along the branches and floating through the air. They all seemed to have the same goal, to reunite Fjona with their sobbing companion.

The throng of pixies were chatting and laughing sweetly. It was a cosy sound and Fjona couldn't help but smile as they headed to a wide opening in the trees.

There, sitting on a rock in the middle, was Fjona's sad golden pixie. Her arms were wrapped around her knees and her head was dipped.

Fjona cautiously stepped towards her. "Hi," she said quietly, "I'm really sorry for upsetting you. I hoped you might forgive me."

She reached out a tentative hand, but before she could touch the pixie, it suddenly went very quiet.

Fjona held back. "Are you okay?"

Then the pixie turned instantly on the spot. She started to laugh again, but not sweetly. It was piercing and maniacal, and the surrounding pixies had picked up the cry too. Her face was gaunt, her eyes red and veinous, and her head was tilted as she smiled with pointed, razor-like teeth.

Fjona stumbled back, clutching her wand in her hand.

The golden glows of the pixies turned to a purply black and a coldness stirred in the air.

A new sound could be heard above the laughter. It was deep and guttural, almost sticky. The leaves around the glen started to rustle and Fjona could track something moving around her. Light yet firm steps of multiple legs tapped against the ground.

The steps seemed to stop immediately before her, hidden behind a wall of vegetation that glistened with slime, as if an army of slugs had traversed it.

There was a moment's silence; even the pixies were holding their tongues. Then, from behind the bushes, an enormous hairy black leg appeared. It was twice Fjona's height, and easily her width.

Another appeared alongside the first and thumped against the floor, quickly followed by a giant spider-like head.

Soon, the whole beast stood angrily before her. It had six legs in total, and a long thorny tail, like that of a scorpion's, which hung over its swollen, prickly body. Two large eyes, each with a smaller eye beneath them, stared through Fjona, and atop its head it wore a crown of white spines.

The beastly arachnid opened its mouth to reveal a spiral of sharp teeth, dripping with a shiny mucus.

Fjona slowly retreated, keeping her eyes on the four staring back at her.

On heavy legs, the beast bounded up close to her, towering above Fjona. It roared from deep inside its belly and dribbled viscous slime over her. It was ready to pounce.

Instinctively, Fjona aimed her wand at the beast's jaw, but managed only to conjure a wisp of smoke that did little to deter it.

As she took a step back, Fjona tripped on a rock behind her and fell onto her rear, fortunate enough to evade the beast's tail as it swung at her.

Around the glade, the pixies were goading on the beast with piercing cheers and chatter.

A leg swiped at Fjona, narrowly missing her, and lodged in the earth beside her, followed by another which landed on her opposite side. She was trapped between them and only able to shuffle back a little.

The beast leaned over Fjona. Her eyes were tightly shut and she held her Raw Wand outstretched above her, delivering as much energy to her hand as possible.

She could hear the creature chewing on its gums, then the sound of it spitting. Fjona expected to feel hot, clammy saliva pour over her, but when she tentatively opened her eyes, she found that a perfect sphere of mucus was suspended just beyond her wand.

Amazed, but determined not to lose control of it, she thrust her Raw Wand towards the beast and the mucus exploded over its face, temporarily blinding it, and allowing Fjona a moment to escape from beneath its legs.

The beast cried out in agony as its own venom burned through its eyes, and it attempted to wipe it away with its front legs.

Fjona could feel her shoulder burning and realised that the slime it had previously dribbled on her had eaten a hole in her cape and was now dripping through onto her skin.

She hurriedly pulled off her cape and shirt, left in just her vest, and saw that her shoulder was red raw. The pain was agonising, but the threat of the beast had not yet subsided.

Although unable to see, the monster clumsily waved its legs and tail about in a frenzy, and its scream echoed around them.

Feeling a little more confident having already injured it, Fjona used the art of manipulation to lift a sizeable boulder. She was able to latch on to it and just about raise it from the ground, though it felt heavy and barely moveable through her wand.

She knew it was only a matter of time before the beast returned to her, yet no matter how hard she tried, she could not raise the boulder any higher than her knee.

Fjona gasped in exasperation as her strength waned and she lost connection. The beast turned to her and charged forward with its tail raised, raring to strike.

Before it could, however, it was pushed away by a powerful,

invisible, though deafening, force. It was thrown onto its back, a safe distance away from Fjona. A burst of energy then shot into the beast from behind Fjona and ravaged its body like electricity.

For a while, the monster continued to writhe and twitch until, eventually, it stopped and lay dead in a heap in the middle of the glade.

"What did I tell you about not being ready?" Perciville scolded. "Did you think I was joking? Are my teaching methods ill-fitted to your almighty needs, oh great Fjona Sarsen? Thought you could seek better guidance alone, did you? The audacity! Engaging in a one-sided battle to the death with a Mother? Sages save me! Did you really believe that you could take on a Mother, of all creatures? What in the Arvum is the matter with you?"

"A what?" Fjona asked.

Perciville ignored her, his tone swiftly shifting from angry to elated as he gestured to her wand. "Look!"

In her hand, the lesser branches of her Raw Wand were beginning to shift, wrapping around the middle. They intertwined and weaved among one another and Fjona could feel them twisting beneath her grip. The branches became ever tighter – then, as they stopped moving, they glowed pale white for a moment.

"It seems something good has come of your foolishness," Perciville mused.

"I'm not sure I'm following," Fjona said. "What was that thing? What happened to my wand?"

"Here," Perciville replied, pointing his staff at Fjona's shoulder. It glowed red at the end and Fjona's skin began to heal. "Left much longer, the venom from a Mother would likely have necessitated amputation."

He conjured a small cup of water and handed it to Fjona, who nodded in thanks.

As she drank, the sage continued. "You wouldn't be the first person to have been lured by Wistful-Eyed Pixies. Had I not intervened, they would most likely be feeding on you by now. As it happens..." He gestured over to the beast, which was now swarming with pixies, all hungrily tearing into its flesh.

Fjona shuddered. "How can something so sweet-looking be so ugly at heart?"

"This is far from unusual in the animal kingdom!" Perciville replied with a laugh. "The same way a cub becomes a bear, and a baby becomes an assassin. It all comes down to survival, in the end. Be that as it may, your cunningness to disable it has earned you a Woven Wand!"

Fjona acknowledged her wand. It was longer and thicker with the entwined branches. Even just holding it, the wand felt more powerful.

"The second progression in a long line of manipulative instruments and, best of all, you are now ready to leave Willow's Brush," Perciville explained.

It suddenly dawned on Fjona what the sage had been telling her all this time. "You mean we physically couldn't have left before, even if we'd wanted to?"

Perciville nodded.

"And the Tree of Birth was waiting for me to prove I was capable enough before it would allow us to leave? By advancing to this... Woven Wand? That's what it was waiting for?"

The sage nodded again and recited, "'Only with a Woven Wand may a sage be permitted to leave Willow's Brush'. That is what was taught at Caeznor. What has it been, a week? That's pretty good going. Same as me, as it happens. There have been tales of sages waiting years before their wands progressed and, let me tell you, they were scarcely among the most talented of sages in the end. You should be very pleased."

"A rare compliment," Fjona acknowledged. "So, how will I progress further?"

Perciville took Fjona's hand and led her back towards the woods, away from the festering pixies. "As a general rule of thumb, it takes twice as long to progress to the third instrument as it did to the second. So, if you keep up your practice, in two weeks or so you may have a proper wand."

"That's it? Keep up the practice? More of the same?"

Perciville shook his head and smiled. "Miss Sarsen, nothing will ever be the same."

CHAPTER 3

BEYOND THE FOG

Marseiha had spent what had felt like a considerable amount of time searching the chapel for another hidden door. Her efforts had proven to be fruitless, though at least she had become desensitised to the gloom that had taken over.

She had tapped on every brick in hopes of finding another concealed chamber like the bell tower, and even reluctantly upended every rotten pew, but it was all in vain. Marseiha seemed to be trapped between some kind of monster in the corridor and a ghost inside the marble altar.

Her mind cast back to the two iridescent meteors, which had somehow become free of the stained-glass window above the door, then disappeared high above her, piercing the ceiling in a dazzling display of red and blue. Perhaps, somehow, her ringing of the bell had released them... and, in doing so, stolen the light from this deathly place.

She stared up at the grand window, now baring only a wilting tree and pile of bones, and an idea came to her.

She quickly glanced around at the other windows, trying to pick out the least disturbing. She settled for the image of the ships out at sea. Sure, the burning ships were sinking into the depths of a red ocean, but it was less unnerving than any of the other frames, and at least death was only implied.

Marseiha wasted no time. Starting with the pew nearest the window, she dragged the bench up against the wall. It was heavy and strained every fibre of her body, but she was spurred on by the prospect of escaping.

She grabbed another and, with yet more might, managed to lean it against the first and push it part way up the wall, lessening the distance between the window and the floor. Then again with another pew, and another, before barely managing to drag the next one up onto a second tier.

Before long, she had precariously stacked enough benches for her to scale the wall and, just about, clamber up to the window. She made the ascent, feeling one or two of the pews wobble as she climbed, but she was soon able reach the narrow sill.

"Okay," she said, detaching the mirror from her belt – the mirror which had already opened a door and that Marseiha hoped would now open a window.

With as much force as she could muster from her position, Marseiha whacked the mirror against the glass. It reverberated up her arm and shattered the mirror itself, but failed to leave even a chip in the window.

She hit again, screaming as she exerted all her strength and, after several powerful attempts, the window began to crack. A fracture split off from the nearest corner and splintered up into the middle of the frame. She smiled then hit again, and again, and again.

The crack grew ever bigger and Marseiha was certain it was close to breaking. In fact, in the middle of the frame, she could just see beyond the window where a small hole had appeared. She aimed at it, steeled herself, then threw the mirror with all her might at the hole.

Sure enough, the mirror penetrated the glass and the window shattered before her. Her movement, however, had destabilised the benches and, as Marseiha clung on to the sill, the pews beneath her collapsed leaving her swaying from the wall.

She yelled again as she pulled herself up onto the ledge.

The air outside was surprisingly stagnant, she realised, as she sat down on the edge of the window and gazed out at a vast ocean. It was strikingly blue beneath a cloudless sky without even a speck of a passing ship or island over the horizon.

"A chapel on the coast?" Marseiha said to herself, trying to remember if she knew of such a place, though nothing came to her.

Now that some of her strength had returned, there was a new problem to address. The chapel had been constructed on the very tip of a high cliff meaning that the drop down to the beach was greater even than the height of the wall. Falling from the wall alone would surely have resulted in a few broken bones at best. Down was simply not an option.

Marseiha studied the outer wall as best as she could from her position. A short way beneath her, there was a lip that ran along the edge of the wall, presumably the top of a frieze. If she could just reach it, she may be able to follow it around to the opposite side of the chapel where she may be able to climb down. It wasn't the most ideal alternative, but her choices were somewhat limited.

Carefully, Marseiha poked a leg over the edge of the sill and stretched as far as she could until she was just able to tap the frieze. Then, squeezing her back as tightly to the wall as possible, she dropped.

"Don't look down," she whispered to herself, judiciously keeping her head up and taking short, nervous breaths.

The lip was relatively deep, though Marseiha's toes just crept over the edge. Still, there was enough room for her to steadily sidle along the seemingly pristine white wall as it curved slowly around its vast circumference.

Soon, Marseiha found herself bending around the wall and away from the cliff below. She felt hopeful that maybe there would be a tree or something else for her to climb down as she worked her way along the frieze.

Her expectations came to an abrupt halt as an enormous crenelated wall loomed high above her. It appeared to divide the tip of the coast and was aligned so that it abutted the chapel. At the end of the fortified wall was an immensely tall, multifaceted tower adorned by hundreds of arrow slits.

To Marseiha, it seemed somehow familiar, but she could not place it.

The sound of crumbling stones caught her attention and she turned to see the lip, where she had just walked, beginning to collapse.

"No, no, no, no..." she repeated as the disintegrating frieze spread towards her.

Marseiha started to shuffle with more urgency, unperturbed by her toes slightly overhanging the ledge. At first the frieze seemed to disappear steadily, just a gentle fluttering of rubble disappearing to the cliffs, but before long, it seemed as if the entire chapel was falling apart behind her – as if her escaping it had triggered it to collapse in on itself. The way the chapel wall was falling was almost graceful, like it had been built out of sand. Even the glass windows seemed to disintegrate into fine dust.

Not that Marseiha had the time, nor the inclination to consider this. She was much too focused on trying to keep her footing and quietly praying that she may be able to get onto the wall if only she could make it to the other side.

The collapsing frieze had nearly caught up with her and now she was having to battle her way through debris falling from above.

Her mind raced back to the face she had seen in the painting and a pit opened up in her stomach as she realised it may no longer be trapped behind that door.

There was nothing she could do about that now but keep sidling along the chapel.

Then hope was on the horizon. She reached the point where the crenelated wall joined the chapel. Not only that, but for whatever reason, someone had hung a rope down from the wall and it dangled tantalisingly close to the chapel.

Without so much as a moment's hesitation, Marseiha leaped for the rope, praying that it could take her weight.

No sooner had she vacated the lip of the frieze did it collapse behind her, and Marseiha found herself swinging idly, grazing her knee against the rough masonry of the crenelated wall.

Using her feet as breaks against the stonework, the rope steadily lost momentum and came to a gentle halt.

Marseiha clung to the rope with all her remaining strength, then began to ascend yet another wall, though this one was far taller than the previous and with absolutely nothing beneath her to break her fall. She pushed that thought out of her mind and kept her focus solely on her hands as, little by little, she dragged herself higher.

All the while, the once idyllic chapel was crumbling into a heap of sand only a short distance from her, and Marseiha was hopeful that whatever cruel affliction had caused it to collapse would not spread into this wall.

Further she heaved, as the rope burned into the palms of her hands, her arms aching in sharp pulses as if they may pop out of their socket at any moment. The air felt thinner nearer the top too, though it may just have been that Marseiha's lungs were struggling to keep up with her. Her legs felt like dead weights and her abdomen screamed with tension, but still Marseiha forced herself to persevere.

Then, just as the final reserves of her energy were about to concede, she looked up to see the top of the wall only a short distance above her.

Little remained now of the chapel but a mountain of sand and rubble, though it was obscured by a thin sheet of mist.

Marseiha cried into the silence as she pulled herself up and over the edge of the wall and lay on her back against the cold stone, clinging for air like she had clung to the rope.

She lifted her head, just a little, to observe her surroundings. Deciding it was safe and that there was no one else around, she lay back down on the ground to rest.

When eventually the adrenaline had settled and she was able to breathe normally again, Marseiha pushed herself up onto her legs and wandered about the top of the wall.

Along the side where she had climbed, she was able to see through the mist and out across the empty ocean. Towards the chapel, the wall appeared to abruptly stop then continued on the other side, and at the opposite end was the immensely tall tower that Marseiha had seen from the frieze.

She crossed over to the leeward side of the wall and was surprised to find that it was completely concealed by a dense, grey fog. There may have been an entire metropolis beneath her and Marseiha would have been none the wiser, especially as it was deathly quiet at the top of the wall.

As was becoming a common theme, her options were limited and Marseiha, on weary legs, headed towards the tower.

The top of the wall was completely barren with not even so much as a few discarded tobacco leaves or a forgotten coat. It seemed less like no one had been up there for a while, and more like nobody had ever been up there at all.

For Marseiha, the most important thing was to find a safe way down and get further inland, away from this chaotic place.

Further surprise met her when she eventually made it to the tower. Despite its enormous height, the tower was just a single, empty room but for a plain, rectangular chest in the middle. It was lit up by pockets of light that squeezed through the arrow slits, all the way up to the ceiling, just visible from the ground.

The chest was long, about the length of a coffin, with a simple flat lid that was barely discernible from the rest of the box. It appeared to be made of stone, like a tomb, but lacked the ornamentation that would usually have decorated a place of rest.

As Marseiha inspected the object, she noticed a slight crease, where the lid met the container, was faintly glowing. She ran a finger along it. It was cold and sent a disconcerting shiver down her spine, but at the same time it was deliciously enticing.

She placed her hands near the top of the chest and pushed. Little by little, golden light spilled out as the lid eased back. Her arms pulsed with exertion and she was forced to squint as the light burst out of the stone chest.

Then, after all her efforts poured into her arms, the lid fell and clattered onto the ground. The explosive impact echoed all the way up the tower before it faded into cold silence.

Soon, the intense light began to dissipate and Marseiha was able to see what lay at the bottom – a long wooden staff inlaid with swirls of jade that twisted up the shaft towards the head. At the head were four curved hooks that folded towards each other to form a rough sphere, and, beneath it, two arms spiralled out of the neck and encircled the head.

The wood was smooth, dark ebony of exquisite carpentry.

Before Marseiha could even reach in to touch it, the staff rose out of the chest by its own accord, then rotated upright and hovered before her. She was compelled to grab it and, no sooner had her hand touched it did a wave of memories flood into her.

This was her staff and within her clutches were powers beyond comprehension.

She had abilities that exceeded those of her peers, whoever

they were, and a hunger to be revered and empowered in equal measure.

There was a darkness inside of her too; she could feel it, knocking on the door of her soul and begging to be let inside.

Perhaps it would all make more sense to her had her memories restored any sense of identity, but that remained hidden like a sheaf of parchment flattened between two tomes on an enormous bookshelf.

With great purpose, she left the tower and returned to the wall.

She innately held her staff high above her, felt tides of energy wash through her body and watched as an eruption of green light exploded out of her staff and illuminated the landscape.

When the power subsided, so too had the fog and, not for the first time, Marseiha was beyond surprised at what lay on the other side of the wall.

CHAPTER 4

THE VILLAGE OF COLT

Now that Fjona was no longer under the protection of the Tree of Birth, it didn't take long for her and Perciville to find their way out of Willow's Brush.

They stood at the top of a stony ridge with their backs to the forest, looking down to a small village in the near distance.

"I've completely lost my bearings. Is that Rosensted?" Fjona asked.

Perciville scoffed. "Rosensted? We should be so lucky! No, I'm afraid Rosensted is a way further south. That down there is Colt, a small farming village. In centuries long past, new aspiring sages would stop over to recuperate after escaping Willow's Brush. They didn't always get it as easy as you…"

He began to descend the steep bank, kicking up loose gravel as he went.

"As easy as me!" Fjona exclaimed, following in his footsteps. "Are you kidding? Or perhaps you've already forgotten about the pettywolves, the walking corpse, the… Mother, was it? Not to mention the dying, putrid tree that gave me my wand!"

"You never mentioned that the Tree of Birth was dying."

"You never asked!"

Perciville looked pensive for a moment, remaining quiet until they neared the base of the ridge. "Be that as it may, your experience was vastly better than many of your predecessors. There were rumours of one sage, many thousands of years ago, who spent three years wandering around Willow's Brush before his wand progressed. Three years of total isolation and evidently lacking the skills to do much with the art of manipulation. Can't remember his name... anyway, by the time he did get out, he was clinically insane and had lost all touch with the Arvum."

"What happened to him?" Fjona asked, though she already sensed where this story was headed.

"Apparently a spring elf cleric nursed him back to sanity and he threw his wand in the Arvumium Strait."

"Oh, a happy ending then? I thought you were going to say that he couldn't become accustomed to the world outside of Willow's Brush and took his own life."

Perciville grinned. "Not quite! Although they say he developed a deep-rooted obsession with his discarded wand, dived into the strait one night and drowned. Washed up on the beaches at Sallisai'Mae. Anyway, let's see if we can finally get some breakfast."

Fjona paused, stunned by Perciville's callousness, and watched the sage jovially cross a narrow bridge that led into the village.

Colt was an unusual place. There was only a smattering of buildings: mainly houses, an inn and a couple of shops, but every one of them was vast in comparison to those on Marrow Myre, with the exception only of the Paddolgolian Brothers' General Store.

Furthermore, the architecture was exquisite and, frankly, bizarre. One house had a wide ground floor and was connected to a first floor by only a narrow staircase which seemed far from sufficient to hold it up... and yet it did. It was like balancing a brick on a pin, upon another brick.

Their neighbour's house was a similar unlikely design, though taller still and, so far as Fjona could tell from the ground, had a roof garden with several trees.

Not only were the houses unusual in style, but they also represented a range of fine building material. One was constructed of smooth sandy stone and supported by curved ebony beams that criss-crossed the façade, another out of blue slate and topped by a golden thatched roof.

There was one house adorned with marble pillars, decorated with intricate carvings of local flora and fauna.

Every building along the single wide street shared this same meticulous beauty. Many were fronted with flowers in bloom and delicately trimmed hedges. One house had incorporated a stream which flowed between the walls and was brimming with fluorescent purple fish, while another had waterfalls flowing endlessly down the walls from a spring on the roof.

Even the road itself was properly paved with clean red stones that followed around to a stable at the furthest end of the village.

It was idyllic and bountiful, as if an artist had been commissioned to create their perfect, nonsensical vision of a village and this is what they had come up with.

Such perfection and yet there was an unsettling feeling in the pit of Fjona's stomach.

"Where is everyone?" Perciville mused.

It was true. There was no sign of anybody. Not even so much as a broomstick or an empty tankard. No sound of children playing or the clucking of a brood of chickens.

"Is Colt normally this quiet?" Fjona asked.

"I haven't stopped by for many years, but it was bustling the last time. A street market, music, hundreds of visitors..." Perciville trailed off as he glanced around at the vacant buildings.

They came to a halt at the far end of the road where the Colt Inn occupied a dishevelled courtyard. Dried grass came up to Fjona's knees and wilting flowers drooped around the vine-covered walls.

Being only a single storey, the inn was much smaller than the houses although it did have a substantial clock tower above it, indicating that it was approaching midday.

"Listen," Fjona whispered.

Faintly, voices could be heard coming from inside the inn.

As Perciville opened the door, raucous conversation spilled out from, it appeared, the entire population of Colt.

"We must act now!"

"We'll all be dead come the winter!"

"Winter? We'll all be dead come tomorrow!"

The entrance hall to the inn was by no means a big space and squeezing in all the villagers did it no favours. They were gesturing and yelling, doing all they could to be heard over one another, though it was far from clear as to who they were addressing.

"We can't just kill 'im," a Marrowborn man shouted into the fray.

"If we don't, he'll kill us first," a young spring elf retorted.

Perciville slammed the door behind him, startling everyone inside. They all turned towards the entrance with a mixture of gasps and screams.

Fjona felt her cheeks flush.

Once the commotion had died down, an awkward quietness hung in the air.

Typically, Perciville was the one to break it. "Sorry to interrupt, but I don't suppose we could get something to eat? My companion and I are rather famished."

A few dozen blank faces stared back at them.

"Who is it?" somebody called from the back of the crowd, and as Fjona watched, a tall, stern-looking autumn elf, owing to his rust-coloured skin, pushed his way through the rabble. He glowered at them through dark eyes, his jaw as tight as a stingy man's wallet. "You're not welcome here, outsiders!" he hissed through clenched teeth.

"Maybe we should go?" Fjona murmured, gently nudging the sage, but Perciville was too stubborn to take heed.

"That braised duck you used to do here was delicious. Oh, and a milk-coffee would go down a treat! Fjona...?" He turned to her as if expecting her to make an order.

She did not.

"Did you not hear me, louse? We don't welcome outsiders here," the elf repeated, taking an intimidating step towards the pair.

He was certainly muscular, and Fjona, despite knowing the strength Perciville contained in his staff, could feel sweat forming on the palms of her hands.

"Outsiders helped build your town," Perciville replied. "Heck, I helped build this town!"

"We care little if you mixed mortar or carved wood; Colt no longer welcomes you." The elf moved closer still, a hand resting on the rusty axe in his belt.

Perciville seemed completely oblivious, and persisted. "Mixed mortar? Please! Too archaic for my peoples. Now either you, my big buffoon, step aside so that we may have something to eat or I will move you myself."

The autumn elf snarled and drew his weapon, just as Perciville pulled his staff from behind his back. Though knowing there was little she could do, Fjona whipped her wand from inside her pocket, just in case.

The axe swung down, meeting an invisible wall several feet from Perciville's head as the sage pointed his staff towards the elf. Around the room, the hubbub was beginning to escalate, with angry and frightened villagers raising their voices in alarm.

The elf's eyes narrowed in confusion as he once more attempted to swipe at Perciville's head.

Again, his axe rebounded off the shield, issuing a drum-like reverberation.

As the autumn elf adjusted his position, Perciville fired a short, sharp bolt at his leg and the elf crumbled to the floor, twitching in pain.

He may have gone on to inflict serious pain to the elf, had a controlling voice not captured the attention of the entire inn.

"Stop this now!" it yelled from deep within the room.

Perciville looked up to the sound of creaking and watched as the crowd gently parted.

Through the middle aisle, a heavily aged island elf hobbled slowly towards him. On one side, she leaned on a stick connected to a single wooden-spoked wheel that rolled slowly with her cautious, uneven steps.

Her eyes were clouded and her hair was grey and thin, but otherwise she appeared to be surprisingly vital.

When she finally approached Perciville, she looked him up and down – at his face, his robe, and the staff in his hand.

Her face portrayed no emotion, merely careful, meticulous calculation.

Then, as she slowly turned on her wheel, she uttered simply, "Come." Her tone was firm and authoritative and she headed back down the aisle.

"Happy to," Perciville said with a smile, gesturing with his head for Fjona to join him.

As he went, he carelessly bumped the autumn elf on his head with the bottom of his staff, a knowing smirk upon his face.

Fjona followed with her head slightly dipped, tracing the hem of Perciville's robe as they walked past the villagers.

The elderly summer elf led them through a low door behind a bar and into a cramped, poorly-lit chamber, containing only a table, chairs and bookcase.

She sat on a stool at the table and leaned her wheel-frame against the wall, then stared at Perciville and Fjona until they took the hint and seated themselves.

She then scrutinised them with the same intense stare with which she had given Perciville before, while a child spring elf appeared from the main room with a tray, jangling with a teapot, cups and saucers.

He wordlessly filled the cups with a ruby, aromatic tea, then disappeared back out of the room like a shadow.

The elder opened her mouth as if to speak, then took a hearty sip of the hot tea, before delicately returning the cup to its saucer. "I don't recognise you," she stated, her tone near-accusatory.

"It has been a long while since I last visited," Perciville replied. "Admittedly, I hardly recognise you, Falavei."

The elder's eyes widened just a fraction. "Tell me, what is your name?"

"Perciville Harper," he said as he took a sip of tea.

Falavei's eyes rolled up as if trying to pull a memory out of her head. "Harper? Hmm... now that does ring a bell..." She trailed off, lost in her thoughts. Then her eyes snapped to Fjona. "And you are?"

Taken aback, Fjona stuttered her own name.

"Sarsen? Perhaps that also rings a bell... but then, I cannot be sure."

"Forgive my interruption, but... who are you?" Fjona asked, willing this interrogation to end as swiftly as possible.

The elder raised an eyebrow. "Ah, I see. Failed to mention old Falavei to your new companion, did you, Harper? How often I am forgotten here, living out my final years as if I never once offered respite to a weary sage."

"You mean you used to look after the new, aspiring sages when they left Willow's Brush?"

"Indeed, indeed," Falavei said, nodding at Fjona, "and in return they may visit from time to time to share their abilities and offer them to the village. But alas" – Falavei's tone suddenly soured – "this is no time for meaningless conversation. We are in the midst of a crisis."

"Which is precisely what brings us to your door," Perciville explained. "I trust that you are well versed in the Eight Afflictions?"

Falavei nodded solemnly. "Indeed I am, but most others have either forgotten or are too young to remember. I see the signs, though. The wilting crops, but a night separating green from grey. The rumours of friction between the elven holds. Now, a villager, clearly tormented. I believe that descendants of faithless men and women may now be vulnerable to the affliction. If that is so, then we may expect a plague of tormented elves and sacrificial mothers, worse even than at the time of the turned-sage. This villager, the others think is merely fevered. But a fever that beckons a thirst for blood? I think not, but none listen to tales of an old woman such as myself."

"Is that what they were debating when we came in?" Fjona enquired.

"Indeed, indeed." Falavei breathed a heavy sigh. "And others have muddied the truth with their own misguided beliefs. Across the Arvum they speak of the *Great Afflictions* or the *Eight Ascensions* with no respect for what lies at its heart. There have even been whispers from Rosensted of some wishing to awaken the Sleeping Giant. Can you imagine? Are they fools?"

"The Sleeping Giant? That's one of the Eight Afflictions, isn't it? Perciville mentioned it once before. What does it mean to 'wake the Sleeping Giant'?"

Perciville, who had been surprisingly quiet, spoke up. "There is a city in the desert: Panamaya. The most ancient city across the Arvum, in the heart of the continent. It is found on a rocky mountain known by the locals as the Sleeping Giant."

Falavei picked up the story. "It is believed that long before the cities of the Arvum were conceived, a lonely giant was tricked by a deceitful sage into draining a great lake, forming the Pentari Desert, and bringing suffering to the villagers who depended on the waters. Ashamed, the giant begged the sage for mercy. The sage cast the giant into a deep slumber and buried him in a mound. Over time, sand accumulated above him and built up into the mountain we know today. It is feared that when the Eight Afflictions return, the giant will awaken, destroying the city as he does. Some say the cruel sage who deceived him will also return and chaos will ensue across the Arvum."

"So why would anyone wish to wake the giant themselves?" Fjona asked.

"Because stories get lost in translation," Falavei replied, a look of frustration further creasing her wrinkled face. "For one thing, the tale of the Sleeping Giant is a myth that transcends generations, and far exceeds the lives of those inhabiting the Arvum today. The conception of the Eight Afflictions, though far more recent, still alludes the vast majority of people. You and I may know the truth of what happened three centuries ago, but many just know the loose threads that have been weaved over time. As to why someone may believe that good may arise when the Sleeping Giant does, I cannot tell you. What I do know is that the threat caused by fear and misunderstanding should not be underestimated, even though it may pale in comparison to the threat of the Eight Afflictions."

Evidently tired of the conversation, Perciville pushed up from his seat. "Be that as it may, it matters little to us. I don't intend to go around the Arvum preaching the truth of the sages. We have bigger fish to fry, like trying to stop the Eight Afflictions from truly coming into fruition."

"And how, may I ask, do you intend to do that?" Falavei asked, her eyebrows raised; her head tilted to one side in question.

Fjona was instantly alert. She wondered how much Perciville would be willing to divulge.

His answer was swift and certain. "By training up a new demi-sage and searching for the one weapon that can stop it."

It wasn't the most satisfactory response, neither for Fjona nor Falavei.

"I don't know that anyone can stop what has already started," the elder mused, "but if I were to place my trust in anyone, it would be a sage such as yourself."

Perciville's mouth twisted into a wide grin.

"I have little to offer, but say what you need and I will help where I can," she added.

"Something to eat would be nice," Fjona interjected, holding a hand over her famished stomach. "He can conjure port and coffee, but draws the line at a bowl of porridge."

"It's more complicated than that," Perciville snapped, then turned to Falavei. "We need to get to Rosensted as soon as possible. If you can provide any transport then both we and the fate of the Arvum would be incredibly grateful."

"Very well. Souley!" she yelled towards the chamber door.

Moments later, the young spring elf poked his rosy round face around the corner.

"Go now to the stables and find these two a cart and driver. Make haste! Time is of the essence. Oh, and go via the stores and pick them out some breads, fruits and meats. Fill a sack, they will be on the road for a few days. Now scurry!"

Diminutive footsteps faded away as the serving boy raced obediently away from the chamber.

"I pray to the sages of old that the time we meet next will be in blessing," Falavei offered with a comely bow of her crooked neck, before reaching for her wheel-frame.

Fjona made to help the elder to her feet, but was met with a wave of frustrated hands and a grunt.

Instead, to avoid the awkwardness of watching Falavei struggle out of her seat, Fjona broke the silence. "Thank you for your wisdom and assistance. When I have practised a little more, I promise to return."

The villagers had largely dissipated now. Some seemed to have helped themselves to a drink around the inn, though most had evidently returned to their houses.

Fjona noticed the muscular autumn elf tucked away in a corner with a half empty tankard of dark ale. He was staring begrudgingly at Perciville as they followed Falavei towards the door. Scowling, the elf raised his left hand then thumped the palm three times with the inside of his right fist. A strange gesture, and probably not one wishing love and good fortune, Fjona didn't doubt, though at least he remained in his seat.

Perciville was completely oblivious to the entire display.

Outside, on the steps to the inn, Falavei pointed them towards the stables. "Go now, Souley should have made all the arrangements. Perciville" – she studied his face again – "you have but one chance to save the Arvum from these atrocities. Don't cock it up." With that, she turned on her wheel and disappeared back inside mumbling, "Harper," over and over as if still trying to place his name.

"Come on," Fjona urged, spurred on by the rumbling of her tummy.

They crossed a stone bridge over a wide river, on the other side of which was a small farmstead comprised of the stables, a barn, and a red windmill.

There seemed to be nobody around. Even the boy, Souley, had disappeared.

"Hello?" Fjona called, straining her ears for a response.

"That sounded like a horse," Perciville murmured. "Follow me."

A herd of cattle was grazing on a plentiful supply of hay as they passed the barn and made their way through the farm.

Then, as they rounded the corner next to a modest house, which evidently lacked the craftsmanship of a sage, they found the cart, loaded with a long white crate and several sacks.

"Looks good to me," Fjona said, swinging Perciville's somewhat dwindling satchel on to the back and clambering on.

Before boarding, Perciville walked around to the front of the cart to greet a dumpy, hooded man.

"I gather you are taking us to Rosensted," the sage commented. "I trust you know the way."

The driver glanced briefly at Perciville with half-open eyes, nodded slowly, then returned his gaze to the two horses, reaching for the reins as he did.

He whipped them both and the cart began to roll gently forward.

"Whoa, hold up!" Perciville yelped, swiftly making for the rear and leaping on, falling into Fjona as he did so, who was halfway through a roasted chicken leg.

"Steady on!" she complained through a mouthful of food. She swallowed the large piece of meat, then asked quietly, "What's he like?" She gestured to the driver with her eyes.

"Remember Moki? Led our horses to Willow's Brush? Well he's just as quiet, but more of an arse."

"Well at least he'll get us to Rosensted in good time," Fjona said, reaching for another chicken leg. "Hey look, it's that boy, Souley!"

She smiled at the lad, who had appeared from somewhere on the farm. He was waving excitedly with both hands.

Fjona smiled and waved back. "Sweet kid in the end. Must be happy to have helped us."

She took a hearty bite into the chicken, feeling immensely satisfied. The sun was shining, she had something to eat, and they were well on their way to their next destination. For the first time in a while, it felt as if everything was going to plan.

CHAPTER 5

THE KELNISH CONUNDRUM

The gulf in wealth between the Upper Gate and the Lower Gate was bigger than the hole in a poor man's pocket, but the gulf between the Upper Gate and the Outer Gate was immeasurable. For those who lived in the more impoverished districts of Panamaya City, any service that may earn a bassal or two was scarcely ever sneered at.

For many, it came down to stealing and selling on at any price, particularly food off an unwary seller at the forum. Others, both men *and* women, turned to prostitution, servitude or low-level companionship, while many still would seek any odd job that may yield something to eat by the end of the day.

Work was hard, but if you had the means, one may be fortunate enough to bear the role of the town crier.

From down in her hovel in the Lower Gate, Kaikura could hear the relentless clanging of the handbell from outside and the tedious, strained wail of a pubescent boy desperately trying to draw in customers with his increasingly dramatic headlines.

Only since yesterday, *bread shortage from Rosensted* had evolved into *Sultan fears for desolate granaries*.

Still, it could be difficult to not be sucked in.

Kaikura reluctantly pricked up her ears. Even Bobassa, who had been having a quiet snooze under the table, poked his head out and turned it up to the hatch.

"Noble guard dismissed from service, hear 'bout it for a

bassal!" the boy practically screamed. "One bassal, is all, who wishes to hear it?"

The tinny bell rattled somewhere near to Kaikura's house.

The boy called again. "Canal carnage! Hear 'bout the latest from the recen' attacks for just a single bassal!"

Kaikura could hear muffled conversation and the bell ceased ringing for a moment. Evidently someone had offered the boy a coin for his news.

After a short while, he piped up again. "More reports of earthquakes *frough*-out the city, is your home at risk? One bassal!"

Now that one did catch Kaikura's attention. During the past week, she had heard fervent chatter of earth tremors from people out on the street and she was certain she'd felt another only the day before. Whatever was happening, it was undoubtedly spreading, though was it newsworthy? Certainly not worth a bassal in Kaikura's mind.

"Mystery at the Archivus!" the crier announced.

Kaikura suddenly found herself straining her thin, pointed ears.

"News on *Prietor* Bouwer!" he continued. "Just one bassal!"

That was it. Kaikura swiped for her purse, grabbed one of only a few bassals and leaped up the ladder. She pushed open the hatch, squinting at the burned white walls around her.

She spotted the crier from the roof.

"You!" she shouted down to him. "I have money for the news."

"Most obligin' to you, San," the boy responded as Kaikura clambered down the frontage and stepped out onto the street.

Bobassa had followed her up the ladder and was watching her keenly from the roof.

"What will it be for ya? Empty granaries? Bandits on the canal? A bassal each, of course."

Kaikura thrust the small bronze coin into his hand. "The

proprietor, please, quickly."

"Ah yes, *Prietor* Bouwer. I am reliably informed that she 'as not been seen in or around the Archivus for over a week. None of her students or fellows have met with her."

"That's it?" Kaikura asked, her face twisted with disappointment. "I could have told you that."

The boy shook his head. "No, San, there is a little more. A *Prietor* Isiah Fethen paid a visit to her home in the Upper Gate and reported she was not there either." The crier's pale eyes glimmered with intrigue. "He's said it's unlike *Prietor* Bouwer to travel unannounced and most unusual that she not be seen in her chamber or home. Very strange, I should think you agree!"

"And most dissatisfying," Kaikura grumbled.

"Please, forgive me, for most that would have been breaking news. Perhaps I can redeem myself with a one-time offer for my most esteemed new customer...? One bassal more and I will share with you two more articles from Panamaya's most reputable news source?"

Kaikura looked the scruffy-necked boy up and down. His garments were torn and tattered, and they were smattered in the same dirt that covered most of his pockmarked face. She dug into her pockets and found another bassal.

"Most kind, San! What'd you care to hear?"

Kaikura smiled. "Dealer's choice."

"As you wish! Well let me tell you 'bout food shortages. It is known that most of the city's imports come from round the Paddock and the farms near Rosensted. I am reliably informed that, despite good weather and long days, many crops have failed this season and there's been an increase in dying livestock— deadstock, I s'pose. Granaries are mostly full, but if a bad harvest is to be expected, they will only last so long."

"Concerning," Kaikura conceded, "though I trust we can

trade elsewhere in the Arvum."

The boy nodded. "Of course, I'm sure there ain't nothing to worry 'bout. Unlike the earthquakes." He segued smoothly into a new topic. "P'raps you've experienced these minor rumbles too? There've been countless reports from all across the city of at least twelve recorded instances of quakes during this last week. Nat'rally, many people fear it is the waking of the so-called 'Sleeping Giant' and a small minority 'ave already made to packing their b'longings, heading down through the Outer Gate and making for Havensend. I have my opinions, of course, but it would be unprofessional to push my *foughts* on my listeners." The boy glanced around and noticed a gathering of folk heading up to the forum. "A pleasure sharing with you, San. I wish you a fine day."

With that, he ran off in the direction of the crowd, frantically waving his bell and yelling out his headlines in a strained, cracking voice.

Back inside her hovel, Kaikura prepared herself a cup of tea and returned to her book-littered table.

"Where in the Arvum could Proprietor Bouwer have gone?" she asked Bobassa, who was now grooming his soft scales with his tongue. "The perplexing nature of this city is somewhat frustrating. Even this proved to be useless!"

She slammed a heavy, red-covered tome on the table, a ripple of dust puffing out of the pages. It was the alluring book that Proprietor Bouwer had left for Kaikura, entitled *The Compendium of Sages.*

"This language, I do not recognise at all," Kaikura ruminated. "Why the cover in one language but the content in another? And these swirly letters – they resemble Kelnish, but these ones; they're like nothing I've ever encountered before. I suppose it must have been re-bound...?"

She leaned over the table, running her long fingers through her hair.

"Am I simply wasting my energy over nothing, Bobassa? I have my own work to be focussing on, yet I cannot get the Sultan's harrowing dream, and the drying spring, and all that mythology out of my head!"

The sandkat brushed up against her legs and purred.

They were distracted by a gentle knocking against the hatch above them.

Kaikura sighed. "Oh, please not again."

Bobassa darted up the ladder, whimpering quietly.

Kaikura had expected the visitor to open the door and invite themselves in as Oolia, the Sultan's steward, had done before, but instead there was simply another quiet, though firm, knock, followed by a muffled, "Hello? Is this the home of San Kaikura Kendi?"

"Umm, yes. Who precisely are you?" she called up to the ceiling hatch.

"My name is Elian Sole, ranger for the Fourth West Division of the Noble Guard of the Sultan. May I please open up?"

A soldier, Kaikura mused, *and a very polite one at that.* Hesitantly, she replied, "Of course, Ranger."

A distorted rectangle of sunlight filled the hovel as the hatch lifted up and revealed a slightly uneasy looking Marrowborn man. He was smartly clad in a long white coat, the gleam of a sword at his hip.

"Please forgive my intrusion, but I am in need of assistance and—"

"May I suggest you come on inside?" Kaikura interrupted. "It will make for easier conversation."

The soldier was taken aback. "Well, if you don't mind..."

He slowly descended the ladder to the grumbling of Bobassa,

who had slinked over to the bedroom floor and was staring at the visitor intently with bulging yellow eyes.

"Oh, how wonderful!" Elian exclaimed. "A sandkat! I haven't seen one of those in years. My grandmother used to keep one, though not nearly as handsome as you..."

Whether Bobassa could understand the soldier's words or was merely soothed by his intonation, Kaikura could not tell, but for the first time, the sandkat relaxed in the presence of an outsider. His grumbling ceased and he hopped down from the ledge to join Kaikura at the table.

When Elian reached the floor, he removed his helmet and tucked it under his arm. He then put a fist over the emblem of his coat, took a knee and bowed to the scholar.

Kaikura blushed. She had never been treated with such respect before.

"Please, *Sun* Sole," she said politely, "do not feel obliged with such formalities. How is it that you came to find me?"

Elian stood, a domineering yet not intimidating figure. A face that was weather-beaten and stretched, though still with the complexion of youthfulness.

"I had been sent to find the Sultan's steward, umm...?" His eyes looked up as he tried to recall the name.

"Oolia Khamun?" Kaikura offered.

"Yes, Oolia! I was instructed to find her in search of counsel and, when I did, she recommended I speak with you."

"Counsel? Not more dream interpretations, is it? Because I really am not an expert; that was a one-time thing for the Sultan and—"

Elian waved his hands. "Whoa, no this has nothing to do with dreams. We need your help with something down at the canal."

"The canal?" Kaikura wondered how any morsel of her knowledge could possibly offer anything of use to the construction.

"Yes, in the excavations. The Kelner elves... well, they've found something... unusual..."

Elian offered Kaikura a headscarf and shawl to keep away the dust, and vacated the saddle of his horse for the scholar. He led them down through the streets of the Lower Gate on the reins, chatting casually as they followed the cobbled labyrinth of streets and alleyways down the mountain.

"To put it simply, yes, I like being a member of the Noble Guard. It's quite a privilege, which is something my family never had growing up. That's not to say that it doesn't come without problems, mind..."

"Problems? Like what?"

"Politics mainly."

"Is that not inevitable? I mean, you are employed directly by the Sultan. You couldn't get much closer to politics without being the Sultan yourself."

The soldier huffed. "Good point, but I mean the politics within the Guard itself. Only this past week, my corporal was suspended because the captain has it in for her. Claimed she'd abandoned her post, caused unnecessary harm to the workers, and acted irrationally without thought. Nonsense, if you ask me, but now she is facing full dismissal and may be banished from the Upper Gate."

"Wow, what could she have done to warrant that?" Kaikura asked, surprised at herself for being so intrigued.

"If you ask me, nothing at all. She and captain Lahsilli have some complicated history, so I'm told, and since she joined the Guard, he has apparently combed every opportunity to get her kicked out. I don't know the details though. I only joined a few years ago. Now my division is being led by Ranger Holden while the corporal awaits her sentence. If the Sultan declares that she had abandoned her post then dismissal is the best Corporal Stone can hope for. She wouldn't be the first corporal to be executed, even this year."

"You speak very freely."

The ranger smiled. "Fortunately there's no punishment for voicing an opinion, else I'd be locked away in the belly of the keep!" He chuckled at his own comment.

Kaikura felt warm inside. She could hardly remember the last time conversation had been so easy with someone who wasn't a sandkat.

"So what about you?" the soldier enquired. "Long days poring through books in the Archivus? Not for me, personally, but an impressive place to study, I can imagine."

"It's all I've ever known," Kaikura replied, "since I was recognised as a child for having an acumen for learning. I've dedicated my entire life so far to study..."

She suddenly felt very lonely as she spoke.

"I envy you," Sole said. "Your pursuit in life is an endless open book. For me, well, suffice to say the role of a ranger isn't endless."

They were most of the way through the stinking streets of the Outer Gate when Sole's horse abruptly pulled up on its hooves, tugging the ranger back on the leather reins.

"What's wrong, you silly old thing?"

"Excuse me?" Kaikura sat upright in the saddle, her nostrils flaring.

"Not you. My horse. We come this way every day. What troubles you?" The ranger spoke softly and gently stroked the horse's face.

The horse seemed to relax for a moment before shaking the

ranger's hand away and braying deeply.

"Is everything okay?" Kaikura asked, feeling more than a little uneasy herself.

"I'm not really sure."

Suddenly, the horse bucked, his front legs kicking frantically around while uttering a guttural, pained cry.

"Whoa, whoa!" Kaikura yelled, toppling from the terrified animal's back and landing in Elian's arms.

"Careful, girl!" Elian called at the horse, but his words were useless.

Around them, other animals had too been disturbed. Dogs were barking, birds screeching. Hoofbeats echoed around the street as a stampede of horses and cattle charged down the mountain.

The ranger's horse joined the chase and disappeared off into a sandy haze.

"Come back here now!" Elian shouted, preparing to follow before the ground beneath him began to tremble and he lost his balance.

People nearby began to scream as the mountain quaked and several poorly constructed sand houses began to crumble.

Kaikura was thrown into a nearby wall and narrowly missed a falling rooftile that clattered and smashed on the cobbles. Elian swept in beside her and held his shield over their heads as detritus rained upon them from above.

The whole event didn't last long and, within minutes, the mountain stilled and a calmness returned.

Dust and sand floated through the streets, but it seemed most of the houses in their vicinity had remained unharmed, at least on the outside.

They waited, just to be sure the quake had passed, and a concerned chatter of people nearby replaced the screaming.

"Are you alright?" the ranger asked, returning his shield to his back and offering Kaikura a hand.

"Yes, I think so," she replied, sweeping dust off her shawl.

"I've heard talk of quakes, but that's the first time I've actually felt one myself."

Kaikura was too shaken to reply.

The ranger offered her a canteen of water from his belt. "I'm sorry if you are feeling distressed, but we need your help urgently at the excavation. Are you at all hurt or do you think you will be alright heading out to the desert?"

The scholar shook some loose brick out of her shawl. Something was nagging her, but she couldn't quite put her finger on it. It seemed ludicrous that the quakes, the canal and the missing proprietor could somehow be connected, and yet...

Whatever the Kelner elves had uncovered in the trench, there was a possibility that it may solve one of her questions.

"With everything going on around here, I think we best get a move on," she said, and led the way.

CHAPTER 6

THE ROAD TO ROSENSTED

The day was wearing on and Perciville was dozing at the back of the cart, his head resting on a conjured pillow of hay.

Meanwhile, Fjona was sitting with her legs dangling over the edge and practising elemental spells on passing objects. Since progressing to the Woven Wand, she had noticed that smaller rocks and stones were easier to latch onto, and that she could now manipulate larger ones too.

Currently a boulder the size of her head was suspended in the air behind them and was bobbing up and down, seemingly following the cart.

Fjona steeled herself, then flicked her wand away from her. In doing so, the rock flung aside and landed in a pool of bubbling mud.

"Nice control," Perciville murmured, though his eyes appeared to be closed.

Fjona smiled then turned her wand towards the air, focused her energy, and took hold of a gentle spring breeze. The coolness kissed her neck and sent a tantalising chill down her spine.

"I can't believe I can affect the weather like this," she grinned, beaming from ear to ear, before using her wand to change the direction of the breeze.

"Yes, well, be careful. We both know full well the impact manipulation can have on the environment."

Fjona wanted to argue that a slight breeze such as this must surely be safe, but she knew Perciville would find some way of picking holes in that.

Instead, she shrugged. "It all makes for good practice."

"Agreed," the sage replied, just as the cart bounced off a sizeable pothole in the road and the driver's large box knocked into Perciville's head. "Hey, watch out now!" he yelled at the driver. "Are you completely blind?"

The driver gave no response. He just kept his head down, and the cart continued to amble along the stone track.

"What's in this crate anyway?" Perciville asked, intrigued. "It's ridiculously heavy."

He pushed it back to its position and started fiddling with the lock.

The driver grunted loudly. It was the first sound he had uttered since they had departed from Colt.

"Leave it alone, Perciville, he doesn't want you playing with it."

The sage huffed. "Very well." He turned back to the driver. "Just keep your eyes on the road, alright?"

They were travelling along one of many long, indistinct roads that criss-crossed a wide expanse of the Arvum known as the Paddock. It was a landscape distinguished by the fact that it was largely indistinguishable, with vast plains of open fields, occasional pockets of bracken and woodland, narrow streams and the odd farmstead.

Every so often, the road would lead them past a herd of wild boars and sheep, or by horses that would gaily trot off in the opposite direction.

For the first time since leaving her home, Fjona felt a sense of familiarity. A connection with nature that wasn't influenced by magic, but by the hands of local peoples passing through.

"When will I be able to conjure?" Fjona asked, turning to

Perciville, who had wasted no time relaxing back into his snoozing position.

"Not for a while," he grumbled. "You need to progress again first."

Fjona sighed. "So it's just elementals until then?"

"Mmhm, it's the first school of manipulation."

"And how come you can conjure drinks but not food?"

The sage groaned. "Can you not tell that I am trying to sleep?"

Fjona raised her eyebrows and mouthed 'sorry', returning to levitating rocks on the side of the road.

"Look," Perciville offered, "there are few laws when it comes to the art of manipulation, but there is one. Sages cannot create life. To those who follow a doctrine, it is this law that separates a sage from a god. When it comes to conjuring, the closer a material is to life, the more difficult it is to craft. A new sage may conjure small objects made of stone or metal, but wood is a little more complex, though far from impossible. Food, drink and cloth are among the most difficult items to conjure as they derive from living things: plants *and* animals. They are known as *Artisanal Spells*. With experience, skill and years of practice, it is well within the abilities of a sage to conjure these things. I've even met sages who could conjure meat which, I can tell you, is an exceptionally intricate and challenging skill."

"So port and coffee are easier to conjure?"

Perciville scoffed. "No, not necessarily easier. They just happen to be what I dedicated years of practice to. I guess I have my own priorities. Be that as it may, I have never failed to find food wherever I visit, but Autumn Elf Old Port and a good cup of coffee are really only in Havensend, and the city itself does very little for me."

"That's it, then? You can't conjure food because you spent your time learning to make drinks?"

The sage smiled. "Essentially. Although, if you hadn't noticed, I can also do bridges and a half decent campsite!"

"Or half a bridge and a mud hut," Fjona teased.

Perciville had to agree. His abilities were certainly lacking these days.

The cart rolled down a steep hill and skirted a field boundary with a ranch on one side and a gurgling brook on the other.

Fjona shuffled back and found a spot next to Perciville.

"So what about the other schools of manipulation? Like attaching the staff to your back?"

"Funnily enough, you need a staff to do that one."

"Does it not work with wands, then?"

"No, but perhaps you can conjure a pocket to put it in," the sage replied, his tone rich with sarcasm.

Fjona frowned. "It was only a question." She idly pointed her wand at the lock on the driver's box and it started to rattle.

Again, the driver grunted and Fjona shied away, her face red.

Perciville smirked. "Leave it alone."

"Ooh, how about the compass?" Fjona asked. "Can I do that with a wand?"

"Now that one, you can do," the sage replied, "to an extent anyway. With a Woven Wand, you should be able to make it glow when it points north."

Fjona sat up excitedly. The elemental spells had been rewarding, but she was always willing to try her hand at something new.

"Focus your energy and let your wand show you the direction," Perciville instructed.

Fjona closed her eyes, held her wand relaxedly in her hand, and felt her energy course through her body. She felt the power itch along her arm and tug at her hand.

An instinct told her to open her eyes. She gently pointed her wand around her until a faint yellow glow flickered at its tip.

"No, no, you must be doing it wrong!" Perciville admonished.

Fjona was dumbfounded. "What do you mean? It's working, isn't it?"

"Hardly. You're pointing west."

"No I'm not! I can feel it. This is north," Fjona insisted, struggling to keep her frustration at bay.

"How can that be west when we are heading southeast?"

Fair point, Fjona conceded. She sunk back into her seat, feeling deflated.

Perciville whipped his staff up from the dusty floor of the cart. "Look, I'll show you." He focused his own energy, pointed the staff before him, then froze, a confused look on his face.

"What is it?" Fjona asked.

"You were right all along…"

"Ha! I knew it! That's good, right?" The reality started to dawn on her. "That's not good, is it?"

"No," Perciville fumed, his jaw clenched. "Hey, stupid oaf of a driver, you've bloody taken us in the wrong direction! How thick are you? You've taken us even further from Rosensted, you degenerate, swamp rat of an elf!"

There was no response.

"Can you even hear me?" Perciville shouted, tugging the driver's hood back.

The driver suddenly rotated his head so that it was unnaturally twisted on his neck like an owl. His eyes were gleaming yellow, and foam was frothing at his black lips. His skin was ghostly pale and veinous.

"Perciville, what is that?" Fjona's voice wavered like an untuned fiddle.

"Get back!" Perciville exclaimed. "He's tormented!"

In the driver's manic state, he had whipped the horses relentlessly and now the cart was racing down a steep hill at an unprecedented speed.

The driver started to laugh. It was high-pitched and hysterical, the kind of laugh that sent a chill down Fjona's spine. Utterly void of humour. He turned on his seat, sat up on his haunches and prepared to leap at them when the cart hit a collapsed tree at the foot of the hill and spun off on its wheels.

One horse, now loosed, galloped off towards a nearby thicket while the cart tumbled across the track and careened into a tree. The other horse lay in a pool of blood.

In a maelstrom of splinters, timbers and the contents of the now-ripped satchel, Fjona was propelled from the back of the cart, and landed in an ungraceful heap behind it.

Holding her head and blinking away her dizziness, she rolled onto her side. A piercing, flickering light was probing her eyes and Fjona could only squint to see what it was. When she came to, she realised that the light was from the sun reflecting off the glass core of Todie's amulet, which had slipped out of her pocket in the chaos and fallen just a few paces in front of her.

Todie had thrown the amulet to Fjona when she'd stood upon a partially-materialised bridge spanning Aserae's Lip, the intention being to bring her good fortune, or so he'd said. Though as Fjona's scraped and bleeding hands reached for the metallic heirloom, she felt somewhat failed by Todie's gift.

"Perciville?" she yelled, resentfully pocketing the amulet as she pushed herself back onto her feet. "Are you—"

She cut herself short when her gaze fell upon the driver's crate that had tipped onto its side and lay within the debris. During its fall, the lid had given way and its contents, a portly naked man, had toppled out of it. The corpse's skin was blue and smeared with dark congealed blood.

Fjona was too terrified to scream.

Even the deranged laughter of the tormented driver failed to pull her from her stupor. The driver hopped over to her like a predatory animal, his face twisted with desire and hunger.

As he leaped at her, a purple bout of energy met him mid-air and flung him down into the wreckage.

Fjona was unable to move, barely conscious of Perciville walking through her field of vision, his staff pointed down as if he were carrying a sword.

In a blurry daze, she could hear energy firing out of Perciville's staff like a flat drum, obscured by the unbearable, incongruous screams of the driver.

It was unrelenting, unmerciful. A pop-like sound from the staff, followed by a screech. Again, and again, and again, until Fjona snapped out of her confusion.

She shook her head to clear it. "Perciville, stop!"

She hopped over to where the sage was standing and felt the bitter taste of bile in the back of her throat at what lay before her. The driver, if indeed that was ever who he was, lay in a heap in the middle of the wreckage. His skin was a pale green and translucent, and it was writhing as if a colony of termites was beneath it. Now his eyes were vacuous black pits and, across his body and ragged doublet were, what looked like, scorch marks from all the places he had been hit from Perciville's enchantments. Of that, there were a lot.

"You executed him!"

"He was tormented," Perciville said quietly.

"And? Could you not have saved him?"

"Saved *him*? I was more preoccupied saving *you*! Do you not realise he would have had your neck had I not intervened? Or perhaps you failed to notice the corpse we have been travelling around with for the best part of a day...?"

The image of the body rolling out of the box filled Fjona's mind. She threw up on the ground beside her, narrowly missing Perciville's feet.

"As I thought..." the sage sighed as he conjured a clay jar brimming with water. "Here."

Fjona graciously accepted the drink as Perciville disappeared around the demolished cart.

"I don't understand," Fjona said, as she followed around to where Perciville was examining the blue corpse.

"It would appear that Falavei's tormented villager has killed our original driver and taken it upon himself to deliver us to god's know where," the sage replied through gritted teeth. He was sullen for a moment. "Poor bugger."

Fjona watched through blurry eyes as Perciville used his staff to pick the original driver up in his box, and carefully lay him next to the tormented man. He then did the same with the dead horse, at all times his face stoic and stern.

"What are you doing?" Fjona asked, but the sage didn't reply.

Instead, he whispered, "May peace be restored to you in the heavens, where it failed you in the Arvum."

He lifted his staff high above his head, then released an immense flame that engulfed the wreckage and all it contained.

Wordlessly, he stepped away from the cremation, pointed his staff around him, then settled on a direction and started walking.

Fjona stared after him. "That's it? Where are you going?"

Without stopping, the sage replied, "We let down our guard and we have been punished for it. If you haven't noticed, we are a long way from our destination and now we have to get there on foot. Let's not waste any more time."

Fjona turned her head to the wreckage. "May the Four Good Gods spare you," she uttered softly, before swiftly walking towards Perciville.

With the sun already beginning to set behind them, and with only the clothes on her back, Todie's amulet in her pocket and her wand in her hand, Fjona followed Perciville.

CHAPTER 7

THE FONT OF SUCCESSION

From behind, Sanjin Baerita was a startlingly alluring island elf with a neat bob of silvery sandy hair, decorated with threads of glass beads and fine jewellery. Her neck was as narrow as a drainpipe and her loose-fitting, exquisite drapery left her golden, pointed shoulders basking in the morning sun.

Oolia felt uncharacteristically envious as she stood obediently in the corner of the audience chamber, listening to the elf's chocolatey voice and perfect, poetic diction. At least the face was more enigmatic, Oolia considered, although the mask that concealed half of it probably attracted more suitors than the half without, and rumours of scarring, rotting, and rashes beneath it did little for the steward's jealousy.

All she could do was stand tall, look assertive, and wear an expression that feigned interest in what the architect had to say.

"Your Divine Excellency, swift and cohesive has been our progress, from my heart I must assure you. Now ready your eyes and I may impart..." Sanjin said, pointing a ringed and manicured finger over a map sprawled out on the table. She ran it over a region to the west of the Pentari Desert labelled The Precipitous Mountains. "By the skill of ours surveyors have the examination of all five aqueducts been concluded, and soon shall commence the restoration of two: Aserae and Aulden."

She paused as the Sultan creased his eyebrows and gave her an enquiring look.

"My assistant architect is of Marrowborn blood," Sanjin explained succinctly, though the Sultan's expression only grew more confused. "Being five aqueducts, my assistant named them for the Myrish gods. Be that as it may, Aserae is of fair condition and in a few weeks shall flow water, yet Aulden requires more effort for the turning of the wheel. Of Yore and Beale, I've been assured that restoration is feasible, but for the commencement of work. Kalzeth is, fittingly I'm told, too derelict to use. By word of our surveyors, the cost to reinstate it would vastly outweigh any benefits."

The Sultan clapped his hands together. "Your report pleases me very much. I am impressed by the speed with which you have served me. I trust you are still confident the canal will be completed by the end of the year."

There was a hint of urgency and trepidation to the Sultan's tone that Oolia picked up on, but that seemed to have eluded the architect. Either that or Sanjin was too experienced and too wise to say anything.

The architect rolled up the map. "My blood runs with confidence, my Sultan. Of several floodgates, the first is to open by week's end, and inwards shall flow the waters of the Ulestic Ocean. When time has blessed the construction to be finished here, the nearest floodgate will be opened and complete will be your canal. Allowing for the Havensend shipyard to have ready your trading vessels then, come the tides of winter, wares of the Free Capital, and now spring water of the mountains will be delivered directly to your door."

A toothless grin stretched across the Sultan's face. "Well, San Baerita, I will be going into my next meeting in a very good mood. When first I commissioned your help, I had expected my successor to be the one to reap the rewards, but it seems fortune will befall me."

Successor. The word resonated around Oolia's head and an unlikely thought occurred to her. It was so implausible, yet how had she not considered it before?

"Oolia, please show our esteemed architect to the door," the Sultan requested.

Mulling over her thoughts, the steward forced a smile and led Sanjin Baerita out of the audience chamber.

The door had hardly closed when the Sultan added, "A talented architect, but must all these damned island elves speak in such a pathetically frustrating way?" His face was a picture of annoyance and his jaw was as clenched as the bottom of a spanked child. "I mean would it be so hard of them to speak plainly? She's lucky her skills outweigh her irritating nature. We should have some proper summer elves apprenticed to her. If I had it my way, we wouldn't need be bothered by our cousins. The Arvum would be much better off if it was left to the hands of our people, wouldn't you agree?"

A sweaty chill ran down Oolia's spine. She wasn't sure she did agree, but the Sultan's question seemed more rhetorical than asking for her opinion.

Fortunately, the Sultan spoke again before Oolia had the chance to voice her concerns. "At least the progress of the aqueducts has left something positive on my mind before I meet with the general. Tell me, Oolia, what did that ranger want of you this morning? Seeking favour for his corporal before I determine her fate?"

"Actually, no," the steward replied. "He was seeking guidance from a proprietor, but didn't know where to look. I sent him to San Kendi, your dream translator, if you recall?"

The Sultan's amber eyes glimmered. "Ah well, I have taken her advice and, although my dreams still haunt me, I can sense a new era or prosperity on the horizon." He caught Oolia's eye then briskly changed the subject. "I hear the corporal has been wasting her days in the wind spa, no doubt ruminating over her poor decisions."

"Is that so?" Oolia asked politely, distracted by her own thoughts.

The doors to the chamber opened to General Kheller, pristinely clad in ruby and gold. He knelt courtly before the Sultan before an invitation to sit at the table.

"A grave discussion indeed to be had," the Sultan mused.

"Perhaps, though Captain Lahsilli has been very transparent about his feelings on the matter," Kheller replied.

Oolia was barely listening. She was replaying a scenario in her head, aware that she needed an opportunity to skulk away and satisfy her contemplations.

She forced a loud, strained cough, but was ignored by the two superiors.

"Though we cannot excuse Lahsilli's biases," the Sultan pointed out.

Oolia coughed again, warranting a brief glance from the general.

"Nor the testimonies of his rangers," Kheller added.

The steward coughed louder still, turning both the heads of the Sultan and the general.

Kheller grimaced. "This counsel is likely to last a while and I cannot focus with this incessant hacking."

"Agreed," the Sultan said coldly. "Oolia, perhaps you should get some air. You may join us back here for lunch."

Trying not to look pleased with herself, Oolia nodded politely and hurried out of the audience chamber. She could hear mumblings behind her as the two most powerful men in the city recommenced their conversation.

Without hesitation, the steward headed out along the

corridor, through a pillared hall, up a flight of stairs and along a windowless passageway to a guarded door at the far end. It was one of the oldest rooms of the palace – formerly a tower; now part of the fifth floor. The masonry was ancient and built of hard desert stone before wealth and trade allowed for the use of marble elsewhere. Along the walls were paintings depicting different elements of the Pentari Desert including the Sleeping Giant, bleak, sandy landscapes, and the canyon borders to the north.

It was a part of the palace where visitors were not welcomed and Oolia had kept her distance out of respect for the Panamayan sultanship. Today, however, her respect was forced aside by her burning curiosity.

She approached the Home Guard on the door.

"Name and status," the guard demanded, no hint of a question in his tone.

"You don't get many people up here, do you?" Oolia replied.

The guard was unmoved.

"Very well. I am Oolia Khamun, Steward to the Sultan. I request admittance to the Hall of Succession."

"I'm afraid while stewardship may open many doors in the city, this one it cannot."

"And why is that?"

"Because it has been decreed that a steward may not enter alone. This is an ancient law and not one that I can overlook."

Oolia tightened her fists with frustration. She only had so much time before needing to return to the Sultan.

"Look, I am here on behalf of Ayermune Dhaller Sé. That should be reason enough for being granted access." She spoke with an urgency that flirted with rudeness.

The guard tilted his head, then stepped to one side. "As you wish."

"Excellent." Oolia brushed past the guard, reaching for the

doorknob.

The moment she touched it, a sharp pulse raced through her hand and forced it away. Her arm spasmed as she turned to the guard.

"Like I said, your admittance has not been decreed."

"And you didn't think to tell me that it would hurt if I even tried to open it?" Oolia noted disdainfully.

The guard shrugged. "As you said, I don't get many visitors up here."

The steward huffed. "So who can get inside?"

"Well, the Sultan of course. The General, I presume, most Home Guards save for the doorkeeper, that's me, and any Noble Guard above the rank of ranger. The door was enchanted centuries ago and those were the conditions. My role is to make sure nobody attempts to break in. Now, if you will, I have an afternoon of standing quietly by myself and resisting the urge to piss."

Time was short and Oolia was determined to get inside the Hall of Succession. She raced down the steps of the palace, crossed over the spring and navigated the streets lined by boutique shops, artisans and wealthy establishments. It was a busy morning, though no more than usual, and squeezing between horse-drawn carriages and throngs of snooty dignitaries only made Oolia's temperament worse. Frustration swam through her veins, but eventually, the steward tumbled into a wide, open rock garden. It was delineated by a golden wrung iron fence that swirled up into a heavy gate with the words Bezenar's Luxury Wind Spa engraved on the open doors.

Oolia's tunic clung to her clammy skin and the prospect of visiting a wind chamber was suddenly very appealing.

She followed a flagstone pathway adorned by statues and pillars, and passed several local elves berobed in flowing white gowns, ambling along with seemingly little care in the world.

At the far end of the garden was the wind spa, a concave tower of four storeys that, from the inside, funnelled the desert breeze over its patrons. A regular spot for many, particularly southern elves who struggled with the heat of Panamaya.

Another refreshing element of the wind spa was that Oolia would frequently accompany the Sultan and, unlike the Hall of Succession, here was a door where her status would allow easy admittance.

No sooner had she entered the polished, cosy foyer was she greeted by a courtly autumn elf on the door. He glowed with health and vitality, and wore a perfectly clipped dark beard, matching his perfectly clipped dark hair.

When he spoke, it was soft and warm like freshly baked bread. "San Khamun! What an absolute delight to welcome you to Bezenar's this morning. Will the Sultan be joining you?"

"Good morning, Wilek. I'm afraid the Sultan is in counsel and I myself will not be staying long."

"That's too bad," he replied. He really did seem disappointed. "We've just received a fresh import of ice and they are preparing some cool *lamna* in the kitchen as we speak."

The thought alone of the sweet, strong tonic made Oolia salivate, but her nearing deadline required snappy decisions and a clear head.

"Soon," she assured, "but I'm here on prompt business and need to be swift. You haven't by chance seen a Corporal Lais Stone here this morning?"

The autumn elf grinned warmly. "This morning, yes. Yesterday afternoon, the evening before, the morning prior to that and so forth. She has barely left her bed and I can only imagine how much of her funds she has left to pay for it. Still, I can tell an elf in distress and she certainly is in distress."

Oolia began to feel a little optimistic. "Please, Wilek, may you show me to her?"

She was led through halls draped with fine silken sheets and lain with ornate carpets, so plush that Oolia had been advised to remove her sandals so that she could feel the craftmanship under her feet. Water trickled down ornamental gullies that circumnavigated the walls and floors, and every corner seemed to house a plant – mainly cacti and succulents, but also several leafy imports that required scrupulous care for them to thrive in the desert.

They stepped out into a colonnade that curved around the ground floor chamber. Immediately, they were embraced by a refreshing cool breeze, flowing in through a cavernous opening that peered out over the desert. This far down in the tower, pockets of sand would be carried in with the wind and it was up to the servant children to sweep it off over the sheer edge with a dusty broom. On the top floor, where the Sultan would reside, the wind would be far more intense and free of sand ingress.

"The corporal is over there, close to the edge," Wilek explained, gesturing with his hand. "I hope she is compos mentis enough for your business." He smiled warmly, then disappeared back out the chamber.

Oolia glanced around at the surrounding visitors. In one bed was a vastly corpulent autumn elf, entirely naked but for his member hidden by his own gut. He snoozed while ale spilled over the lip of his glass as it dangled precariously from his pudgy fingers.

Beside each other rested two male spring elves whose fingers toyed with one another's between the two beds. One was slender and toned, the other very slim, and both naked but for a short towel around their waists. They were chatting softly to one another and relishing in the cool breeze.

The remaining guests were summer elves, including one elder who had discarded her towel and was sitting with her legs uncomfortably apart.

Averting her eyes, Oolia headed over to where Wilek had pointed.

"Corporal Stone?" she asked, tentatively.

"Jus' Lais," the corporal replied, "'nother *lamna* please..."

Oolia stepped around her. Lais was lounging on the bed with a near-full glass of tonic and a spindle of drool hanging from her mouth. She wore only a short towel and her moderate breasts sat firmly on her broad chest.

"Lais, please. My name is Oolia Khamun. I need your—"

Before she could finish, the ground began to quiver and Oolia fell into the wall. There was a sound of smashing glasses, screams from outside the tower, and nervous mumblings from within.

"Hmm, you've really upped your service," Lais groaned in a satisfactory voice, stretching out her legs and curling her toes.

Consternation was picking up around the room. The spring elves had sat up from their beds and were clutching one another's hands more tightly, and two of the summer elves had dressed back into their robes and were preparing to leave. Meanwhile the fat autumn elf slept through the whole event, while the elder appeared to be enjoying it even more than Lais.

A potted plant near to the mouth of the chamber was shaken over the lip and fell down the sheer edge to the streets below, while the servant children huddled in a corner furthest from the opening.

When the earthquake subsided, the door swung open and Wilek ran in. He looked flustered, even a little scared, though he was too conscious about the wellbeing of his customers to care for his own misgivings. He proceeded to navigate the room, checking in on the guests and offering reassuring words.

Once Oolia had regained her composure, she persisted with her enquiry.

"Look, Lais Stone, I need your help. I need a corporal to permit me access... somewhere."

"I'm not a corporal no more," Lais mumbled, though she did at least squint her eyes open briefly to acknowledge the steward.

"You have only been temporarily dismissed," Oolia replied, struggling to resist adding 'for now'.

Lais began to speak a little clearer. "You an' I both know what that'll lead to. Now please let me wallow in my own stupor while I await my fate and, while you are up, please find me another drink."

That was the last straw. Oolia reached for a barrel of icy water, removed the bottle of wine that it contained, and emptied the water over the corporal's head.

Lais's reaction was instantaneous. She leaped up from the bed, screaming out of shock and turning the heads of everyone in the room. Her towel fell to the floor and she stood unashamedly naked before Oolia, grimacing and clenching her fists.

The steward was suddenly aware of how fierce the corporal's body was, even like this. Her richly dark skin was bursting with muscle – arms, abdomen and legs. She sported several deep scars, of which one ran up the inside of her thigh. Oolia could only imagine what experience had led to that.

Before the steward was a powerful woman, whose passiveness could lead to aggression over a barrel of water.

The corporal raised a fist, but was restrained by Wilek and a second servant who had come over when they saw the commotion.

"It's okay," Oolia said firmly, as Lais tried to shake them off. "Release her, now!"

They did as Oolia demanded and Wilek apologetically offered Lais her gown, which she gratefully put back on.

"I'm sorry it came to that, *Corporal* Stone." There was no objection from Lais this time. "But I desperately need your help."

"I'm done offering help," Lais hissed through gritted teeth, glaring at Oolia. "Especially for the Sultan and his damn army,"

Oolia was unfazed. "Well you may just be in luck. What I need you for may not help the Sultan. In fact, I'm afraid for my sake that it might just do the opposite. And if I'm right, then it might just save your life."

Lais's demeanour changed in a heartbeat. Her shoulders relaxed and any residual aggression floated away. "What do you need?"

"Back so soon?" the doorkeeper said sardonically. "And I see you have brought a friend this time." He looked Lais up and down. She was wearing plain clothes: a simple white tunic, cotton trousers and sandals. "Was I not clear before about who may gain admittance? Sultans and soldiers. She is neither."

"Are you sure about this?" Lais whispered to the steward.

"Since we aren't going to try and take the door off its hinges, you may as well let her try and open it herself," Oolia replied to the doorkeeper.

"Doesn't hurt *me*," he replied flippantly, then stepped aside.

Oolia gestured for Lais to try the knob.

Lais looked a little confused. "What's the big deal? It's either locked or it isn't." She reached out and grabbed the knob, clasping it and evidently feeling no resistance.

Oolia breathed a sigh of relief. In explaining to Lais what she had needed of her, she had failed to mention the part about the pain-inflicting doorknob, and could only wonder how Lais may have reacted had she not been able to touch it.

Lais twisted and pushed, and the door eased open.

"Very well," the doorkeeper conceded. "I hope it was worth the trouble."

Lais and Oolia stepped through into a chamber so poorly lit that they could not see the walls. The only thing visible was a large stone bowl that hovered above a stone slab in the middle of the room.

"What is that?" Lais asked.

Oolia headed straight towards it. "The Font of Succession, created millennia ago to determine the heir to the throne after each sultan. Ancient laws dictated that the sultans must be pure of virginity, so there may never be a familial succession. At the time, the sultan would choose a summer elf who they knew to be worthy, powerful and merciful enough to succeed them, but that led to too many disputes. The sultan's word wasn't proof enough when they died, or else the successor was often just the highest bidder." Oolia was inspecting the bowl. It contained a clear, viscous liquid, but nothing more. "The Font of Succession removes all ambiguity. Whoever the Sultan truly believes to be worthy of the throne will be represented here."

"And you want it to be you?" Lais asked.

Oolia chuckled. "No, absolutely not! I have dedicated my servitude to the Sultan and I want nothing of his power. That is not the purpose of this visit."

"Then what is?"

Oolia didn't reply. She was busy sweeping dust off the stone slab beneath the font, revealing an inscription.

Calis for'un eilech
Reveal thy face of merit.

"This language is ancient Pentari elvish from before the

Arvum was unified," Oolia revealed, but her excitement fell upon deaf ears.

"We didn't learn much history in the academy," Lais explained, waving away the comment.

The steward stood before the font and peered over it. "Calis for'un eilech," she said boldly.

The thick liquid began to swirl as if someone had removed a plug – though it didn't drain. It rippled and splashed against the sides, glimmering in the soft light within the bowl. Slowly, a face began to appear.

Oolia's mouth dropped open as she stared into the font. "Oh Ayermune, what have you done?" she murmured grimly, like she was scolding a child.

Lais peered over the steward's shoulder. "Who is she?"

"I don't know her name, but I have seen her in the Sultan's chamber."

"So she's his successor. What's the problem?"

"The problem," Oolia explained, stepping back from the font in disgust, "is that it is impossible in Panamayan law for anyone but a summer elf to inherit the throne. Even had the Sultan believed another elf to be more worthy, the font would still reveal the next most worthy summer elf to be his successor. Panamaya is a proud home to all races, but the sultanship abides to the heritage of its local people. I don't know how she did it, but this spring elf, whoever she is, has somehow manipulated the Sultan so that deep in his soul he believes her to succeed him."

"What does this mean for the Sultan?" Lais asked.

Oolia sighed. "It means he has been corrupted, and the last time a sultan was found guilty of corruption they were executed in the desert by being tied to a post, coated in goats' blood, and fed to the dalachites."

The gravity of the situation was beginning to dawn on the

corporal. "Can you imagine the reaction of the locals if they were to find out that a spring elf is lined up to succeed the Sultan?"

"Rioting, segregating, persecution…"

"This might be a leap, and don't think I'm making associations just because of race, but do you think the bandits may have something to do with this?" Lais proposed. "We killed one and he was a spring elf."

"I suppose it's possible that the elf in the font is working with someone else. Do you know what happened to the bandit's body?"

"Last I heard, the Warden of the Archivus had it in his cellar for examination."

Oolia looked contemplative. "Look, let's keep this between us for now. If the wrong ears hear us then we could find ourselves in trouble, especially as the Sultan is prone to making rash decisions. If the attacks on the canal are related to all this then we may be on the precipice of war with Rosensted. I suggest you go to the warden and see if there is anything on the dead bandit that may link them to the elf in the font. We could do with tracking her down and finding out what she wants. Meanwhile, I'm going to return to the Sultan's side as his dependable steward and, if the opportunity presents itself, gently probe at his ambitions."

"Well, I have nothing else to do before my hearing, but don't expect me to keep quiet in court if the judge is preparing to sentence me to death," Lais muttered bitterly. "Time is running short, and not just for me."

"What do you mean?" Oolia asked, confused.

"These tremors are becoming more frequent and more violent. Even I am beginning to suspect that the tales of the Sleeping Giant may be true."

CHAPTER 8

A TIME FOR REFLECTION

Fjona wasn't used to the sage being so quiet. He walked purposefully along the dirt track, holding his staff out in front of him for navigation. She decided it best to leave him to his sulking and save him the trouble of answering her questions.

Besides, Fjona was struggling to relieve her mind of the tormented cart driver. She kept picturing the way he had leaped at them, his hunger for death, even the vacant look in his eyes which seemed startlingly familiar. The hysterical laughter, the scream.

Then, of course, there was the mangled corpse of the original driver, whose death could surely have been preventable had they only arrived at Colt a little sooner and not wasted so much time with Falavei. Even the image of the dead horse flashed through her mind. It hadn't chosen to accompany them and now it burned to ashes in the same cart it had been forced to pull.

Without realising it, Fjona's spiralling thoughts had overwhelmed her to the point that she stopped in her tracks. How long they had been walking for since the cart and how long she stood alone on the track, she could not have said. Time appeared to have frozen for her. Her head swam with harrowing laughter; horrible eyes; congealed blood; orange flames that had consumed everything but her memories.

Perciville was yelling, but the contents of his words were lost on her. His tone sounded angry, but Fjona didn't care. She was physically and emotionally incapable of caring. She wanted nothing else but to wake up in her loft and find that everything had been one strange, lucid dream. Right now, even the wand in her pocket and all the possibilities it bore could be a part of that dream for all she cared.

The yelling got louder, certainly closer. A few words, something like, "Are you kidding me, we don't have time for this," managed to penetrate Fjona's brain fog, but they had no effect on her whatsoever.

The sage was practically screaming at her until, suddenly, he wasn't. She could feel his presence before her, but could no longer hear him shouting.

That's when she realised her cheeks were cold with her own tears.

Before she knew it, Perciville had embraced her. She could feel dew on her face as she nestled against his robe. He felt so warm, so unexpectedly nurturing.

Fjona cried into the sage's shoulder and she wasn't entirely sure that Perciville wasn't sobbing a little too.

When eventually he let go, she saw a flash of light issue from his staff. Then, he wrapped a ragged blanket over her shoulders and gently eased her onto a log stool in front of a fire.

The warmth was blissful. Fjona hadn't realised just how cold she had felt. Her senses were beginning to return to her and, when she looked down, she realised she was holding a jar of steaming hot coffee. Not that she had the energy to drink it right now, but it felt glorious in her hands.

Perciville had been quiet until now, but when he began to talk Fjona could finally make sense of his words.

"Harri Lodin was my favourite barista in Havensend. No, across the whole damn continent."

Fjona looked up and managed to take a sip of coffee. It was like smooth, nourishing lava coursing through her body.

The sage continued. "He made the absolute best coffee anywhere in the Arvum. Beans came from the Bouandan jungles, the cream from Elkensen mountain goats, and even the water came from the springs of the Precipitous Mountains. It was like drinking your greatest love affair, mixed with your wildest fantasy and warmed with your fondest memory. Even the jars in which he served it came from the potters of Rosensted. I tell you, Miss Sarsen, no drink has come close to matching what Harri Lodin could brew and, before you wonder, no – what you are drinking now is my own concoction and it pales in comparison."

Fjona didn't mind. It did more than hit the spot right now.

"Harri poured as much love into his coffee as he did to his customers and he was revered by everyone who ever set foot in his café. When the turned-sage created the Eight Afflictions, there was a period of time when they had yet to take effect – before the Afflictions were consumed by Santhé."

Perciville was silent for a moment.

When he next spoke, his voice was gentler still and wavered a little. "There were tormented men appearing everywhere. Sallisai'Mae, Elkensen, you name it, there was trouble. They were ferocious, and armies could only do so much to defend against them. Local civilians had no chance. It takes more than a pitchfork to combat them. A sword or an arrow can deter them, but really the only way to kill a tormented man is with dark manipulation. Spells intended to kill. Oh Harri..." He began to sob. "He was loved so much by the sages and was determined to stand up to the turned-sage, but he never got the chance. I paid a visit to check up on him and I saw the signs immediately. The eyes, the anger, the frothing at the lips. I tried to talk sense back into him; then I tried using manipulations to contain him, but my limited skills at the time failed to hold him. He leaped at me and, to be frank, I was prepared to let him devour me, but he dived straight over

73

me. Straight over me and towards a child taking refuge in the café with her parents, hiding under a table. My instincts got the best of me and I used dark manipulation, just in time, to slaughter my beloved friend. My poor, poor Harri Lodin."

For a while, the only sound was the crackling of the fire.

"I'm sorry," Fjona whispered.

The sage shook his head as if to say 'don't be'. "That was the first time I ever had to kill," he told her. "Before a horrible series of culling tormented men. Before the cities went to war, and long before our friendly cart driver. Fjona, please forgive me if it seems I can kill without care. Every death by my staff chipped away a little part of my morality, but it still weighs down on me. The driver is no exception. We have a long journey ahead of us and I know I can get wrapped up in my own ambitions, no matter the cost. If at all you need to talk about what you have experienced then please know, I am here to listen."

This time, Fjona got up to join Perciville and embraced him, enveloping them both in her blanket.

"Thank you, I feel better now." She really meant it. The sage's stark honesty had restored some of her faith in him and their mission. Although the image of the tormented driver still pervaded her thoughts, at least she could take comfort in the fact that his death meant something to his killer.

When she released him, Perciville spoke up again. "Since we have stopped for a break, you may as well get some more practise with your wand."

Fjona smiled, extracted her Woven Wand from her pocket, focused her energy, and levitated the empty coffee jar off the ground with seeming ease . Every day her skills were improving and she was becoming a bit more of a sage – for better or for worse.

CHAPTER 9

THE WELL BENEATH THE PALACE

"You must forgive my steward," the Sultan apologised as Oolia vacated the audience chamber. "It is most unlike her to cause a disturbance."

The general simply grunted and picked up from their conversation. "In respect of Corporal Stone, we need to remember that the role of a Noble Guard is highly exclusive. With the treaties in place, we cannot afford to keep a position occupied by a gung-ho, disobedient thrill-seeker when there are many thousands of Panamayans on the waiting list to join the cadets. Whether the judge rules the corporal to have broken her oath or not, I am still concerned that we may have a division led by somebody completely out of control."

"Hmm..." The Sultan considered the general's words with his fingers resting on his narrow chin. "You make a very true point, Sigmund. I already feel as though my control over my people is waning; I dare not lose it with my own army."

The general nodded approvingly.

"Very well, we must wait to hear what the ruling is, but be prepared to consider promoting a ranger to the position of corporal, and training up a new ranger in their stead."

"Consider it done, my Sultan."

"And Captain Lahsilli," Ayermune continued. "Competent?"

There was no hesitation from Kheller. "One of the best, and highly revered by the locals. He is currently out at one of the outposts – Salamander, I believe – responding to a report of dalachite pups. A dozen or so have been seen encroaching on the town which suggests there is a parent somewhere close by. I trust Beric, and I value his judgement, as do the other captains and many of the rangers."

The Sultan nodded. "Very good. My feelings too, but I wanted to hear your own. I gather the bandit raids have ceased?"

"For now, yes. There has been no disturbance since the corporal's faux pas"

"So it may be that her actions have deterred them?"

Kheller chewed his lip in contemplation. "It is possible; though don't forget, the bandits broke through her defence. It may be foolish to believe we have seen the end of them. The one bandit who was killed had no belongings or skin brands or indeed anything to reveal who he was, other than being a spring elf. I handed the body over to the Warden of the Archivus for closer examination."

"Though one spring elf doesn't mean we are at odds with all of Rosensted," the Sultan pointed out.

"So you say, but is it not feasible that the spring elves may feel threatened by our new trade route with the Free Capital?"

"Feasible? Certainly," Ayermune replied. "But likely? No. I have spoken only recently with a prestigious ambassador for the Governess and she assured me that Rosensted have no intentions to tarnish our good relationship. I trust her sincerely: a spring elf in fact. Whoever led, or is leading, the attacks are low-level tyrants trying to cause problems. It is almost certainly a dispute with the Kelner elves rather than with Panamaya City."

"Then I have no cause to disagree, especially as I too have met with a Rosensted official, a beauty of a spring elf herself, and she was most—" The general smiled boyishly as if reliving a promiscuous memory "—encouraging."

The Sultan was quiet for a moment, chewing on his lips and

studying the general's expression. *A beauty of a spring elf?* What were the chances that two elves of such description had visited the Upper Gate?

A simmering feeling of suspicion and jealousy stirred within him, though the Sultan only forced a smile of his own. "Excellent, indeed. You see, Sigmund? Not every conflict beckons the brink of war. With that in mind, let's not assume the threat has completely subsided. I'd like you to shuffle around some of your divisions and increase the sentries around the construction. I have just met with Sanjin Baerita and she is confident the canal will be fully functional by the end of the year. Let us do everything in our power to aid its success."

"It is done, my Sultan. I have enlisted two of the south divisions to help, but I can reassign some from the east. They have been getting restless with little to occupy them so I am sure the change of scenery will do them some good. Anything else?"

"I believe that is all my agenda," the Sultan replied. "Here, let us share a toast to prosperity."

The Sultan stood from the table and proceeded to a wooden cabinet with a golden trim, in the corner of the audience chamber. He extracted two small chalices and a bottle of *lamna*, then carefully poured the green-blue liquid into each glass.

"I'm afraid I've no ice, but I like it all the same at this temperature." The Sultan returned to the table and handed one of the glasses over to the general. "To prosperity," he said, raising his cup.

"To prosperity," Kheller concurred, and they clinked their glasses together.

Just as the two chalices made contact and the sound of glass resonated, the ground beneath them began to shake. The crystal chandelier above them started to rattle and the heavy audience table shimmied a short way across the polished floor.

Outside the audience chamber, they could hear the

murmuring of frightened voices. Then the door swung open and two Home Guards, blue coats billowing in the tremors, fell into the chamber.

"Are you okay, Your Divine Excellency?" the first guard asked.

The quake subsided and the four elves stood on legs of jelly.

"Yes, yes, we are quite alright, be gone!" the Sultan snapped.

The two Home Guards gave one another an abashed look, then retreated back out of the chamber and closed the door firmly behind them.

Kheller was the first to break the silence. "I have felt only one tremor before, but it was barely a wobble. Are they perhaps getting worse?"

The Sultan felt faint and on the verge of vomiting.

"My Sultan, are you unwell?" the general asked.

When the Sultan replied, his voice quivered as the floor had done moments before. "I have heard rumours, but people talk all the time. I had always believed the tales of the Sleeping Giant to be just that: tales. Perhaps there is more truth to the myth than I ever accounted for. Come, I believe it is time we pay tribute to our elusive god."

Before Kheller could argue, the Sultan headed purposefully towards the door and the general was obliged to follow. They descended the two flights of marble stairs leading down to the entrance hall. It was dusty following the tremors and the servants were already cleaning up, chatting to one another in hushed, scared voices.

Ordinarily, the Sultan would have reprimanded them for talking while at work, but he was far too preoccupied on this occasion to pay them any attention.

They rounded a corner and followed a tight, pillared hallway down to another flight of stairs that descended into the cellar rooms and servant quarters. It was foggy with dust and bore a musty smell like that of old books.

"Is this really necessary?" the general asked as the Sultan led them through a simple door at the end of a dank corridor. On the other side was a spiral staircase that twisted down yet further into darkness, save for a few dim candles along the walls.

The Sultan responded as they descended. "I fear that there may be some truth to the history of the mountain. How often have you come down here to pray to the giant?"

Kheller didn't reply.

"Nor I," the Sultan continued, "though it is said in the doctrine of Panamaya City that the sultan should regularly pray to the Sleeping Giant in return for good fortune, and that the general of the army should do the same, but for longevity. So far as I know, no sultan has been down to the cellar for centuries, let alone down to the shrine."

Kheller ran his hands along a sharp iron banister. "The story of the Sleeping Giant is a fairy tale. These tremors are circumstantial."

"Let's hope so..." Ayermune offered uncertainly as they reached the bottom of the stairs and stepped off into a small chamber before an incongruously large and ornate arched door.

The Sultan reached under his robe and pulled out a tangle of brass and silver keys. He fumbled through them and began trying them each in the lock, though with little success. He seemed to lack any method too and the general was sure the Sultan had tried the same key at least twice already.

Kheller collected his own keys, of which he had far fewer, from his belt.

"Here," he said, "I think it's this one."

He brandished a thick copper key that was larger than the rest and had stumpy, long teeth, then twisted it stiffly in the lock until it clunked open. The Sultan pushed Kheller aside and heaved the door open himself.

On the other side was a small cavern. They were inside the

very peak of the mountain, just beneath the belly of the palace. The cavern was lit by tall stone lanterns spaced evenly around the room, all of which burned with a strange green flame that leaped up the rocky walls.

A circle of sandstone pillars reached up to the ceiling of the cave and surrounded a simple stone well, up a short flight of steps, in the very middle of the chamber.

Kheller followed the Sultan up towards the well until he abruptly crouched down before it. Awkwardly, the general knelt beside him and, together, they bowed their heads.

Then the Sultan spoke. "Oh mighty Giant, he who sleeps beneath us. I am Sultan Ayermune Dhaller Sé and, with me, General Sigmund Kheller. On the surface we can feel your strength and we beg for your mercy. For though we are small, we the people of Panamaya City are virtuous and spiritual, hardworking and tenacious. To you I offer my respect. Guide me to appease your will and allow me to fulfil my duty to you as the Sultan of Panamaya City. I will do whatever you wish. All I ask is that you spare this city and its people. Oh mighty Giant, hear my plea."

His voice filled the cavern and echoed off the tight walls. It was so powerful that the silence that followed was palpable.

Only when the general grunted did the Sultan open his eyes to see Kheller peering down the shaft of the well.

"Sigmund, get back from there!" Ayermune commanded. "Have you no respect?"

"Don't you think it's odd?" the general mused, blatantly ignoring his superior.

"Don't I think *what* is odd?"

"That you can see a long way down the well, but there's no sign of anything down there."

The Sultan joined Kheller and peered in beside him. "I guess we're looking past the giant's head and down to his feet. I'm sure if you were to drop a torch down there you'd see his toes."

Kheller shook his head. "Your Divine Excellency, please hear me. You know I have nothing but profound respect for you, but this is madness! There is no such thing as the Sleeping Giant. It is a story told to children to make them behave, that is all!"

Ayermune tightened his jaw. "You think me mad?"

The general suddenly found himself on the back foot. "I think you are under a lot of pressure and that you are looking for something of which you can gain control. Quakes happen all the time across the Arvum; it is just a natural movement of the earth."

"Maybe so…" Ayermune said, taking a cautious step away from the stone-walled chasm, "but why take the chance?"

The general began to turn as two firm hands pushed him from behind and he tumbled over the edge of the wall in a cloud of ruby and gold.

Screams reverberated up the shaft as Sigmund Kheller plummeted into darkness. Before the Sultan knew it, the general had gone. He had fallen so far into the crust of the mountain that not even a thud could be heard when he hit the bottom. If, indeed, he had hit the bottom.

When the Sultan spoke again, it was in a venomous tone. "Oh mighty Giant. I offer you my finest soldier as a sacrifice to you. I pray for many more years of slumber." Then, in a softer voice, he added, "Forgive me, Sigmund."

Whatever morsel of grief the Sultan felt was fleeting, and he was quick to vacate the chamber, locking the door carefully behind him. He needed to return to his own chamber to make plans. After all, he now had a new general to find.

CHAPTER 10

UNEARTHED

They had found Elian's horse only a short way around the corner and, by mid-afternoon, it had taken them the rest of the way through the Outer Gate and down to the base of the mountain.

Kaikura took a deep breath as they descended the final part of the slope and crossed under the stone entrance canopy that marked the threshold between Panamaya City and the Pentari Desert.

The ranger turned to her. "Is everything okay?" He had a look of consternation across his face.

Kaikura hadn't realised just how audible her breath had been. "Just preparing myself."

"For the Kelner elves?"

"For the desert." Kaikura gazed around at the vast, empty horizon. For an immeasurable distance, all she could see was sand, clouds of dust and perfect blue sky. The stark nakedness of the landscape was as refreshing as it was unsettling. There were no clustered houses or gatherings of people, no smell of street sewage or sounds of arguments, wailing, or relentless complaining about the wealth gap.

Instead there was nature and stillness, and terrifying vastness.

"You've never been down to the desert before?" Elian asked, his eyes wide.

Kaikura shrugged. "I've never had the necessity. My life's sphere revolves around only the Archivus and my home. I am learned enough to know that the desert is dangerous and unsuitable to navigate without a guide."

The ranger tugged on the reins and the horse began to amble gently across the hot sands on its strangely wide hooves.

"There are dangers, of course," Elian agreed, "but what is a dalachite pup or the odd bandit compared to the thieves, delinquents and drunks in the city?"

Despite the immense heat, Kaikura shivered. "I try not to think about them."

"The traffickers and the troublemakers who call themselves gangs?"

"Please, if I'm to sleep well tonight, my thoughts best not be swimming with the images of ghastly men trying to sneak into my hovel to kill me." She was surprised by how casual her own words sounded. "Besides, I have security."

At first, the ranger scrunched up his eyes, until he realised what Kaikura meant. "The sandkat?"

Kaikura nodded. "Bobassa."

"Bobassa. Handsome creature indeed, and vicious, I bet, when he wants to be. Why not bring him to the desert with you?"

"He's a true companion and has proved to be very protective at times, but without a ranger and a horse to lead me, the desert is off limits." She let out a longing sigh. "As much as I'd like to visit some places other than Panamaya City. Have you heard of the Carved City of Bouanda? Buildings quite literally cut into the cliff face."

The ranger shook his head. "To be frank, I've not heard of Bouanda."

Now it was Kaikura's turn to be dumbfounded. "What! Well, if I might divulge, Bouanda is a jungle-covered island, situated in the far north of the Arvum. Sallisai'Mae, the local name for the Carved City, is the native home to the island elves."

"An interesting race, I must admit," Elian replied. "Just had no idea where they came from. I was only ever taught about Panamaya City and our nearest neighbours: Rosensted, and Havensend, and the town where the little elves come from."

Kaikura beamed at Elian's innocence. "They're called tipids, a species derived from the diminutive village of Nouwa. When I say *diminutive*, I mean that the houses and streets are all in proportion to the tipids themselves. So I've read, anyhow. I've never been there." She sighed again. "I haven't really been anywhere."

"Hey, how about we go together?" The ranger's voice was warm with kindness.

Kaikura sat up straight on her saddle. "Really?"

She couldn't remember anyone extending an invitation to her, with the exception of Sialah Bouwer offering her to join the Archivus.

"Why not?" Elian continued. "When the canal is finished it's likely my duties will be reduced. I could consider it, what do they call it...? An *ambassadorial expedition* of the Arvum."

"The general would permit that?" Kaikura struggled to keep the scepticism out of her voice.

"I don't know, but I can always ask."

Kaikura burst into laughter. "You know, at a time when our workers are being needlessly attacked by bandits and the Sleeping Giant is seeming to awaken, you are a very optimistic man."

"Life can be hard," the ranger replied solemnly, "so I think it's good to be positive where you can. Who knows? Maybe I'll speak with the general later and he might permit me to go on a drinking spree in Rosensted, you know, as an ambassador!"

When eventually they arrived, it appeared that most of the Kelner elves had got back to work after their discovery that morning and were once again occupied excavating the trench and batting the sides.

"Wow..." Kaikura gasped as Elian pulled the horse up around the sandbank.

"Yep." The ranger smirked, raising his eyebrows. "It's pretty big!"

"It's gargantuan!" Kaikura exclaimed. "I mean, I have observed it from the city, but from up there it just looked like a narrow scratch running through the desert. I hadn't appreciated its vast width, and depth for that matter."

A deep, bold voice came from behind them. "You can understand now why the other cities might feel intimidated by it."

"Ranger Holden," Elian smiled, then swiftly shook his head. "Forgive me! *Corporal* Holden, let me introduce you to San Kaikura Kendi, a student of the Archivus." As he spoke, he offered a hand to Kaikura and gently helped her from the saddle.

"San Kendi, it is a pleasure indeed," Holden replied with a polite bow of his head.

He towered over Kaikura and, for a second, a pang of fear shot through her, until she remembered the circumstances in which they were meeting.

"Thank you, Ranger Holden," she replied, "and thank you, Elian, for delivering me safely." The scholar found herself staring at Holden's face. Specifically, the navy tattoo that had been inked onto his cheek. "Your family must have served in the Arvum War. I can only imagine the losses..."

Her voice trailed off and she regretted opening her mouth the moment Holden returned her a steely gaze.

"It was long before my time," he replied in a tone utterly devoid of emotion. "I wear my signet with pride."

"Of course," Kaikura replied.

"As do the remaining descendants of the war."

"Indeed, I know."

Kaikura's blood suddenly felt very hot and she could feel her ears reddening.

Fortunately, Elian was quick to relieve her discomfort. "We should show Kaikura to the trench immediately. The workers are very concerned with the artefact."

Artefact. The word rang in Kaikura's mind. "What is it?"

"Best you come see for yourself," Holden replied, the awkwardness of their conversation seemingly forgotten.

The interim corporal led Kaikura and Elian around the bank where the sounds of the excavations seemed to amplify tenfold. The clattering of mattocks and axes, the squeaking of pulleys, the general construction hubbub of easily a hundred labourers. Some of the workers were singing as they dug, others just passed the time with inane chatter, as much as Kaikura could tell from their language.

She looked up, away from the trench, and caught sight of several other rangers around the construction and on the banks. There seemed to be at least two divisions on sentry, and possibly more dotted around the outskirts. She shuddered at the thought of the bandits returning and her fears of the desert coming into fruition.

"San Kendi?"

It was Holden. Evidently, he had been speaking to her, but she had become too entangled in her own contemplations to pay him any heed.

The ranger looked at her glazed-over eyes, then gestured to a bony young elf beside him. The elf had bright eyes and a funny, wispy beard in the middle of his chin. He wore only a ragged pair of shorts and sandals, and his bare chest was mottled with a paste of sweat and sand.

"This is Starless'Sky," Holden informed her. "He'll guide you down into the trench."

"Excellent, thank you – sorry, guide me where?" Kaikura was suddenly feeling a little dizzy.

"I head back down to trench," Starless'Sky explained, in slow, careful Arvish. "You follow. We have item found from dig."

"All clear?" Holden asked.

"You're not coming with me?" Kaikura tried not to sound as desperate as she was.

"I'm afraid I am more useful on the surface," Holden explained, his fingers twitching with agitation as if he were tired of their conversation and wanted to get away to more pressing duties.

"I'll accompany you," Elian offered.

She felt a fraction reassured, though still very apprehensive about descending into the depths of the desert.

Holden turned to Elian. "Is that so, Ranger? We need you at your post." The interim corporal stood tall and intimidating like a statue as he glared at the younger ranger. The sword at his hip glinted in the sun.

For a moment, it seemed that Elian was going to buckle, but he caught Kaikura's eye and winked. "My instruction was to find an expert from the Archivus, deliver them safely to the artefact and accompany them back to the city. I still need to fulfil my task." He spoke with an assertiveness that steered well clear of rudeness and sat firmly within the realms of obedience.

Holden's thick frame relaxed. "Very well, Ranger Sole." He gave Elian a respectful nod. "I trust you will be of good use to the labourers." He turned to Kaikura. "We appreciate you coming down for this."

Before she could respond, he kicked his horse and galloped

away from the trench.

"Thank you," Kaikura whispered, once Holden was out of range.

Elian nodded, quickly tying his horse up to a post before heading towards a rickety ladder that dangled down to the first step of the excavation.

"I'll meet you at the bottom," he said, then led the descent, followed closely by Starless'Sky.

"It is, ah, safe!" Starless'Sky reassured Kaikura, as he looked up from the top few rungs to see her looming nervously over the tip of the trench. "Only one, er, die? Umm, no, only one death! One death from ladder fall."

It wasn't exactly comforting, but one death in miles and miles of construction and many thousands of ascents and descents wasn't too bad, considering. She knelt down on the edge of the trench, feeling the abrasive, grainy sand on her knees, then swivelled carefully around and reached for a rung with her foot. Gently, she retreated backwards, then gripped onto the rope handles. It shook with the movement of Elian and Starless'Sky beneath her.

She tightened her grip and focused her vision on the trench wall, determined to keep from looking down.

"Wish me luck," she said to Elian's horse, who appeared to bray a response to her.

With every wobble of the ladder and every spray of sand against the side of her face, the descent down to the first of the two steps was very trying.

Starless'Sky tried to help distract her. "*Kaikura* is nice name. What does meaning?"

The scholar was so preoccupied with not missing a rung and falling to her death that she barely heard the labourer, and didn't offer a response.

Her silence didn't deter him.

"You city elves have funny names," he continued. "They make no, umm... uhh... sense! Your names make no sense."

"And yours do?" Kaikura retorted, though more out of politeness than to further the conversation.

"Kelner elves give names on the err... circum..." He trailed off as he tried to remember the word.

Before Kaikura could offer a suggestion, her foot reached a hard stone surface. She had made it to the top of the first step, though there was still a fair way to go.

"Circumstances?" she suggested to the labourer, who had waited for her on the step before descending the next ladder.

"Yes, circumstances! We are named by *circumstances* of birth," he replied, before beginning the next descent.

Kaikura followed hastily, eager to get down to the surface, offer her expertise, then get home to the safe confines of her hovel and have a nice cup of tea.

"I was born in small camp near Barracuda, near sea. No rain in desert, but big clouds in sky sometimes in summer. I came at night, but so many clouds that no stars were seen so they named me *Starless'Sky*."

"That's a delightful story," Kaikura murmured between nervous breaths, hoping she sounded more genuine than she felt.

"And my brother!" the labourer added excitedly, "born of famed winter in the camp, ahh, cooking tent. Have guess. What did they name him?"

Kaikura shook her head. "I have no idea."

"Please," Starless'Sky insisted, "have guess."

"I don't know, umm... Chilly'Sands?"

The labourer laughed heartily, shaking the ladder as he did. "No, but nice try! No, they call him Frozen'Pots!"

Kaikura tried not to snigger, but the surprise got the better of her. "Really?"

"Don't worry, he laughs at his name too! When born, they put him in a cookpot filled with, er, blankets, to keep warm. Before then, it had been too cold to touch, so they say."

They proceeded down to the second step, then the rest of the way down to the base of the trench. Starless'Sky had continued to list the names of his family and close friends, explaining their origins and suggesting alternatives. By the end, Kaikura was grateful to the labourer for keeping her preoccupied while she climbed down.

"How come your names aren't in Kelnish?" she asked, once they reached the bottom.

Starless'Sky shrugged. "They were 'til the magic-makers took the world."

"You changed your names into Arvish after the Sagedom was formed?"

The labourer nodded. "Now we speak Kelnish, but our names are yours." He glanced up at the ladder. "You must be glad not to fall today."

Kaikura nodded. "I calculated my chances of falling to be slim if only one labourer has died during the entire construction."

Starless'Sky's face scrunched up with confusion. "Ah no. Only one has died this *week*. Many, *many* more have fallen here. We dig and we build, but our ladders don't last." He shrugged, seemingly unbothered by this terrifying revelation.

Before Kaikura could react, Elian Sole interrupted them.

"So, where is this mysterious artefact?" he asked, wiping a bead of sweat from his forehead.

Indeed, without a breeze to cool them and with the increased heat from the workers, it was much hotter down at the base of the trench than it had been on the surface. So much so that the ranger had removed his helmet and now carried it under his arm.

The noise of the workers reverberated around them and Kaikura's head pounded with the sharp clanging of metal on stone.

"Yes, please show me," she said, hoping to get a move on.

Starless'Sky led them along the rocky, sandy base, passing through labourers and around wheelbarrows piled high with spoil. The sides of the trench loomed high above them and Kaikura was starting to feel more than a little claustrophobic. At least, she acknowledged, the labourers had shored the trench face with wood and stone to prevent it from collapsing.

They came up to where the main excavation was happening. Dozens of labourers were lined up along the base and on the steps, and were systematically breaking through the face of the trench. Kaikura observed the form of what they were digging through with great intrigue. A geological record of the Pentari Desert tracing back centuries, if not millennia, with each layer holding environmental secrets from an era long forgotten. From the top, down to just beneath the second step, the face predominantly consisted of sand, though the strata was distinguished by different shades: golden browns, paler whites and red browns in the middle. Then, strangely, a dense layer of blue clay with streaks of what appeared to be preserved organic material. Beneath that, several layers of buried soils, then down onto rock.

"What are you looking at?" the ranger asked, evidently disinterested in the geology.

"Nothing," Kaikura replied, "just my own fascination. Now, where is this artefact?"

"Over here." Starless'Sky pointed to a tattered cloth with the bulge of an object beneath it.

Kaikura carefully removed the cloth and was surprised, if not a little disappointed, by what lay beneath.

"What is it?" Elian asked. If he was disappointed too, his voice hid it well.

"I'm not exactly sure," Kaikura admitted.

It was a long, curved object – thick at one end, then bent around towards a sharp point. If stretched out, it would have been the length of Kaikura's arm, and the widest end was about the circumference of her waist. It was the colour of a raincloud and heavily worn like the glaze peeling away from a pot.

"May I?" she asked the labourer, gesturing to pick it up.

Starless'Sky nodded.

In her hands, the artefact was heavy, though still light enough to carry. Its skin was hard and smooth, and the pointed end was viciously sharp.

"Where precisely was the artefact discovered?" Kaikura asked as she gently rolled it over in her hands.

Starless'Sky called over another labourer. They exchanged a brief conversation in Kelnish, pointing at the strange object and over to the excavation. Then the labourer was dismissed and returned to shovelling loose stone into an already overfilled wheelbarrow.

"He say it fall from blue, err... we say *Lutuma*," Starless'Sky explained.

Kaikura tried to interpret what he meant based on where he was looking. "The blue clay?"

Starless'Sky nodded gleefully. "Yes, yes! *Lutuma*: clay! From blue clay."

The scholar looked contemplative, glancing from the object to the clay.

"What are you thinking?" Elian murmured.

"That blue clay, I think, is alluvium," she said, as if it explained everything.

Elian stared at her, like a hound waiting to be fed.

"It is sediment formed by moving water, often associated with flooding," she explained.

"Flooding? In the desert…? How is that possible?"

"The layer is deep in the stratigraphy, indicating that it formed a long time ago, prior to the formation of the desert as it is known today. In other words, it means that this" – she gestured to the artefact – "pre-dates the desert. Now, as for what it is…"

Starless'Sky spoke up. "The workers say a horn from demon! Is why some are scared."

Kaikura smiled. "A horn, indeed, almost certainly. But I think only a wild imagination would connect it with a demon. A more likely conclusion is that it once belonged to an *aurik*, a sort of ancient cow, or else some other long-extinct mammal. It's interesting…"

Elian exchanged a bemused look with Starless'Sky. "Forgive me for asking, but how exactly is an ancient cow interesting?"

Kaikura rolled her eyes. "Do you not understand? The city is suffering moderate earth tremors to which the locals are retelling the tale of the Sleeping Giant. Now, you and I both know that it is a myth… except that maybe it isn't. This horn and that blue clay prove, undeniably, that there was a landscape here long before the desert was formed."

"Yes, but you said it was a floodplain, not an entire lake like in the story and, if it had been a lake, how would a cow have lived in it?"

Kaikura shrugged. "Stories get lost in translation and change faster than the seasons. Perhaps there was never a lake, but an enormous river surrounded by floodplains, or there *was* a lake and we are standing on a long-lost island, or perhaps a peninsula? Whatever the case, this proves there was an inhabited landscape here before the desert was formed."

"I don't know, it all sounds a little far-fetched to me. A giant, buried beneath a city? A harbinger of doom, soon to awaken?

Maybe it is just a cow." Elian gestured again to the horn.

"Believe me, I'd have made the same assumption only a couple of weeks ago, but there is something strange going on around here and, as a scholar, I do not believe in coincidences. To find evidence of a buried landscape here at the same time the mountain is quaking? Call me crazy, but there is something bigger at play here."

Elian breathed out a long, controlled sigh. "In the grand scheme of things, I hope you are crazy."

CHAPTER 11

SCARRING

After her encounter with the steward, Lais had decided it best to head home to fully sober up before paying the warden a visit. Since her, supposedly temporary, dismissal from the Noble Guard, she had moved her modest belongings out of the barracks and into a cramped inn on the edge of the Lower Gate. For a bassal a night, she had her own room, and it came with a lock. She had thought that if that failed to keep the thieves and horny men away, then the Pentari knife she had pinched from the barracks ought to do the trick.

By the time she had returned to her room, drained several jars of cold coffee, cleaned herself up, and changed into a fresh tunic and trousers, the day had worn on, the sun was starting to sink, and the moon was already peering over the horizon.

She grabbed her purse, although it was significantly lighter than it had been the week before, and tied it to her belt. After all, she wasn't sure how easy it would be to get into the Archivus and her ticket that usually allowed her into the Upper Gate may no longer be accepted.

The air was warm and dry outside as Lais exited the inn and cut through an alleyway beside a tavern called The Sleeping Giant's Wife. The swinging sign over the door sported an indecent adaptation of the sultanship's Giant emblem, instead portraying it with long, dark hair, comically large breasts, and lying provocatively over the city. Naturally, the crowd clustered around the entrance were balding, beady-eyed elves who could barely hold themselves up for the ale.

As Lais walked past, one of the elves reached out a sweaty palm and grabbed her arm. "You owe me a kiss," he slurred through purple gums.

Repulsed and simply not in the mood, Lais thrust the hilt of her knife into the man's ribs and he keeled over in pain.

"Argh, you whore!" he yelled, spitting up a mouthful of blood and beer onto the ground.

The man's dreary friends looked up from their tankards.

"Bozzie's been attacked by that bitch," one of the elves jeered, reaching a hand beneath his tunic.

"He attacked *me*," Lais corrected, despite doubting these drunks would care for her perspective.

"How dare you speak to us, *woman*," an autumn elf replied, snarling through stained teeth and gesturing rudely with his fist against the palm of his hand.

Lais dismissed them and tried to move further along the alley, but one of the more agile elves hopped across the tables, hand on his belt, and impeded her.

"You ain't going nowhere without first getting on your knees," he growled, whipping a short blade out from his hip.

Lais snarled at the knife with a look of derision. "If your manhood is anything like your sword, it wouldn't be worth anyone's time to get on their knees."

The elf tightened his jaw and his eyes burned like fire. "I gave you a chance to yield."

Lais was quick to react as he waved his sword at her, parrying the blade with her curved Pentari knife. She pushed forward with all her force until the elf stumbled back along the alleyway.

"I suggest you lower your weapon before you get really hurt," Lais snarled through a jaw so clenched she could form pearls between her teeth.

The elf didn't heed her warning. Instead, he lunged towards her with his blade raised above his head, and targeting hers. Lais was fast to react and ducked to one side. As the elf fell past her, she stabbed him firmly in his calf and he slumped ungraciously in a heap next to his friends. Blood gushed out of the wound as the elf cried out in agony.

"Had I missed my aim, you'd be bleeding blue and nobody recovers from that," Lais sneered, sensing that she had finally made her point.

Her senses were very much mistaken. The sad gang of drunkards reached for their weapons – knives, maces and hammers – and made towards her. They no longer looked like they wanted her pleasure; more like they'd settle just for her head on a spike.

Lais took one look at them, quickly calculated her odds, then turned on her feet and scarpered in the opposite direction, cursing under her breath.

She sprinted along the alleyway with the antagonised elves closing in on her from behind.

Just as they seemed to be gaining on her, Lais tumbled out onto the street, narrowly missing a tall grey horse.

"Whoa!" the rider called out, wrapping her hands around the horse's neck to keep from falling.

"Corporal Stone?" A ranger stepped around the front of the horse.

"Elian?" Lais gasped, catching her breath as the elves threw themselves out of the alley in rough formation.

There were six of them in all and, though they had evidently been drinking throughout most of the day, they seemed to be able to hold themselves upright.

"Why d'you run, sewer rat?" one asked.

"Should've warmed my sheets when you'd the chance," said another.

"Lower your blades," Elian demanded, brandishing his own sword.

"Piss off, Ranger, this ain't your fight," the first elf grunted as he waved his knife at Elian.

"If it's the corporal's fight, then it's my fight."

"Corporal?" the elf said, glancing Lais up and down with a look of disdain. "Don't seem like no corporal to me."

Lais thought they were technically right, but was wise to keep her mouth closed.

"Sheath your weapon, and return to wherever it is you came from," Elian commanded, stepping up to the lead elf.

The elf scrunched up his thick, dark eyebrows. "And if we refuse?" He turned the knife point towards Elian.

"I'm afraid that isn't an option."

The elf spat in his face. Long, viscous strands of saliva crawled down Elian's cheek. The ranger didn't flinch; didn't even show a hint of disgust or discomfort.

He merely grunted. "So be it."

In one swift movement, Elian threw his cutlass to his side and Lais grabbed it by the hilt. With his other hand, he whipped out a short sword and cleanly cut through the elf's hand. The elf's knife clattered against the stone paving as hot blood fountained onto the street. The shock and pain seemed to be so excruciating that he couldn't utter a noise, other than the thud of his thick frame on the ground as he fainted.

"Hey-hey! Go!" Elian called to his horse, tapping it lightly on the rear. The horse neighed, then cantered slowly out of harm's way.

"Whoa, what are you doing?" the rider panicked.

"Keeping you safe, San Kendi," Elian replied. "I'll be back

shortly."

The horse had barely moved out the way before iron met iron.

Elian pushed back one of the assailants with his shield while Lais sparred with two swordsmen. She used her strength to hold them off, but failed to get close with her sword. Then she pushed them apart, fending one off with her sword and the other with her knife. Slowly, the elf defending against her knife edged closer and closer until it seemed certain he was going to land a fatal blow. Just as the elf stabbed forward for Lais's head, Lais ducked out of the way and the two elves stabbed each other. One had a sword through his eye, bursting it like a soft-boiled egg. The other took the blade firmly through his shoulder. It wasn't likely to kill him, not if it could be safely removed, but until then, all his strength vanished and he cowered away.

All the while, Elian was feeling the wrath of a mace as it pounded relentlessly against his shield. The ranger held his ground, biding his time. He was feeling the rhythm, counting the brief interval between each hit. Again, again, again, the mace thundered down on the emblazoned iron. Then, calculatedly, the ranger heaved forward, causing the attacker to temporarily lose his balance. In that moment, Elian swiped at his legs with his shield and the elf crumbled to the floor.

With the odds of success dwindling, the remaining elves took one look at their fallen comrades and fled back down the alleyway.

Elian stood over the mace-wielding elf who lay in a bundle on the ground with the ranger's sword pressed into his neck.

"Tell me why I shouldn't push this the whole way through," Elian demanded, applying a little extra force and gently cutting into the elf's leathery flesh.

"Because you don't have the bollocks for it," the elf sniggered, then choked on the blade as it slipped cleanly through to the back of his neck.

Elian turned to the elf whose hand he'd pierced with his sword. The elf, still with a dazed expression, had at least come around from fainting, though his skin was as blanched as his winter brethren. He was crouched on the floor, fumbling with his shirt and attempting to stem the flow of blood wasting from the wound.

"Clean this mess up," the ranger said firmly.

The elf looked up at him with disbelief. "But I've only one hand." His injured hand was now tucked in his arm pit, blood still seeping through the makeshift bandage.

"Should've thought about that before you attacked a member of the Noble Guard."

Again, Lais realised it best to keep her mouth shut. The maimed elf didn't need to know that she was due in court in a couple of days with the verdict almost certainly to be guilty and the punishment to be, at best, release from the Guard.

"You" – the ranger turned to the elf whose shoulder was skewered on his friend's sword – "help him. I know your faces. If I return to find you haven't pulled your weight then you'll wish I'd put you down like I did your pathetic friends."

The elves looked terrified. Even Lais wore an expression of surprised fear.

The two elves fumbled around in pain and attempted to move the first of the bodies.

"Thanks for saving my butt," Lais murmured. "It's good to see you, Elian."

"You'd have done the same for me," the ranger replied. He embraced her warmly. "It's damn good to see you too. Walk with me..."

They started up the hill to where Elian's horse waited patiently outside a bookstore.

"I've never seen you like that," Lais commented.

The ranger shrugged. "With everything that's been going on lately, I guess I'm reaching the end of my tether. The bandits, your dismissal, these drunks attacking you just for walking past their turf. This city frustrates me…"

"It's not the city, just a small minority. I'm glad you appeared when you did. I'm not sure how long I'd have fought them off with my knife. Where were you headed?"

By now they had caught up with Elian's horse. "I was escorting San Kaikura Kendi back to the city. San Kendi, please forgive me for abandoning you." He bowed his head to Kaikura, then gestured to Lais. "This is my friend and leader, Corporal Lais Stone of the Noble Guard of the Sultan."

Kaikura smiled at Elian. "You are of course forgiven. It quickly became apparent that you had only my safety in mind." She then appeared to scrutinise Lais from top to bottom. "It's a pleasure to make your acquaintance, Corporal."

"Likewise," Lais replied, bowing. "How is it you know each other?"

"The Kelnish workers excavating the new canal have uncovered what transpires to be the horn of an ancient animal," Kaikura explained. "However, prior to my assessment, it had stirred some distress. Elian came to me to ask for my opinion on the artefact."

"San Kendi is a student of, if I remember correctly, anthropology and mythology at the Archivus," Elian added, looking to Kaikura who nodded in confirmation.

"The Archivus?" Lais repeated. "You wouldn't happen to be heading that way, would you?"

Elian shook his head. "I was returning Kaikura back to her home. Why do you ask?"

Lais picked her words carefully. After all, she didn't want to draw too much attention to her sleuthing, even in front of a trusted ranger. "I heard the body of the bandit that Fayne killed out in the desert has been moved to the care of the warden. I was hoping to see it to help gather some evidence to support my case to the judge."

Elian seemed convinced by her mixture of fact and fiction. "Well, I'll be soon heading up to the barracks. Why don't you accompany us and we can visit the Upper Gate together?"

"I can take you to the Archivus," Kaikura offered. "The curators are rather strict about who can enter, but if you're with me, you'll have no problem."

Lais considered the offer for a moment. On one hand, involving more people may put them at unnecessary risk, especially if the Sultan were to hear of it. Then again, having a seasoned scholar who could get her into the Archivus without hassle and introduce her to the warden could only be beneficial.

"Very well, thank you," she replied.

They continued to the Upper Gate. Kaikura was mostly silent while Elian filled in Lais on all the latest news from within the Guard. When eventually they passed through the wall, Elian walked them up to the Archivus before bidding them farewell and returning to the barracks.

Kaikura, with the animal horn wrapped in a sheet and tucked under her arm, led Lais through the garden and into the Archivus.

"Have you ever visited the Archivus before?" she asked, holding open the grand door for the soldier.

Lais shook her head as she passed through into the low-ceilinged vestibule. "Never."

Lappili and Desmée seemed to never go home to sleep and were still slumped in overly sized chairs at the front desk, though Desmée had nodded off and was snoring with impressive gusto considering his size.

Lappili meanwhile stared at Lais with beady eyes as Kaikura ushered her through.

"She's accompanying me," Kaikura explained to the elderly tipid.

"Hmm..." was the only reply.

As they stepped through into the main library, Lais looked around in astonishment at the vast ceilings, decorated pillars and row upon row of bookshelves.

"Come," Kaikura urged. "I shall give you the full tour another time, but we best get a move on."

"Okay," Lais mumbled, too mesmerised to offer anything more.

The scholar led them around the ground-floor gallery to a dark and narrow corridor towards the rear of building. It was hidden away behind the books and had gathered enough dust to suggest that people scarcely ever came this way.

"This is where the warden studies?" Lais asked sceptically as she brushed past a tangle of spiders' webs.

Kaikura shook her head. "No, this is the way to the basement where I believe the warden has stored the body that you are looking for."

Lais noticed the scholar shudder, and the image of a decrepit body stuffed into a crate, then hidden beneath the Archivus, sent a chill down her own spine.

"So we're not meeting with the warden?"

"Let's just say Warden Newblood has been acting a little strange of late. A little aloof and not his usual spirited self." She paused. "He creeps me out a bit."

They came up to a low wooden door, unlocked but stiff in its frame. It needed more than a little strength to push it open. It was so low that both Kaikura and Lais had to duck to avoid hitting their heads on the lintel, and they had to continue down a narrow, spiralling staircase with their heads tucked in and their shoulders squeezed against their chests.

"Are you sure we're allowed to be here?" Lais whispered, surprised at herself for being concerned over breaking the rules.

"I never said we *were* allowed..." Kaikura replied. "But since the door has been left unlocked, nobody could blame our intrigue."

At the foot of the stairs, they stepped into a round vault, somewhere beneath the Archivus. It had high ceilings with an intricate truss and small windows right at the top, with only a shaft of moonlight creeping in.

Around the vault were shelves crammed with old books and strange objects, wooden crates and barrels, metallic instruments and unusual tools. It was liking stepping into the mind of a scholar's chaotic passions.

In the middle of the basement was a round stone table, stained with blood. Above it, a low-hanging candle chandelier.

Kaikura found a rusty oil lamp and used it to light the candles, inviting a golden gloom into the room.

"Are you sure the body is in here?" Lais asked, shivering in the cold space.

"So I've heard," the scholar replied as she distractedly pried through the warden's belongings.

At the far end of the vault, Lais came across two lead caskets, each with a padlock the size of her hand. They were cold to the touch and she imagined them to be unimaginably heavy.

"Over here," she called to Kaikura.

The scholar joined her and she vainly attempted to tug one of the locks away.

"Have you some hidden strength that allows you to break metal?" Lais asked wryly.

Kaikura sighed. "You're welcome to give it a go yourself."

They both suddenly froze in horror when a gravelly voice came from behind. "You'd be wise t-to leave that b-be. And tell me, who do I have the pleasure of reprimanding for breaking into my study?"

Slowly, Kaikura and Lais turned around. The scholar jumped at the sight before them. Warden Daemund Newblood stood facing the two women. His skin looked ghostly pale, his eyes sunken and pallid. A wiry, dishevelled nest of hair buried his chin, and his white-and-gold robe hung loosely over a wilting frame.

Lais wondered if the warden's sickly appearance was merely a product of the poor lighting in the basement, but she knew she was kidding herself.

"Sa-San Kendi! Ah, a p-pleasure of course," the warden said, his tone dramatically shifting to a pleasant timbre, "and you m-must be…?"

"*Corporal* Lais Stone," Lais replied, emphasising her former title for all it was worth.

"A friend of our es-esteemed scholar, I don't d-doubt?"

Kaikura hurriedly spoke up. "Warden, the corporal wishes to see the body of the spring elf who was killed in the desert. She is hoping to find some…" She paused, suddenly aware that she might be compromising the soldier.

"Evidence as t-to who he m-might be?" the warden finished.

"Actually, yes," Lais confirmed. "Can you help me?"

Daemund laughed. It was a cold, eerie laugh that sent a reverberating chill across the spines of the truss and down the walls.

"No. But not because I don't w-want to. Because there is nothing to see. Allow me to show you…"

He hobbled unsteadily towards them, leaning on the stone table for support. Then, he moved them aside with cold, clammy hands and stood before the second of the two lead crates.

"Are you feeling unwell?" Lais asked, battling to keep the repulsion out of her voice.

The warden ignored her, instead too focused with the lock.

There was no keyhole, nor numbers to twist into a code, but rather dozens of tiny brass switches that could each be moved in four directions. It was mind-bogglingly complicated, even for someone who evidently already knew the code.

Despite a severe lack of dexterity, Daemund fumbled at the switches until he found the pattern and the lock clicked open.

As he heaved the lid open, an icy mist spilled out of the casket.

"If perhaps you'd b-be so kind…" He gestured vaguely towards the contents of the container behind them.

Kaikura and Lais exchanged a concerned look.

"You want us to—"

The warden cut Kaikura off before she could finish. "Move the body onto the t-table," he commanded, clapping his hands together. "This is your project a-after a-all, is it not? Besides, I have examined the b-body from t-tip t-to t-toe and found nothing to distinguish him from anybody else."

The thick smell of rotten meat poured out of the casket and it was enough to make Kaikura's eyes water.

"I'm not sure I can do this," she protested, but Lais simply returned her a steely gaze. "Fine, but I'm taking the feet." Kaikura placed her animal horn carefully to one side, peering into the frozen casket.

Lais took the shoulders and, together, they lifted the stiff, naked body out of the crate and carried it over to the table.

Kaikura retched at the sight. Pale green skin like the flesh of an apple, with a network of cuts and stitches from the knife of a coroner. A tapestry of death. The eyes were dark and hollow, and every bone seemed to be pressed up against the skin as if it were about to burst through. Of course, there was a deep gorge through the neck where Fayne's arrow had struck, though the arrow had subsequently been removed.

Lais, however, was less concerned by the smells – the only

aspect of the dead bandit's appearance that did bother her was the lack of anything that may explain where he came from.

"I t-told you," Daemund stuttered. "The boy holds no secrets. He had on him only an axe and these *hibernigot* beans." He handed Kaikura two oval beans, no bigger than the size of a fingernail. One was blood red, the other a bright green.

"What exactly are hibernigot beans?" Kaikura asked, pressing the smooth, hard legumes between her fingers.

"A coward's way out," Lais replied, not even looking up from the body.

Kaikura looked to the warden for an explanation.

"Not very c-common these days. They are incredibly d-difficult to grow. They require perfect acidic soil, exact levels of s-sunlight and only a finite amount of w-water."

"Yes, but what do they do? Why might a coward eat them?"

"To avoid a more g-gruesome death by the blade of an axe. Individually, the b-beans have no effect on the body. But consumed in a p-particular combination will result in one of two consequences. Take the red before the g-green and it will only simulate death. Your heart stops beating, your b-blood stops flowing and several hours later, you will aw-waken as fit as fiddle, though a little groggy. Take the g-green before the red and you will perish within minutes, experiencing no ounce of p-pain."

"Red before green and you'll only dream; green before red in a moment you're dead," Lais recited, still carefully examining the corpse.

Kaikura returned the beans to the warden. "So he had these on his person for what reason? To avoid interrogation? Execution? Torture?"

"Exactly." The warden's pale eyes brightened with excitement. "Most likely enforced by a g-gang leader. I've not come across them for a long time. Not since I witnessed a whole b-battalion take their lives during the War for the Arvum..." He trailed off then, unwilling to relive the tale, and he dropped the beans in a silver dish away from the body.

Kaikura shivered again in the cool of the basement, then changed the subject back to the matter at hand. "What precisely are you looking for?" she asked Lais.

"Most gangs, at least in Panamaya City, have some kind of initiation branding. Body art, ink tattoo, burn stamps," Lais replied, catching the scholar's shudder as she spoke.

"Most g-groups take pride in their associations. They want to be recognised for their c-crimes."

"But it shows the authorities who to incriminate," Kaikura added.

"True," Lais replied, carefully examining the body's face and neck, "but the authorities, at least in this city, are scarcely powerful enough to imprison or execute every gang. Historically, they've tried, but each time they cut the head from one leader, another two seemed to replace it." She ran her fingers down the body's shoulder, looking for marks or signs, or anything. "So now most of the gangs just pay off the Sultan. After all, why would it bother him if a local, hardworking shopkeeper was murdered in his own store because he refused to serve a killer, if the fees paid by the gang funded a new wing to his palace?" She rolled the bandit onto his back with a thud.

"You'd b-best be careful to not speak so f-freely, Corporal. A Noble Guard, no less, bemoaning our leader. You could l-lose your position for that."

Lais seemed unmoved. "Quite likely," she said simply, staring down at the dead bandit whose arm shone iridescent in the moonlight. "Nothing!" she shouted. "How can he have nothing?"

"You failed to take heed of my caution," the warden replied.

Kaikura wore a look of disgust, though no longer for the

rotting corpse in front of her. "How can our Sultan be so corrupt in plain sight without anyone protesting? He should be dethroned for allowing such behaviour to exist."

Lais turned to the scholar, her eyes burning with frustration and anger. "Look, the Arvum isn't the pretty little place described in the history books. It's complicated and messy and nothing really makes sense. Out there in the real world, there are cruelties and atrocities, death, deals, and corruption. Just because your sheltered little world in this library protects you from it all, doesn't mean it isn't out there. You want to learn about it? Put down your papers and pick up a damn sword."

Her voice rebounded off the stone walls until fading into tense, awkward silence. Kaikura appeared too shocked by the soldier's response to even speak. Tears were welling in her eyes as she stood there, silent as a grave.

The warden started muttering behind them. "Well who would have b-b-believed it..."

Kaikura finally found the courage to retaliate. "My life isn't all about books."

"Corporal! Look!" Daemund exclaimed, apparently oblivious to the whole tense conversation.

When Lais turned back to the table, the moonlight had climbed up to the bandit's chest and a white crest, carved into his heart, glowed through his skin. It was a single line that came up and around to form a rough triangle, before cutting back up through itself. A crudely etched sword through a mountain.

Lais's face glowed with excitement. "A brand!"

"What does it mean?" Kaikura asked, her voice still quivering.

The warden blocked the streak of moonlight with his body and the shining emblem vanished. Then, when he stepped aside, the sword and mountain immediately glowed through the skin again.

"How could this even have been made?" Lais pondered.

Daemund addressed Kaikura first. "It means this b-bandit worked for an organised cult. The a-attacks on the canal m-must have come from someone with a r-real agenda." He then turned to Lais. "As for its conception… I cannot say. It seems somehow familiar, but blocked deep down in my memory. Alas, if p-perhaps I could recall, I should find you and share the knowledge."

Lais shook her head. "That might be difficult."

"And why is that?" the warden asked.

"There's nothing left for me in this city. In a little over a week, I will likely no longer be with the Noble Guard. I've found myself a new mission." Lais looked down at the bandit. "I'm going to Rosensted to find out who this elf worked for and bring a stop to it." She turned to Kaikura with a faint look of shame. "You are right, San Kendi. Somebody needs to stand up to these gangs."

CHAPTER 12

THE PADDOCK

It transpired that the tormented coach driver had led Fjona and Perciville further west than the sage had originally thought and, even after a full day of hiking across the plains, Rosensted was still a long way off.

The evening had pressed in and Perciville had conjured a new camp in the crease of a hillslope where there was at least some protection from the wind. Even here, in the vast openness, the sage was still reluctant to manipulate the weather and he knew his apprentice lacked the skill to do it herself.

He rested against the wall of a conjured mud hut, juggling a wooden ball between his hands, and watched Fjona attempt to start a fire with her Woven Wand. He had challenged her to start the fire that evening and was adamant he wouldn't bail her out and do it himself. It mattered little to him anyway since his robe was enough to keep him warm.

Considering Fjona was yet to develop the ability to conjure materials for herself, she had collected some kindling from a nearby thicket of oak trees and had carefully assembled the branches and twigs into a neat pyramid. Perciville had offered to conjure some firewood for her, but Fjona had been too stubborn to permit it.

She sat cross-legged in front of the pyramid with her eyes tightly shut and the wand pointed firmly at the sticks.

A stiff breeze shook the tip of her wand and she opened her

eyes excitedly.

"Well, that's disappointing," she said as her whole body slumped forward, fireless kindling staring back at her. "Why can't I do it?"

The sage tilted his head, then took a hefty draught of conjured whiskey. "It will come in time. You know *what* to do, all you need is to break down the barrier that is preventing you."

Fjona sighed. "I just don't know how to do *that*. Maybe my wand is broken!"

"Typical Myrish, blaming her tools!"

"Is that a real stereotype on the mainland?"

The sage chuckled. "Absolutely! The elves always mock the Myrish and, to a lesser extent, the Marrowborn for blaming our tools. It's intended to be light-hearted of course, but they'll say things like 'maybe if they made better tools, they would live longer'!"

Fjona looked back, confusion etched across her pale face. "I don't understand. Is the Myrish life expectancy that much lower?"

"Relax, Miss Sarsen, the elves are merely poking harmless fun. Blaming your tools, never moving away from home, being particularly chatty; those are the main things they say of the Myrish. Equally, summer elves are said to be stern, island elves are lavish beyond their needs, and spring elves are free-spirited. I could go on, but I'm sure you get the point."

He took another swig of whiskey and closed his eyes.

"How long do the elves live for?" Fjona asked, having given up on lighting the fire and instead levitating a stick off the pile of kindling.

"It varies across the species and of course wealth and lifestyle play a huge factor." The sage appeared to be weighing up the values in his hands. "But generally speaking, up to about five hundred years."

Fjona's eyes widened. "What! Five hundred years?"

"Yes, well, that really only applies to the summer and autumn elves. Island elves can be even longer, but spring elves are more like one hundred and fifty. Then, at the other end of the spectrum, there are the tipids who live to about thirty or so years, but they cherish the time they spend in this life."

"So then, surely most elves remember the collapse of the Sagedom?"

Perciville's expression turned sour and he shook his head. "Sadly not. During the collapse, with the onset of the Eight Afflictions, and in the war that followed, the blood that was shed across the Arvum could fill an ocean. Generations were wiped out in all the cities. There are a few, like Falavei in Colt, who were around at the time and do indeed remember, but most of the populations are born of the children who took refuge at the time. Any remaining sage will of course remember, but I don't know how many are left."

They were quiet and reflective for a while. Only an owl hooting in the nearby thicket and the chirping of evening crickets in the fields could be heard.

Perciville noticed Fjona shivering. Wordlessly, he took his staff and ignited the kindling. He almost expected Fjona to object to his interference, but she didn't say a word.

"How long will I live for?" Fjona asked tentatively.

"Again, there's no clear boundary for a sage's life expectancy. As a general rule of thumb, harnessing the art of manipulation may increase one's life tenfold, but with greater variation."

"So I might live to eight or even nine hundred?"

Perciville just nodded and watched, as he had seen many times before, somebody process the cost of longevity. First, the smile. The knowing that time is no longer a threat to one's existence. That a day lounging around and achieving nothing equates to an insignificant speck in a vast lifetime. The chance to really see, experience, and learn everything before it's too late. To fall in love, bear children, and grow up to see generations and generations of one's own bloodline thrive and... then the look of realisation. He'd seen it in Caeznor when new sages were initiated. The sudden awareness of those whom one would outlive. One's parents, siblings, friends, lovers and all those generations of children, unless they all happened to train up as sages. The conflicts, sufferings or relentless mundanity that surpass all lifetimes.

He watched as Fjona's eyes and mouth processed everything she may be sacrificing for the sake of adventure, power and curing the world.

She ran her hands down her legs for comfort and stopped when her palm met an object in her pocket. She pulled it out and held it before her. Todie's amulet.

"If I'm to live so long, I'll be leaving so many behind," she said, running her fingers over the intricate depictions. "I must learn to forgive him."

"A long life isn't always what it's cracked up to be," Perciville told her. "Though nor is a short life, a medium life, or anything in between. Fjona, listen to me carefully..." He sat up and waited until Fjona's eyes and his met. "It matters not how long we live. It is how we spend our time that is important, not how much time we have to spend. Do you understand me? Take each day as it comes and cherish all that we have to learn."

Fjona took a deep breath, then pointed her wand at the fire. A brief but forceful wind appeared and expelled the flames, plunging them both into a darkness that had quietly crept in while they were talking. Then, moments later, a spark appeared at the tip of the pyramid. Then another, deeper into the pile, and soon embers were growing. Before long, the fire was reignited and the warmth returned.

Fjona smiled. "I did it!"

"Manipulation is like writing," Perciville explained, smiling back at her. "You have the words inside of you and the dexterity in your fingers to articulate them, but you still need ink, a quill and parchment to write them down. In the same way, we have the root of all spells within us, but it is only with a wand that we can harness them. Your wand is not broken, Fjona, you just need to learn to write."

Fjona looked the sage up and down. Her smile turned into a grin, her grin into laughter and soon she was in a fit of hysterics.

"What did I say?" Perciville asked, feeling his face reddening.

"You're a talented and wise man," Fjona replied, "but boy can you be pretentious!"

Perciville broke into laughter and soon they were both in fits, each with a jar of whiskey, giggling like children into the night.

The proceeding days followed the same rhythm. They would awaken with the sun, tidy away their campsite, have something to eat if it was available, and then set off for a long day's hike. In the evenings, they would find a suitable place to nestle down for the night and Fjona would take the opportunity to practise her skills with some guidance from the sage, if he was in the mood to assist her.

They were working well together and, in doing so, had managed to travel a good distance through the Paddock. With every rise and fall of the moderate landscape, every brook and river that had to be crossed, and every thicket of woodland that had to be passed, Perciville could sense they were nearing their destination.

They had even been fortunate enough on a couple of

occasions to stumble upon a lonely farmhouse, whose occupants were nearly always obliging to offer food and fresh milk whenever the sage withdrew a bassal or two from his robe.

As they journeyed south, the days started to become longer and the air was feeling humid and warm. The weather had attracted midges and flies that had started to pester the pair, and Fjona was becoming irritable as they swarmed around her. The insects seemed to be bothering the wild cattle and horses too who were regularly seen charging around the pastures, trying to shake the pests away.

The flies had, however, encouraged Fjona to practise her manipulations and she'd found that summoning a nearby lofty breeze worked well at disbanding the swarms, though the effect only lasted so long before another cloud of midges would appear.

Despite these nuisances, both Fjona and Perciville's spirits were high and both were noticing vast improvements in Fjona's abilities with her Woven Wand. She was beginning to manipulate the elements with more confidence and sustain the manipulation for longer. Naturally, the more progress Fjona made, the better a mood Perciville was in and this had a crucial impact on both their states of mind, particularly on the long wet days without any trees or hills to shelter and too little time to make camp.

The urgency to make Rosensted in good time was only heightened the nearer they got to the town.

They had both noticed it, but it was Fjona who pointed it out first.

"All the crops are dying," she said as they circumnavigated a field of endless wilting plants. As far as the eye could see lay blankets of brown, rotting stems on beds of mulch, with a putrid smell for accompaniment.

Perciville sighed. "We are running out of time."

They followed the farmstead down to an old, well-travelled

road and were able to pick up the pace now that the ground was level.

"How long after we open this box will it take for the Eight Afflictions to disappear?" Fjona asked.

The sage didn't reply.

"You have no idea do you? Do you even know if this plan of yours will work?"

Perciville let out an exasperated huff. "Ultimately, yes, it will work. I was there at the conception of the Eight Afflictions and I know what it will take to control them. I can't be sure how long it will take for the vessel to take effect. All I know is that this is the best – the *only* – shot for the Arvum." He turned to Fjona and looked her in the eye. "You have to trust me."

Fjona shrugged. "I do trust you, Harper. You've been right up to this point."

The road they now followed was once a major trade route between Rosensted and Colt, though it had long since fallen into disrepair and now a single wagon may have struggled to navigate it, let alone a convoy of a hundred.

For Fjona and Perciville it was a welcome change from trudging across fields. Over the next few days, they followed the road as it wound down the hills towards the coast and would set up camp to one side of it.

Every so often, they would meet a fellow traveller heading the opposite way, often with a sack full of food or a cart loaded with milk or alcohol. They would stop to exchange for food and hear any local news that the traveller may be bearing from the town, though more often than not, their tales generally involved people neither Fjona nor Perciville had ever heard of, committing some kind of crime or grievance that didn't interest either of them, and resulting in minimal punishment that would never come to impact them. Merely a waste of time, though Fjona did enjoy meeting a few spring elves and listening to the sweet tones of their unusual accents.

As they walked gradually nearer to town, the traffic started to increase a little and Perciville insisted that they come off the road to prevent Fjona from starting up conversations and wasting more time. He claimed it was further evidence of the Myrish stereotype and that they simply couldn't afford to hang around.

After some debate, Fjona agreed to follow Perciville off the road which, according to the sage's staff, was a more direct route anyway.

Naturally, the sage received an earful when the sun began to set and an immense storm set in from over the Near Sea.

"Look," Fjona yelled over the wind, "it's your fault we're off the road and there is no shelter. Use your staff to calm the rain!"

"You know how dangerous that can be!" Perciville shouted back, inhaling a mouthful of icy rain, and ducking his head away from the onslaught of weather.

"There's nothing around here! Who is it going to harm?"

The sage was about to give in when he caught the glow of a lantern up ahead. "Look, there's a farmhouse! Chances are they'll let us warm up inside. Nothing I conjure will be as cosy as a fireplace and a proper bed."

Fjona squinted through the harsh rain. "Fine, but if you're wrong, you'll be hearing about this for the rest of our excursion."

Together they pushed themselves along through the mud, barely able to hear or think over the wind that enveloped them.

They followed a dirt track between two pastures that led straight up to the door of the stone cottage.

Perciville knocked, but Fjona didn't even wait to be let in. She pushed past him, threw the door open, and tumbled inside.

The door slammed behind them and the screaming wind was shut outside.

Fjona removed her soaked cape and wrung it out on the floor. "I feel like I can breathe again."

"Hello?" Perciville called. "Is there anybody in?"

There was no reply.

"Perhaps they're away in Rosensted for the night?" Fjona suggested.

"But then who lit the lantern?"

Confused, they followed the corridor down to where the light was coming from. It led them to a pantry where a tall lantern spat light upon a table near the window. The candle within had burned low and there was barely any wick remaining.

"Perhaps they forgot to put it out before they left?"

Perciville tilted his head. "Maybe, but keep close."

It was cold inside the farmhouse and Fjona wished they could have just kept to the road, found a quiet spot to set up and camp, and had another night like all the previous.

Alas, that was not the case.

Suddenly, the sound of something being knocked off a table came from deeper inside the cottage.

Fjona jumped. She was about to say something, but Perciville put his finger on her lips.

The light in the room began to flicker, then disappeared altogether. The candle had burned out and they were, not for the first time, plunged into darkness.

"Don't scream," Perciville whispered. "I'm still here."

The tip of his staff began to glow and some visibility returned to them, faint though it was.

"Let's just get out of here." Fjona's voice trembled.

The sage considered for a moment. "Alright, let's head back towards the door."

They vacated the kitchen and headed back into the corridor, following the modest glow of Perciville's staff. As they passed another door, they again heard the sound of falling objects.

Perciville put his hand on the doorknob, but Fjona pulled him away.

"Don't!"

Heavy footsteps echoed from the room beyond. It was too much for Perciville to resist. He gripped his staff, held the doorknob in his sweaty palm and gently pushed the door open.

The sight within horrified Fjona and she held her hand over her mouth. Hunched over a table was the bloodied and mangled body of a woman. Half her head seemed to have been torn open and flies buzzed around it, fighting over a meal.

Perciville stepped inside, pointing the staff around the living room to illuminate every corner.

"It's okay, Fjona, it's just the one."

"The one what?"

A purple flash erupted from Perciville's staff and Fjona knew exactly what he had meant. An animalistic cry came from within before fading again into silence.

Fjona followed the sage into the living room to see the dead tormented spring elf, mouth covered in bloodied foam, slumped in the corner. He was probably a farmer, judging by his rough-spun dungarees and cap. In one hand, he held the bones of an arm which Fjona realised had belonged to the woman slouched at the table, presumably the elf's wife.

"Let's just get out—" Fjona was interrupted by Perciville shouting.

"Ahh cockles, it's got me!"

Another elf had crawled from behind the table and grabbed Perciville by the legs, causing him to tumble to the floor. In doing so, he released his staff and it sailed through the air towards the door.

"Quick, get my staff!" he instructed Fjona as he writhed and kicked against the elf.

The tormented elf was grotesquely skinny, and his hair was thin and mottled with blood. Venomous yellow eyes stared at the sage as the elf cried and whimpered and tried to bite at him. It was clearly injured and unable to push itself up on its two rotten legs.

Fjona hopped around the table towards the staff, but another tormented spring elf slumped in through the door. It took one look at her and its head suddenly twitched up.

"No, no, no..." Fjona repeated as the elf flailed its bony arms at her.

"What are you waiting for?" Perciville shouted above the cries of the elves.

The standing elf leaped at Fjona, but she was quick enough to duck out of its way. Its head collided with the wall and the stones surrounding it began to crack. It seemed to twist its leg and uttered a pained cry.

Perciville was screaming now as he battled against the elf on the floor. Fjona whipped her wand out of her pocket and pointed it at her elf. She focused her energy, bravely closed her eyes, then felt the wand come alive in her hands. When she opened her eyes again, she had latched onto a glazed vase on a mantlepiece. Without any hesitation, she flung the object at the elf, and it shattered into pieces against the elf's taut skin. Ceramic shards ripped into its body and streams of blood oozed out of the cavities, but it did little to deter it.

Fjona repeated the spell, flinging trinkets and crockery, books and candles at the elf, enough to frustrate it and cause minimal pain, but hardly enough to disable it.

"Think," she said to herself, aware that she had only so many skills with her wand. She wracked her brain, digging for some ability that may come to her aid, though her thoughts were foggy under the pressure, and all that came to her was the knack of using her wand as a compass. Quite how that could save her, she didn't know.

Her mind flicked back to Willow's Brush, when she had begged Perciville to change the weather and he had, despite his own cautions, listened to her. That time, it had been reckless, but... an idea came to her.

She closed her eyes, focused, and pointed her wand forward.

The tormented elf hobbled closer towards her, unperturbed by the wand being waved in its face. Then, just as Fjona could feel its hot, stinking breath, the tormented elf stopped in its tracks. It could sense a vibration that seemed to be shaking the whole cottage. It turned its head to the window and stared in horror as the glass shattered and an immense gale and rain billowed into the living room, following the trace of Fjona's wand. She directed it into the tormented elf and it flew back against the wall behind her, clashing into a cabinet adorned with crockery.

"Nice! Now grab my staff and use it!" Perciville shouted, smacking his own tormented elf with the shoe of the dead farmer.

"How can I use your staff?"

"Just do it!"

The elf in the cabinet was beginning to recover and was pulling itself out of the splintered wood and shattered glass. It was screaming in agony, tensing its translucent arms with rage. Fjona could see its thick veins bursting against its thin skin, as it turned its furious yellow eyes at her.

She quickly reached for Perciville's staff and pointed it at the elf. It felt heavy in her hands and she knew little what to do. She thought of her training and imagined that it was just like using her own wand. After all, the spells were already in her, as the sage had said before.

She closed her eyes to help her focus and she felt the weight of manipulation erupt from the staff. When she opened her eyes, she saw a bright maelstrom of white light fire into the now helplessly overwhelmed elf. It screamed again, far louder and more piercing than before, then fell to the floor, panting like a hound.

Fjona took a second to catch her breath, but was quickly reminded of the sage battling away beside her.

"Umm, hello? Come rescue me!"

Fjona hurried around to Perciville, pointed the staff at the elf and released the same chaotic white light. The elf flew off the sage in a whirl of screams, and plummeted against the wall.

Perciville quickly leaped to his feet and snatched the staff away from Fjona, who was standing stiffly still and lost in shock.

He quickly fired a flash of dark manipulation at each of the two tormented elves and they slumped to the floor, dead.

"You did well," Perciville said, wrapping an arm around Fjona.

"Wh-what was that? The white light..."

"Let's get us warmed up and tidy away these bodies. I will explain everything in the morning, but we need to get some rest."

His response seemed to snap Fjona out of her stupor. "You can't be serious! How can we possibly stay here now? It's not safe!"

"It's safer than it was and no less safe than out there, believe me. Besides, I'll use my staff to make a shield. It looks like the residents will no longer mind that we are here. We'll do a quick sweep of the rest of the house, dump the bodies outside and maybe get a proper fire started. What do you say?"

Fjona glanced out the broken window at the storm and watched as a wooden bucket flew through the air.

She took a deep, resigned breath. "Fine," she conceded, "but since this is your fault, you can deal with the bodies."

CHAPTER 13

HOME FROM HOME

Fjona had been reluctant to sleep in one of the beds of the deceased occupants of the farmhouse, but the allure of warm blankets and a soft feather mattress was too much for her to resist. Despite the comfort of the bed and the reassurance of Perciville's shield, which enveloped the entire house, Fjona nonetheless suffered a long, sleepless night. She tossed and turned for hours, desperate to be taken away into slumber, but the harder she tried to drift off, the more difficult it was to do.

She was amazed, though not completely surprised, to hear Perciville snoring the moment his head hit the pillow. Somehow the killing of tormented elves, though it may weigh on his soul, did little to hinder his ability to fall asleep.

The moment the sun was creeping through the window slats, Fjona leaped out of bed. She was prepared to do everything in her power to get away from this place as soon as possible.

She started by making the most of a small washroom at the rear of the house where she could clean herself up properly for the first time since she had left home. Then she collected her clothes from downstairs. Before bed, she had completely stripped down, away from the eyes of Perciville, wrapped herself in a blanket and washed her clothes in a basin. The sage had kindly conjured a small green fire in the kitchen over which Fjona had hung her cloak, trousers, shirt and undergarments. To her delight, she found in the morning that her clothes had completely dried through and were warm and pleasant to put back on. She ran her hands through her messy, curly hair and pushed it away from her eyes.

Fjona had left Todie's rose amulet on the table so that she could hang her trousers up. As the morning light flashed off the amulet's heart of glass, it caught Fjona's eye and reminded her to put it back into her pocket. Feeling more refreshed and well rested than she had in weeks, Fjona couldn't help but feel that Todie's wish for the amulet to offer her good fortune was finally coming true.

Being in a house like this felt as if she were back home in Wychwold and an idea came to her. Fjona rummaged through the pantry and found a tray of brown eggs, a stale loaf of bread, and some chilled meat which still smelled good. There was even a jar of milk which had yet to go off and some hard cheese.

"It would only go to waste," she reasoned as she lay it all out on the kitchen table.

With a little effort, she used her wand to light the hearth and found a knife to cut the meat into thin slices. It was a joint of wonderfully fatty pink pork, and the sight alone made Fjona salivate. She threw it into a cookpot above the hearth and it started to sizzle, filling the kitchen with a sweet, tantalising aroma.

Before too long, the fragrance of cooked food had travelled up to the loft and Fjona could hear light footsteps coming downstairs.

"This. Smells. Divine!" Perciville exclaimed theatrically from the doorway, wiping the sleep from his eyes.

"Morning greets you," Fjona replied. "Please..." She gestured to the table, laden with cooked pork, scrambled eggs, fried bread and cheese.

"My absolute pleasure," the sage said, taking a seat. He looked around the table with a curious expression.

"I couldn't find any so I thought you could conjure some,"

Fjona explained, reading his mind.

Perciville grabbed his staff and pointed it at the table. One at a time, he conjured a mug of coffee for them each and passed one over to Fjona.

"You know," Fjona said after taking a hearty sip, "there is an amazing coffee plantation on Marrow Myre. It's at the base of the Infant Mountains where they grow the richest, smoothest beans I've ever had. Granted, until recently it was the only coffee I've ever had, but it stands up!"

"I know the one," Perciville replied, "and I agree, it's very good, but I've had better."

Fjona took a big bite of pork. "Well I like it. Perhaps my parents will pick some up on their return from their pilgrimage. I look forward to having a cup when I get home. That's if they don't completely despise me for running away."

"The Myrish are also known for being forgiving," Perciville mumbled through a mouthful of toast.

Fjona smiled and tucked into her eggs before asking the one burning question that had been plaguing her mind since the night before. "That white light. What exactly was it? I didn't exactly choose to create it."

"Ah, yes." The sage wiped his mouth on a long, floppy sleeve. "It is called *untempered manipulation*. When somebody wields a wand or staff to whom it doesn't belong, they are able only to cast this chaotic form of manipulation which has no capacity to conjure or heal, but can cause harm. As I said before, we all have the spells within us, but it is only with our own instrument that we have the means to express them. Yesterday, you cast untempered manipulation to disable the two tormented elves and, in doing so, saved our lives."

"So anybody can harness untempered manipulation, so long as they have access to a wand or staff?"

"Pretty much, but it can be dangerous and wildly unpredictable. Innocent lives have been lost by persistent abuse of another's instrument of manipulation, and it can permanently affect a living person's soul. It served us well last night as a last resort, but what we really need to do is train you up to cast dark manipulation so that you can protect yourself," Perciville explained.

"How long will it take to learn dark manipulation?" Fjona asked as she shovelled the last mouthful of eggs into her mouth.

The sage shrugged. "How long is a piece of string?" When Fjona didn't respond, he added, "There is no real timescale to progression, but there was once a sage with a proficiency for arithmetic who sought to calculate it. He found that it took twice as long to progress from a Woven Wand to a Wand, then three times as long from a Wand to a Long Wand, the latter of which enables you to cast inflictions."

Fjona's eyes were glazing over.

"Anyway, from that point you can start working your way towards dark manipulation, but it could take as long as ten, fifteen, even twenty years before you can really cast anything effective."

"Twenty years! I thought you were going to say by the winter solstice, or maybe next spring at the latest."

Perciville chuckled. "Miss Sarsen, how many times have I to tell you? The journey to becoming a sage is a long and tumultuous one, though mind-bendingly rewarding! Take my word, the best way forward is forward."

Fjona rolled her eyes. "Wow, how philosophical..."

"My point is, don't let the journey intimidate you."

"I'm not intimidated by it. I just want to get there."

"Well, that seems like a perfect segue. Rosensted isn't far. If we leave now, we can be there by early evening."

CHAPTER 14

THE WOMAN AND THE SHADOW

Nothing at all. With all the immense, unchallengeable power that had unleashed from the top of Marseiha's staff – that which had enveloped the landscape and vanquished an impenetrable fog – all that it had revealed was nothing. Nothing at all except the boundaries of an empty, lonely island in the middle of a vast, empty ocean.

Marseiha looked down at a barren and overgrown grassland with not so much as a tree or pond to intervene the monotony. In the not-so-far distance, sheer cliffs leaned over a rock-infested sea – the kind that experienced scramblers would have been wise to avoid.

She held the staff forlornly in a limp, sad hand.

Then she screamed. Not a terrified scream or one even of surprise. She screamed because, what else was there?

Here she was, stranded on a cursed island which was crumbling at her feet, lonely and confused with no notion of how she came to be there.

It was infuriating, and only by yelling from the belly of her lungs was she able to express at least some desperate morsel of herself.

Perhaps it was just as well that there was nobody else around for it spared them from hearing the string of expletives that rolled out of Marseiha's mouth.

When she was finished, she rested an elbow on the edge of the wall, put her head in her hand, and wept.

Exactly how long she remained like that was impossible to tell, but when she did eventually lift her head, she felt that her emotional well was all but dried up. A sense of pragmatism washed through her and she decided that all was not lost. After all, she was alive.

It was then that she scanned the desolate plains, and was stunned to see something buried in the luscious grasses on the far side of the island. From high on the wall, it wasn't possible to tell exactly what the object was, but it was vaguely shaped like a small building. Where there is a building, Marseiha reasoned, there must have been people for she would surely have remembered erecting it herself, wouldn't she? Surely...

Of course, she pondered, *whoever built it may no longer be here, but they must have come from somewhere.* Whatever the case, it was pointless to remain where she was so she decided to head back towards the tower where she had found her staff. It was only too likely that within it was a staircase that would lead her to the ground.

As she made again for the tower, her attention turned to the unwelcome sound of shifting sand behind her. She looked back to see that the fate of the chapel had indeed now befallen the wall and it too was starting to crumble.

Though her legs still twinged with the exertion of having climbed the wall, she found herself running as fast as they would allow towards the tower. No matter how hard she pushed herself, however, she could not outpace the rapidly disintegrating wall and it was surely catching up with her. Her misfortune then plummeted yet further as the tower itself started to crumble. It was like the contents of an enormous hourglass, gently pouring away into dust.

Marseiha skidded to a halt as larger blocks of stone started to rain down from high up on the tower, only narrowly missing her. One moment she could see the stone casket, illuminated in its soft glow, the next it was buried beneath a heap of sand and debris.

The wall was disappearing on either side and Marseiha was intrinsically aware that there would be nowhere left to stand before too long.

It may just have been her imagination, but she was sure that, partially muted by the sounds of collapsing walls around her, she could hear the cackling of the portrait demon and a horrible chill raced down her prickly spine. Perhaps it had indeed escaped and there was no knowing what intentions it had for her.

Unfortunately there was little time for Marseiha to worry about what may or may not be lurking on this island with her. With every brief second that passed, more and more of the brittle wall slumped away into a heap of sand – it was quickly closing in on where she stood.

She held the staff before her, then leaped from the wall. Now that she was submitting to gravity, she could feel the wind lapping at her dress as she fell. All her faith fed into the staff and she quietly begged it to spare her from falling to her death.

A sense of familiarity and security bled through her veins and Marseiha, though tumbling ungracefully towards the ground, held the staff upside down and found the strength to focus. In doing so, a strange yellow light spilled out of the upturned head and formed a disc beneath it. As Marseiha cautiously planted her feet on the disc, she and her staff stabilised and she remained suspended in the air.

Relieved, she expelled the breath she had been holding.

The fall had covered about half the distance between the almost entirely disintegrated wall and the ground, but there was still a fair way to go. She clutched tightly to the staff and steeled herself; she felt her body and her mind intertwine, then released her energy. Swiftly and smoothly, Marseiha drifted down to the ground, a safe distance from the demolition behind her.

When she landed on the surface, she hopped down onto the tall, squishy grass and planted an affectionate kiss on the neck of her bejewelled staff.

"Thank you, you beautiful thing."

The yellow disc faded away and Marseiha flipped the staff back upright and scanned the horizon.

On the surface, the landscape was just as stark as it had seemed from high up on the wall. Empty, but for a sea of tall grass and the speck of a building on the far coast.

With the prospect of a lengthy hike across the island, Marseiha felt that she was not dressed appropriately for such an endeavour. She held her staff above her and allowed her spirit to flow into the dark ebony wood. The head glistened with a silvery-turquoise glow and a swirling mist of colours enshrouded her. As it spiralled down towards her toes, her sullied, ragged dress transformed into a clean sand-coloured doublet, black trousers and sturdy leather boots. Now with her creative juices flowing, Marseiha thrust the staff forward and cleared a perfectly straight avenue through the grass. In its stead, an elegant stone pathway appeared that led directly to the distant building.

She may have continued to conjure had she not felt a pang of fatigue, deciding it best to leave her ambitions there for now. With more gusto, she strode along her pathway with a sense of optimism that answers would be awaiting her at the end.

In her head, she attempted to piece together the series of events that had led her here in hopes that she might recollect who she was and how she came to be on such a remote, desolate island.

From waking up on the floor of a cabin, to the ghastly corridor of empty portraits, the chapel and the altar, the mirror and the bell. Nothing seemed to make any sense and now it had all disappeared into a lifeless heap on the top of a cliff.

It was only for the reprise of a definite cackle that Marseiha snapped out of her daydream. This time, there was no doubt the laugh belonged to the portrait demon and that it was getting nearer with every terrifying beat. She paused and held her staff longways, turning gently on the spot and surveying her surroundings.

Then she saw it, though not the demon itself. What she saw was a path of dead grass that cut through the meadow in an erratic loop towards her. It moved like the wake of a ship, spreading through the pasture as a disease. The nearer it approached her, the more intense its laughter became.

The dying grass came nearer and nearer until the demon reached the conjured pathway, though no monster appeared from the meadow. Instead, a black shadow in the vague shape of a hand loomed across the paving. It was twisted and distorted, and moved with the suddenness of an arachnid. Long spindly fingers reached out as if it were trying to find Marseiha. When one digit did eventually point in her direction, the whole hand quickly raced towards her.

There was little time for Marseiha to react. She instinctively pointed the staff at the shadow and released a deafening pulse of energy that targeted the very centre of the hand. The demon seemed to freeze on the spot, apparently disabled by the attack.

Marseiha breathed, believing the danger to be over, but it didn't last long.

The shadow started to twitch and writhe on the paving, shifting back and forth like a dog trying to shake away a flea. Slowly, it rose out of the ground: a somehow three-dimensional shadow, still with grotesque long fingers.

To the sound of more horrifying laughter, the hand shadow started to spin around itself – a tornado of blackness. For a brief moment, it seemed to have transformed into a different shape altogether. To Marseiha, it appeared to be a long coat or a robe, though with no body beneath it. When she released more dark pulses at the shadow, they seemed to no longer have an effect. Conversely, her efforts seemed only to feed the monster's fury as it towered high above her.

"What are you?" Marseiha cried out. "What do you want?"

Her words fell on deaf ears, if indeed it had any ears, and her distress just encouraged further demonic laughter.

She screamed louder still and continued to expel a spectrum of colourful spells, though without any concept of what they were. Yet the shadow continued to grow, unperturbed by her efforts.

Just when all hope felt to be gone, the monster darted towards Marseiha with the velocity of an eagle and she felt it brush past her pointed ears.

When she turned around, she caught a glimpse of the demon climbing higher and higher into the sky until it was completely beyond her field of vision and had faded into the unknown.

With the shadow monster disappearing, so too did its harrowing laughter, and a peacefulness returned to the island.

Scars of dead, rotten grass were all that remained of its presence in this deserted place.

Marseiha could feel her blood boiling. She didn't feel scared or even anxious about who or where she was. Instead, she felt anger. Anger, frustration and an aching hunger for answers.

She looked back to where she had come from to see only an enormous heap of sand, and then looked the other way where, in the distance, she could make out the silhouette of the only landmark that existed here. One tiny building on an otherwise unremarkable island.

CHAPTER 15

BOSMAR FODD

"So much for 'Rosensted isn't far'," Fjona groaned as she and Perciville climbed yet another steep hill, having departed the farmhouse that morning.

After much discussion, she had persuaded the sage that they should return to the road to avoid any further incidents like that from the night before and, since then, they had followed that route for the best part of the day.

Perciville had huffed and puffed every time a fellow traveller stopped them for a conversation, though even Fjona had started to get fed up with the same monotonous exchanges. 'Where have you come from?'; 'What is your trade?'; 'Why is your companion staring at us with such scorn?'.

It didn't help that Fjona had hardly slept the night before and her legs were beginning to feel the fatigue from the miles of walking she had endured since leaving Port Widow at least a couple of weeks before. Although she could never admit it to Perciville, it really helped to now be relieved of their satchels, and her growing confidence in the sage's ability to provide meant that she could travel with nothing but the clothes on her back, her Woven Wand in her belt and Todie's Myrish amulet in her pocket.

Perciville seemed to be struggling too, Fjona noticed. His staff was no longer hovering behind his back with an attachment spell, but was instead being implemented as a walking stick to help drag him up the hill. The sun was already beginning to set and it cast a long shadow of the sage back down the hill towards Fjona.

He paused when he reached the brow and turned to Fjona with a wide grin. "I see our destination," he called back down to her.

Fjona was panting by the time she reached him. She wondered if the salty air from the Near Sea was affecting her lungs. "Thank the Four Good Gods. I'm looking forward to a—"

She stopped herself the moment she pulled up next to Perciville only to see the twinkling of lanterns in a town across a wide-open valley, and up on an even steeper hill beyond.

"I thought you said we were nearly there!"

Perciville smirked. "I think you will find I said only that I could *see* our destination. Don't be disheartened; we are doing well. I reckon we can be there before sundown."

Fjona just groaned, then led the way on two heavy legs.

For all his faults, and of that there were many, Perciville could at least be right on occasion and he proved himself so when they did eventually arrive in Rosensted to the dying flickers of the sun.

To Fjona, Rosensted was enormous as they followed their way through a jungle of narrow, winding streets, lit by candle lamps and adorned by rows of large detached square houses. Many were several storeys tall with wooden verandas and balconies, chimney stacks and great windows. Others were squatter, though with peculiar ornate beams that criss-crossed the facades. Some of the houses had their own stables and ranch, while at least a couple had a small orchard or chicken coop. It seemed to be a very functional, self-sustaining place in the same way Wychwold was, but on a much grander scale.

Having never visited a place of such breadth and grandeur before, Fjona caught herself often referring to Rosensted as a city. However, the sage was quick to correct her each time.

"It's a large town, granted, but Rosensted is no city," he would say. "Just wait until you see Havensend or Panamaya City. They are in a whole other league."

The road led steeply down to a wide river with many houses built up against the clear flowing waters. Even at this hour, there were small boats carrying passengers or wares downstream towards a marina up ahead.

"Where exactly are we headed?" Fjona asked, fed up with aimlessly ambling along.

"The promenade," Perciville replied succinctly, then continued along the leafy riverside.

"And where is that?"

The sage pointed in the direction of the marina. "It's up ahead. Not far this time, I promise."

Fjona sighed.

"It will be worth it, believe me. The place we are seeking serves the nicest seafood. Cockles, mussels, crab..." Perciville was already salivating as he spoke. "Decent ale too. Actually, mead is the thing Rosensted does better than anywhere else. Sweet but strong, like the spring elves they say."

Fjona could believe that. The nearer they got to the promenade, the more spring elves she saw along the riverbank, and they were exactly as she had remembered from those celebrating Lullatide back in Port Widow. They were generally very trim, with chiselled, almost gaunt, faces – skin of olive, and eyes of the sea. The women wore flowing dresses as long as their hair, and the men wore smart, though not elaborate, coats that were always pressed and clean.

"That all sounds great," Fjona replied, realising just how hungry she was, "but what about your friend? The reason we've come all this way. Will he be there?"

"Yes," Perciville answered. "Hopefully."

"Hopefully? I thought you said you knew where to find him?"

The sage shrugged. "I haven't seen or spoken to him for years."

Fjona pulled on his shoulder. "Wait, are you saying we have travelled half the continent on a mere hunch that your friend *might* be here in Rosensted?"

"No. We haven't travelled anywhere near half the continent."

Fjona's jaw tightened. "You know what I meant."

"Miss Sarsen, please, let's not make a scene." Perciville looked around at a handful of elves pottering about, though nobody was paying them any attention. "The last time I saw Bosmar Fodd, he said he was heading to Rosensted for work. It's possible, of course, that he has moved on since, but this is our best shot."

Fjona just huffed and continued along the river. "You better be right," she called back to him.

The marina was crammed with boats of all sizes surrounding a small island in the middle which supported a marble sculpture.

"It represents the four pillars of spring elven religion," Perciville explained as they circumnavigated the marina. "The sphere at the centre is the sun; the waves over the top are the sea; the arms around the edge represent the wind; and the plinth on which it stands represents the soil. Unlike the summer elves or the Myrish, the spring elves worship the Arvum."

Fjona admired the intricate artwork and nearly tripped up on a paving stone after gawping at the sculpture without paying attention to where she was walking.

On the far side, they arrived on the promenade which was thriving with partygoers. Music was flowing as much as the alcohol and there were hundreds of spring elves dancing and singing, expressing every bead of merriment.

Fjona's mood dramatically improved as she and Perciville were swept up in the festivities. She found herself being pulled from one dancer to another, spun on the spot and embraced by wondrous choreography.

"What are they celebrating?" Fjona called to Perciville, whose face was as emotive as a bare wall.

The sage was busy keeping his head down and slapping away every hand that welcomed him to join in. "We don't have time for this, Miss Sarsen," he replied, devoid of expression.

"But it's fun!" she protested as she was swirled around a dangerously handsome elf with arms that could break waves.

Several other elves jeered at the sage as he attempted to drag Fjona away from them.

"There will be plenty of time for frivolity once we've saved the world, now come on," Perciville insisted through clenched teeth.

"Ahh let her stay," one of the dancers pleaded.

"Don't be such a sourpuss," said another.

Fjona noticed the sage's hand grip his staff out of the corner of her eye and thought it best to spare the dancers a nasty infliction. She quickly thanked them for their hospitality, then hurriedly shuffled alongside Perciville.

"You need to learn how to have fun," she teased as they pushed through the energetic crowd.

"Perhaps," Perciville grumbled, "but there are other matters at hand. When this is all done, you may return here at your leisure to dance with the spring elves. I assure you, you haven't missed anything. They do this every evening."

He ushered Fjona away from further distraction and along a series of narrow alleyways that bent around towards the cliffs.

As they walked, Perciville explained that Rosensted was often referred to as the mainland sister town of Port Widow and Fjona could see why. Both were situated on cliffs overlooking the Near Sea, with dockyards down on the coast, and each shared a propensity for street parties and an eclectic local population. Spring elves were prominent in each town, though less so in Port Widow, and trade by sea was very common. Had it not been for the need to visit Willow's Brush first, it would surely have been an easy boat ride from one port to another.

"If they are indeed sisters, Rosensted is certainly the classier, more elegant and sophisticated sister," Fjona said, "whereas Port Widow would be the sister who never gets invited to family weddings in fear of her overindulging on wine, causing a scene, and ruining the whole occasion."

It was true enough that between the promenade, streams, parks and grand architecture, Rosensted was really quite a marvellous town.

The tone did start to shift, however, as they neared the coast and Fjona noticed there were more and more derelict houses and one or two shady characters hanging around the parks.

"And naturally, you are leading me to the dodgy end…" she said quietly, so no unsavoury ears might hear her.

"Don't worry, they tend not to bother outsiders. Most of the tension is between different families," Perciville reassured her, "though keep your head down. It would be unwise to attract unwanted attention."

It was hardly the comforting words Fjona had hoped for, but she took the sage's advice and pretended there was nobody else around.

They followed some steps down to a cosy courtyard belonging to a tavern which had certainly seen better days. The roof was bowing steeply in the middle and the weathered brickwork was mottled with algae. Despite its unflattering appearance, it sounded as though it didn't deter customers.

From outside, they could hear raucous laughter and singing that spilled out of every crack, so loud that it was a miracle the tavern hadn't yet collapsed in on itself.

Fjona pictured the promenade around the marina and let out a long, disheartened sigh.

"Trust me," Perciville assured her, "the Crypt Keeper's Keys is a damn sight better on the inside than out here."

As he opened the door, they were enveloped in an explosion of music that pricked up the hairs on Fjona's spine, and before long they were squeezed together on a cramped table in the corner of the tavern, each with a plateful of seafood and a heavy tankard of ale.

"Well I hate to admit it, Harper," Fjona mumbled through a mouthful of white crab, "but you were right about this place."

The sage wiped his mouth with his sleeve. "You just needed to have a little more faith," he said smugly, before tucking into a portion of fried prawns.

For a short while, both Fjona and Perciville seemed to forget about their reason for travelling all this way and gladly feasted to the backdrop of merry elves and Marrowborns.

The bard this evening was a short and squat spring elf with clipped brunette hair on one side of her pockmarked face and down to her shoulder on the other. Her voice was rich and bold, and she sung from deep inside her portly frame. Accompanying her were a tall, lanky lute player, whose slender fingers raced up and down the neck of his instrument; a muscular percussionist, who beat her flat, wide drum with jovial enthusiasm; and an older spring elf, whose cloudy eyes insinuated he was blind, performing on a strange curved reed instrument that Fjona had never seen on Marrow Myre.

They were a lively band and the audience could barely drown them out as they rose their drunken voices to a song, Perciville explained, called Groogal the Grugan.

Groogal the gregarious Grugan
greeted everyone he met
with a grievous grin, from his eyes to his chin,
and so all the little folk wept.

Groogal the gracious Grugan
gave greatly all his wealth,
to gambling; drink, but he failed to think
of the grinding on his health.

Groogal the gritty Grugan
tried back to steal his gold.
They grabbed him with a sack o' coins
and banished him, behold!

I knew not why he came to me,
except I had a sail.
So Groogal joined me at the stern;
I welcomed him with ale.

Groogal the greedy Grugan,
gorged gaily on a goat,
and when I said 'you've had too much!'
he gorged upon my boat.

Now that is why,
please listen friend, for this it has to be,
you may greet a Grugan anywhere,
just never out at sea.

For Grugan's are a gleeful sort,
when greed is kept in hand,
and Groogal was the greediest,
To e'er walk the land!

It was an unusual song, Fjona thought, though clearly popular among most of the tavern except for a sheepish-looking fellow with waxy orange skin on the opposite side.

"Well, this has been fun," she said, slumping forward and casting a chiding look at Perciville, "but evidently your friend is not here."

"And why do you say that?"

"Had he been, I'd have thought you would have invited him over already."

The sage leaned in over the table. "Wrong you are again, Miss Sarsen. He is indeed here and has acknowledged my presence with a brief nod of the head. I haven't invited him over as I consider it to be poor form to disturb somebody when they are at work."

Bemused, Fjona glanced around the tavern. There was an older man serving drinks at the bar to two women. Perhaps he was Perciville's friend, but she couldn't imagine how someone of his apparent age could be of any use to them. Then, of course, there was the band. She scrutinised them with a furrowed brow.

"Okay then, which one is he? The gangly one with the lute or the blind one with the...?" Fjona paused, trying to find the word.

Perciville chuckled. "Ha! Them? Not likely, and it's called a reedaphone. Don't you have them in Marrow Myre?"

"Then who?" Fjona asked crossly.

Perciville gestured towards the bar with his forehead. Clinking their glasses together were two spring elves, one with a long beard tied up in a knot as if it were rope; the other with a plump belly that poked out the bottom of his shirt.

"Really? Which one?" Fjona was unsure as to how either of them might be useful.

"Ignore the spring elves, they are just a distraction. Look carefully."

Fjona snapped. "Perciville, what are you talking about? I'm getting tired of these stupid games. Just show me who your damn friend is!"

142

The sage opened his mouth, as if he were about to retaliate with the same ferocity, but took a deep breath instead, his voice taking on a softer tone. "Please, Miss Sarsen, this is the only way. Do you remember me teaching you about staff shielding? About casting a spell that would make me... not invisible, but entirely unnoticeable?"

Fjona nodded slowly.

"Well, Boglanders are an ancient species of elf who have evolved to carry that trait, irrespective of manipulation."

"Boglander? I've never heard of such a thing."

The sage shrugged. "I wouldn't be surprised. You haven't heard of a lot of things." Before she could react, he quickly continued. "Look again towards the bar."

With a degree of reluctance, for fear that Perciville was just trying to wind her up, Fjona looked back towards the two spring elves.

"Now," Perciville whispered, "look really carefully. Tell me, what do you see?"

Fjona huffed, then inanely described her menial observations. "One elf just took a sip of ale; another is laughing at a joke. The old elf behind the bar is now talking to them with, oh wow, look at that..." she paused for effect "... a ragged old towel over his arm!"

Her sarcasm goaded no response from the sage.

Frustrated, she continued. "The elf with the belly just spilled his drink and is now lapping ale off his collar like a dog. The bearded one is bent over double, and shaking with laughter, and this all seems like a waste of time."

"Keep going..." Perciville insisted.

"The barman has turned to serve another customer and now..." Fjona paused as her vision caught something strange, though she wasn't sure what it was.

"Now?" the sage encouraged.

"I feel like something is wrong. I can't quite put my finger on it, but… there!" She was looking intently at the bearded elf's doublet. "His pocket. It looked like it moved, just a fraction. Again! Did you see that? His wallet is poking out the top of it. It wasn't doing that before."

Perciville hummed in agreement.

"And now it's disappearing back inside his pocket. I can see…"

Suddenly, literally in the blink of an eye, Fjona could see a peculiar-looking fellow with his hand in the pocket of the bearded elf. He had seemingly appeared from nowhere. Nobody else seemed to be paying him any attention as he slumped over to the bellied elf, reached into his trouser pocket, withdrew a handful of coins from his wallet, then dropped it back in.

"I don't understand…"

"That, Miss Sarsen, is Bosmar Fodd the Boglander," Perciville informed her, "and, believe it or not, the key to saving the Arvum."

Fjona was barely listening. She was far too preoccupied watching the Boglander skulk between the patrons with bare floppy arms, dipping into their pockets with deft fingers. He was a curious looking elf with long floppy ears that hung down from his perfectly bald head to his neck. His skin was a pale blue, almost translucent, and Fjona imagined it would be greasy to touch. Evidently being completely unnoticeable to people negated the need to dress appropriately, sporting instead just a simple loin cloth to hide his manhood and a leather belt with a sheath for a knife.

What stole Fjona's attention the most, however, was the smooth, almost slippery way he glided between the patrons as if his body weren't constrained by his bones.

Sure enough, he ducked around an elbow, squeezed between two shoulders and fell into the pocket of a Marrowborn woman with perfect execution. His spatial awareness and timing were impeccable.

"Impressive, isn't he?" Perciville commented, watching Fjona's gaze.

"Impressive, but entirely unethical," she replied. "How can you sit and watch your friend steal like that?"

The sage shrugged. "It's a difficult world in which to make a living, especially for a Boglander on the mainland. What would you rather? That he sit outside on the street and beg to people as they walk past him?"

Somehow Fjona was feeling sorry for the strange little creature as he pinched a coin out of the reedaphone player's jacket mid-performance.

"I guess not," she conceded, "although I can't believe there's no other work out there for him that may help people instead of stealing from them."

"Well that is exactly why we have come to him," Perciville replied. "I think you'll find that the job we require from him will do wonders for his morals."

CHAPTER 16

REUNITED

By the time the band had finished performing, most of the patrons of the Crypt Keeper's Keys had finished their drinks and gone home to bed, leaving behind the debris of frivolities as if the tavern had been hit by a small hurricane.

Perciville and Fjona had stuck around until the end and now only a smattering of guests remained. Besides a mixed group of elves around one table in the corner, a hooded figure at the bar and a couple of women by the door, there was hardly anybody left.

Fjona watched as the Boglander, Bosmar Fodd, pinched his final wallet for the night, tucked it into his own pouch and shuffled over to their table.

He wore a stern, disapproving expression upon his slippery, translucent face.

"You have some cheek turning up here unannounced," he grumbled, his tone was just as unfriendly as his eyes.

"It's good to see you too, Bosmar," the sage replied nonchalantly.

"Keep it down," the Boglander hissed back. "I don't want anyone else to see me."

Perciville remained impassive.

"Judging by your face, I can only presume that you have spotted me?" Bosmar asked, turning towards Fjona.

Fjona hadn't realised she'd been staring at him this whole

time. "I'm a friend of Perciville's," she explained quietly.

"A friend, eh?" He scrutinised her from head to toe before taking a seat next to her. "You're a little plain compared to his usual taste, but I can see how you might be pretty. How long have you been...?" He gestured crudely with his fingers, then whispered to Fjona, "You realise he's nearly four hundred years old, right? I'd be impressed if he can even get things started."

"Hey, no! It's not like that!" Fjona's face reddened and she suddenly became too nervous to make eye contact with the sage.

Bosmar broke into phlegmy laughter and waved a flimsy hand at her. "Forgive me, I didn't mean to offend!"

"We met on Marrow Myre," Perciville interjected. "I believe you know it well."

The Boglander suddenly stopped laughing. His eyes dropped and he cowered away a little.

"You know Marrow Myre?" Fjona asked.

Bosmar took a deep breath then swiftly changed the subject. "So what brings you to me, Harper? Here to gamble away more money to me or to manipulate some honesty into my bones?"

"He's from the Myre of Maw," Perciville informed Fjona, forcing the subject back around.

Fjona's face lit up. "*You* are from the Myre of Maw? I didn't think anyone lived there. Are there more Boglanders? Perhaps some friends or family?"

Bosmar put a clammy finger on her lips and Fjona immediately stopped talking, mostly due to the invasion of her personal space. She moved her head back, but the finger remained.

"She talks a lot," Bosmar muttered to Perciville.

"Don't speak as if I'm not here," Fjona mumbled.

"She has a lot to say," Perciville replied, "and if you value your finger, I suggest you move it from her lip."

Taken aback, the Boglander did as the sage advised. "Let's not speak of my history," he continued, "and instead get straight to business. Why are you here?"

Perciville looked Bosmar keenly in the eye and spoke two simple words. "It's time."

At first, Bosmar Fodd didn't react, but slowly his face morphed into an expression of recognition. "Are you sure?"

The sage nodded.

"And how prepared are you? How much do you know?"

Fjona wanted to pipe up and ask them to speak with some transparency, but she was too intoxicated by the tension between them to even open her mouth.

"Fjona is training up to be a sage, but still needs time. She has only a Woven Wand," Perciville explained.

"A Woven Wand! Damn this! Come find me again when you are ready for my help."

"Bosmar, the threat is too imminent to waste time going back and forth across the desert. There is still much to do, granted, but I have faith in Fjona. She is our best shot."

Her name had been thrown around too much now for her to not speak up.

"What are you talking about?" she asked with frustration. "I'm making good progress. Whatever it is you need, I can do it." Fjona whipped her wand out of her pocket and pointed it at Bosmar.

The Boglander's eyes shot open and he snatched it away from her, then fondled it between his clammy fingers. "Silverwood? Like the first sage's..." he murmured.

Perciville nodded in agreement.

After closely examining the Woven Wand, Bosmar returned it to Fjona. "Its colour doesn't necessarily mean anything."

"I know," the sage replied.

"But then maybe it does..." Bosmar pondered. "Okay, fine!

You have my attention. What else?"

Perciville continued. "There was a book, from way back during the Sagedom. It was said to contain the history of the sages and the secrets of the desert. Before he died, Sagen Master Herak Siadonis ensured that the vessel could only ever be found should the Eight Afflictions require it to be. It was said that he hid the vessel according to a location recorded in that ancient book, before casting a shielding spell over it so that it would only reveal itself to a worthy Proprietor of Intellect during a time of desperation."

"Wait. So you know where to find this box – this vessel?" Fjona asked.

Perciville nodded. "I believe I know how to locate it, sure."

"So where? Panamaya City?" Bosmar asked.

Perciville smiled. "The Archivus. Indeed. Specifically to meet Proprietor Sialah Bouwer."

Bosmar leaned in close. "Look, I will join you. You have my skills and my word, but there's something you should know." He glanced over to the table in the far corner of the tavern. "They call themselves the Covenant of Creation. They're a cult who tread the blurry line between freedom fighting and terrorism. I don't know their intentions fully, but I've overheard them plotting something against the Sultan and the palace."

"We were warned of their kind by an island elf in Colt," Perciville replied. "Said there's talk about the Eight Ascensions or something?"

Bosmar nodded his round, squishy head. "Yes, that and many other variations. My point is, their new leader, Lucinda Denvillier, just took over following the death of her brother. She is very clever and highly persuasive, and I know she is up to something. They've employed the help of somebody they refer to as the Contact. Now I don't know for certain, but I have reason to believe that the Contact may be a sage and one of a cruel disposition."

"Could they be working with the turned-sage? Perhaps they've already returned," Fjona suggested.

Perciville shook his head. "No, if this Contact were the turned-sage, we'd all know about it by now. A sage can still be cruel and deceitful and evil without turning. There's a big difference between a turned-sage and just a bad person."

Fjona felt a chill descend her spine.

Bosmar continued. "There *is* talk of your turned-sage of old, though. Probably just rumours, but there's no smoke without fire, after all. I've heard whisperings of the Foreboding One, or Kal'Set in the Kelnish tongue, returning to life from the Isle of Exiles. That name, Kal'Set, may sound familiar to a Myrish woman, such as yourself."

Fjona wasn't sure what the strange Boglander had meant at first. She repeated the name in her head, even sounded it out with her tongue, until it hit her.

"Kalzeth," she replied timidly.

Bosmar Fodd nodded. "Some Marrowborns, perhaps those who are more astute, have made reference to Kalzeth Reincarnate. They say the Afflictions are beginning and the Arvum is in peril, that Kalzeth Reincarnate is the harbinger of death, returned in physical form. People are afraid."

"Hardly looked like it," Fjona said, "judging by the mood in here no more than an hour ago."

"Not everyone has noticed the dying crops or the new mothers dying shortly after childbirth with no explanation, but take my word, there are many who sense it is coming."

"That's all very interesting," Perciville interrupted, "but it adds no weight to our shoulders. This cult, this Covenant of Creation, they're just one of a hundred groups across the Arvum who have got their facts twisted and are willing to die for it.

Whatever squabbles they may have with the Sultan, best we just leave it to them. We have bigger fish to fry. Same for the talk of this Foreboding One. Talk is just talk. Granted, there may be an echo of truth to it, but to suggest that they have returned is ludicrous...!"

Fjona caught the sage briefly glance away.

"Whatever else is happening in the Arvum, I couldn't care less," he added. "All that matters is that we find the box and bring an end to the Eight Afflictions. Then Fjona here can go back to partying with the spring elves and you can return to exploiting every dumb-wit who enters this place."

"Suits me," Bosmar replied, interdigitating his slender fingers.

There was an awful lot for Fjona to take in and she felt somewhat overwhelmed by the whole conversation. She asked the only question that was on the forefront of her mind. "So what next?"

"Are there beds here?" Perciville asked Bosmar, who duly nodded. "Then we rest up well and head out first thing tomorrow morning. If Bosmar is right about this cult causing trouble, then it could do us some good to get to Panamaya City as soon as possible. Then we go about finding this ancient book."

"An actual city?" Fjona gasped. "I can't wait!"

Perciville and Bosmar Fodd exchanged a quick look, then each took a sip from their tankards before an oblivious Fjona.

An awkward silence fell between them and Fjona took it upon herself to break it.

"So how come you left the Myre of Maw?" she asked Bosmar.

In a heartbeat, his eyes burned with fury, he whipped his knife out of its sheath and held it at her throat. She could feel his horrible breath in her eyes.

"I told you not to—"

His venomous words were cut short as a strong arm appeared

from behind him and pinned his knife-wielding hand to the table. At the same time, the mysterious newcomer, hidden beneath their cloak, held a small but sharp hand-axe to the Boglander's neck.

"Don't," they said simply, in a voice that sounded strangely familiar to Fjona.

"Very impressive," Bosmar conceded, "but it takes more than that to get the best of me."

In one slick and perfectly judged movement, the Boglander slumped away from the axe, slid off his seat, pulled another knife from somewhere in his loin cloth, and pointed it at the newcomer. The newcomer was just as quick and managed to hold back the knife with the blade of his axe.

It was a stalemate.

"Stop this!" Fjona hissed at the pair, leaping to her feet. "This isn't worth the commotion!"

The few remaining heads in the tavern had turned towards them and Fjona couldn't be sure whether that meant they had now spotted Bosmar or if this newcomer appeared to be holding an axe in thin air.

"The price for disrespecting me is blood," the Boglander spat, "and you, my strange, hooded friend, have disrespected me."

Perciville remained in his seat, watching the display like a spectator at the theatre.

"Are you not going to stop this?" Fjona asked.

The sage just shrugged. "It's not our place to get involved."

Fjona huffed. "Well I disagree."

She moved over to the pair, both sporting a combative stance with a leg forward and their arms raised.

"Lower your axe and Bosmar will sheath his knife," she said to the newcomer.

"No," they replied firmly.

"This isn't worth it," Fjona argued, but there was no response from beneath the hood. "Very well."

She extracted her wand from her pocket, focused herself, then latched on to both the axe and the knife. For the first time, she was manipulating two objects at once and it seemed to be quite effective. She was able to pull the two weapons apart, despite the strength of the two wielders as they resisted. They were too strong for her, however, and managed to overcome the manipulation. The axe and the sword clattered back against one another.

"Nice try, but no magic can stop me," Bosmar boasted, leaning his knife against the head of the axe.

Desperate, Fjona turned to Perciville. "You have to do something about this! We're supposed to be keeping a low profile. How is a bloodied corpse right next to us going to help that?"

At first, the sage's reaction was so minimal that it wasn't apparent as to whether or not he had heard Fjona. After a moment's thought, he took his staff, pointed towards the lacklustre fight, and effortlessly conjured a force that pushed them apart.

"Argh, why did you do that?" Bosmar complained. "I could've had him!"

"That is precisely why," Perciville replied. "Now be civil. There are still people about."

Whether it was because they were tucked away in a quiet nook of the tavern or because the remaining punters were too inebriated to pay them much attention, it mattered little. Whatever the reason, nobody had come over to break up the fight.

Fjona turned to the newcomer. "Now reveal yourself. Lower your hood and explain to me why it is you would risk your life so needlessly to help a stranger in a tavern."

The newcomer was hesitant at first, but then spoke up. "Very well, but please don't get mad..." he murmured as he pulled down his head to reveal a tangle of soft auburn hair.

Fjona's jaw dropped. "Todie!" she exclaimed, unsure whether to hug him, kiss him or scream at him.

"You know this fool?" Bosmar jeered before Fjona waved a hand, signalling for him to shut up.

"What? How? What?" It was all that Fjona could utter before her confused, disparate emotions collided and she realised how glad she was to see him.

She embraced him tightly and planted a heavy kiss on his cheek. As she held him, she could feel Todie's body relax.

"So you're not mad?" he asked tentatively.

"Of course I'm mad at you! I begged you not to follow me and you evidently ignored that, but I cannot tell you how pleased I am that you are here."

"You know I didn't mean what I said on the cliff—" Todie began, and would likely have said more had Fjona not interrupted him.

"I know, and a lot has happened since then. Water under the bridge. I forgive you for it all."

Todie smiled warmly and Fjona invited him to sit with them.

Perciville was surprisingly inert throughout the whole reunion and remained unmoved in his seat, staring intently at Todie while Fjona playfully interrogated her friend.

"I have so many questions! How did you get over to the mainland? How did you find me? Just... how?"

Although clearly feeling more than a little uncomfortable beneath the sage's unrelenting gaze, Todie proceeded to regale his experiences from the previous weeks.

"Well, after you disappeared across to the mainland, I felt a horrible sense that I may not ever see you again. I was so conflicted. Part of me, a really big part of me, wanted to find a way across Aserae's Lip, track you down and bring you home. Then there was this other voice inside of me saying that you would never forgive me if I forced you to come back when you were so excited and desperate for adventure. I felt too guilty about what I'd said that I decided to leave you be. I was going to head back to Wychwold so that Evelyn could be relieved from housesitting for you and I could explain to your parents where you had gone, but instead I was drawn towards the Whistling Lake. I walked the whole way there. Had to sleep in an old wood store that I found on the way. When I arrived, I located the shrine to Aserae and I prayed."

Bosmar sniggered at the mention of prayer and received a sharp look from Fjona.

"I firstly prayed you would be safe and that you would find what you were seeking, and that you would return home when you were ready. I prayed that your parents would forgive you for leaving and would continue to admire you for who you are. Then I prayed for me. I prayed for guidance. Should I follow you and assist you, and one day bring you home, or should I leave you to follow your own compass? Now, I wouldn't say that Aserae spoke to me, it might just have been that I'd the chance to process all that had happened, but in the end I decided to find you. Before that, I knew I must be prepared so I visited the Paddolgolian Brothers' General Store in Swirleybucket and..." He paused for a moment. "I'm ashamed to say that I arrived after dark and broke in. I stole, although I intend to later pay for it, some equipment so I could survive out in a foreign place alone. I stuffed a satchel with tools and food, clothes, this cloak, and canvas to pitch a tent. That's also where I got this axe. Figured I may need something to protect myself with."

"That was very wise," Fjona assured him.

"Anyway, I left Swirleybucket immediately and headed straight for Aserae's Lip, setting up camp a way out of town. Do you remember the conditions when I caught up with you the first time? Well, this time it was much, much worse. The rain was ferocious and the river was as wild as I have ever seen, but I was driven by my fear that I may never see you again. So, I clambered down the cliff and found an old raft. Admittedly, it was a little worse for wear, but it was my only option, so I boarded it, and paddled as best I could to the other side. The current was vicious and I had to lie on my belly to avoid tipping off. You of all people will know how hard it was for me, considering what happened to my brother and father."

Todie's face turned dour and it was only Fjona squeezing his hand that enabled him to pick up the story.

"The waters were terrifying. They lashed about the raft and, at times, entirely swallowed me, to the point that I really thought I might have drowned. In the end, I was carried a long way down the creek where I was able to grab onto the cliffs opposite. I managed to climb up using tree branches that hung down from the top, but had they snapped, I can only imagine what fate I may have suffered. As it happens, I made it to the top in one piece, though I was completely soaked through to my bones, which was around the same time the rain stopped. You would have been in hysterics at the sight of me! Then things got frustrating..." He paused for a while as he tried to recollect. "I was in the woods."

"Willow's Brush," Fjona explained. "I'd been there too."

"Right, Willow's Brush then. Well that place is an enigma, I swear. It seemed that whichever way I walked, I kept returning to the same point. Seriously! I would see a distinct tree, follow a ridge in one line, then return to the same place. Then I'd take a different turn, maybe a rocky path between the bracken, and still end up at the same tree. It was infuriating."

Todie was so busy telling his story that he was oblivious to the intrigued look that Fjona and Perciville exchanged.

"Anyway, I had to camp for several nights in the woods because

I kept going around in circles. Got attacked by tiny rabid dogs at one point which was the first time my axe had really been of any use. Eventually, the trees became thinner and I stumbled out of the woods somewhere south along the coast. I could still see Marrow Myre across the sea. I had no idea where to look for you so I decided to stick to the coast so that I could at least see home. How many days I walked south for, I can't say. Maybe I camped for three nights, maybe four? After a while it all becomes a bit of a blur. Whatever the case, I arrived at Rosensted a couple of nights ago and paid for a proper bed with a few coins I'd pinched from the Paddolgolian Brothers. I promise, I will repay them. I've been exploring the town and asking if anyone had seen you, but everyone thought I was crazy. I was going to stay for one more night, then head west to the next town, if there is one, but it never came to that. I saw you the moment you walked through the door."

Fjona was amazed at Todie's story. It seemed so relatable at times, yet so drastically different at others. "So why then did you not speak to me when you saw us arrive?"

Todie looked a little abashed. "I was still unsure of what to do. I was so happy to see you alive and well, and I felt reassured enough that you are safe to leave you as you asked. I couldn't bring myself to go, though. Ended up staying much later than I'd intended. I kept wanting to come over and speak to you, but I was afraid you were still upset with me and that you would never forgive me for following you. It was only when I saw" – he paused – "your *friend* with his knife at your throat that I was compelled to intervene. It just came over me, without even thinking about it. Even after that, I was still contemplating disappearing into the night and letting you go without you ever knowing I was here."

"Oh, Todie, I'm sorry I've put you through so much." Fjona squeezed his arm comfortingly. "Well, you are with us now. I have too much to tell you and show you, and I am so glad you can experience the last part of my adventure with me!"

Perciville forced a loud cough and everyone turned to him. He was grimacing with his eyebrows raised, leaning on an elbow with an upturned hand.

Before the sage could speak, Todie interjected. "Look, Perciville, I don't know enough about you and nor do you about me, but let me make this clear. If Fjona would like me to accompany her, then I will, whether you approve or not."

Todie looked at Fjona and she nodded her consent for him to join her.

Perciville sighed heavily from his nose, then wordlessly stood up and walked around to where Todie was sitting. Todie's eyes were wide and alert, and the sweat on his palms shimmered even in the low light.

The sage grabbed Todie's axe from the table, despite some resistance from Todie, then held it in front of him. A bright cobalt light poured out of Perciville's staff and enveloped the axe. Slowly, the axe started to grow. Its shaft extended to the length of Todie's arm and to a similar breadth while the head stretched out to at least three times its original size. When the spell faded, the axe still glowed as if it had been recently polished and the lethally sharp tip glistened in the candlelight.

Perciville handed it to Todie. "You'll need this," he said with a glance towards Bosmar Fodd, "especially if he has any objections."

Then he headed over to the bar to get a drink.

CHAPTER 17

VERDICT

The crowd had already started to file into the gallery. Such was Panamayan law, court hearings were made to be heard by whoever may wish to attend so that no ruling may be passed without complete transparency. As a consequence, the court itself was built to be open-air in a design similar to the theatre only a couple of streets away. It was a hexagonal stone structure with rows of benches around the top with enough space to seat a thousand spectators. Far fewer than the theatre, though neither failed to reach capacity. The main difference between the two, and perhaps the main reason that so many periodically turned up to spectate at court hearings, was that it was the only event in the Upper Gate that was opened up to the entire city. Granted, visitors from the Lower and Outer Gates were ushered through their own entrance so that they weren't able to sully the grounds of the Upper Gate, but it at least gave many the opportunity to participate in citywide conversations with their superiors who were otherwise segregated.

Generally, the gallery attendants were scarcely aware of the case they were watching and would merely come along for the experience. To them, it was a form of entertainment that didn't revolve around a tavern.

Around the rim of the court were high marble pillars with blazing beacons on top, signalling a hearing was soon to open.

In the middle, at the foot of all the seats, was the judge's podium. A tall stone plinth that loomed over the defendant's square, who was required to stand for the entire session. Sessions that had, in the past, exceeded an entire day.

Behind the podium was the raised seat of the Sultan, beside which were chairs for his steward and relevant leaders depending on the case in hand. On the opposite side was a row of benches for the witnesses.

Although the gallery was still filling up, the judge headed out to her podium to commence the session. She was a portly summer elf whose face was obscured by a red mask, the symbol of jurisdiction. After all, she would be speaking not for herself, but on behalf of the people of Panamaya City. She wore a long black robe that dragged along the ground beneath her, and in her hands she carried a two-headed drum beater.

When she had climbed to the top of the podium, she hit the beater against a wide drum, producing a single loud bang that echoed around the entire court. Such were the acoustics within, that one could fart on the ground floor and it may be heard by a spectator at the furthest end of the gallery.

The judge spoke with powerful, stern conviction. "Welcome all in the gallery. I am Eminent Judge Welanina Eradin, empowered by you, the City of Panamaya, and appointed by Sultan Ayermune Dhaller Sé. We have been summoned by the Sultan, following consultation with General Sigmund Kheller of the Noble Guard, to deliberate the case of a corporal, alleged to have failed to maintain her duty and accused of putting the lives of our citizens at risk. The status of a Noble Guard is in fact written in the name: to act nobly and with pride, to defend our city and its people. Failure to act with the conduct of responsibility may incur a breach of oath, which itself would warrant a suitable punishment."

Judge Eradin paused for suspense and a silence fell across the gallery.

"Much like the Kelnish workers down at the construction, we must dig into the details of these accusations so that I may fully understand the circumstances and pass judgment. In order to do so, I must introduce the relevant parties to the court floor. Firstly, it gives me great pleasure to invite our High Excellency, Sultan Ayermune Dhaller Sé…"

The judge gestured to the side of the floor from where the Sultan emerged. His grand, ornate azure robe did little to detract from his stressed and wizened face. Despite his evident fatigue, he nonetheless walked gracefully towards his seat behind the judge's podium, with a deeply unamused expression.

Behind him followed Oolia Khamun who had donned a smart black doublet. She received no formal invitation from the judge, behaving as something of a shadow to the Sultan as she followed him across the floor.

As they walked, some in the gallery cheered, others booed, and many sat in silence and watched with beady eyes.

The judge continued. "In addition I would like to welcome, to the witness stand, those of the Noble Guard who were present on the day in question."

Again, she gestured across the floor where only Elian Sole of the Fourth West Division emerged along with Storm'Dune of Lahsilli's division. They were both berobed in white, though Storm'Dune was still swamped beneath his coat, as they each walked sheepishly across the floor in stark silence.

When they had taken their seats, Judge Eradin added, "And finally I must present to court the accuser, Captain Beric Lahsilli of the West Division, and the defendant, Corporal Lais Stone of the Fourth West Division."

The gallery attendants provided a theatrical entrance for the captain as if he were the protagonist in a dramatic production. As he crossed the floor with a confident and powerful gait, the spectators cheered and whistled. The captain waved his appreciation to them, no doubt aware of the fact that he had received a grander welcome than even the Sultan.

A long, quiet pause followed after Lahsilli took his seat.

Oolia shuffled nervously on her chair, gazing around the floor, but there was no sign of Lais Stone.

Mumblings could be heard drifting down from the spectators in the gallery as the villain of the story failed to appear.

"Coward must have fled," the Sultan spat through cruel lips, but Oolia didn't reply.

She was too busy agitatedly tapping her fingers on her trousers and leaning forwards to get a better view. Even Judge Eradin had stood up on her podium and was glancing about the court through the slits in her mask.

Then, as the whispers of consternation among the gallery died down, the sound of jangling and scraping rang out from the entrance tunnel. From the gloom, Lais Stone appeared, weighed down by heavy iron manacles around her ankles, her hands bound by shackles behind her back. She had been forced into a tattered, soiled shirt and trousers, and her feet were bare except for the chains. Her face was an expression of anger, perhaps overcompensating for the shame that enshrouded her as she dragged herself across the dusty floor.

For the gallery, it was an exciting new addition to the stage and they jeered enthusiastically, despite not knowing any details of her alleged crime.

When eventually Lais pulled herself up to the defendant's square, the judge welcomed her with a sardonic smile. "Nice of you to join us."

She received a polite smattering of chuckles from the gallery.

Lais, like her namesake, was as immovable as a stone. She said not a word and instead remained still, glaring at the podium and trying to mentally drown out the echoing boos that surrounded her.

The judge banged the drum and the heckling from the gallery petered out into quiet.

"I announce this hearing commenced," she stated, then looked down at Lais with steely eyes. "Corporal Lais Stone, you are under trial for the following accusations: insubordination, insufficient and dangerous leadership, engaging in rogue action, and abandoning your post when on duty during the construction of the Pentari Canal. While patrolling your designated region to the west of the Sleeping Giant, you allegedly led your division to engage in combat to a minimal threat, only to act provocatively and unsuccessfully, costing a great deal of damage to the construction, including several fatalities and multiple casualties among its workers. Corporal Stone, please regale to court the oath that you pledged when granted servitude to the Noble Guard?"

"This whole situation is a farce," Lais responded, to the shock of the gallery. "I have not failed my role. I acted as I swore I would to protect—"

The judged banged the drum, immediately cutting Lais off. "Thank you for sharing your thoughts and feelings on the matter, Corporal Stone, but I didn't ask that of you. I asked you to recite the oath you pledged when you joined the Guard. Are you able to do that?"

Lais remained quiet.

"Corporal Stone, your insolence is doing your case no favours. I suggest you participate, else you may find it increasingly difficult to have your arguments taken seriously."

Still, Lais Stone was unmoved.

"Very well," the judge conceded, "perhaps I can prompt your memory?" She retrieved from her podium a sheath of well-weathered parchment, its gold-leaf border glistening under the

Panamayan sun. "I have here the oath that was read by Lais Stone to General Sigmund Kheller, who I am told is currently away on an expedition, on the day of her appointment to the Noble Guard."

She read it to the court.

Behind the podium, Oolia whispered to the Sultan, "The general is on an expedition? Where? You said he was taken ill last week."

The Sultan waved a hand at his steward. "Hush now. His whereabouts are of no concern to you."

"Well, he should have made an effort to be here," Oolia insisted. "This is a hearing for one of his finest soldiers."

"What do you care for this guard?"

Oolia bit her tongue and feigned interest in the judge's recital.

"... I solemnly swear my *life* to the Sultan of Panamaya City, its people, and to the Noble Guard, so that I may never break my allegiance to my service and live by the shame that I might cause. I vow to follow every order without question or trepidation, to act with conviction, and to never endanger my comrades or those who entrust in me. I will never cower from, or abandon, my post, nor will I ever wear my robe in vain. Under the watch of the Sleeping Giant, I give my life to the Noble Guard." The judge's voice rebounded from every wall and pillar. "Corporal Stone, I trust you understand the severity of this situation and might you perhaps refrain from referring to it as 'a farce'? You offered your life to the Noble Guard and, hence, should it transpire that you broke your oath, then your crime may be punishable by death."

Heckles rained down to the floor from the audience.

"General Kheller isn't even here to prove I took the oath," Lais announced to the court.

"As I said, the general was unavailable to attend today's session; however, Captain Lahsilli was present at your appointment and can attest in his stead." The judge turned to the captain.

Lahsilli snarled at Lais. "San Stone pledged the oath and I'll be damned if she gets away having broken it."

There was more jeering from the gallery and the judge had to beat the drum to calm them down.

"Thank you, Captain," the judge replied, then turned to Lais. "So you see, Corporal Stone, there is little doubt so far as to the promise you made to the Noble Guard. The question that remains is whether or not you have broken that promise."

"I have broken nothing," Lais insisted, but the judge just waved a hand at her to signal silence. Lais felt her fury brimming to the surface. If not for her military discipline she would have struggled to hold her tongue.

"I would like to invite Captain Lahsilli, the accuser, to converse with the court and guide us through his claims."

To an excited gallery, the captain left his seat and stood before the judge, smiling cruelly at Lais as he walked past her.

"Captain Lahsilli, you claim that on the day in question, Lais Stone was on sentry at the canal construction when she saw travellers on the horizon."

"Indeed, a long way in the distance, and merely crossing the desert."

"And where exactly were you?" the judge asked.

"I was further south on patrol with my division. We could also see the travellers who appeared to be heading south."

"Very good. Then what happened?"

"San Stone, formerly Corporal Stone," Lahsilli announced derisively, "took it upon herself to ditch her position by the canal. She assembled her division and raced towards these travellers, equally aggressive and severely underprepared."

"They weren't travellers!" Lais interrupted, but the judge beat the drum again and reprimanded her.

"Speak out of turn again, Corporal, and I will have you gagged."

Lais immediately shut her mouth and resisted the urge to go up to Lahsilli and slap him across his smarmy, arrogant face.

"Captain, please continue. What happened after the corporal had left her post?"

"Certainly," Lahsilli said with a forced smile. "My division and I happened to be coming around the construction when we saw San Stone and her five comrades attack the travellers. This unwarranted act of aggression provoked the travellers to retaliate and they did so, first bisecting Stone's division, then continuing along the canal where they needlessly attacked the workers who would otherwise have been left alone, had it not been for Stone's actions. Several workers were killed during the attack and much of their machinery was destroyed. Many who were left unharmed have since lost faith in our protection and have resigned from service, shunning and disrespecting the Noble Guard. All this comes as a result of Stone's recklessness."

His testimony prompted more calls from the gallery and Lais noticed Elian shouting his disapprovals at the captain before Storm'Dune forced him back to his seat.

"Had I not shown up when I did and driven the travellers away, who knows how much more damage they might have done?" Lahsilli was battling with the noise raining down from the spectators, and was practically shouting by the end of his testimony.

"Silence!" Judge Eradin shouted as she banged the drum yet again. "This hearing will go on for days if you keep yelling every time somebody makes a claim. Now, before we hear from the defendant, we have just two witnesses who have offered their time. Captain Lahsilli, you may take your seat and Storm'Dune, please approach the podium."

A hush fell over the crowd as they watched Storm'Dune move towards the raised podium.

"Do you corroborate the narrative that Captain Lahsilli has detailed?" the Judge asked.

"He speaks true," Storm'Dune replied.

"Can you elaborate at all on the events we have heard?"

"Err no," he mumbled, attracting a murmur of giggles from the gallery, as he nervously glanced around the court.

"There is nothing more you can add that may aid the outcome of this hearing?" the judge persisted, but Storm'Dune just shook his head. "You are Kelnish, I presume? Storm'Dune – very much a Kelnish name."

The witness appeared even more uneasy. "Yes."

"So your ability to communicate with the labourers of the canal is much greater than, say, Corporal Stone or even Captain Lahsilli?"

"Er... yes. I speak often with them," Storm'Dune replied, uncertain as to where the judge was leading him.

"So tell me then, what do the labourers believe of the attacks on the canal? We have heard reports of bandits. How do the labourers feel about them?"

Storm'Dune now looked very uncomfortable and he exchanged a nervous look with Captain Lahsilli behind the podium. "The reports," he said nervously, "of bandits have come from just one mouth." He looked behind him at Lais whose eyes were burning like fire. "They, the Kelner elves, don't believe they are targeted. They say the Noble Guard is overstepping its mark, that they tire of staring at the empty desert and seek combat where it doesn't exist. They say travellers are attacked needlessly and the Kelner elves suffer as collateral."

"He lies!" Elian Sole shouted from the witness stand as the court erupted into further hysterics.

"Your turn will come," the judge retorted sternly, turning her masked face to the ranger. When peace resumed, the judge said to Storm'Dune, "Thank you for your statement. It is certainly a shame that none of the labourers came forward as further witnesses, but to have you speak for them is most appreciated." She dismissed the guard and invited Elian Sole to the floor. "We will now hear from a witness of the defendant, Elian Sole, a ranger of the Fourth West Division of the Noble Guard. Ranger Sole, you say that Storm'Dune is lying about the feelings of the Kelner elves. Why?"

Elian was a pedestal of etiquette. He bowed courtly, straightened himself up and neatened the collar of his coat. Then, perfectly composed, evidently rehearsed, and carefully conveyed, he spoke. "Eminent Judge, please. What we have heard today so far has either been misconstrued or entirely misconceived. Corporal Lais Stone is a loyal and highly competent soldier. She is brilliantly talented, masterfully skilled with her blade, and a pillar of diligence and nobility. These accusations are, to be frank, an insult to one of the finest soldiers in the Guard, and it pains me that these events have soured her reputation. Corporal Stone is fierce, and disciplined, and is revered by her division—"

"Yet only you show up to her hearing?" the judge intervened, coldly.

Elian looked sheepishly at Lais, then faced the judge. "My comrades harbour mixed feelings towards all this. They fear that this situation may tarnish their own positions in the Guard, and they are cautious to not step on anyone's toes. They were anxious that their words may be twisted and cause more harm than good and so they decided that saying nothing would be better than to say the wrong thing." He turned back to Lais and mouthed, 'I'm sorry'.

"Quite the sentiment," the judge replied sarcastically. "And what is your take on the situation?"

"Well, on each occasion, these were not merely travellers but bandits."

"On *each* occasion?"

"Yes, we have been attacked twice. The first time, Corporal Stone and I went to the Sultan to—"

The judge interrupted Elian again. "So you are telling me there have been two claims of bandits — though the Kelner elves agree they were travellers— and two occasions of Corporal Stone leaving her post?"

Elian cursed to himself. "See, this is why the others didn't want to attend. We needed to report the attacks to our superior, but the captain was indisposed and we were unable to locate the general. Eminent Judge, Corporal Stone is the finest guard I have ever had the pleasure to stand aside. It would be a travesty to expel her from the Noble Guard, let alone..." His voice quivered a little and the ranger held his tongue. "My point is, she is a Noble Guard through to her blood and wouldn't have it any other way."

"Except I would," Lais interjected.

"Corporal?" Elian replied, his brow nearly flying off his face.

"Elian, Judge Eradin, I have been quiet long enough. Please permit me to speak."

Elian looked abashed and was duly dismissed by the judge. He walked solemnly back to his chair, then looked over to Lais, guilt and shame etched across his face.

"Very well, Corporal Stone, the floor is yours," Judge Eradin announced.

Lais took a moment to gather herself. "Thank you, Elian, for your kind testament, but I fear it is in vain. For years, for my entire life, I have grafted in this god-awful slum of a city."

The gallery joined in a mutual hush as they were shaken into silence by the starkness of Lais's words.

"Like many, if not all of you up in the gallery, I grew up on a disease-ridden street, littered with rats and flowing with sewage. I strived for years to become someone and finally –finally! – I was welcomed to join the Noble Guard by a dear friend—"

"Don't go there!" Lahsilli interrupted, attracting more than a few looks from those around him.

"A sore spot, is it, Captain? Perhaps the reason you have begrudged me all these years?"

The captain leaped from his seat. "You have no right to go there, Stone!"

"What in all the Arvum are you talking about?" the judge asked sternly.

"She doesn't know what she's talking about," Lahsilli hissed.

"You blame me for your own mistake!" Lais yelled up at him.

"That is an outrageous accusation!" Lahsilli exclaimed.

This time, the Sultan interrupted them. "End this now!"

His words echoed around the entire court, bouncing off the pillars and stinging Lais's ears.

"We are here to discuss the future of Lais Stone, not some pitiful disagreement from your past. It is not relevant to the matter at hand. Leave it be!" the Sultan demanded.

Silence fell under the weight of authority; not so much as a squeak could be heard from the gallery.

When the dust settled, Lahsilli returned to his seat with a huff.

"Corporal Stone," the judge continued, "you have been accused of breaking your oath to the Noble Guard. If you have nothing to say that might prove your innocence, I will have no choice but to bestow upon you a suitable punishment."

Lais stared intently at Lahsilli, then replied to the judge. "Beric's disdain for me is at the root of all this, but the Sultan is right. It's not relevant. Nothing is relevant! Look at me!" She started to laugh hysterically. "Look! I cleaned latrines with my bare hands, carried full barrels up the mountain on my back. I was a donkey, and a filth picker, and I was a nobody. Then I was appointed into the Noble Guard and, yes I took the oath and I meant every damn word. I was dedicated to the core. My body is a tapestry of scars from the teeth and claws of dalachites from defending the outposts, and my eyes are burned with heat and dust from staring out at the desert. My shoulders ache from the shield I wore proudly on my back, and my buttocks sting from the chafing of my horse's saddle. I led my division with pride and we never turned our backs on our duty. I don't care what Lahsilli and his lapdog say, the Kelner elves know that we defended them and without us, they would nearly all be dead."

"What precisely is your point, Corporal Stone?" Judge Eradin asked.

"My point is – look at me now! I bled for this city and you thank me by draping me in rags, chaining my limbs in shackles, and parading me around like a criminal to hide the fact that there is something truly rotten going on around here. I don't believe that General Kheller has just gone away for a few days and I don't believe anyone here really cares whether or not I acted recklessly or that I left my post. You are all aware of something unsettling beneath the surface and you are trying to pin it on me!" She paused, then looked up at the Sultan. "I have seen the Font of Succession."

The Sultan's face dropped like a stone in a pond.

"You want the truth?" Lais continued. "I don't want to be with the Noble Guard anymore. There is too much corruption in the Upper Gate and I shall no longer be a part of it. You can execute me for all I care. There is nothing else to live for. Eminent Judge, Your High Excellency... Beric, you don't give a damn for anyone else below your precious Upper Gate. You can all rot in the desert."

Stunned silence became a drizzle of chatter, became a pouring of approving and disapproving shouts, became a storm of chaos among the gallery.

Lais's impassioned speech had resonated with the attendants, many of whom she knew could relate to the hardships that she had endured over the years.

No matter how many times the judge banged her drum, it proved ineffective at restoring a sense of decorum to the court. It was only when the Sultan signalled for the Home Guards up in the gallery to silence the attendants with stern words and sterner weapons that the silence resumed.

"Corporal Stone, I think it is apparent that we have failed to establish the true events that occurred on the day in question and that a severe lack of, and conflicting, evidence and witness accounts mean that we have no way of proving whether or not you are guilty of the charges made on you. Therefore, I revoke the accusations and declare you innocent of insubordination, insufficient and dangerous leadership, engaging in rogue action and abandoning your post."

Lais could hear applause from the gallery, but she sensed the danger was not over.

"However, you have spoken out and disrespected the Sultan, in his presence no less. You have accused us of corruption, and wished ill upon your superiors. Lais Stone, you are irredeemably treasonous and a threat to the fabric of this *fine* city. With the approval of our High Excellency, Sultan Ayermune Dhaller Sé, I sentence you to immediate execution."

There was further outrage in the gallery, while Lahsilli grinned from ear to ear.

"Execution is the least this traitor deserves," the Sultan replied, offering his approval.

"My Sultan, this is unacceptable," Oolia whispered to him. "Is this really how we treat a valued member of our military?"

"Valued member? She told me to rot in the desert!"

"She is scared and ashamed. We shouldn't punish someone for that," she urged, but the Sultan was unmoved. Oolia took a deep breath. "Revoke this decision or I will tell them what I saw in the Font of Succession."

The Sultan paused. "What *you* saw?"

Oolia's blood suddenly felt very cold and her hands felt sticky, but she had come too far. "I used Lais to get me into the Hall of Succession. I had my suspicions and they were painfully correct. You are in deep trouble. Have the judge overturn this decision now..." She didn't need to say any more: the threat was enough.

"Judge Eradin, I urge you to retract your decision," the Sultan stated, though Oolia could hear the panic in his voice. "Let's not be hasty. We need not punish San Stone with immediate execution. Her previous value as an esteemed soldier in my Noble Guard should not be undermined. Therefore, I permit her two days of incarceration during which she may get her things in order, prior to her execution later in the week. Court is over."

As the crowd departed, the Sultan stood to exit the chamber, walking past Oolia.

"You don't know what you have done," he spat, the fury in his gaze sending a chill down Oolia's spine.

This trial was far from over.

CHAPTER 18

POLLEN

They had retired to bed a short while later, squeezing into a tight loft room above the Crypt Keeper's Keys. It hadn't been the most comfortable of stays, but Fjona had been so wrung out from the journey to Rosensted that she had fallen asleep the moment her head hit the pillow.

Come morning, the four travellers: Fjona, Perciville, Bosmar Fodd and Todie, had been true to their decision to head out early and were already on the road before the rest of the town had awakened.

They were heading to the village of Pollen, half a day's hike south of Rosensted where, as Bosmar had assured the others, there was a stable that kept Pentari camels. If they were lucky enough to commandeer a camel each, they could halve the time the journey through the desert would take on horseback, let alone travelling on foot. It was a strong argument for the slight detour.

The journey was straightforward for now, simply following a road that weaved through the hill scape, gradually winding away from the sea and skirting around several small lakes.

Bosmar, with a bulging satchel of 'essential gubbins', as he put it, led the way alongside Perciville. A short way behind them, Fjona and Todie took the chance to really catch up with one another, barely pausing between one topic and another. Todie had been particularly interested to hear Fjona's chain of events since parting ways at Aserae's Lip and they soon realised that, certainly for a few nights, they had both been in Willow's Brush at the same time.

Fjona retold her experience with the pettywolves, locating the Tree of Birth and receiving her wand, to which Todie was amazed, not least because it meant that all Fjona's talk of sages was actually true. She spoke of Falavei and the strange but wonderful town of Colt, though she left out the part about the tormented coach driver. In fact, she avoided the subject of the tormented elves altogether, feeling that it may be overwhelming for Todie to learn of the attacks, especially as she was still coming to terms with them herself to a degree.

"So he's kept you safe, then?" Todie asked, gesturing to Perciville.

"I've kept myself safe," Fjona replied defensively, "but Perciville has stepped up when he's needed to."

The road was leading them along a high cliff between two lakes that appeared moody in the reflection of a grey sky. Although it was early in the morning, they could see several fishermen casting lines from their dinghies, hoping to reel in a decent catch for the market.

"I still don't trust him, you know," Todie murmured.

"Just give him a chance. Sure, he can be a little eccentric at times and even a little senseless, but his intentions are good, you'll see. I mean, he welcomed you to join us, didn't he? Even provided you with a proper weapon." Fjona patted the long-shafted axe that Todie carried on his back.

"That may be true, but I still get a bad feeling about him."

"Look…" Fjona turned, grabbing Todie by the shoulders. "You trust me, right? And I trust Perciville. You can trust him vicariously through me for now, until you come to realise that his only intention is to save the Arvum."

"From what?" Todie started off again along the road. "You

both keep claiming that the Arvum is in danger, but how exactly?"

"If you'd seen the things I have during the past few weeks, and heard the tales from Perciville and Falavei, then you would have no doubts as to what threats are lurking in the shadows."

"Don't misunderstand me, I came all this way to offer you my support and that's precisely what I intend to do. I just find it hard to put my faith in something so intangible."

"What!" Fjona exclaimed. "You're a cleric! Your whole life has been dedicated to nurturing your faith in something intangible!"

Todie's face turned red. "Yes, well... that's different!"

"Is it? How different is it to believe in a family of almighty gods who crafted the Arvum out of nothingness, and the misuse of power by an ancient sage which, though once ensnared, is now threatening to return and cause mass grief and destruction if not stopped?"

Todie's face warped into a brooding expression. "Okay, I take your point. Talk me through it all again. Who is this Foreboding One, the supposed Kalzeth Reincarnate, and what exactly did they do?"

While they followed the road over a wide bridge, spanning a river that looked like it could use a drink, Fjona proceeded to explain the story of nearly three centuries ago that had ignited this whole affair. Though she struggled with some of the details, particularly the names of many of the sages, Todie soon had a fair understanding of the Eight Afflictions, the vessel which was built to contain them, and the signs that they were trickling back out.

"So Santhé died in her effort to prevent the Eight Afflictions from spreading?" Todie clarified, his expression sombre.

Fjona nodded. "Yes, and Perciville speaks very highly of her. Apparently she was an immensely talented sage with incredible, though short-lived, potential."

"You say that there are signs of these Eight Afflictions all around us, but what exactly have you seen?"

"Well the fields of dying crops for a start. You must have passed them yourself? Granted that doesn't necessarily mean they relate to the famine caused by the Eight Afflictions, but it's a heck of a coincidence if they don't. Falavei mentioned sacrificial wives in Colt and then there's the—"

She paused, unable to find the words.

"What? What have you seen?"

"Tormented elves," Fjona replied. "It's a cruel and grim affliction. Their minds had been irretrievably stolen by this awful disease. They'd become angry, hungry for flesh, highly aggressive. Horrible yellow eyes that stared right through me and were near-impossible to vanquish without the aid of a staff. I had to fend one off while Perciville was impaired by another and it came pretty close. Todie, as much as I am glad to be on this adventure, there were times when I was praying to be back home in the comfort and familiarity of Wychwold. Thank you for finding me." She planted a soft kiss on Todie's pale cheek.

Blushing faintly, Todie's lip wobbled as if he wanted to speak, but no words came out.

Eventually, he spoke again. "I couldn't stand the idea of bumbling around the village when I knew how much of the Arvum you were getting to experience!"

They caught up with Perciville and Bosmar Fodd at the edge of a lake. A long wooden bridge crossed to an island in the middle which was occupied by the village of Pollen.

"Nice of you to keep up," Bosmar grumbled, though his eyes had a teasing glint to them.

Perciville gave Bosmar a stern look. "Play nice. We have a fair journey ahead of us and it wouldn't do any of us any good if we've a falling out."

Fjona was taken aback. She wasn't used to seeing such a

diplomatic side to the sage.

"Ahh, they know I'm only tickling their nerves," Bosmar replied with a boyish grin.

They followed the bridge over the lake that rippled and splashed with bright orange fish, and paused when they got to the gate. The doors were closed and chained together with a big rusty lock. Above it, written in white paint, were the words 'DO NOT OPEN!'.

It was as if the blatant caution and deterrence were as unnoticeable as the Boglander himself, because he immediately proceeded to pick the lock.

"Whoa, what are you doing?" Todie exclaimed, clearly unnerved. "Can you not read?"

"Of course I can read, princess!" the Boglander hissed.

"Then why are you ignoring the warning?" Fjona asked.

Moments later, the lock clicked open and the chain dropped to the ground with a heavy clang and thud.

"Because we need camels," Bosmar replied, as if that were reason enough. He heaved open the stiff gate door.

"Come on, let's see what's going on," Perciville commanded, pushing past the Boglander.

Fjona shrugged and followed, her wand out at the ready.

"Hey, you can't be serious?" Todie looked stunned. "There could be tormented elves through there!"

"That is exactly what I think is through there," Perciville replied with a strange smile, "but if we can't get any camels, the journey to Panamaya City will take weeks. Besides, we have my staff, Fjona's wand, your flashy new axe, and Bosmar has a few neat tricks of his own. We'll be fine."

Todie huffed. "If the villagers have abandoned this place, what are the chances they left their camels anyway?"

His point was ignored by everyone, even Fjona, who just

threw him a sympathetic smile before disappearing into the village. Reluctantly, Todie followed, brandishing his axe.

There wasn't much to Pollen. A main street surrounded by a jumble of timber-framed houses and shops, and a number of hidden alleyways. Besides the detritus that littered the road, there was nothing around. It was deathly quiet.

They walked slowly along the road, hardly making a sound of their own for fear of drawing attention.

A throaty rumble deep inside the village broke the eeriness.

"Aha, see, I told you there'd be camels here!" Bosmar grinned.

It was a strange sound; a rich, gurgling moan, like nothing Fjona had ever heard in Marrow Myre. The camels' calls echoed along the streets, the sound muted by the surrounding houses. It was impossible to pinpoint exactly where it was coming from.

"We should split up," Bosmar suggested. "Be quicker to find them."

"And more likely to get someone killed," Fjona pointed out.

Before Bosmar could comment, Perciville piped up. "Fjona's right. If there are tormented elves here, while you can all deter them, I'm the only one who can finish them off."

"What do you mean?" asked Todie. "Can I not just lop its head off with the axe?"

Perciville shrugged, glancing down a side road. "You can try, but if they've been around for a while, the bones in their necks will have fused to such a degree that no metal can slice through it. Your best bet is to aim for the legs and disable them until I can get to it with dark manipulation."

Todie frowned. "Gee, nice of you to tell me that before we entered the village."

Perciville smirked. "I'm telling you now."

"What is that awful smell?" Fjona interrupted.

A fetid, rotting fragrance had filled the air, like old fish at a market.

Todie pinched the end of his nose while Bosmar and Perciville simply exchanged a horrified look.

They rounded a corner that led to a small plaza and immediately stopped in their tracks.

Where once there would have been festivities and music, food and wine, the plaza now held only a heap of charred, rotting corpses.

Todie threw up instantaneously on a grassy verge while Fjona just managed to hold herself together.

"What happened here?" she asked, but her question was quickly answered when she noticed a tormented elf, crouched at the far side of the heap and scraping on the remnants of flesh and tissue from the bodies.

"Oh, I knew this was a bad idea!" Todie's voice quivered with fear, drawing him a disapproving look from Bosmar.

The Boglander started towards the tormented elf, brandishing a long, dulled knife, before Perciville stopped him.

"Best I deal with it. You'll only end up causing a fuss if you merely hurt it."

Bosmar yielded and allowed the sage to move past him.

Perciville inflicted a bout of dark manipulation that instantly killed the tormented elf. "Now let's get a move on," he insisted. "We don't know how many more of them are lurking around here."

Todie suddenly yelped. He had tried so hard to contain his surprise, but it slipped out.

"Shh!" Fjona whispered.

"I told you he was a lightweight," Bosmar muttered to Perciville, before turning on Todie. "You're going to get us all killed!"

"L-look! The corpses... they're moving..."

Fjona glanced over at the heap and, sure enough, there seemed to be a murmur of movement. It was faint, but it was certainly there. A pulsing, like a twitching heartbeat.

"Don't!" Todie exclaimed as Fjona edged closer to the corpses, her hand tightly gripping her Woven Wand.

"Are you still alive?" she asked the trembling bones, to which there was no reply.

"Probably just the worms—" Bosmar began, before the heap erupted from the middle and four tormented elves emerged in a maelstrom of charred bones and cartilage. Their teeth were covered in dried blood and ashes, having evidently been gnawing on the remains from inside the pile.

They leaped out, yellow eyes flitting from one intruder to another, screaming out hysterically as they charged towards them.

Perciville was quick to take one of them down, but the other elves moved too quickly and too erratically. To make matters worse, their cries attracted dozens more who emerged from the deserted buildings and streets around them.

"Four Good Gods, spare us!" Todie yelled, swinging his axe around; failing to land a hit.

Fjona was using her wand to latch on to the bones and thrust them at the elves, managing to blind one and deter another, but it wasn't enough to stop the elves from closing in on them.

Perciville, in the meantime, had killed another two, one of which was leaping through the air towards Todie before being hit in the side by the dark manipulation.

"There are too many," Fjona cried as she inched away from the chaos. "We need to retreat."

Meanwhile Bosmar had slashed away at several of the tormented elves and impaired three of them. He was surprisingly agile and able to duck and slide between flailing arms and vicious teeth.

Todie and Fjona found themselves being pushed back by the advancing elves. One lost a leg to Todie's axe; another suffered debris being propelled into its eyes by Fjona, but still the elves pressed on.

"Quick!" Fjona yelped, dragging Todie along a network of narrow streets and alleyways. Behind them, screams and hysteria rebounded from wall to wall.

They rounded a corner which led them to a dead end, except for a strange tower of a house at the far end.

In the same letters as those scribed on the village gate were the words 'KEEP OUT!', but Todie and Fjona had no option other than to seek refuge inside.

The front door was locked, but they were able to break the latch with the aid of Todie's axe.

Once inside, they slammed the door shut, then leaned their bodies against it. They had entered into a circular lobby of what once might have been quite a lavish home, but which had since been torn apart and stripped of its belongings. A mezzanine floor followed the circumference of the room above, though the stairs were not visible, presumably hidden behind one of the many entranceways splitting off from the lobby.

Moments later, the tormented elves were pounding against the door from the outside and Fjona and Todie could feel the harsh impact against their backs.

Todie's face was a portrait of terror. "I don't know how much longer we can hold them for."

Fjona surveyed the room, looking for anything that she may be able to latch on to with her wand, when her eyes caught something on the floor above. "Hey, what's that?"

It was a mysterious flickering silvery-blue light that had started to move around the mezzanine floor.

"Maybe somebody still lives here?" Todie offered, through

quivering lips.

He was about to open his mouth to get their attention, but Fjona placed a hand over it. "Don't! That could be anything up there. Remember what it said on the door..."

Todie nodded in agreement, then replied in a hushed voice, "What do we do?"

The tormented elves continued to pound against the door with, if anything, increased ferocity.

Again, Fjona looked around the room. Against one wall stood a vintage wooden dresser, bare of ornaments and trinkets. It was bigger than anything she'd lifted before, but her options were somewhat limited.

She extracted her Woven Wand from her pocket, focused as best she could, considering the circumstances, and pointed it at the dresser. A green energy poured out of the wand, drifted across the hall and embraced the dresser, simultaneously illuminating the room.

A terrifying shriek echoed down from the mezzanine floor. It was horrifying and shrill, and sent chills down Fjona's spine. It seemed to be coming from the strange light.

"What in the Arvum is that?" Todie asked shakily, but Fjona didn't reply.

She had somehow managed to drown the noise out and maintain her concentration on her spell. Slowly, the dresser edged towards them, scraping clumsily against the wooden floor, leaving a wake of white scratches in the boards.

Still, the tormented elves hammered on the door, desperately trying to break in to feast on fresh blood.

Todie, starting to feel useless, scanned the room for an escape. He noticed a rug on the opposite side to the dresser, which had been moved aside to reveal a trap door. Somebody had evidently had the same idea, based on the way the rug had been twisted up and pushed to one side. When he looked up, he saw that the silvery-blue light was edging around the floor and getting brighter as the screeches got louder.

"You need to get a move on," Todie urged, but Fjona was diligent with her concentration.

When the dresser was close enough, Fjona said, "When I tell you to, move out of the way of the door, okay?"

Todie nodded in affirmation.

"Okay." Fjona took a deep breath. "Move!"

Todie rolled to one side, and Fjona to the other. For a moment, the door opened letting in the animalistic cries of the tormented elves, and their fingers wrapped around the doorframe. With her wand, Fjona quickly thrust the dresser into the door. This time, the tormented elves cried in pain instead of malice as the door slammed onto their fingertips.

From above, the silvery-blue light was nearly blinding, and the shrieks, deafening.

"We need to be quick!" Fjona shouted over the chaos.

Without a word, Todie grabbed her by the wrist and tugged her across the room to the trapdoor. He flung it open and allowed Fjona to climb down first.

He quickly followed, casting one final peek at the front door before descending into uncertainty. He saw the dresser bouncing under the force of the tormented elves before they soon got the best of it and it clattered to the floor in a cloud of nails and splinters.

Todie didn't wait to watch the tormented elves pile into the lobby. He dropped the trapdoor down and listened to the cacophony of shrieks and cries, heavy footsteps and thuds. Silvery-blue light shone through the cracks in the floorboards above in short, sharp flashes.

It sounded as if there were a storm in the room above with

the shriek of the light and the cries of the elves. However, the tormented cries slowly petered out and heavy thumps resounded against the floor as the elves fell, one by one, until, after a final thud, only the shriek remained.

Todie and Fjona, holding their breath, watched intently at the floorboards as the mysterious light seemed to move around the lobby. Then the shrieks faded, but the light remained.

One thing was certain – there was no going back up.

CHAPTER 19

THE LIGHT THAT KILLS

They descended the ladder in near darkness, save for the specks of dusty light slipping between the floorboards above them.

When Fjona reached the bottom, only a short distance below, she used her wand as if latching onto something. A faint green light flowed out of the tip, illuminating a small basement beneath the house. It was bare but for a table in the middle, upon which lay a scroll of parchment and a pot of ink.

"What was that thing?" Todie whispered.

Fjona shook her head. "I have no idea."

"Do you think it killed them all?"

"Sounded like it."

"I can't tell if it's a blessing or a curse." Todie looked up to where the silvery-blue light was still just visible. "I don't trust your friend Bosmar."

Fjona turned to Todie with eyes of steel. "Firstly, he is no friend of mine. You've known him practically as long as I have. Secondly, what has this got to do with him?"

"Can't you see? He's the one who insisted we come to this village, and for what? Camels? Are you kidding me? Surely we could have found some camels somewhere else, but he insisted! Besides, what are the chances that the people who lived here would abandon their homes but leave their rides? They sounded weird too. I bet they're lame or blind, or else entirely unrideable! He led us here to get us killed... or at least get *me* killed."

Fjona pondered Todie's idea, bizarre though it was, then shook it away. "It's plausible, but I think you're just being paranoid, Todie. Bosmar Fodd is a friend of Perciville and he trusts him."

"Yes, and Perciville even agreed that there were likely tormented elves in Pollen."

Fjona shrugged. "So what? He obviously hadn't realised there would be so many. He must have calculated that the risk of a couple of tormented elves against his staff was worth the benefits of finding camels."

Todie scoffed. "Well, if we get out of here alive, we'll see whether his miscalculation was worth it. I'll tell you what, if we manage to find these camels in this godforsaken village and all get away in one piece, I will never voice my distrust in either of them again."

Fjona frowned. As much as she would like to prove Todie wrong, it was difficult to believe there had been any reason for stopping in Pollen, considering their current situation.

"Fine," she replied, "but if we do find them in one piece, I expect you to live up to that."

Todie smiled in the subdued light. "I'm a cleric. We keep our word."

Now they had caught their breath and cleared the air, Fjona pointed her wand around the basement. As she cast it over the table, it latched onto the scroll and pulled it towards her. While she unfurled it, Todie explored the rest of the confined space, though there was little else to see but for the cold stone walls.

"Hey, listen to this..." Fjona squinted at the scroll in the low light. She read aloud: "'To you who didn't take heed of my warning, nor the warning from the first phase of leavers, then may the Four Good Gods spare you'."

"The Four Good Gods?" Todie repeated. "They were Myrish."

"Marrowborn, probably," Fjona replied, receiving a confused

look from Todie. "I'll explain later. Anyway, it says: 'I cannot foresee what reason may have compelled you to visit Pollen, not least enter this house, but since I cannot imagine this place surviving, I owe it to the people who once lived here to leave an account of its demise. Understand that Pollen was once a simple fishing village that opened its doors willingly to travellers and provided a home to a few hundred villagers. Mainly Marrowborn and spring elves, but we were far from exclusive.'

'The village was established many hundreds of years ago, where fishermen from Rosensted could live and work, then travel to the town to sell their catch at the market. It was a peaceful place until the Sagedom collapsed and before the war that followed, though that was long before my time. Shortly after the treaty, Pollen became a sanctuary for many refugees from Havensend who had lost their homes. Among them was a sage from the Rock of Caeznor who moved in and built this very house.'

'At first there was some reluctance to allow her in because of the destruction that seemed to follow her people, but with the skills to help and heal, she quickly became an asset to the villagers and was revered long into her life. We knew not her real name, for she had changed it when she left Caeznor. To us, she became known as *Sola*, which translates as *healer* in the ancient tongue of the spring elves. That's how the village managed to thrive for the past couple of centuries until the events that consumed us no more than a month ago.'

'The problem was that nobody knew what to do in the event of a sage's death and Sola, being of relative youth hadn't divulged this. Her passing was unexpected and there's no way of knowing what happened. All I can say is that no ceremonial rites were performed and never was her soul permitted to rest. The energy that a sage consumes during their lifetime has to go somewhere and if their death is not properly mourned, so it lingers in this world. It is volatile, somehow aggressive, and deathly to touch. That's even after the frightening shrieks and the horrible light. We had no name for it so it was just referred to as the Light That Kills. Before we were really aware of its threat, we lost nearly a dozen good people in one gruesome attack. After we cremated the bodies, many of the villagers fled. Who can blame them? They left a warning on the gate and locked it shut to prevent others from falling into our peril'."

"Hold on," Todie interrupted again. "That message at the gate wasn't about the tormented elves?"

Fjona shook her head. "Apparently not." She continued reading from the scroll. "'Those who remained, like myself, knew the risk we were taking by staying, but we felt a duty to Sola to help find a way for her to rest, however cut off from the rest of the world. We failed, of course, and while we were busy scratching our heads and searching for a solution, a new threat appeared. It started with just one, but soon there came another, and another, until more than half the remaining men, notably descendants of the Havensend refugees, had turned into monsters. They looked like themselves, but were at the same time totally different. Fiendish, bloodthirsty, unnegotiable beasts made from the husbands and fathers we once loved, and nobody could figure out why.'

'At first we thought perhaps our drinking water had become contaminated with disease, so we cut off the supply. Still the men turned. Then we thought it might be in our food, so we fasted for weeks, but even that failed to prevent it. Eventually we concluded that it must be something in the air. That was when the last of us decided to leave. Forgive me, Sola. I served as your ward for the past two decades and when you needed me most, I failed you.'

'To you who reads this note, get out of here now! Leave the Light That Kills alone and GET OUT! There is a hidden passageway designed by Sola when she was well should she ever need a quick getaway. It is in this very basement, through which the last villagers and I will have fled. Face away from the ladder, walk three paces forward, parallel to the wall, turn right and look closely at the wall, about halfway up. You will see a tiny white cross. Tap four times in quick succession on the cross and a passage will open for you. It will close behind you so be quick! Follow it all the way down and it will lead you to the stables. From there you can get around to the main gate.'

'Please return this note to the table should any other poor soul stumble down here alive. May the Four Good Gods protect you. RM'."

"I can't believe this," Todie said. "That light... that was..."

Fjona nodded solemnly. "The price for becoming a sage." She looked down at her body, as though she might be able to see her own light on her skin. She felt terrified.

"Hey, don't worry about it, Fjona," Todie tried to reassure her. "The note said there's a way to prevent that from happening. The ceremonial rites. That's not necessarily going to happen to you."

"But why didn't Perciville mention that? Why was there no 'you'll conjure and toy with the fabric of the Arvum and when you die, you'll become an unstoppable entity that will consume everything in its path'," Fjona questioned nervously, mimicking the sage's voice.

"Fjona, you trust Perciville, right? Then trust that he has your best interests at heart. Maybe you're not powerful enough yet for that to be an issue or maybe he just hadn't got around to telling you. All I know is that we need to get away from this place before that Light finds us and this whole conversation becomes obsolete."

Fjona pulled herself together and returned the scroll to the table, whispering, "I hope you got away safely, RM."

Meanwhile, Todie was carefully following the instructions out of the basement. He returned to the ladder, walked three paces forward, turned to the wall and looked carefully. Sure enough, inscribed in chalk and no bigger than a fingernail was a tiny white cross. Todie carefully tapped four times with his finger.

Moments later, the wall stretched apart from each point of the cross, revealing a tunnel lit by candles burning with a green flame.

Todie's mouth hung agape. "Wow."

"Come on," Fjona urged, "let's get a move on."

They hurried down the tunnel as the basement door closed behind them. The passageway twisted and turned beneath the village until they came to the end, where they found another ladder that led up to a plain ceiling.

Todie led the way again, clambering up the ladder to find another tiny cross. Again, he tapped it four times with the tip of his finger and the cross spread apart, revealing the stables above.

When he'd climbed through, Fjona heard him curse.

"Todie! Are you okay?" She raced up the ladder as quickly as possible. When she climbed out, she found Todie petting a camel and feeding it hay. "For Aserae's sake, I thought you'd been attacked or something!"

"Worse," Todie replied glumly, "turns out Bosmar was right all along."

"Of course I was right," the Boglander exclaimed, appearing from behind one of the stalls and making Todie and Fjona jump. "You needn't look so afraid – my eyes aren't yellow and I'm not trying to rip you apart."

"I see you weren't too worried about us then," Fjona said crossly, noticing that Bosmar had already dressed his camel and was busy attaching his satchel to the saddle. She looked around at the rest of the camels. There were four in all, as well as a three horses, all dwarfed in comparison. It was like looking at Shagwell standing next to Evelyn's palomino back home.

The camels were not only tall, but much bulkier than the horses, made to appear even larger with their long, swanlike necks and humped backs. Their coats were a sandy colour, most befitting for a desert-roaming mammal, and they seemed far more elegant to Fjona than she'd imagined from the stories told to her in childhood.

"May I ask, what have you done with Perciville?" asked Fjona.

The Boglander scoffed. "Me! Done with *him*? He ditched me to chase you to your inevitable deaths the first chance he got."

Fjona cursed, racing towards the door of the stables. "We need to find him before he finds the—"

The door suddenly swung open and Perciville fell inside, his face red and sweaty. He took one look at Fjona before embracing her in a tight, almost suffocating hug.

"Thank. The. Stars," Perciville choked out between short breaths. "I thought I'd lost you. Did Todie make it out as well?"

"Yes, yes, we're all fine," Todie replied shortly, prising Fjona and Perciville apart. "Now would you mind explaining to me what in all the Arvum we are up against, because—"

Perciville waved his hands at Todie. "Yes, but later. For now, we need to get out of here."

"But why? It's such a paradise—"

"Not now, Bosmar," Perciville interrupted, pointing a demanding finger at him. "We need to go!"

There was a brief discussion as to what to do with the three horses: release them into the Paddock to run free, or leave them as the villagers had done in case somebody else should stumble upon them. The latter, of course, ran the risk of them starving before that somebody might get to utilise them. In the end, they agreed that releasing them was the morally better decision.

They quickly prepared their own camels, although Perciville

had to conjure a couple of saddles, since the stables seemed to be lacking. He also performed a couple of tricks with his staff to help settle Todie's camel, who'd been batting the cleric away with its head and spitting in his face. Evidently the camel's recent incarceration in the stables had done little for its mood.

Besides being a little higher off the ground, Fjona found that riding a camel was much the same as a horse as they headed on out to the street. Its gait was a little unsteady, causing Fjona to rock from side to side, and it required notably more force to steer, but it felt otherwise familiar.

Before too long, they were briskly riding back through Pollen, past a fresh heap of dead tormented elves that had already attracted a swarm of plump buzzing flies.

At the entrance to the village, Bosmar pulled the gate firmly shut and Perciville conjured a succession of chains and locks, binding the doors together like the seam of a doublet. He then conjured a brief flame and burned the word 'SERIOUSLY' underneath the message 'DO NOT OPEN!'.

"That should keep any more fools from entering," he muttered when he was finished.

"Oh quit your whinging!" Bosmar exclaimed. "We got our camels, didn't we? And we all made it out alive."

"Yeah… just about," Todie mumbled.

They hurried across the bridge and back to the lakeshore where they parted ways with the three horses. Perciville used his staff to create a pulsing red symbol in the air in front of the horses. One by one, he directed it into their long faces, then pointed it away in the vague direction of the Paddock. The moment he was finished, they raced off in a plume of dust, as if they were chasing a fox.

Fjona admired the sight. "Neat trick."

"It's called a *commanding charm*," Perciville explained,

hopping back onto his camel and kicking it with his heels. "Admittedly, one of the more difficult manipulations to perform. I can only direct a horse like that to a rough destination. I've got it to work on small dogs too, and a rooster once, but I've mainly practised on horses."

"Why can't you do the same to our camels and have them take us directly to wherever we're headed?" Todie asked.

Perciville chuckled. "Truth be told, I'm far from mastering the charm. They won't stop until they arrive, which has more hazards than you might expect. It's far wiser to be in control yourself."

Fjona frowned. "Does the charm work on people?"

"Theoretically, yes, but the only sage I've ever known to have the capability was Sagen Master Herak Siadonis and his morals were greater than his skill. Now, we best ride. We have lost half a day and we've a long way ahead. I suggest we follow the road down to the old quarries to set up camp. We can make it by sundown if we leave now."

They set off at a swift pace, following the perimeter of the lake and quickly turning Pollen into a distant memory behind them. Already the air was feeling just a little bit drier, the grass just a shade or two browner and the distance between the trees just perceptibly further. Although the desert was some way up ahead, the arid boundary known as The Cusp was only a full day's ride ahead, particularly at the pace they were travelling now.

Since the road was relatively flat and straight, the camels were able to gallop at a fair speed, meaning they were able to cover a lot of ground, but the chance for conversation was somewhat limited. It gave Fjona the opportunity to reflect on the events in Pollen and try to make sense of the Light That Kills. She would have to ask Perciville about it when they stopped.

Then there was the matter of Todie. She was certainly glad to have him back in her company, but he still seemed to resist the fact that she had an important role to play to prevent the Arvum from collapse. Still, he had promised to withhold his distrust now they had their camels, and Fjona had never known Todie to fail to keep his word. Besides, as she watched him up ahead, his long axe rocking gently on his back, she couldn't help but admire him for the arduous journey he'd made alone in order to find her.

As evening rolled in and the road become narrower, they dropped to a steady pace. They wound around the edge of a long disused quarry, now partly filled with milky white water. The excavation was expansive and Fjona could only wonder how many thousands of elves may have worked here over the centuries it was in use.

"A lot of the marble used in the Sultan's palace came from here," Perciville commented, but since neither Fjona nor Todie knew who the Sultan was, and Bosmar simply didn't care, nobody responded. "I used to come up here when I was younger to practise my elementals," he added, hopping down from his camel and pointing his staff down at the stagnant pool.

He focused his energy and released a fiery burst of green, down to the base of the quarry. A great plume of water rose upwards like a snake and swirled around, twinkling in the starlight.

Todie and Fjona stared, mesmerised. Then Perciville swooped the water back into the pool with such care and dexterity that it barely made a splash.

Wordlessly, Fjona plucked her wand out of her pocket and pointed it down at the waters. Like Perciville, she focused her energy and released a bright flicker of green that pulsed down. From the top of the quarry, it was only just possible to see the diminutive thread of water that Fjona pulled out of the depths. Still, even when compared to Perciville's, she felt powerful.

"Incredible..." Todie said, wide-eyed.

"Impressive, indeed," Perciville agreed.

"Not exactly Arvum-saving ability," Bosmar grumbled, receiving a scornful look from the others, "but you've got to start somewhere I suppose."

They set up camp a safe distance from the edge of the quarry between two rockfaces to shelter them from the wind. Between the four companions were varying degrees of preparedness. Todie managed to erect a half-decent tent using his canvas and some long sticks that he'd acquired on the ride down. Perciville, of course, had only his staff, but with it he could conjure his mudbrick hut and basic amenities to be shared with Fjona. Bosmar, however, had neither canvas nor the ability to manipulate. While he was prepared to sleep on the bare ground, he was able to persuade Perciville to fashion a wooden bath for him and fill it with water. It wasn't the rich, viscous bog water that he was once accustomed to, but it would serve him just as well out on the road.

While Bosmar bathed, the others sat around a campfire, feasting on fish that Perciville had caught from down in the quarry lake, and sharing a conjured whiskey or two.

When they were feeling more relaxed and settled, Fjona finally brought up the topic that had been plaguing her mind.

"Todie and I saw something odd back in Pollen." She immediately grabbed the attention of Perciville and Bosmar. "We'd been chased by the tormented elves into a house that once belonged to a sage known as Sola, according to a scroll we found in the basement. We could hear this awful screeching sound upstairs and there was this bright light that seemed to move around."

Bosmar suddenly sat up in the wooden tub and glared at Perciville.

"It wasn't worth the risk," Perciville explained to the Boglander, as if he'd spoken.

"For you maybe! I could have pocketed that thing without hesitation," Bosmar replied.

"You barely have enough vessels as it is! It would have been a needless waste."

"That wasn't your call to make."

"And it wouldn't have been your risk to take!"

Bosmar Fodd pointed a long pale finger at Perciville. "You came to *me* for help. Let's not forget that!"

"And you will be fairly rewarded," Perciville replied. "When the time for your help has come and passed, and that time was not today. Let's not also forget that I can just as easily dematerialise that bathtub as I did conjure it." He was clutching his staff and leaning it intimidatingly towards the Boglander.

Todie interrupted their stand-off. "I'm sorry, but what in the Arvum are you two bickering about?"

There was a moment's silence before the tension between Bosmar Fodd and Perciville faded, and Bosmar relaxed back into this bath with a scoff.

Perciville rested his staff, took a deep breath and then started to explain. "Fjona, you may recall me mentioning these beings before. I know precisely what it is you and Todie witnessed because I saw it myself when I went in search of you. That light – that horrifying, deathly light is what is known as a Gaeya'San. Incredibly deadly and…"

"And incredibly lucrative!" Bosmar interjected, rubbing together his thumb and forefinger.

"What does he mean?" Fjona asked.

"If you might all stop interrupting me then perhaps I can explain!" Perciville snapped. "Thank you. Now, when a sage dies, all that energy they harvested and nurtured over countless centuries doesn't just disappear. It needs to be abated in a ceremony by another sage else it lingers in a powerful and unstoppable purgatory state. Had the Gaeya'San reached you, we would not be here having this conversation. They are known for killing from the inside out and, judging by what I could see through the window, it showed no grain of mercy to those tormented elves. My greedy friend here—"

"Unnecessary adjective," Bosmar said, twisting up his face as if he had actually taken offence.

"Has acquired several objects known as Soulless Vessels. Since he is capable of sneaking up on Gaeya'San without being noticed, he is one of very few elves who has the capacity to capture them."

"Why would he want to?" Todie asked. "We chained up the gates and it couldn't seem to escape from that house. Why not just leave it locked up?"

The Boglander laughed. "Boy, you really are a naïve dimwit. A captured Gaeya'San fetches a high price among some irreputable buyers throughout the Arvum. Had I known there was one on our doorstep, I'd have bottled it up in one of these."

From his satchel he pulled out five tarnished trinkets made of a strange dark metal. They were like pocket watches, though a little deeper, with a latch on the side that pushed up a glass prism in the middle. The vessels came in different shapes too: a couple like crescent moons, another like a rounded hexagon.

"You really are a swine," Fjona argued bitterly, "making money from such a devastating being. Have you no idea what your buyers want them for?"

The Boglander scoffed. "Look, farmgirl, the first rule of business is to never ask questions. I fetch the product, I receive a bounty. That's what it's been for decades and I don't intend to change it."

"Be that as it may," Perciville interjected, "I am under the strong belief that the box we are looking for that can rid the world of the Eight Afflictions is guarded by Gaeya'San. That is why I enlisted Bosmar Fodd to join us, but we cannot squander those Soulless Vessels before we finish our mission as I cannot say how many we may need."

"How many have you got?" Todie asked.

"Six," Bosmar replied, shoving the vessels back into his satchel.

Fjona frowned. "That doesn't sound like a lot."

"They're hard to come by. I can only do what I can do," Bosmar explained dryly. "If need be, I can capture the Gaeya'San and release them in the desert."

"And put lives at risk?" Todie exclaimed, horrified.

Perciville sighed. "Look, we will have to cross that bridge when we get there. We've got enough on our plates as it is. Think of all those tormented elves. I've not seen numbers like that since the Sagedom collapsed."

"At the rate we're going, there is going to be *a lot* of bloodshed," Todie said, sombrely resting his head on his knees.

Fjona looked equally dejected. "There's no other choice. You've seen how aggressive they are. Their minds are totally lost. It's either kill, or be killed."

"And even if we could get them to Beale Cahn, there's no guarantee," Bosmar said matter-of-factly.

A strange feeling washed over Fjona.

"Very true," Perciville agreed, raising his tumbler towards the Boglander and taking another sip of whiskey.

"Wait, what's at Beale Cahn?" Todie asked, consternation written across his face.

"It's an ancient stone circle where tormented elves were taken to be blessed," Perciville informed him. "If you got there in time, they could sometimes be cured, though often with great compromise."

"Like losing memories or bodily functions, paralysis – that kind of thing," Bosmar added.

"NO!" Fjona suddenly shouted as the realisation came to her. "No, no, no..."

Todie gulped, the same truth dawning on him. "Fjona it's okay, we might be able to stop this before anything serious happens to him."

"What's going on?" Perciville asked.

Fjona was in too much of a state of shock to reply. She got to her feet and started pacing anxiously around the camp, her fingers embedded in her hair. When she eventually turned back to the others, her face was as pale as the moon and streaked with tears. Her eyes burned with fear and anger.

"Beale Cahn is where her parents were travelling to. Her father..." Todie paused, unable to find the words. "Her father is tormented."

CHAPTER 20

BEALE CAHN

This was never supposed to have taken so long. Dharla Sarsen couldn't help but wonder how worried Fjona must be feeling, watching the door expectantly and waiting for her parents to come home. She could picture her daughter, at first pleased to have some space to herself. Probably had Todie and that helven girl, Evelyn, visiting every day to entertain her, but sooner or later she would find that she missed the company of her parents. How dull it must be for Fjona back in Wychwold without her.

Had it not been for the clouds, Dharla imagined that she'd have been able to see her home, but they were well above them now.

Her back ached, her legs were running on reserves, and her wrists burned from the rope tied around them. Of course, she had hoped it wouldn't come to that, but since binding herself to her husband, they had covered much more ground. It still pained her, though, when she occasionally turned to check on him, only to see the shell of the man she loved, slumping through the snow and ice, eyes yellow and mouth frothing.

It had been two days since he'd last tried to attack her. The outbursts were becoming less frequent, but much more violent, and now she had to re-dress the bandage on her arm twice a day.

Dharla pulled Ascerat along the ridge, causing loose angular rocks to scuttle down the slope. She tried not to look down. One slip, one misplaced step, and these past weeks of travel would all have been for nothing.

It had been a very long time since Dharla had last come this way, practically a lifetime ago, but it still seemed familiar. If she were right, and she was desperate to be right, then her destination should be around the next bend.

"Arghhh!" Ascerat moaned from behind. He was starting to feel hungry again.

"I know, I know, my love. We are nearly there…"

Dharla tugged at the rope and Ascerat stumbled forward. They passed through a blanket of fog which shimmered with specks of ice. The ice crystals stung Dharla's face in spite of the numbness. It was so cold it almost felt hot.

Finally, as they trudged through the snow and rounded the edge of the slope, a sense of hope washed through her. During the course of her life, long before Fjona was born, Dharla had visited much of the island of Marrow Myre, and Beale Cahn remained to be the most wondrous location of them all. It consisted of three concentric rings of tall granite pillars, capped by long, flat lintels. The middle ring stood the tallest with three tiers of stone, the next with two tiers, and the outer ring with just the one. Salt crystals embedded in the fabric meant that the snow never settled on the monument so it remained pure in the frozen landscape.

Standing in its shadow, Dharla felt a pang of guilt for her daughter. A daughter who she had tried so hard to protect from the cruelties of the world that she had neglected to show her the beauties beyond her village. She had raised Fjona to be so sheltered that her daughter had barely seen what lay beyond the parish boundaries.

Right there, Dharla bent a knee into the crusty snow and made a vow.

"My wonderful, precious Fjona. My own fears and insecurities have bested my judgement and now I leave with the regret of shielding you from the entire world. I only hope now that I can be redeemed for hindering your experience in this life and, should time and health permit, then I will make amends. I promise that, when your father and I return home to Wychwold, I will take it upon myself to show you everything that exists out there. You and I will, together, visit every town, lake, forest and mountain throughout the entire island of Marrow Myre."

Although Fjona was a long way down the mountain and far out of earshot, Dharla hoped that, somehow, she might just have heard her.

Ascerat moaned again, reminding Dharla of their real purpose for hiking this deeply into the Infant Mountains. She stood, dropped her satchel and dragged him forward along an avenue of sorts through the concentric rings, towards the middle where lay a stone altar.

Dharla urged Ascerat to sit on the altar, but he was too resistant. Some mutated instinct seemed to whisper to him that he was in danger, and he lashed out angrily.

"I'm sorry, my *derin*," Dharla whispered, retrieving the staff from her back.

As she had done many times during the past couple of weeks, she released a shocking flash of white energy at her husband, forcing him to keel over and whimper like a puppy.

"I love you," she whispered in Ascerat's ear as she unravelled the heavy body and lay him carefully on the altar with his arms drawn across his chest and his feet neatly together.

The tears had started to freeze on her cheek, though Dharla took no notice of them. She stood behind Ascerat, held the staff up through the middle stone circle and dipped her head.

Eyes tightly closed, she recited, "Beale, God of emotion, King of healing, I beg of you the gift of replenishment." Then she opened her eyes and uttered the words, "Relieve this soul of abandonment!"

She thrust the staff upwards, but instead of chaotic energy erupting from the tip, it drew in a golden light from the sky. Dharla held on with all her might until the light stopped flowing into the staff, and the staff started to glow from head to tail. With the power to heal now harnessed, she waved the staff over Ascerat's stiff body, issuing the same golden energy. The light enveloped Ascerat, filtering through his skin and flowing through his veins.

He suddenly jolted up, eyes closed; mouth wide open as he screamed in agony. A ghostly, guttural scream from deep within his chambers. All Dharla could do was watch in tears and restrain herself from rushing to his aid. She could hear the cracking of the bones that had fused as the cruel affliction waned under the strength of Beale.

Then Ascerat's pain subsided and he slumped back down onto the altar, still glowing as though he'd swallowed the sun.

Dharla allowed herself to walk over to him. He seemed so peaceful, but she knew it was far from over. She kissed him gently on his golden cheek, then returned to her satchel and proceeded to set up a canvas shelter between the pillars.

The fate of her husband was in the hands of Beale now. All she could do was wait.

CHAPTER 21

THE CONTACT

In the centre of Rosensted, between the derelict orphanage and the Gambler's Tavern, was a shielded avenue with a sign reading 'Indi Street'. A sign one would only get to read should the proprietor of the avenue permit it. Not that anybody should want to pay Indi Street a visit since the only residence was a single dilapidated hut with barred windows and a leaning chimney stack, one breeze away from tumbling.

"Is this the right place?" Lucinda asked with urgency.

Horse Leg grunted in reply. "Do you know another invisible street, San Denvillier?"

Feldin, buried beneath his cloak, spat back, "How dare you speak to Lady Denvillier with such disrespect! I should have your head put on a spike."

"Try me, imp."

Lucinda snapped her fingers. "Now boys, let us not bicker over petty ordeals. We have more important issues to address."

With that, she tapped her staff against the front door and waited. There was no response. Impatiently, Lucinda reached out to knock again, but Horse Leg intervened.

"No, the Contact does not like that. Your brother taught me to be patient here."

Lucinda turned up her nose, then took a deep, resigned breath.

After what felt like a tediously long time later, the door swung open, seemingly of its own accord.

"Thank you," Lucinda said, inviting herself in.

She hadn't been at all sure what to expect on the other side, but she certainly hadn't been expecting this. Inside the hut was a grand orangery, filled with exotic plants, the trickling of streams and waterfalls, and the tweets and trills of rare birds. It was like stepping into a Bouandan rainforest. Outside had been a cool, overcast morning, but in here, the sun seemed to radiate through the glass ceiling and it felt as warm as a hot summer's day.

Lucinda gazed around the expansive room, many times larger than the exterior. "Extraordinary..."

"Indeed," said Horse Leg. "When I came before, I thought I was delirious from the pain."

They followed a pristine flagstone path that weaved past leafy bushes and tall, sprawling palm trees with vibrant round fruits. A bridge crossed over a pond of the clearest water, home to long orange fish and little green frogs.

"How exactly are we supposed to find this *Contact* in all this...?" Feldin asked.

He was immediately met with a response by their elusive host. "Left past the honeysuckles," a soft voice informed them, "straight on under the blossoms, right by the wisteria and follow the Bouandan Perygroves. Watch out for the bees, and don't go near the *Hibernigum*."

Lucinda and Feldin exchanged a bemused look.

"That's him," Horse Leg said simply.

They followed the Contact's instructions and found him in a small courtyard, conjuring a rosebush with his staff. He stood with his back to them, wearing a grey robe embroidered with green vines and swirls of butterflies.

Lucinda cleared her throat. "You must be my late brother's notorious Contact."

The Contact froze. "*Late* brother?"

"I'm afraid Benjamin was murdered in a tavern in Rosensted. I am his sister, Lucinda—"

"Yes, yes I know who *you* are," the Contact replied. "Why is it that you have come to me?"

"San Denvillier, there's something you should know," Horse Leg whispered, but Lucinda waved him away.

"You were assisting my brother with a project regarding the Sleeping Giant. I was hoping you could tell me what you and he had discussed?"

Horse Leg interrupted again. "Please, San Denvillier. The Contact. I should've mentioned before—"

This time, Feldin instructed him to remain quiet, jabbing the hilt of his knife firmly beneath Horse Leg's ribs.

"Well, Lucinda, sister of Benjamin Denvillier, perhaps you and I should have a conversation," said the Contact.

Lucinda tried all she could to not jump as the Contact turned to face her. Much like the orangery, the Contact's face was extraordinary. The nose, mouth and right cheek were the rusty hue and smooth complexion of an autumn elf. The eyes, forehead, left cheek and chin seeming instead to resemble a blue-feathered bird. The look was startling, though the transition between the two was neat enough that it didn't appear entirely wrong. Just very, very unusual.

The Contact led them up to a plush living room that overlooked the orangery and poured his guests a cup of sweet, fragrant tea. They nursed their drinks quietly, unsure of exactly the words to say.

The Contact smirked. "I suppose you are wondering about the face?"

"No actually, I was more interested in the crockery. Is this ceramic from Havensend?" Feldin asked sarcastically, receiving an admonishing look from Lucinda.

The Contact ignored the remark. "I was gravely injured during the collapse of the Sagedom, some three hundred years ago, give or take. I received a nasty infliction that tore away half of my face. Fortunately, I was, and am, a very skilful sage, particularly at *Splicing Charms,* and so I repaired the wounds with the face of a silkstar, perhaps the most elegant of birds in all the Arvum. Sometimes I miss my old face, but I've become rather accustomed to this one."

"I bet that took some getting used to," Feldin muttered under his breath.

"Likewise, I provided your brother with some rather cunningly amplified camels, a creation I was particularly pleased with. From my understanding, they faired well against the Noble Guard. I also had the pleasure of repairing your friend's leg. How are you finding it?" The Contact peered at Horse Leg with his strange, avian eyes.

"I can walk well enough," Horse Leg replied.

"I've become quite fond of it," Lucinda added, tracing the inside of the leg with a delicate, provocative finger and grabbing his manhood. "Though it's a shame you stopped there."

Horse Leg batted her hand aside and Lucinda laughed cruelly.

"So tell me, Miss Denvillier, what brings you to my home?" the Contact asked, bringing the subject back around.

"I want to know exactly what you and my brother were plotting."

The Contact chuckled warmly. "I'm afraid I may not be at liberty to do that."

"No? And why is that?"

"Because, were I to tell you too much, the sequence of events that should follow would be rather unpleasant."

"Speak plainly," Feldin demanded.

"I would, but I dare say you would not understand."

"Unpleasant how?" Horse Leg asked.

"Ah-ha! Now that is the kind of question you should be asking. I liked you the moment I spliced that horse's leg onto you. Let me demonstrate..."

The Contact took his staff, made of dark green wood, and pointed it at the table. Feathers of red and green light spilled out of the head and twisted about the table, conjuring a complicated web of vines. At points, the vines crossed over one another, then split off in separate directions where occasionally a black or red rose would appear.

"What is this?" Lucinda questioned, unimpressed.

"This," the Contact explained, "is the future. Or, rather, our possible futures."

"How—"Feldin began, but was immediately cut off.

"Allow me to elaborate. This bed of vines shows the present. Now this reading doesn't allow me to see what you are going to have for dinner tomorrow, but it does allow me to see what fairness of prosperity or austerity the Arvum is facing, and the pivotal events that will determine its fate. I cannot tell you whether we are looking at days, years or decades, but only that ahead of us we have periods of peace and war, surplus resources and famine, long life and death."

The Contact pointed to different vines: some plump and vibrant, others dried and wilting. Some of the vines were a brush of thorns, while others were naked and bare to the flesh.

"So what is our future?" Lucinda asked, still sceptical of the sage's intentions.

"Well, if you follow every possible alternative, you will surely see that all the routes have, at times, periods of austerity and many, though not all, pass through this black rose, indicating a catastrophic event, after which very few vines survive. There is one, however, that after the chaos, appears to regenerate and thrive, thus producing this silver rose, here."

Feldin frowned. "So we are inevitably headed towards a catastrophe, and only one leads to survival?"

The Contact shrugged. "Essentially."

"How can you know what to do from this?" Horse Leg asked, his face as gormless as his adopted name.

The Contact held his staff up in one hand and touched a point on the vines with his other. "By reading it."

His staff lit up while his eyes glazed over. He remained like that for a moment, his eyes twitching as if he were dreaming. When he released the vines, his pupils returned.

"But I cannot foresee specific details, merely snippets of moments that will occur at that point in time, at that particular alternative."

"This is nonsense," Feldin snarled. "How can we trust that you aren't just making this all up?"

"For what gain?" the Contact asked.

"Money? Power?" Lucinda suggested.

"Perhaps these are what you seek, but I have all the money and power I could possibly want at the tip of my staff. You should also be aware that I had foreseen the death of your brother and that I know who was responsible for it, though it would punish the future if I were to tell you."

Lucinda stood abruptly, her eyes ablaze. "Don't speak of my brother in vain. He was a good man."

The Contact gestured for her to calm with his large, wrinkled hands. "I agree. He fulfilled everything I asked of him."

"Oh yes? And tell me, what exactly was that?" Lucinda demanded.

"Well..." The Contact looked intently at Lucinda with his piercing, birdlike gaze. "He brought you to me..."

Silence filled the space, but for the birds and waterfalls, as

Lucinda, Feldin and Horse Leg tried to calculate whether this sage was a brilliant genius, or a manipulative lunatic.

The Contact answered the question none of them had dared to ask. "The key you stole from the general and which Feldin cast into a counterfeit allows access to a room beneath the palace of the Sultan. That room contains an ancient well that tunnels deep into the belly of the mountain. The fate of the Arvum rests in the waking of the Sleeping Giant, and it cannot happen solely by itself. I had feared that the admirable tenacity of the Kelner elves constructing the canal may have prematurely awakened the giant and plummeted the Arvum into a far bleaker fate. The efforts of your bandits to hinder the workers and scare many of them away has bought us more time, though we are still on the precipice of darkness. What is needed is for a wielder of untempered manipulation to drop a staff — the staff I had given Benjamin and that you now hold — down the well and deep into the belly of the mountain."

"Will that not destroy the city?" Horse Leg asked.

"I cannot say."

"And why is that?" Feldin snapped at the Contact.

"The degree to which I inform you of the future, of itself determines the future. You have all the information you need in order to follow the right path."

"Which leads us towards the silver rose?" Lucinda questioned.

The Contact looked at her keenly. "I'm afraid I cannot tell you that either."

They were contemplative again as they weighed up their options. Trust the man who their former leader, Lucinda's brother, had trusted, or dismiss him as being clinically insane.

Suddenly, the Contact clapped his hands together. "Well, this has been very productive indeed! I suggest you get back to your *den*, as your brother referred to it, and digest all that I have shared with you today." He gestured to them to rise and pointed them towards the exit.

Lucinda stroked the shaft of her staff, almost feeling the power which it contained within. "I will carefully consider what you have asked of us."

"Oh," the Contact replied with a wry smile, "I know you will."

As they made their way towards the orangery path, the Contact grabbed Lucinda's arm and whispered in her pointed ear. "Be cautious though, Lady Denvillier. The trajectory of the Arvum comes down to you. Your powers of persuasion, though they don't work on me, nor did they on your brother, very much work on the Sultan, and the games you played when you visited Panamaya City last have repercussions. *Prestigious ambassador to the governess*, I believe it was? That was a personal favourite of mine."

Lucinda's ears pricked up and she coyly dipped her head away.

The Contact continued. "I wish I didn't have to tell you this, but having looked into the future, I know that I *have* to, so listen carefully. When next you visit the palace, follow the stairs up to the Font of Succession. The guard will say that you cannot get in, but you can. Read aloud the inscription and gaze into the font. Then you have a big decision to make and I know not what that will be."

Lucinda didn't reply. She just turned on her heel and followed her two companions back along the path with one realisation: the Contact was a brilliant genius *and* a manipulative loony.

CHAPTER 22

ILLEGIBLE

Elian sat with his head in his hands, his long fingers combing through his hair.

"I can't believe they're executing her," he said into his palms, as Bobassa's soft scales brushed up against his leg.

Kaikura joined Elian at the table, clasping a hot cup of tea in spite of the weather. "I know."

"I did all I could, but that damned judge twisted my words!"

Kaikura reached out and patted the ranger's shoulder. "I know, I was there."

"How can that be it, though? Surely there's something I can do..."

"Like what?" Kaikura asked. "Break into her cell and rescue her? Then what? You'll end up both being killed before you even got out the city."

Elian slammed his fist on the table, making Kaikura flinch and back away from him.

"I'm sorry, I shouldn't have..." he stuttered, his face reminiscent of a chided dog.

"You really cared for the corporal, didn't you?"

The ranger nodded. "She's fierce, ambitious, not someone I'd want to get on the wrong side of or—"

"Have a relationship with?" Kaikura asked, the words slipping out of her mouth before she could stop them.

For the first time since the ranger had knocked on her hatch door that morning, Elian laughed. "No, indeed! An amazing woman, don't get me wrong, but I only ever valued her as my superior. Immensely talented in the sand. Bold and brazen and genuinely one of the best. Seems like such a waste..."

He trailed off, and even Kaikura's mind flicked to his helpless leader, imprisoned somewhere in the Upper Gate.

She sipped her tea awkwardly for a moment. "How is the excavation coming along?"

"They've made good progress since you visited. And they've found a few more of those aurik horns. Not as big as that one, but still impressive." The ranger gestured to the horn, quietly serving as a bookend on a shelf beside the table.

"I suppose it stands to reason that there may have been a herd of auriks living around an ancient river," Kaikura postulated as she retrieved the archaic bone and placed it on the table in front of them. "I feel such a connection to the past when I touch it. Do you feel it too?"

Elian closed his eyes and touched the smooth skin of the horn.

"How vastly different the Arvum must have been back then," Kaikura added. "A wide open landscape with rivers and lakes, and who knows what else! These giant, beautiful auriks roaming around, grazing on luscious grasses and drinking bountifully from a river."

Elian sighed dreamily. "It sounds wonderful."

Their fingers touched then, only for a moment, and Kaikura instinctively retracted her hand.

Nervously, and a little red in the face, Elian continued, "Well... I... umm... what exactly does an aurik look like?"

Kaikura frantically got to her feet, returned the horn to the shelf, then started leafing through a pile of books underneath the table.

"Allow me to show you," she said, covering her embarrassment with excitement. She grabbed a couple of dusty old tomes and dropped them on the table with a heavy thump, running a finger down the spines, then settling on a thick volume with a faded yellow leather cover. "The most accurate depiction is in here, I believe."

The tome was named, simply, *Ancients* by Marssen Tilar, and the front portrayed a spread of bones, laid out in the shape of some extinct creature.

"I've not indulged this particular tome for some time," Kaikura said as she blew away a sheet of dust, then opened it in front of Elian.

She began peeling through the pages, stopping on occasion to show her guest an eclectic mix of ancient fauna, including a strange amphibious camel and a six-winged bird.

"Ah-ha, here it is! The aurik. 'An ancient mammal of the bovine family. Remains found in waterlogged deposits throughout the Arvum...' And here's a reconstruction of what it may have looked like."

Kaikura flipped the book around so that Elian could see.

"Wow, it's big! I see what you mean about that horn. It's very similar..."

"Yes," Kaikura pondered, "similar, but not the same."

She flipped the book back around and continued reading. After a while, she stood and retrieved the horn again.

"What is it?" Elian asked, but instead of answering, Kaikura smacked the horn against the edge of the table, creating a booming thud and leaving a chip in the artefact.

Bobassa screeched at the sudden sound, his scales flared as if ready to attack. When he realised that Kaikura was the source of the intrusive sound, he settled and returned to dozing underneath Elian's chair.

"What are you doing?" Elian cried, his fingers briefly twitching in the air above his hilt.

"It would seem my original assessment has been disproved," Kaikura replied. "Had this artefact been a horn, then we would find it to be hollow, but it isn't. It's solid bone…"

"So if it isn't a horn, what is it?"

Kaikura couldn't quite believe it herself, judging by the sheer size of the object, but she could not deny what it was. "It's a tooth."

"A tooth!" Elian exclaimed. "Surely it's too big to be a tooth?"

"I'm inclined to agree," Kaikura replied, "but its shape, form, fabric; everything about it, besides perhaps its size, proves unequivocally that it has to be a tooth."

Elian inspected the artefact again more closely and ran his fingers along its smooth surface. "If indeed it is what you say, then can you image the creature it belonged to?"

Kaikura nodded. "Impressive, indeed. I wish my mentor, Proprietor Bouwer, hadn't vanished out of the city, for she would know exactly what it is, I assure you."

"Did she not tell you where she was going? Even leave a note?" Elian asked.

"No. Well, hardly. She left this for me, but I've yet been able to make heads or tails of it," Kaikura replied, replacing the tooth on the table and pulling out another book. "*The Compendium of Sages.*" Kaikura read the title aloud, then noticed Elian's face drop in awe.

"You can *read* that! What language is it?"

"It's Arvish. The Common Tongue. The same as everything else, except—"

"No, it isn't!" Elian interrupted. "It's a load of strange symbols. I've never seen anything like it in my life."

Kaikura paused, then opened it to a random page. "Do you see the same symbols here?" she asked.

Elian nodded. "Yes, pretty much identical. Why?"

"Well, to my eyes at least, the front cover has been written in Arvish, as clear as day, but the rest is in this strange, illegible language that I've never seen before. What is utterly unfathomable, and intrinsically fascinating, is that, to you, the front page is also cryptic..."

"I swear by the Noble Guard I cannot read a single word of it. How is this possible?"

Kaikura considered Elian's question for a moment, the tips of her fingers pressed against her temples. "I don't know. Perhaps a sage had something to do with it? Maybe even the same one who created the Panamayan spring..."

The words rolled off Kaikura's tongue, like a loose wheel racing down a hill.

"Wait, really? The spring isn't native to the mountain?"

"Well... possibly not," Kaikura replied. "I heard it from the Sultan when I was providing him counsel. If it's true, however, then it's rumoured that the enchantment placed upon it should only sustain the spring for three hundred years and it is now soon to dry up. The Sultan is reinstating the ancient aqueducts in the Precipitous Mountains so that we can ship freshwater here instead. That or to simply relieve his mind of the fear."

"Why go to all the trouble? Surely he could just find another sage to replenish the old spring?"

"There aren't any, I suppose. At least not in Panamaya City and the Sultan is hardly likely to go begging Havensend to let us borrow theirs, if indeed any remain. Be that as it may, for thousands of years the sages spread their influence throughout the Arvum. I suppose, maybe a sage enchanted this book so that it couldn't be read." Kaikura rested her hand in her chin as she tried to make sense of it all.

"But why allow you to read the cover and nothing else?" Elian asked. "It's like its mocking you."

Kaikura shook her head. "No, I don't believe this to be an act of mockery. I think it's more likely an act of desperation. Wherever Proprietor Bouwer went, she wanted me to find this, but perhaps the book had been originally intended for her eyes? Maybe the book is trying to get me to read it?"

Elian chuckled despite himself. "Please don't take any offence, but this all sounds ridiculous!"

"I know, but with all the ludicrous happenings going on around here, an emotive book is hardly incongruous."

In a flash, the scholar fished out a sheath of parchment and an inkwell from a cabinet in the corner of the room. She spread the parchment out on the table and began writing.

"What are you doing?" Elian asked.

Before Kaikura could reply, the earth started to quake, gently at first then gradually heavier, and dust trickled down from the ceilings. The tremors had started to become more violent, forcing Elian out of his seat. Bobassa was equally unimpressed. His scales were pricked up and his claws dug into the wood of the table to avoid being shaken across the room.

"These... are... becoming... more frequent," Kaikura uttered over the vibrations as she clung to the table. "Are... you... okay?"

Her teacup bounced across the table, tipped over the edge and shattered against the floor in a pool of ruby. A stack of books collapsed into a heap on the floor and the pans in the kitchen clattered together like a dissonant windchime.

"Yes, I think so," Elian replied between breaths as he pulled himself up off the floor and was plunged unsteadily forwards into the table.

The lantern above swung freely around their heads and the ranger had to duck to avoid being bludgeoned in his skull.

After a short while, the tremor eased into a peaceful stillness and only the sprinkling of dust from the ceiling and debris across the floor pertained to it.

They could hear scared murmuring outside as the concerned neighbours reassured one another. Children cried, but most of the parents had become used to quakes and were able to soothe them.

Elian dusted off his coat and helped Kaikura to her feet with a kind, gauntleted hand. "Droves of elves have already left the city. Perhaps you should consider the same?"

"And go where? I have no family to seek elsewhere, no friends. I wouldn't even know where to begin. My life belongs with the Archivus and I couldn't bear to leave it unless I had to, nor could I abandon the children at the alleyway school. They have only each other to keep them safe. What of yourself? Have you considered fleeing?"

"I'm a ranger with the Noble Guard. I am bound to this city, and this city to me. The soldiers will be the very last to evacuate, should it come to that."

They were pensive for a while, listening to the consternation beyond the walls while Kaikura imagined the fate that might befall Panamaya City.

Then, as if nothing had even happened, she reached again for her inkwell.

"If we are staying here then we need to figure out what's going on and I think there may be answers in this very book."

"What exactly are you doing?" Elian asked again, twisting his neck so that he could just make out what Kaikura was writing. It turned out to be the alphabet in a precise, neat grid.

"With your assistance, I'm going to decode it," she explained, turning the parchment around to Elian. "Now here is the word *the*. What I'd like you to do is draw the symbols that you see next to each letter. As best as you can manage. Can you do that?" She held the quill towards Elian.

The ranger smiled. "Absolutely."

He proceeded to translate the symbols. His writing was neat and surprisingly graceful as he copied the swirling lines and irregular twists that comprised the enigmatic script.

They continued to work together until they had transcribed the whole title and had nearly all of the letters they needed. With most of the language translated, Kaikura was able to slowly, but surely, decode the chapter listings and, through the process of elimination, figure out several more of the remaining letters.

She was making good progress when one chapter heading caught her attention: *A Chronology of the Sleeping Giant.*

Kaikura hadn't even realised that her mouth was hanging open when Elian asked, "Are you trying to catch flies?"

She didn't reply, instead frantically flipping through the pages to find the chapter. The moment she peeled back the page, her eyebrows furrowed into a look of befuddlement.

"What is it?" Elian peered over Kaikura's shoulder. "Wait a second..."

"Indeed," Kaikura answered, as if Elian had spoken his mind.

Among the page of cryptic prose was an illustration depicting an unusual creature. It wasn't entirely unlike an elf, with arms, legs, torso and head; however, that was where the similarities ended. For one thing it was far more muscular, particularly across its wide chest and arms. Then there was the fact that instead of hands, it had claws and instead of feet, it had talons. Although this was just an illustration, its face seemed intimidating, not least for the small horns on its head and a ferocity in its eyes.

It wasn't for these frightening features that Kaikura and Elian were taken aback, however. In actual fact, what they had both noticed was that the terrifying creature had two particularly long, overhanging, deadly pointed teeth that grew out of its upper gum and curved down towards its waist.

Elian was the first to speak. "That doesn't look particularly friendly."

"Whatever this monster is, it would appear we have one of its teeth." Kaikura quickly turned to her parchment and began translating as much of the page as possible.

Slowly, the words unfolded before her.

Whence Yilsommen had ensured peace amongst the elves of autumn, then she did travel forward to the Pentari Desert where disparate families of the elves of summer lived in fear of the vicious elves of sand.

"I've never even heard of the elves of sand. They used to live in the desert?" Elian asked, reading Kaikura's scrawled writing over her shoulder.

"Sand elves, I suppose," she replied, then continued to transcribe.

These elves of sand were a vile incarnation of the species. Bloodthirsty, aggressive, and destructive. When the elves of summer had first emerged and reasoned to live alongside, the elves of sand had resisted with aggression. With claws great and teeth long, they did spill the blood of thousands of elves of summer before drifting into the territories belonging to the elves of spring, autumn, and river. Death and chaos ravaged the land akin to disease. The elves of sand became known by a name in the tongue of the elves of summer. Raithers.

"Raithers?" Kaikura read aloud. There was something about even the name that sent a chill down her spine.

"I've never heard the term before," replied Elian.

Thus the raithers believed they held dominion over the Arvum for they'd resided in the Pentari region for many thousands of years, long before it had even deteriorated into a desert.

Yilsommen, mother of the sages, used unprecedented force to cease every single living raither in an attempt to rescue the other populations. She fought them in the Pentari Desert and it was there that she laid them all to rest, piling them atop one another in an immense burial mound. This mound later became known as the Sleeping Giant.

"Does this mean what I think it does?" Elian asked. "That there's no giant buried beneath the mountain?"

Kaikura nodded. "I believe it does. Oh how exciting, and something of a relief!"

Elian looked at her, bemused. "A relief how, exactly?"

"Do you not see? All that sits beneath the mountain is a great pile of raither bones from many thousands of years ago. There's little more down there than the tooth the workers had uncovered in the trench. It's perhaps a little spooky to be living atop a burial mound, but whether one is walking on the mountain, on the sand or on the soil, we are always walking over the dead. What remains a relief is that there is no giant destined to awaken and destroy the city!"

"So the earthquakes are circumstantial?"

"They must be," Kaikura replied enthusiastically. "Everybody fleeing from a waking giant is simply fleeing a natural event. Earthquakes have been recorded throughout the Arvum over generations. This is nothing unusual or to be afraid of."

The ranger smiled. "Well, that is a relief, I suppose, although it doesn't mean that the city isn't going to collapse anyway."

"That is true, but like we agreed, you and I aren't going

anywhere."

"I wonder why your mentor wanted you to read this book? Surely it wasn't just to find out about the raithers." Bobassa hopped up onto Elian's lap, interrupting his train of thought. He started petting the sandkat.

"It's an exhaustive tome," Kaikura told him. "There may be something more important in here."

"Well good luck translating all that."

They were disturbed by a firm knock on the hatch door.

Bobassa immediately leaped from Elian and onto the table, growling up at the ceiling.

The ranger stood and rested a hand on the hilt of his sword. "Are you expecting any visitors?" he asked Kaikura, who duly shook her head. "Who goes there?" he called up to the hatch.

There was a muffled reply from outside, to which Kaikura frustratedly answered, "Oh just open it up!"

The hatch door lifted and, not for the first time, the Sultan's steward, Oolia Khamun, peered down inside.

"San Kendi, Ranger Sole, forgive my intrusion, please, but I am in need of your help." She sounded distressed.

"What do you want?" Elian asked.

"Corporal Stone doesn't deserve her fate. I intend to break her out of jail and I need your help, Ranger."

CHAPTER 23

RELEASED

A lot could be said for the ingenuity and artistic flare that Panamayan architects once held when creating the impressive city that now occupied the Sleeping Giant. From the intricacies and beauties of the palace to the sheer startling wonderment of the Archivus, and the acoustically remarkable judiciary court, Panamaya City had an abundance of formidable buildings.

Inevitably, contemporaries of these architects were, more often than not, commissioned to design buildings of a more sordid nature. Many hundreds of years later, it was still discussed over a *lamna* or two whether the decision to build the city prison beneath the Upper Gate sewage latrine was based on logistics or to act as a passive form of punishment.

Lais had spent just one night and, to her best guess, a full day in her cell, yet already the rotten stench of faeces above her was making her welcome her pending execution.

So much for having time to get her things in order. She had been permitted just half an hour, under the watch of a guard, to clear her stuff out of her inn room, and dump it in the streets to be distributed among the poor, before being shuffled unceremoniously into a dank, stinking cell.

Now she sat on the cold stone floor with her back to the hard mountain rock, staring aimlessly through the bars, waiting for the guard to come and take her to her death.

From somewhere along the corridor, Lais could hear the

sound of murmuring. There was a firm, though not raised, voice, and a brief discussion.

"My executioner?" Lais wondered, as she dragged her tired, chained legs across the cold floor. She strained her pointed ears, but was unable to hear the details of the conversation.

Then clipped footsteps echoed along the corridor and the gruff, monotonous voice of the gaoler grunted, "This be your prisoner, sir."

The blue coat of a Home Guard lingered behind the bars, facing away from Lais with their hands behind their back.

"Thought the execution was tomorrow," the gaoler said.

"I'm only checking in on her," replied a strangely familiar voice.

"Not many visitors down here," the gaoler added, "least of all a Home Guard. Anyway, this is her. She don't do much but sit with that frown. Can't blame her. Waitin' for death must be damn tedious."

"I dread to think," the Home Guard responded, then turned on the spot in a flurry of blue.

Lais realised why she had recognised that voice. For a moment, she wondered if the sewage fumes had inhibited her senses and she had spiralled into a state of delirium.

She had to blink twice to regain herself and, when she had, there was no mistaking the face of Elian Sole standing above her. He was not clad in his usual white Noble Guard coat, but had somehow acquired the blue coat of a Home Guard. When he looked down at his former corporal, his face was passive and stoic as if he didn't recognise Lais, or was at least trying to make it appear that way.

As Elian turned back to the gaoler, he gave Lais a barely perceptible nod. "Very good," he told the gaoler assertively. "A guard will be with you first thing tomorrow to collect the convict and take her for execution."

While he spoke, he surreptitiously uncurled his fingers to reveal two hibernigot beans; one red, one green. Lais watched keenly as he carefully squeezed his hand between the bars and dropped the beans on the floor, just inside the cell.

"I'd appreciate it if you could keep my visit to yourself." Elian reached into his pocket and extracted a small purse, which the gaoler gladly accepted.

"You were never here," the gaoler replied, his voice fractionally more expressive than it had been.

As the two walked away, Lais swiped for the beans as swiftly as she could with the manacles bound to her legs. She blew the dust away from them and put one in each hand, glancing from the red bean to the green.

Had Elian provided her with a comfortable, though cowardly, way out? Or had he concocted a plan for her to escape? Did he intend for her to take the red bean first, feign her own death and spare the need to execute her, or was he enabling her to take her life into her own hands?

Even if Elian intended her to fake her death, that didn't mean she had to. After all, what would her life become after being disbanded from her service to the Guard and exiled from her home?

All these thoughts swam through Lais's head and she found that she was starting to favour the idea of ending it all there and then. That was until the image of Beric Lahsilli's smarmy face crossed her mind. To take the coward's way out and leave Lahsilli with the satisfaction of knowing that Lais Stone died in a stinking cell beneath the city was too humiliating to pursue.

In the end, it was an uncharacteristic lust for revenge on which Lais based her decision.

"I hope you've got a plan, Sole," she whispered in the dankness as she ate the red bean first.

It tasted surprisingly salty and had a creamy flesh inside its tough skin. It left a faint taste of iron in her mouth as if she'd bitten her tongue and made it bleed. When she had swallowed it, she tentatively ate the green bean. It was extraordinarily bitter and it took an inordinate level of discipline to keep from throwing it up. Now her mouth felt horribly parched as if she'd inhaled a sandstorm and her eyes had become sore and difficult to keep open.

When she had successfully swallowed that too, she started to feel really strange. Initially came a light-headedness as if she'd had one too many drinks at a tavern. Then she started to feel cold, but only on the inside, beneath her skin, like her blood had started to chill. Her vision became cloudy and her heartbeats became far less frequent and with far less vigour. Before there was any time to panic, Lais passed out on the hard floor and fell helplessly into a dreamless state of unconsciousness.

Had she had any sense of her mind at all, Lais may have considered that 'red before green and you'll only dream' was entirely misleading and in fact 'red before green and you will lose all sense of being' would have been more apt.

An unknown length of time later, she became vaguely aware of somebody standing above her. There may have been voices too, although it was impossible to know what was being said. There was a definite shift in light and Lais could almost feel herself being carried somewhere outside of the prison.

As her senses became faintly more readable, she was aware that the cold stone floor of the cell had been replaced by a cold, soft yet bony surface. A primal part of her mind was telling her she was in motion and that she was trapped beneath something heavy.

She was on the brink of consciousness, somewhere in the void between awake and asleep, completely unable to move and with only a minimal degree of thought. That minimal degree was enough for Lais to know that she was currently buried in a pile of corpses and she was being carted down the mountain towards the mass grave in the desert.

In her head, she started to panic, desperate to push the bodies off her and escape, but she was entirely incapacitated. As she panicked, she depleted what little strength she had recovered and, perhaps to her fortune, completely passed out again.

Judging by the shroud of night, Lais came to a long while later. She was bleary-eyed, cold to the touch, and was as dehydrated as the Pentari Desert.

Muffled, familiar voices filled her head.

"What else does the book say?" somebody asked softly.

"Oh, read her the bit about Yilsommen – did I say that right? – and the raither."

Someone replied, "Yes, Yilsommen, the first sage. She combated the ferocious monsters known as raithers, or sand elves, and buried them in the desert. It says here that she defeated them and laid them to rest beneath the mountain."

"Incredible... you got all this from a mysterious book?" the first voice asked.

"I did. It was left for me by my mentor."

"Fascinating."

"Indeed."

"She's awake."

A shuffling of feet and pages of a book.

"Good. Let's get her up and on the road," the softer voice replied.

"You can't be serious! She's in no condition to be wandering through the desert by herself," another said, accompanied by the slamming of a book.

"Either she leaves as soon as she's up or she risks being recognised by a ranger and carted back to the Sultan."

Lais achily waved her hands at them to be quiet. She knew that they were barely whispering, but to her ears it was deafening, and giving her a headache.

She managed to push herself up and squinted at the piercing light of a single lantern.

"How do you feel?" the first voice asked. It was Elian, and Lais's eyes had adjusted enough to just make out a big, relieved grin on his face.

"Horr-end-ous," Lais croaked back.

"Oh, here, have this," the third voice said, a peculiar book with strange letters tucked beneath her arm while she eased a jar of water into Lais's quivering hands.

It was the scholar from the Archivus. Lais tried to place a name to the face. Kaikura. She was surprised to see her here, considering the way Lais had spoken to her when they had last met. She found herself staring at the spine of the book, in an attempt to pull back her senses, but saw that it was written in an entirely alien script, like nothing she had seen before. She wondered if perhaps the effects of the hibernigot beans were still hampering her mind.

"Tha... nks," Lais said, taking a cautious sip of the blissfully cool water. "Where am I?"

"We're in the evacuation camp, a short way from the mountain," said Elian. "There are hundreds, even thousands of tents here, pitched by folk who've fled the earthquakes. It's got pretty bad in the last day or so."

"How long have I been out?" Lais asked, her voice starting to come back to her.

Oolia spoke up next. "Two days, which is why we need to

get you out as soon as possible, particularly now that it is dark. The guards have been inspecting the tents to keep an eye on the evacuees and it's only a matter of time before they come to us."

"She'll only get herself killed if she leaves in this state," Kaikura reiterated. "That would defeat our whole endeavour."

"You don't need to travel far tonight," Oolia said to Lais, "just beyond the patrol area of the North Divisions. After that, you can set up camp and recover, but you need to go as soon as you can walk."

Kaikura was about to argue, but before she could speak, the corporal had pushed herself up and perched on the edge of the makeshift bed.

"My strength is coming back to me," she said. "I'll be fine so long as I have some supplies."

Elian swiftly reached for a satchel and dropped it beside the bed. "We were able to procure some of your clothes as well as a tent, some money and enough food to get you to Salamander. I also managed to pinch your Noble Guard sword from the barracks in case you run into dalachites along the way. I'm afraid I left your old shield. I figured the insignia may draw attention."

Lais nodded, glancing at her equipment. "You've been a loyal friend."

She made an effort to stand up, but immediately stumbled forward as if she were intoxicated. Elian was quick to catch her and he helped her back to the bed.

"Are you certain this is wise?" Kaikura asked again.

Lais nodded. "The steward's right. If the guards come by here and see me alive, we will all be at risk of execution. The best thing is to leave under cover of darkness and seek refuge in Rosensted. I was already planning on heading that way." She looked Elian up and down. "The blue coat was a nice touch."

"Oolia borrowed it from the palace. Was the only feasible way to get into the prison."

"Well it worked very well," Lais replied. "And the beans? I guess they came from the Archivus?"

Kaikura nodded. "They were where the warden left them."

Lais glanced around at her three rescuers. "I cannot thank you enough. Sincerely. I will make it up to you all when I am able to. Oolia, I could hear you pleading with the Sultan to spare my life during the hearing. You didn't tell him what we saw in the palace, did you?"

Oolia didn't need to reply; the frozen expression on her face was enough.

Lais scoffed. "That was bold. What a waste of a bargaining chip, trying to save my skin!" There was no hint of sarcasm in her voice. "Still, I can imagine the past few days have been very tense?"

"The Sultan is treating me as if nothing has happened, but that isn't to say he doesn't wish to interrogate or punish me. He's showing me the cold shoulder a little, but he hasn't brought up our conversation. I fear that he is brooding over what I said and what to do with me. I might need to figure out a contingency before he decides what my knowledge is worth."

"Wait, have I missed something?" Elian asked. "What did you say to the Sultan?"

Oolia took a slow, composed breath as if she were weighing up whether or not to share what she and Lais had seen in the Font of Succession. "Okay, fine, I will tell you. But you need to promise not to act on it, else we will all find ourselves in danger."

"We are already in danger," Elian replied, "but whatever it is, we will keep it between us."

"I promise too," Kaikura said.

"Lais and I paid a visit to the Font of Succession based on a suspicion of mine which transpired to be true. It appears that the Sultan has been fraternising with a spring elf and now she, whoever she is, is destined to be the next sultan of Panamaya City. This is an unprecedented event. Historically, only summer elves have been eligible to rule the desert, but somehow the Sultan has been compromised."

"What!" Elian exclaimed. "Well why don't you call him out on it? Why not take *him* to court?"

Oolia laughed. "Because the outcome would be the Sultan having to abdicate or be executed and the spring elf would have to replace him. The city would be forced into an unspoken alliance with Rosensted, causing friction with the other major cities, and a war would be inevitable. There is something truly rotten at the root of all this and Lais is going to Rosensted to locate this spring elf and interrogate her. We need to keep this to ourselves because spreading the word could be catastrophic."

"I wish I hadn't heard it," Kaikura said, her voice sounding thin.

"Look," Lais interjected, "I will handle it, just keep yourselves safe, okay? I'm feeling well enough to travel. I think I should go now."

Oolia nodded. "Very well."

Lais stood up and helped herself to the satchel, before poking her head out of the flap of the tent. It was still very dark outside, except for the glow of a few lanterns belonging to their temporary neighbours.

"I hope to see you all again soon," she said with a courtly bow, her fist held over her chest.

"Remember, get beyond the patrols tonight and you'll be fine from there onwards," Oolia warned as Lais slipped out of the tent and into the night.

It was a long way to Rosensted, particularly without a horse, and very few who travelled alone ever made it across the desert alive.

Still, as the people of the Sleeping Giant slept behind her, Lais felt a sense that everything was about to change. At the edge of the camp, she turned back to cast one final look at the strange, lonely mountain in the middle of the desert and wondered if she would ever see it again.

CHAPTER 24

THE CUSP

Over the past few days, Fjona, Perciville, Todie and Bosmar Fodd had covered good ground heading south away from Pollen and Rosensted. The air was noticeably drier and Fjona had taken to wearing just a cotton vest in a desperate attempt to keep cool.

The realisation that her father may be on a path towards becoming tormented urged Fjona more than ever to reach the end of this journey and recapture the cruel afflictions that now threatened her family.

Not to mention Falavei's theory that only the descendants of those who opposed the turned sage – this Kalzeth Reincarnate – nearly three centuries ago could become afflicted. That begged the impossible question of how her Myrish father may be ancestrally related to somebody who came from the mainland when the Sagedom collapsed. A question that could only be answered as soon as this quest was over and she could return home.

Fjona led the way, following the slowly crumbling road towards the desert. Todie had learned that offering words of optimism or condolence would only result in a sharp tongue and more than a few profanities. He now rode quietly at Fjona's side, speaking only when spoken to or if he had something actually useful to say, which transpired to be not very often.

They were travelling across a rocky, barren landscape known as The Cusp which formed a natural border between the temperate region to the north and the Pentari Desert to the south. Vegetation had dwindled to a few thorny bushes, cacti and clumps of spindly, dried-out grasses, and the only wildlife they had seen for a long while were scorpions and migrating birds.

As the distant horizon seemed to open up, Todie broke his new golden rule. He spoke without having been spoken to, and without having anything useful to offer. He may have been forgiven, however, for it had been a considerably long time since a resident of Marrow Myre had looked down on the Pentari Desert from the surrounding cliffs of The Cusp.

"Four Good Gods, would you look at that," he gasped as he pulled his camel up and looked out across a blanket of golden brown.

Even Fjona, who had spent the best part of three days in a sour mood and brooding over her father's health, was taken aback by the beauty of the desert.

"It's incredible..." she said, scanning the expansive, undulating carpet of sand and dunes, taking it all in.

"The Pentari Desert." Bosmar gestured towards the sand, as if introducing them. "The most popular way to die in the Arvum. What will it be for us, I wonder? Dehydration? Starvation? Ripped to death by a dalachite, baked to a crisp in the sun, or spiralled into delirium and choking on your own knife because your mind told you it was a baguette?"

Perciville rolled his eyes. "Cut it out, Bosmar, we'll be absolutely fine."

"Well of course we will! We have Mr Sage-boy's magical staff to keep us safe. Who knows, maybe he'll whip us up a *lamna* and we can have a party!"

"What is the matter with you?" Fjona snapped at him.

Perciville answered for Bosmar. "Don't bother, Fjona, he's going to be like this for as long as we're in the desert. Boglanders are highly adaptable to temperature changes. He can walk bare in the desert, in the mountains, in the tundra, wherever. It has no impact. However they struggle with low humidity and the drier the air gets, the more of a whiny git he's going to become."

The entire time, Bosmar was mimicking Perciville's facial expressions behind his back, making Todie snigger at the sight.

"So, where next?" Todie asked through a tight throat as Perciville shot him a stern look.

The sage pointed to a tiny silhouette on the horizon. "Can you see that?"

Todie nodded. "Yes. Is that Panamaya City? It's still so far away…"

Perciville clapped him firmly on the back. "I'm afraid not. Panamaya City is much further than you can see now. That there is Salamander – one of several desert outposts."

"Right…" Todie looked exasperated. "Well, I suppose we best get a move on."

"Before we head down into the desert, I suggest you cover your skin," Perciville added, raising his staff. "Conjuring tailored clothes is a skill beyond mine, I'm afraid, but I can create some simple cloth for you to fashion into a shawl. Put out your hands."

The tip of his staff glowed green and a stream of light spiralled about Todie's hands, materialising a length of white cloth. He repeated the same for Fjona and made a smaller one for himself to wrap around his head.

While they tied them up to create a shawl, Todie casually asked Perciville, "Are you not sweltering beneath that robe?"

The sage just smiled and replied cheerily, "Nope!" He gave no further explanation.

They rode back over to the road which sloped steeply down through a cutting in a rocky promontory. Heading in the opposite direction were several trading caravans that had travelled over from Salamander the day before. They mainly consisted of summer elves, adorned by jewel stones and glass beads, riding muscular horses or camels similar to their own.

The tradesmen offered to sell their wares: pottery, rugs, exotic foods and drinks, but much to Todie's disappointment, who was curious to know exactly what exotic foods entailed, Fjona insisted that they were in too much of a hurry to stop and browse.

They descended the road that levelled out into the baked sands of the desert. Here, there were more groups of merchants converting their carts for the road. These carts, or *desert trawlers* as Perciville explained, had a pair of sleds that enabled them to glide over the sand and, using a clever contraption, a pair of wheels that could be dropped down for use on the road.

"Where are you headed?" one of the merchants asked as she yanked up the final lever on her trawler and the sled clicked into a bracket on the side. She was a summer elf, tall and broad with a gut that insinuated over-indulgence.

"To the city," Fjona replied simply, preparing to move on past the merchant, but the elf abruptly stepped aside from her cart and stood before Fjona's camel.

"Panamaya?" the merchant asked.

Fjona just nodded, irritated by the disruption.

Perciville pulled up beside them. "What's the matter?"

"We have just come from Panamaya City," the merchant explained. "It is not safe. The giant that sleeps beneath it trembles. He is soon to awaken."

Fjona and Perciville exchanged a knowing look, before the sage turned back to the merchant.

"Thank you for the warning." He kicked his camel back into a gentle canter.

"You're still going?" the merchant asked Fjona, her voice wavering with surprise and apprehension.

"Don't worry. You'll be able to go back to your home soon

enough." Fjona too kicked her camel into motion, its wide hooves pressing gently into the sand.

Behind her, Fjona heard the merchant mutter to her companion, "Damn fools."

But if ever there were a time for Fjona to ignore a warning, it was now. There was simply too much at stake.

The heat seemed to have intensified in the short distance from the top of The Cusp down to the desert floor. For Fjona and Todie, it was like nothing they had ever experienced before, and they weren't entirely unfamiliar with the sun. Midsummer days in Marrow Myre were frequently hot, but they never bothered the Myrish folk – so long as there was a jar of chilled mint and cucumber water available to quench their thirsts.

Here in the desert, it was a whole different kettle of dried-up, dehydrated fish. The Pentari sun was oppressive and unrelenting without even a wisp of a cloud to provide a moment's relief. Worse still, there wasn't even a droplet of moisture in the air and Bosmar Fodd's complaining just added to Fjona's frustration.

All she could do was focus on the journey ahead and try to drown out the Boglander's whinging.

At least, she considered, it was a mostly straightforward route here. An avenue of reasonably spaced flags had been established to delineate a single clear path for travellers that, according to Perciville, would take them directly to Panamaya City via Salamander.

So long as Fjona could restrain from throttling the Boglander, they should arrive at the Sleeping Giant in a matter of days with relative ease.

"So what else can you do with that wand?" Todie asked, in a desperate attempt to restore some sense of civil conversation.

"Honestly, it's incredible!" Fjona replied excitedly. "Everything I have learned since I left Marrow Myre has made me realise just how sheltered we were back home. When I got my first wand, the Raw Wand."

"Your *first* wand? You mean you had another?"

"Well, sort of. It grows, you see? I mentioned before how I'd picked it from this ancient, wilting tree in Willow's Brush and how I could immediately feel the strength inside me. It wasn't much" – she chuckled as she remembered her first experience of manipulation – "just very basic elementals. Like using gravity to levitate a leaf or a clay jar, or redirecting the wind to put out a fire, then using the wind again to reignite it. Then, while we were still in Willow's Brush, I was attacked by this grotesque monster called a Mother, of all names, and after I'd defended myself against it, the Raw Wand grew into this." She plucked the wand out of her pocket and showed it to Todie while still clutching onto the reins of her camel. "A Woven Wand," she explained, "and my skills have grown with it. I can manipulate the wind, levitate larger objects, even use it as a compass. I can't wait to see what I'll be able to do when it progresses again. Eventually, I'll be able to conjure bridges and learn dark manipulation to defeat tormented elves, and pour myself a rare drink at my own whim!"

"I'm very impressed," Todie said sincerely. "You know I think I'd like to learn it too. Find myself a wand and use it to help grow crops and create duck ponds and build shelters when there's no wood available. I wouldn't want to play the role of a god, though. I will leave that to Aserae and her siblings, but if I could use the manipulation to serve the gods then that could only be a good thing, right?"

Fjona shrugged. "I guess."

"You don't believe in the Four Good Gods anymore, do you?"

"I'm not sure what I believe anymore," she admitted. "The work and the power of the sages is so tangible. In Wychwold, every good deed was attributed to Aserae and every bad harvest was blamed on Kalzeth. We lived our lives praying that we would be treated fairly so long as we acted as we were told, and when things turned sour we pointed our fingers at the sky and begged for answers. Whereas the sages give and take from the Arvum in equal measure. I'm learning a power with the potential to transform an entire environment, but also the discipline to know when to stop. It's rewarding to no longer require faith to succeed, but to be able to look inwards at what I can achieve by myself. Am I making any sense?"

Todie sighed heavily. "Yes, you're making sense. It's important to feel empowered by one's own merit. I just believe that there is a greater meaning behind what we do and our good and bad decisions are weighed up against each other."

"Well, answer me this. Ditching my family to pursue becoming a sage with a complete stranger in an attempt to rescue the Arvum from a deep-rooted, invisible threat... is that a good or bad decision?"

"Fjona Sarsen, always asking the tough questions!" Todie mused. "Well, your decision is undoubtedly based on the best of intentions. Whether the consequence of those intentions realise to be good or bad, I cannot say, although you know what I hope them to be..."

They rode on for the rest of the day and set up camp for the night a short way off the flag-way. It was still a day's ride to Salamander, but with the added exhaustion instilled by the heat, they settled in early before sunset, not least to give the camels a well-earned rest.

Perciville conjured a light breeze in an effort to cool the travellers down – with the inability to conjure elements herself, Fjona could at least practice latching onto it.

Perciville also conjured a miniature handful of rain clouds with which to cool themselves down, and Fjona was able to pass it around the group using her own wand.

They were all in much better spirits going into the evening, especially when the sun had gone down and they had all managed to settle down too.

"Your old man might be alright, you know," Bosmar said, bathing in a conjured wooden bath with his eyes shut.

Todie shot the Boglander a look of disgust as Perciville rolled his eyes.

"Leave her alone, Bosmar," the sage urged. "Nothing you say will make anything better."

Bosmar shrugged. "I'm trying to be supportive, like you've been asking of me all day."

"Yes, but reminding Fjona that her father is likely on an irreversible path to becoming tormented is not exactly what I had in mind."

Todie slapped the sage on the arm.

"What?" he asked, innocently.

"Irreversible path to becoming tormented? Hardly what Fjona wants to hear."

"It's fine," Fjona reassured her friend. "I understand the severity of the situation and I'm fully aware the best I can hope for is that my mother gets him to Beale Cahn in time. All I know is that we need to bring an end to this mess before it's too late."

"Right, that's what I was trying to say!" Bosmar continued. "Your father, against all the odds, *might* just about be okay."

Without a nod, Perciville pointed his staff in Bosmar's direction and dematerialised the bath. The Boglander collapsed, naked, onto the sand in a pool of rapidly dissipating water.

He pulled his sordid, tattered loin cloth back on and gesticulated crudely at Perciville, his complaints and threats to the sage entirely drowned out by the hysterical laughter of Fjona and Todie.

CHAPTER 25

SALAMANDER OUTPOST

With the exception of Bosmar Fodd, whose mood became drastically sourer, the humour at his expense did wonders for everyone else's morale. That, and the exhaustion from the day before, led to a restful night's sleep, aided by the gentle breeze that Perciville had conjured and which had continued to flow through the shield of his staff.

The sun had awoken them early and, following a snappy breakfast consisting of the last scraps of dried breads from Todie's pack and some conjured coffee in spite of the heat, they were back on the flag-way and crossing the desert towards the outpost.

They rode at a moderate pace so as not to tire out their camels completely and it meant that Fjona could practise with her wand at the same time. Based on the broad timescales that Perciville had mentioned before, if it should take twice as long to progress to the next instrument, then her wand was likely to grow in the next couple of days. Assuming, of course, that she kept up her practice, but with the focus being predominately on travelling, her opportunities were often limited.

Nonetheless, she felt her burgeoning strength every time she cast a spell and Perciville had been surprisingly patient and positive when it came to her development. He continued to offer her guidance and challenges to help spark her abilities and, as a result, her concentration and composure had significantly improved.

While she rode, a stream of desert sand swirled around her as she directed it with her wand. Now, she could maintain focus without the need to close her eyes, and still keep control over her camel.

"That's so cool!" Todie called, startling her and making her lose connection with the sand.

It immediately dumped upon the cleric's head, trickling through the weave of his shawl and down the back of his neck.

"What did you do that for?"

"You distracted me!" Fjona yelled back. "Why did you sneak up on me like that?"

"What do you mean? I've been talking to you all this time."

Fjona frowned. "I guess my focus drowned you out."

Todie opened his mouth as if to speak, but before he could, an unexpected force beneath the ground frightened Fjona's camel and threw it off balance. In a whirlwind of cries, yelps and sand, Fjona toppled out of her saddle and landed in an ungraceful heap.

"What's going on?" she cried, scrabbling for her wand which had slipped out of her hand in the chaos.

"Watch out!" Todie warned as Fjona rolled over to see the gaping mouth of a strange reptilian beast, wearing a coat of glistening grey scales, and with two bulbous eyes atop its head.

It was a sizeable creature; as high as Fjona's waist, with a thick, muscular body that petered out into a long tail. Its hind legs were large and pointed like a frog's, and its front served both as legs and arms as it pounded towards Fjona and made to swipe at her.

It came close before Todie's axe swung down at the creature's barely perceptible neck and severed its head cleanly off with the ease of slicing an apple. The decapitated head rolled to one side, blue blood congealing with the sand.

"What is that thing?" Todie asked as he helped Fjona to her feet.

She shook her head. "I've no idea."

Two more scalic creatures tunnelled out of the sand, the first leaping at Todie, but Fjona reacted quickly enough to repel it away with her wand. It flew through the air and landed several paces away.

Meanwhile, Todie hacked away at the second beast, first disabling it by cutting through its left leg and then lopping its head off. The other beast was quick to return to them, but it was no match for the fine edge of Todie's axe. He swung it vertically with all the strength he could muster, slicing the creature's head longways so that it split open like a nut but remained attached to the body.

So distracted by the carnage before them, they hadn't noticed a fourth beast emerge from the sands behind them. It dived through the air towards Fjona's head, but before either of them could react, it was caught by the fatal blade of a throwing knife.

"Are you two trying to get yourselves killed?" snarled Bosmar, hopping from his camel to retrieve his knife.

As he plucked it from the gut of the dead beast, he instinctively thrust it behind him, stabbing another of the aggressive creatures in its gruesome face.

"What are these things?" Todie asked the Boglander.

"Dalachite pups."

"Be grateful that the parent isn't around," Perciville added, pulling up alongside them. "Your axe would do only so much damage against a full-grown."

Fjona gave him a horrified look as she climbed back onto her shaken camel. "You mean these aren't fully grown?"

"I'm afraid not, princess," Bosmar replied, "and believe me, you'll know when you see one."

Todie and Fjona exchanged a look of consternation before kicking their heels and continuing the ride to the outpost.

It appeared that the herd of dalachite pups was an isolated incident and the party were able to travel with relative ease for the remainder of the day. By the time the sun was beginning to dip below the horizon, they had arrived at Salamander.

The outpost consisted of a timber tower that had evidently seen better days judging by the sun-bleached and worm-eaten wood, though a nightguard still occupied it. Next to the tower was a grand round tent which shook from the weight of music within and glowed with candlelight at every seam. Surrounding it were dozens of smaller tents in all shapes and styles. Some were cut from coloured cloth while others were patched together with whatever the owner could find.

As had become a familiar routine, Todie erected his own tent while Perciville conjured the mudbrick shelter on the outskirts of the outpost so not to draw attention to themselves.

"You know there's plenty of room in my tent if you get tired of his snoring," Todie said quietly to Fjona as he hammered in the final peg with the handle of his axe.

Fjona looked from the squalled tent of Todie's to the far more comfortable conjured hut.

"That's kind of you to offer but—"

"It's a flimsy sheet of canvas. Yes, I know. Still, the offer is always there..." he added, turning his reddening face away from Fjona.

The outpost provided not only respite from the harshness of the desert but also some respite from the adversities of their journey.

Naturally, they were drawn to the music coming from the grand tent and were immediately enraptured by the festivities within. The space was bursting with elves, particularly summer and spring, though there were more than a handful of island and autumn elves too. They were drinking and dancing around a six-piece band performing an intensely rhythmic repertoire at the furthest end of the tent. The music was highly percussive with four of the members playing a variety of drums and cymbals. Of the other two, one fingered a bassline on a hefty ebony string instrument while the other offered a harmonious melody on a reedaphone.

A sweet and smoky fragrance floated across the ceiling and all of the four companions became intrinsically aware of how hungry they were.

"This is more like it!" cheered Bosmar Fodd as he slipped away into the crowd, pinching shreds of meat from unattended plates and sips of ale from unattended tankards.

"He's got no morals, that one," Todie said with disdain.

Fjona patted his arm. "Don't worry about him. Let's get some food, I'm famished!" She turned to Perciville. "Have you got many coins left in your purse?"

"Umm, I should imagine so," Perciville replied, a little sheepishly, as he plucked the velvet pouch from somewhere deep in his robe.

"Huh..." Fjona frowned as she received a handful of bassals from the sage. "Your pouch seems to have replenished itself. Is it enchanted?"

"Shh!" Perciville hissed, swiftly tucking it away. "Would you keep it down? Honest folk don't take too kindly to—"

"Counterfeit money?" Todie finished, crossing his arms disapprovingly.

"*Conjured* money," the sage grumbled, "and don't give me that look. Did you not steal all that you carry from the Paddolgolians?"

Todie blushed.

"Isn't it a little immoral to pay with unearned tender?" Fjona interjected before he could argue.

"Look, do you want it or not?" Perciville snapped.

"I don't really have a choice if I want a cooked meal," she replied, stuffing the coins into her pocket.

"The money's as good as any," Perciville assured her. "And I earned the enchantment, did I not?"

Fjona shrugged. "I suppose. It just feels like we're deceiving people."

"I don't see the harm. You get a good meal and they get paid," the sage replied matter-of-factly. "Anyway, I'm going to stake out the place. I recommend the honey fowl or the fried scorpions. Oh, and don't stay up too late! We have a heck of a journey tomorrow." He disappeared in the direction of some scantily clad, dancing spring elves, close by to where Bosmar Fodd was inviting himself to the pockets of a number of customers.

"What a creep," Todie muttered under his breath.

Fjona raised her eyebrows.

Todie blushed again. "Uh, come on, let's get some scorpion!"

They squeezed through a crowd of elves who were deeply engaged in noisy conversation and pushed through to the bar.

An overly smiley summer elf with teeth as straight as his posture took their order, and they remained at the bar with an ale each, awaiting their food.

While the smiley elf pestered Todie with questions about how a pale Marrowborn had ended up in the desert, Fjona was distracted by a tap on the shoulder.

"I'm sorry to disturb you, San...?"

A dangerously handsome summer elf with eyes of onyx and skin ten shades darker stood before her. His hair was a dense cloud of curls within which his long, bejewelled ears disappeared. She couldn't help but stare at him.

"See, this is where you respond with your name. I am Sun Lothis Dakhar from the Upper Gate. And your name...?"

"Ah, my apologies," Fjona stuttered, her face flushed. "I'm

not from around here! I'm Fjona Sarsen from Wychwold. It's a pleasure to meet you Sun Lothis Dakhar."

"Please, you may call me just Lothis, San Sarsen."

"Hey, Fjona, shall we go for a dance?" Todie urged, grabbing Fjona by the shoulder, but she waved him away.

"Our food hasn't arrived yet, Todie."

"Here," Lothis said, thrusting another ale into Fjona's empty hand, though she had barely sipped her first. "Now tell me, Fjona, where is this elusive Wychwold? I am well-travelled, but I've yet to stumble on such a place."

"She's with me," Todie insisted, trying to squeeze through to them.

His words fell on deaf ears.

"It's a small village on the island of Marrow Myre," Fjona replied, "just east of the Infant Mountains and south of the River Racken."

Now the elf wore a bemused expression, though with a charm that wasn't unnoticed by Fjona. "I know not of these places, but I trust them to be as beautiful and as mysterious as you..."

"Corny, right?" Todie said mockingly, placing an arm around Fjona while clutching a steaming pot of gelatinous scorpions.

"Forgive me, Lothis. This is my friend, Todie Farren."

The elf smiled and reached out a hand, only to be met by the pot of scorpions.

"A pleasure to meet you, *friend* Sun Farren."

"Yes, well, you too," Todie replied. "But I'm afraid we must be going."

The elf placed a heavy, wide hand on Fjona's shoulder. "San Sarsen and I were only just getting acquainted."

Fjona was starting to feel uncomfortable, but was distracted by a woman from across the room yelling, "Somebody has stolen my purse!"

"I think you should remove your hand," Todie warned.

"I think you should remove yourself," Lothis replied through gritted teeth.

Fjona carefully peeled the elf's hand away from her shoulder. "Careful boys, let's not let this escalate."

"It's funny how a divine meal is often followed by a turd," the elf sneered, his dark eyes staring intently at Todie.

"Are you calling me a turd?" Todie's spare hand exchanged Fjona's shoulder for the shaft of his axe.

"Are you calling me a meal?" Fjona added with a look of disgust.

She was ignored, however, the handsome summer elf too focused on the position of Todie's fingers on the axe.

"Careful, turd, you'd be wise to not make a scene," Lothis advised as he pulled aside the hem of his coat to reveal a bronze sword handle that reflected the candlelight.

From across the room, Fjona heard the woman's voice shout, "It was you! You stole my purse!"

Perciville's voice followed. "Please, I've no need for your precious coins."

"I saw you come in with him," Lothis added as he glanced towards the commotion, then back at Todie and Fjona. "Thieves, are you?"

With a grunt, Todie pulled forth his long axe while Lothis drew his sword, meeting in the middle in a perfect stalemate.

No sooner had they drawn their weapons than the music was replaced by the resonate swipe of metal on metal as the entire venue, minstrels included, brandished their own swords, knives and axes.

"Why would I want your money?" Perciville's voice sounded.

"Lower your weapon, turd, or hell will break out," Lothis hissed.

"Todie, this is madness," Fjona said, aware that many eyes and half as many weapons were pointed their way.

Nobody moved. Not Todie nor Lothis, who remained stilled by the weight of their weapons, pressing evenly against one another. The only sound was their heavy breathing as they each deliberated whether to yield or attack.

The cleric was about to surrender when a throwing knife sailed through the air and stuck into a timber beam over the bar with an animated wobble.

After that, panic ensued. Todie's axe clattered against Lothis's sword in fast, erratic motions, as the pot of scorpions fell to the floor with a crash. Meanwhile Perciville threw the woman across the room with his staff and deterred her friend with a shield.

Many of the other customers began sparring among themselves without really knowing what they were fighting for.

There were cries of, "Kill those vile spring elves!" from the summer elves and "Make the Marrowborn bleed!" from the spring elves. Autumn elves screamed "For Havensend!", to which the Marrowborn countered "For the Arvum!"

Swords clanged, axes swiped and knives jabbed as the atmosphere within the tent deteriorated into chaos.

"You see what you've started?" Lothis accused Todie as he swung his sword low towards the cleric's feet.

Todie parried it away with the tip of his axe, then pushed the elf backwards with the shaft.

"Me? You started this!" Todie replied angrily.

Fjona carefully placed her drinks on the bar, only for them to be shattered by the boot of a spring elf who climbed upon it and was throwing empty bottles into the fray.

Irritated, Fjona used her wand to force Lothis's sword back, allowing Todie to smack him on the head with the blunt end of the axe.

"I don't wish to kill you," grunted Todie. "Lower your weapon and we can both walk away from this."

"So she's a sorceress, eh?" Lothis hissed scornfully, casting a dirty look at Fjona.

"I'm a sage!" she stated firmly, before the shoulder of an autumn elf caught her jaw and she lost control of her manipulation.

Lothis, now released from the wand, thrust his sword forward and sliced a deep gash across Todie's arm. The cleric yelled in agony as deep red blood gushed out of the wound.

"Todie!" Fjona shouted in fear for her friend.

Lothis may have delivered a fatal blow had it not been for another throwing knife that caught him in his thigh and caused him to keel over.

Fjona looked over to see Bosmar Fodd dip his head courteously before stabbing a Pentari Marrowborn in the toe beside him.

"Stop this now!" came a voice, though it went largely unheard.

On the far side of the room, Perciville flung the woman across the crowd and into the drums with a loud crash, while Todie wailed in pain over his bleeding arm.

"Stop this immediately!" the voice cried again, this time respected by the whole room.

Some held their weapons where they were; others cautiously laid them down.

The voice came from a corpulent, bearded summer elf who wore a robe of fine cloth. He had big puffy cheeks and moved with a stiff awkwardness as if the bones in his legs had fused together.

"Lower your weapons, now!" he yelled, to which Todie and Lothis, among others, abashedly sheathed their weapons. "This is *my* establishment and I will have none of this pathetic squabbling," the bearded elf announced, his bold voice echoing around the tent. "You three..." He turned his gaze from Todie, to Fjona, to Perciville. "I want you away from Salamander, tonight!

You have brought chaos to a domain that prides itself on harmony. I know not who you are, nor where you are from and I care little for it. Be gone now and do not ever dare return."

"I think this has all been a big misunderstanding," Perciville argued, but before he had even the chance to dig himself deeper, a pair of firm hands grabbed him by the shoulders.

Fjona and Todie were accosted by muscular elves too, all donning tattered, faded white coats and each with a face as expressive as an old shoe.

Bosmar Fodd snuck out with them, though not before pinching a few loose coins from one of the tables.

As they were shoved outside towards their camels, Perciville continued to complain, but the elves had no interest in what he had to say.

"Be gone, little man," one said, as they watched Todie quickly and ungraciously stuff his tent back into his satchel and Perciville dematerialise his hut, though not before he had healed the cleric's arm with his staff.

It was surprisingly cold in the desert when the sun set and as they sombrely and ashamedly rode south away from the outpost, Perciville wore a frown of deep, narked resentment.

"I cannot believe you three utter fools!" he growled. "I mean, was I expecting too much of you to not steal from every damn blasted pocket or pick a fight with the biggest bloody elf in the Pentari? Sages save me, you near as hell started a bleeding race war with your callousness! A nice meal and a proper good night's sleep. That's what the three of you have sacrificed for me, so bloody thanks a bloody bunch."

"I'm sorry..." Fjona began to apologise, but Perciville just hissed at her.

"Save it," he snapped. "Let's just ride in silence until we are a safe distance away from the outpost to set up camp."

For once, everyone, including Bosmar Fodd, took heed of Perciville's request and rode on without a single utterance as a pale moon rose above the horizon.

Fjona brooded quietly as it seemed that the respite promised by Salamander Outpost would have to wait. As her camel trudged across the blanket of grey sand, she couldn't help but wonder why chaos always seemed to follow her wherever she went.

CHAPTER 26

THE NOBLE GUARD OF THE SULTAN

The Sultan was far from unfamiliar when it came to heading council meetings with dignitaries and advisors, but in the past few days following the court hearing, these meetings were becoming increasingly relentless.

He had spoken tirelessly with the treasurer about wealthy aristocrats withdrawing all their funds from the banks and relocating to Havensend, following the increase in earthquakes and damage to their homes.

Even the reassurance from the Archivus geologists, who assured the Sultan that the tremors were just a phase of the Arvum relating to a subterranean shift, did little to convince the treasurer to dissuade the dignitaries from leaving.

He then met with several illustrious merchants to discuss the poor harvests in the Paddock, before sitting down with the architect, Sanjin Baerita, who had yet again requested more funds and many more labourers for the construction of the canal.

Following two early morning tremors, the Sultan took the opportunity to enjoy a relaxing breakfast on the north balcony, overlooking the Panamayan spring.

Young servants presented him with platters of fresh fruits, crusty loaves, and local meats drizzled with Havensend honey. This he washed down with sweet wine and tea.

Oolia, whose occasional absences over the past few days hadn't been entirely unnoticed by the preoccupied Sultan, stood courtly behind him, her shock of white hair tied up into two buns like the bread rolls on the Sultan's plate.

It was there on the balcony, once the servants had returned inside, that the Sultan finally broke the silence and addressed the elephant in the room.

"I haven't forgotten what you said to me in court," he said, as he stuffed a cube of melon into his mouth.

Oolia remained quiet. She knew better than to speak and risk saying the wrong thing.

"Did you hear me?" the Sultan asked gruffly.

Now she had no choice but to respond. "I heard you."

"I have visited the Font of Succession and I can understand your concerns," the Sultan continued, "though considering the implications to my throne, my legacy, even my life; should word of what you saw fall into wrong ears, I may have an inkling as to where they heard it from. I'm sure you realise that, as my steward, your risk may be as great as my own..."

A chill ran down Oolia's spine as the Sultan's threat penetrated the marrow of her bones.

He turned his stern amber eyes towards the steward. "Do you take my meaning, or must I speak plainly?"

"I understand," Oolia replied, breathing slowly to keep her voice from wavering.

"I have a lot of respect for you, Oolia, and it would be a real shame if I had to—" He snapped apart a stiff duck leg and raised his eyebrows.

Oolia winced at the cracking of bone and sinew. "I understand," she repeated. Though she didn't quite feel as if she were off the hook.

"I gather it was the corporal who broke you in?" the Sultan continued. "Well, suffice to say, she won't be an issue any longer. I have been informed of her timely death while incarcerated."

Oolia's lip curled faintly into a half-smile that was so imperceptible to the Sultan, he couldn't have seen it had he been staring directly at her mouth. This time, it was the Sultan who was excluded from a secret.

"A tragedy," the steward managed, conveying a tone of sincerity and resentment.

"If I had you killed, the truth of what you saw in the font would be buried in the desert like that traitorous soldier."

"There are others who can visit it," Oolia pointed out, hoping to reduce the heat on her. "The other corporals; captains; the general when he returns."

"The corporals and captains have no reason to visit the font and, should they wish to, I've instructed the doorkeeper to not grant them permission. If they insist, the doorkeeper will keep me informed and I will have them dealt with. As for General Kheller, well, I suspect we may not see him again."

Oolia suddenly felt very cold. "What do you mean?"

She wondered if the general had discovered the font too; if perhaps the Sultan had killed him.

Ayermune laughed. "He rode out into the desert two weeks ago and hasn't been seen since. You and I both know what that means."

It was true. Unless the general had left the desert for good, disappearing for even a few days usually indicated that dalachites or dehydration had led to an unfortunate demise.

There was a tap on the glass balcony door, followed by the timid voice of a servant boy. "Your Divine Excellency, a guest has arrived for you."

"Ah how fortuitous!" the Sultan exclaimed. "My new general has arrived. Please, send him in."

"You've already appointed a new general?" Oolia failed to keep the surprise out of her voice. "Who?"

"Good morning, my Sultan," said Beric Lahsilli as he invited himself onto the balcony and bowed courteously to Ayermune. "Steward," he added, greeting Oolia with a fistful of condescension and a sly grin as the Sultan gestured for him to take a seat. "I was sad to hear of Lais Stone's sudden death. I understand you were close?"

"We only met for the first time quite recently, actually," Oolia replied stiffly. "I gather you knew her better."

Lahsilli nodded. "To my great misfortune."

"It was rather disappointing to learn that we had such a defiant soldier within the Guard," the Sultan agreed. "I trust your leadership will elevate my army to a new regime."

"I have one or two ambitions that Sigmund Kheller lacked," Lahsilli assured the Sultan, a look of contempt flitting across his face.

"The Arvum is becoming destabilised and I sense that Panamaya City may need to reinstate supremacy across the desert," the Sultan added.

Lahsilli twisted his head in confusion. "What exactly are you asking of me, my Sultan?"

The Sultan leaned in. "Have you yet found a captain to replace you?"

"Indeed. I have promoted Callis Holden, formerly of the Fourth West Division."

"Excellent." The Sultan clasped his spindly fingers together. "And have you found two new recruits for that division? It was already looking sparse with the removal of San Stone."

"I have indeed, my Sultan. A summer elf and a Pentari Marrowborn. Both young, fit and very capable."

"Very wise," the Sultan replied with a grin. Then his grin slipped into a steely-eyed frown. "Now that you have replenished the Noble Guard, I wish for you to double it."

Oolia's eyebrows rose so quickly, they almost flew off her forehead.

"You want me to expand the Guard?" Lahsilli asked, sitting back in his seat and watching the Sultan with intense curiosity.

"You heard me, and when it is doubled, I wish for you to double it again! Then do the same for the Rear Guard, and the Home Guard too."

Oolia's jaw nearly hit the floor, but she restrained herself from speaking out.

"My Sultan, please forgive my ignorance, but your army is already at its permitted capacity. If I expand it any further, we will be breaching the treaty that has maintained peace across the Arvum for hundreds of years. Our elven cousins will see this as an act of aggression. It may spark a war."

The Sultan slammed a heavy fist on the table, forcing tea to fly out of his cup. "Are you questioning my authority? Must I seek out a new general so soon?"

Lahsilli jumped from his seat and knelt before the Sultan. "Your Divine Excellency, forgive my querying. I was asking only for confirmation of what you are requesting of me."

The Sultan smiled, though not with his eyes. "You have heard correctly then, for a third of our city now live beside the mountain in a makeshift camp, while a third have taken their wealth out of Panamaya and fled to the Free Capital. Very soon, the summer elves will be known as a troubled, dwindling species and left to the history books like the river elves of old. Beric, we need to remind our cousins that the summer elves are a proud and powerful population. That we will not crumble, even if the Sleeping Giant does, and that our people cannot simply walk away from their homes and spread their wealth to the greedy capital, just because they are afraid of a few tremors."

"You want me to drag them back to the city?" Lahsilli asked

dutifully.

"Drag, shove, bully; I don't care. Whatever it takes to restore dominion to Panamaya City."

Lahsilli rose to his feet, inclining his head respectfully. "Your army will be twice its size by the time the canal is finished, and twice again by this time next year. We have hundreds of young trainees who are desperate to be recruited into the Noble Guard. So long as we've the coats to drape on their shoulders and the iron to place in their hands, we will have an army."

By now, Oolia was biting her tongue. She wanted to scream at them but she knew that opening her mouth would only be in vain, and the Sultan had already threatened her once this morning.

She couldn't help but picture Elian Sole, the kind ranger who had helped rescue Lais Stone. Would he be embroiled in this war? If she could only warn him, maybe she could persuade him to retire his service and relocate to Bouanda, far from the troubles in the south.

"Very good, General. We need to remind this damned continent exactly who occupies its heart."

Lahsilli cleared his throat, casting a begrudging eye over at Oolia. "I do have one concern, my Sultan. What should I do if somebody interferes with our plans?"

The Sultan looked behind him at his loyal steward. He seemed to be carefully considering what Lahsilli was asking, though his response was far from surprising. "You have a sword, do you not?"

Lahsilli bowed. "Understood."

"You may be dismissed, General," the Sultan said, pointing to the door.

Lahsilli began to depart, before a thought appeared to strike him and he turned abruptly. "I almost forgot. Kheller's horse is still in the stables. Wherever he disappeared to, he went on foot. Strange…"

Without another word, he disappeared back into the palace.

There was a moment's silence before Oolia finally plucked up the courage to speak. "I thought Kheller *rode* out into the desert?"

Her words had barely left her mouth before the Sultan jumped up from his chair, a snarl upon his face. His long, pointed nose almost touched her forehead and she could smell the wine on his breath.

"Do not *dare* question me, steward. I am *your* Sultan; this is *my* palace. *You* serve *me*! Unless you want to return to the slums of the Outer Gate, I suggest you keep your damned head down and your lips sealed tight. Do I make myself clear?"

Oolia had served the Sultan for many years and, in all that time, she had seen him in every palette of sour moods. This wasn't the first time he had lost his temper with her, nor was it the first time he had threatened to kick her out of the palace. In the past, all those threats had seemed baseless and, on each occasion, the Sultan would quickly come around and seek forgiveness.

This time, though, Oolia wasn't so sure.

For the first time in all her years serving the Sultan, she felt truly terrified.

CHAPTER 27

SARSEN AND STONE

Perciville wore a face with as much emotion as a drystone wall. It had been three days since his incompetent travelling companions had managed to get them barred from the outpost, yet he still hadn't the strength to fully forgive them.

Since then, they had ridden in more or less the same estranged formation. He at the front, Fjona and Todie closely behind, and Bosmar Fodd following at the rear.

He had worked so hard to accept that he was no longer a lone wolf and, for the most part, had even come to enjoy their company, but with the weight of the world on his shoulders, and a heck of a lot more to lift besides, the whole journey was becoming tiresome.

Fjona was the other concern; a matter he had very much made sure to keep to himself. While he was truly impressed with her progress so far and admired the fact that she was casting elemental manipulations while riding a camel, he couldn't ignore that she had held a Woven Wand for days more than he'd expected.

From his experience, long ago though it may have been, it took almost half a year to become a demi-sage and, by that point, it may all be too late. The longer Fjona was bound to a Woven Wand, the longer she would remain a novice, and the final destination would be just out of reach.

Perhaps she was a poor choice after all.

As he brooded over his thoughts, he released a long, weary

sigh. Whether Fjona would be ready or not, there was no turning back and he had known that the ambitious timescales would always pose a dilemma. Had there been any alternative, suffice to say he would have thought of it sooner, but there wasn't. The plan would have to remain as it was; train up a new sage, track down Bosmar Fodd, then travel to the Archivus and locate the shielded book that should hopefully lead them to the box. If they could find the book, of course. Another snag in this endless charade, but he'd be damned if he gave up now. At least the Sleeping Giant was in sight, even if it were just a tiny silhouette on the horizon.

Perciville was pulled out of his spiralling thoughts by Fjona calling from behind.

"Harper! Look!"

He glanced behind him. Fjona was pointing out into the desert, away from the flag-way. There, between the heatwaves, a great beast sparred with the glimmering blade of a traveller.

It was strange to see a fully grown dalachite so close to the route, and Perciville watched curiously as it whipped its long, scaly tail at the traveller, sending them soaring through the air. In a cloud of sand, the dalachite pounded towards the traveller, ready to rip apart their flesh with its razor-sharp teeth.

In Perciville's peripheral vision, he noticed the blur of a camel charging towards the fray.

He groaned, muttering to himself as Todie followed closely behind Fjona, wielding his axe high above his head like a war flag as they both raced towards danger.

"I don't think they realise just how much bigger the adults are," Bosmar chuckled, as he appeared alongside Perciville like a shadow. "Ah well, I shall remember them with mostly fond memories..." He kicked his heels as if to continue his journey, only to turn his mount abruptly as Perciville rode off towards the fray. "Oh don't be a moron!"

Perciville could hear Bosmar Fodd chasing after him.

"You better have something clever up that ridiculous sleeve of yours," Bosmar yelled, "else we'll all be dead before lunch!"

Up ahead, Fjona and Todie appeared to have done enough to steal the dalachite's attention and draw it away from the traveller. In doing so, however, the sand-dwelling reptile had turned towards them, spooking their camels. Todie's camel took off at a pace, causing him to lose his grip and topple out of his saddle, the head of his axe plunging dangerously close to his head as he fell ungraciously onto the sand.

Fjona's quickly followed suit, though she was swift enough to leap from it, landing firmly on her feet as the two camels raced away together, grunting with fright.

"Bosmar! Go fetch their bloody camels!" Perciville shouted.

To his surprise, the Boglander turned in pursuit of the two strays without complaint.

To Fjona's credit, her relatively limited skills with her wand were proving useful enough to hinder the dalachite. She was whipping ribbons of sand against its bulging black eyes. Not enough to cause any real pain, but sufficient to temporarily blind it.

Angrily, the dalachite flailed its muscular tail about and flaunted its rows of pointed teeth.

Perciville had almost forgotten just how enormous dalachites could grow as he pulled up close to Fjona and cast a shield before them just as the dalachite leaped at them, baring its teeth and extending its claws. Of course, it rebounded, but was quick to lurch forward again, hammering against the ethereal shield, hefting all of its vast weight against it as if it might prove enough to penetrate it.

"What were you thinking!?" Perciville admonished Fjona, forcing his staff forward with all of his strength.

Fjona huffed at him. "I was thinking of saving that person's life."

She gestured to the slumped body. They didn't appear to be moving.

"Oh and an excellent job you did," Perciville replied sarcastically. "Now we're both trapped beneath this shield until either the dalachite or I tire first and, I'm going to level with you, I drink a lot and hardly sleep. I don't exactly pride myself on stamina."

Fjona looked around for signs of help. Bosmar was way in the distance and struggling to catch the loose camels, while Todie lay on the sand, winded, dazed and utterly useless.

Meanwhile, Perciville continued to scold her. "Every moment we spend not pursuing our goal, the further we have to travel and it's getting to a point where I would rather ditch you all and let the Arvum fall into disrepair than keep you around and prevent the worst from happening."

Fjona wasn't listening at all. The blade of Todie's axe glinted in the sun and an idea came to her. She pointed her wand at the axe and carefully dislodged the weapon from the sand, cautious to avoid accidentally beheading Todie. Then she yanked it into the air and dragged it towards them. It bobbed up and down as if floating in water.

All the while, the dalachite continued to pound at the invisible shield and Perciville continued to berate Fjona. "You will be the death of me, Miss Sarsen. I should never have gone to Port Widow. It would have spared me meeting you and, in doing so, spared my life!"

Still latched onto the axe, Fjona carefully twisted it so that the blade hovered only a short distance above the dalachite's head, before thrusting it down into its thick, scaly skin.

A fountain of blue blood sprayed up into the air as the axe sliced into flesh and cartilage. The dalachite roared in pain and tried to swipe at the axe with its long hind legs.

Fjona looked at Perciville with an expectant expression. "Well? Are you going to finish it off?"

The sage appeared to awaken from a fugue state and looked over at the aggravated and damaged beast.

"Oh. Umm, yes..." he mumbled, wielding his staff in both hands and pointing it at the dalachite.

He released a jet of dark manipulation that enveloped the monster and lifted it into the air. A purple mist swirled around and started to compress the creature, squeezing the dalachite as if it were trapped in a fist.

It screamed in a pitch that was hauntingly high for its size and Fjona almost felt sad for the deadly, uncontrollable monster.

"Can you be at all humane?" she urged Perciville, but her plea came too late.

The mass of beast and energy squashed into a ball and started to shrink until, suddenly, the energy dissipated and a heavy block of what looked like metal dropped to the ground, along with Todie's axe.

"Mine!" yelled a voice from behind as Bosmar appeared, two camels in tow, and leaped from his own to retrieve the object.

"What is that?" Fjona asked, gazing at the shimmering black sphere. It was as big as the Boglander's head and, when he put it into an empty satchel attached to his camel, it bulged at the bottom.

"A perfect, lucrative dalachite orb," the Boglander explained, patting his saddlebag. "Produced when they become embroiled with a sage. These beauties always fetch a high price."

"They get melted down and cast into jewellery or weapons," Perciville elaborated. "Dalachites are just as lethal, whether they are dead or alive."

"I'm fine by the way," Todie grumbled as he limped over, clutching his stomach. "Perhaps we should check on our friend over there." He gestured to the traveller.

They wandered over to find a dark-skinned summer elf with hair as red as blood, her fingers still tightly wrapped around her sword.

"Is she dead?" Todie asked.

Perciville leaned over and placed his ear to her chest, then shook his head. "Her heart is still beating, though it's very faint."

He held his staff above her and produced a red glow, wafting the beacon-like light slowly over the elf from head to toe and back again. Moments later, the elf's eyes sprung open and she began to cough up bloody, sandy phlegm.

She seemed somewhat dazed as she sat up and looked around at the strange companions who greeted her.

"What happened?" she asked, eyes darting around for the dalachite. "Is it gone?"

"More or less," Bosmar replied quietly with a sly grin.

"I'm afraid it got the better of you," Perciville added, "but you're safe now. Can you tell me your name?"

She seemed a little reluctant to reveal her name at first, but after glancing from Perciville, to Fjona, to Todie, she eventually conceded. "Lais Stone, former corporal of the Fourth West Division of the Noble Guard of the Sultan."

"Your first name would have sufficed," Bosmar said under his breath, before heading back to his camel.

"*Former* corporal?" Perciville asked.

Lais nodded. "It's a little complicated. Been forced to leave my home, though it seems many have. I am seeking refuge in

Rosensted."

"Well, travel safely and avoid Pollen," Perciville replied with a half-smile. He turned as if his work was done and they were ready to part.

With a look of disgust, Todie butted through and offered Lais a hand. "Forgive my insensitive travelling companion. He sometimes forgets how to speak with other people."

The elf smiled as Todie helped her up off the baked sand. As she dusted off her tunic, she asked casually, "So, who are you all? What brings you to the desert?"

"We are an unlikely company of travellers. Myself and Fjona here are from Marrow Myre. Oh, and that one too, I think…" Todie looked over at Bosmar Fodd, who was perched on his camel and peeking inside his bulging satchel with glee, not that Lais could see him. "We are journeying south to Panamaya City in search of a Proprietor of Intellect, if I have that right? We believe they may be in possession of a, supposedly, magical book, which contains the location of a mysterious box with the power to recapture the *deadly* Eight Afflictions: a horrifying creation of Kalzeth Reincarnate. If left alone, this powerful curse will sweep across the Arvum bringing death and famine and monsters. Is that about the crux of it?" he asked Fjona nonchalantly, as he looked over his shoulder and faced the others.

The three companions stared open-mouthed and wide-eyed at Todie.

Wordlessly, Bosmar dropped down from his camel and wielded his knife, then approached Lais.

"Hey, what are you doing?" Todie exclaimed as the Boglander barged him out of the way, kicked Lais back down onto the sand, yanked back her head, and held the knife in front of her throat.

"What is this? Where did you come from?" Lais complained angrily, writhing her body, and looking down at the glinting knife past her nose. "What's happening?"

"Are you a complete fool?" Bosmar accused Todie. "Rule number one: don't share your masterplan with a complete stranger. We don't know this woman, we can't trust this woman. Should she share one word of what you just needlessly, stupidly spilled, even to a passing caravan or a bartender, then our entire mission may fall apart!"

Fjona stepped forward. "Bosmar, please. There is no reason to kill her for Todie's mistake."

"Well somebody has to," the Boglander replied.

"Let her go," Todie pleaded, then raised his axe, "or I'll make you."

The cleric inched further forward, but as he did, Perciville cast a shield between Bosmar and Lais, and Fjona and Todie.

"Regrettably, Bosmar is right," said the sage resignedly.

Fjona stared at him incredulously. "Are you serious? We saved her life only to take it?"

"We *risked* our lives to save hers, yet what your friend has divulged in one breath risks more than intercepting a dalachite."

"You're pathetic," Lais spat. "I asked for no part in this! I'm just nobody, heading nowhere. I barely understand what your friend said, let alone have the intention of spreading it."

Perciville appeared to consider this for a moment, but replied in the same saddened tone, "But one cannot control the words that slip out of our mouths from time to time, as Todie here has demonstrated."

"Then kill him, not me!" Lais argued.

Perciville just shook his head.

"Fine then. Kill me. I have little else in this world to live for. But know this... I might've been able to help you."

"How?" Fjona asked, hoping to buy her more time.

Lais was contemplative for a moment. "I happen to know a

scholar from the Archivus. She's brilliant, intelligent—"

"We don't need a scholar," Bosmar interrupted. "We need a proprietor, and unless you happen to know Proprietor Sialah Bouwer then you are as useless to us as—" He glared at Todie. "As he is."

Todie just frowned back at the Boglander, but before he could argue, Lais interrupted.

"Wait! I recognise that name."

"Great, you recognise the name of an esteemed Proprietor of Intellect. Can I kill her now?" the Boglander asked.

"She's missing! Sialah Bouwer... she disappeared from Panamaya City." Lais spoke tersely, barely pausing between brief sentences, the blade of Bosmar Fodd's knife still pressing into her throat.

"You're lying," Perciville accused, but the elf just shook her head.

"No, I swear it. The town criers have been reporting it for weeks. Sialah Bouwer, Proprietor of Intellect in, er... Ancient Cultures and Mythologies, I believe they said? Her whereabouts are unknown. Some fear she went into the desert and was killed, others rumoured she had debt trouble, made a poor deal with a gang leader and has been buried somewhere in the Lower Gate. You're wasting your time in trying to find her."

Perciville lowered the shield. "Bosmar, release her."

The Boglander shot Perciville a sour look. "You're believing this?"

"Sheath your knife," the sage shot back.

Reluctantly, Bosmar unclasped the back of Lais's head and dropped her down into the sand, though he continued to hold his knife by his side.

"Thank you..." Lais uttered through dried lips.

"You're not off the hook just yet," Perciville warned. "Sialah

Bouwer. It was definitely that name? She's missing?"

Lais nodded. "I swear it."

"What does this mean?" Fjona asked. "Would she definitely have had this book in the first place?"

"I've never met Sialah Bouwer, but I've heard a lot about her over the years," Perciville replied, "and she is the only Proprietor of Intellect to whom the book could possibly be revealed to. Somebody with the perfect balance of integrity and knowledge to decipher it and, from what I gather, Sialah Bouwer was the only person who fits the bill."

"So if she really has gone missing and nobody knows where to find her, what can we do?"

Perciville pursed his lips and furrowed his brow as he considered Fjona's question. For the first time since he'd witnessed the meteors collide, he was stumped.

He let out a deep sigh. "I'll think of something. You may kill her now, Bosmar."

"What!" Fjona and Todie exclaimed.

"She's clearly not a threat," Fjona argued. "Is your anxiety really worth taking another's life?"

"You weren't alive when elves fought with elves," Perciville snapped. "You didn't walk the Arvum when rivers of blood flowed between the cities and dead elves were piled in heaps, swarming with flies. You didn't know a time when careless words spoken in the wrong ears resulted in unspeakable horrors. I'm not suggesting that Lais here would purposefully undermine us, but should she utter even a word of what Todie let slip to her then who knows what may follow!"

Fjona shook her head in disgust. "Don't be the monster we're trying to destroy."

Perciville remained unmoved.

"If you do this," Fjona continued, "if you kill this innocent

270

stranger, then I will refuse to follow you."

The sage laughed. "And risk the lives of every soul across the Arvum, not least your father's?"

Fjona opened her mouth as if to reply, but no words came out.

"I thought as much." His voice had taken on a softer cadence. "I'm sorry, but this is the way it has to be. Kill her, Bosmar."

As Bosmar raised his knife, Lais cried out.

"Wait! This ancient book of yours. I may have seen it..."

"Too late, love," Bosmar interrupted, licking his lips.

"It was written in an unknown script. Not Kelnish, not ancient Pentari, but something completely different," Lais rambled desperately. "When I was coming to, I remember them discussing it. Something about a... Yilsommen? And raithers..."

Perciville froze. Yet again, Lais had his attention.

"Where is it?" he asked brusquely.

"Spare my life, release me unharmed, and I will tell you where to look. Or else slit my throat and be done with it."

The sage paused, his face tightening in concentration. Eventually, after a painfully long time, he yielded, and after much arguing, managed to persuade Bosmar Fodd to yet again lower his knife. The Boglander skulked back over to his camel, his head hanging low beneath his shoulders.

Todie helped Lais to her feet and offered her some water, which she graciously accepted.

"I swear that thing appeared out of nowhere..." she said quietly to Todie as she glanced over at Bosmar Fodd.

"He has that effect," Todie said in agreement.

Perciville clapped his hands together, impatient now that new knowledge was in his grasp. "So? Who has the book?"

"A scholar of the Archivus," Lais replied. "Her name is Kaikura Kendi. She lives somewhere in the Lower Gate."

The sage looked at Lais expectantly. "That's it? Somewhere

in the Lower Gate? There are many thousands of hovels in the Lower Gate! How in the Arvum are we supposed to track her down?"

The elf took another long swig of water. "To the west of the city is the construction trench of the new canal. It just so happens that it runs through the jurisdiction of my former division, the Fourth West. They should be patrolling it during the day. When you arrive, look for Ranger Elian Sole. He's the only Pentari Marrowborn in the division so you should be able to spot him. Elian and Kaikura have recently become acquainted and he can show you to her home."

"How can you guarantee that he will lead us to Kaikura?" Fjona asked. "After all, we are just four strangers."

"You can tell him Corporal Lais Stone sent you after you saved her life. He was always very loyal to me."

Perciville bowed his head. "You can't possibly fathom how valuable the information you have shared might be for the good of the Arvum."

Lais didn't reply.

"Forgive my friend for his hastiness with his knife," the sage continued. "These are unsettling times and one cannot be too cautious."

Her expression impassive, Lais sheathed her sword. "I grew up in Panamaya City. Lives have been lost for far less than hearing the wrong words. Let us hope we never run into each other again, else it may be my blade at your throat."

With that, she thanked Todie for his compassion, then began the long walk towards Salamander.

"Oh, and one other thing," she added, turning on her heel, "Kaikura is a kind soul, and Elian a good man. They don't deserve trickery or torture. Once you receive this precious book of yours, I insist that you leave them alone for good and return to wherever it is you came from."

As Lais Stone disappeared into the haze, Perciville couldn't help but watch her in admiration. A rare warrior, fierce enough to threaten a sage. Now there was something he hadn't seen for a very long time.

CHAPTER 28

THE CABIN

She strode with purpose across her conjured road towards the building on the furthest edge of the island. Behind her lay a mountain of white sand and debris – the remnants of the wall and chapel from which Marseiha had escaped.

Now it appeared that she had escaped only into her confinement with the hopes that something useful may reside inside the building.

"If not?" she wondered as she admired the ebony staff in her hand, "then perhaps I can craft a boat on which to sail away."

Somehow, though, the prospect of sailing blindly across an empty ocean was less appealing than being trapped here alone.

Marseiha was about halfway along the road to the building when a whooshing sound caught her attention. Her heart began hammering against her chest as the image of the shadow demon crossed her mind and she immediately looked up to the sky in fear of seeing its unwelcome return.

Sure enough, the sound was coming from above and Marseiha could faintly make out a tiny object falling from the heavens.

It didn't seem like the demon, however. For one thing, the object was enshrouded in a brilliant green glow that grew eye-wateringly brighter as it neared the island. For a moment, it appeared to illuminate the entire sky and Marseiha had to squint just to look at it.

It occurred to her that, whatever it was, it was heading directly for her. She pointed her staff towards it and expelled several instinctive bursts of energy in order to stop it, or catch it, or do anything in order to prevent it from crashing down onto her, but nothing seemed to work. Whatever it was, it bore a power that was greater than her own. Greater, or perhaps merely comparable.

There wasn't enough time for Marseiha to really consider this further. Instead, she clutched her staff and ran towards the coast. All the while the whooshing sound grew louder and the green light more radiant. She felt as if, yet again, she was being chased.

Then, like lightning striking the ground, the object plummeted into her road, barely a step before her, and Marseiha skidded to a stop. Dizzily, she looked down at a sizeable crater surrounding a fist-sized meteorite that pulsed with a, now temperate, green glow. It had appeared so much bigger when it was airborne.

Faint murmurings seemed to be spilling out of the rock and Marseiha sat on her haunches to get a closer listen. The sounds carried the same cadences and pitch to that of a voice, but they were wobbly and distorted, as if she were hearing it underwater. She could feel the pleasant heat radiating from the meteorite as she reached out with her hand and, as she did, the voice became clearer, though still impossible to decipher. It was clear enough, however, to distinguish that there were in fact two voices – as if the meteorite were having an impassioned conversation with itself.

Marseiha's curiosity got the better of her and she brazenly touched the meteorite, feeling its heat kissing her fingertips.

Immediately, the voices filled her head. One, vaguely familiar, the other, completely alien to her.

"Good morning my *derine*," said the first.

"What do you mean?" replied the other.

"I slept on it. I want to make you a sage."

Almost startled, Marseiha released her hand and the strange, ephemeral voices dipped back into imperceptible mumbling.

"What magic is this...?" she asked the rock frustratedly, before glancing up to the sky as if the clouds might drift into an answer. "Whose voice is this?"

She reached out again and grasped the meteorite, beckoning disconnected conversation between the same two voices.

"About bloody time! I've been out here for hours!" the familiar voice exclaimed.

"A Raw Wand?" the other replied.

"It seems something good has come of your foolishness."

"How can something so sweet-looking be so ugly at heart?"

"'When meteors collide, so it will be that the Eight Afflictions have returned."

The words pierced Marseiha's soul like a barbed arrow through the skin of a buck, and she shook her hand away from the meteorite, too frightened to listen any longer.

The Eight Afflictions. Her hands suddenly felt cold and sweaty, her breaths just a little shallower.

"Why?" she wondered aloud, her heart hammering against her chest. "I've never heard of such a thing, unless... unless I had..."

Tightly, she squeezed her eyes shut and rubbed her temples with the tips of her fingers as if focussing her energy might allow her to recollect. She knew not why, but those words had resonated inside of her as if she were bonded to them like a mother sensing harm in her child from afar.

Yet her mind was empty of all knowledge of the Eight Afflictions. Not so much as a crumb of recognition lay in the corners of memory. They were as alien to her as her own existence.

When she eventually gave up trying to remember and opened her eyes, she was shocked firstly to see that the meteorite had vanished, though its crater remained.

What surprised her more, however, was that the building,

previously at the furthest end of the island, had moved to just a few feet away and was now peering down on her, trapping Marseiha in its cold shadow. It was a small log cabin with a roof of wooden slats and only one blacked-out square window to her side.

She walked around the cabin only to find that it had no door.

Furiously, Marseiha screamed. Everything about this place had a riddle and she was fed up with having to jump through hoops only to be faced with yet another conundrum.

"What insanity is this?" she yelled at the cabin. "Who would build such a pathetically useless excuse for a shelter and fail to include a door?"

She was inches away from breaking down in tears, but instead, Marseiha wielded her staff and released an expulsion of energy at the cabin walls. A spectrum of colours and sounds, whisps and swirls relentlessly whipped at the cabin until fatigue intervened and Marseiha slumped to ground, panting. She was too tired to even cry or feel pity for herself.

When the dust settled and her spells subsided, Marseiha looked up to find that an old battened and ledged door had appeared next to the window. It had no door handle or knob, though it was slightly ajar.

Without hesitation, she hurried towards it and prised it open with her fingers. When she stepped inside, her feet had barely touched the flagstone floor before the door slammed behind her. She tried to push it open just to see if she could, only to discover that she was locked inside. It was dark and gloomy within, but Marseiha was able to illuminate the cabin with her staff.

Moments later, her mouth hung open, aghast, as she glanced around the very room from which she had awoken not so long ago. The same red log walls and antique writing desk. The same elegant, though decrepit, cuckoo clock hanging on the wall above the same cold stone floor.

The candlestick that she had removed and left in the corridor had somehow been returned to the table, now burned down to a sad stump. Beside it lay a single piece of parchment.

Marseiha picked it up and held it in the glow of her staff.

Do you know what you did?

It was a short message and yet Marseiha had to read it twice over, and then twice again.

"Do I know what I did?" she asked herself. "Do I—"

A brief memory suddenly flashed through her head. Fire. Screams. Pain. Then, slowly, more memories started to trickle back and Marseiha began to recall what had happened. The faces of old acquaintances, the walls of an old building, the dire consequences of her actions.

Before there was time to properly process her recollections, she heard the creaking of the door behind her and she turned to see a silvery light spill into the cabin.

CHAPTER 29

PANAMAYA CITY

In the days that followed, the tiny speck that was the Sleeping Giant grew ever bigger until it loomed above the four companions like a great leviathan, really living up to its name.

Fjona stared, dumbstruck by the sheer scale of the mountain and the density of buildings that covered much of the surface, all the way to the top. There, right at the peak, she could make out the Sultan's notorious palace that glistened under the setting sun.

It was truly an astonishing sight, not merely for the fact that, until now, the biggest settlement she had ever visited was Rosensted and it could fit into Panamaya City at least twenty times at her best guess.

Two grand walls segregated the city and, even from where Fjona was standing, it was obvious where the wealthy lived. The lowest region, nearest to the base of the city, consisted of thousands of tiny makeshift huts and narrow streets, crammed together like the scales of a dalachite. Above that, the houses were still squat and squeezed in, but at least they were more uniform by design, though far inferior to the tall monastic buildings near the top. Even from way down at the desert floor the buildings at the summit were clearly much grander and of exquisite design.

At the base of the mountain was an expansive camp. It was impossible to guess just how many tents and cobbled-together shelters there were, especially as even now there were many more settlers arriving from the mountain, but it must have been in the thousands.

Most had made do with scraps of fabric held up by sticks, stone, or even their belongings, such as crates and cases. Others just settled for a blanket and the desert sand beneath with nothing else that could be considered a possession.

As they passed through the camp, Fjona was surprised by the liveliness of the inhabitants despite their dire situation. It was an orchestra of chatter, laughter, even quiet music, as well as the bleating and braying of their animals. Now that the heat from the day was waning, families of summer elves and Pentari Marrowborns, among others, sat around campfires outside of their tents and toasted breads, skewered meats and scorpions.

"This place is extraordinary!" Fjona exclaimed to Todie, who had ridden beside her the entire way since leaving Salamander.

When there was no reply from the cleric, Fjona glanced over to see him staring open-mouthed at the enormous mountain covered in a thick skin of buildings and walls.

"The Sultan must be a very powerful man," Fjona said to herself, awed by the scale of the city and palace, whose grandeur was evident even from where she stood.

Perciville pulled up alongside her. "Ayermune Dhaller Sé, I believe. I knew his predecessor, but I am yet to meet him. They say he is equal parts cruel and fair, though in reality I think that just equates to being cruel."

Still quietly fuming at Perciville over his callous treatment of Lais Stone, Fjona simply glared at him before turning to Todie. "Come on, let's go find this canal."

They headed off through the camp, passing weary locals and travellers along narrow avenues between their shelters. Although there was music and laughter emanating from some corners of the settlement, as she drew closer, Fjona became aware of the loneliness, loss and fear written upon the faces of many of the locals they passed. Families huddled together in their tents or sat forlornly out in the dying sun with nothing better to do besides contemplation.

"I told you he was untrustworthy," Todie said, reminding Fjona of their own dire situation.

"I'm aware," she replied through gritted teeth, "though I still trust him for the most part. It's just that I am discovering more about his being and I don't like it."

Todie scoffed. "He threatened to kill an innocent passer-by, simply because I opened my mouth! I know I shouldn't have said what I said, but still..."

"I know, I know! He's... he's under a lot of pressure..."

"Under a lot of pressure? Fjona, wake up and smell the smoke! He's revealed his true colours, and surprise, surprise, it's a bloody shade of red!"

"Well, I appreciate you letting me share your tent the past couple of nights."

Todie was suddenly very quiet. "You're always welcome to sleep with me."

When Fjona shot him a bemused look, he quickly corrected himself. "Alongside me! I mean you are always welcome to share my tent, but sleeping separately, of course..."

Before an enormous hole could swallow Todie up, they were interrupted by a series of beggars, pleading for coin, food or water, none of which they were able to offer.

"I'm sorry," Fjona said sincerely to an elderly summer elf with a missing eye, who sat hunched over outside a tent made from old rugs. "I promise, you'll be able to go home soon."

A young girl ran past them clutching a veiny wedge of cheese and, moments later, a Pentari Marrowborn with a thick moustache came stumbling out from behind a crowd of elves, wielding a cheese knife and a bad temper.

"Where did that little thief go?" he demanded, his moustache twitching crossly at Fjona. "You, Marrowborns! Did you see that brat?"

Fjona and Todie exchanged a coy look.

"Well? Are you both dumb?"

Fjona grinned. "I'm afraid we haven't seen anyone come this way."

"Damn useless fools..." the man grumbled, then charged along the avenue in pursuit of the girl.

The deeper into the camp they got, the more chaos ensued. Loose chickens and donkeys seemed to be around every bend and crowds of people became ever denser. A putrid smell of rotting food and sweltering sewage filled the air and it was enough to make their eyes sting.

"I miss Wychwold," said Todie, in a tone of regret.

"The boring villagers? The monotony of tending the farmsteads and cooking meals, day after day? The same rivers, the same hills, the same mountains on the horizon?"

Todie nodded.

"Me too," Fjona sighed. "Look, we are close to finding this box of Perciville's. Once we've got it, we can part ways with him and head home. We'll relieve Evelyn from tending to my house and I can see my mother and..." She trailed off as she considered the state her father might be in by now.

Knowing better than to offer words of condolence, Todie just smiled sadly. "Perhaps I can finally take you to the Great Forest of Aulden?"

"That would be nice." Fjona removed her Woven Wand from her pocket, pointing it forwards as she focused. "Good, we are still heading to the west of the mountain. I was starting to lose my bearings in all this."

She glanced back to see that Perciville and Bosmar Fodd were still following closely. Although she was still angry with them both, it was reassuring to have them nearby as they ventured further through the camp. For the most part, they had been left alone by the settlers with the exception of the beggars. Had Fjona the skills of her mentor, she would have conjured some fresh water for them at least, if not some clean clothes or even something to eat. Granted it would take a long time to learn the Artisanal Spells, as Perciville had called them, but she could only imagine the good that may come from her staff if only she had the ability.

She was also abundantly aware that the sage following closely behind her had his staff quietly attached to his back and his replenishing purse still hidden deep in his robe.

"Would it really be so hard for him to offer charity to one of these poor folks?" she said to herself. "I suppose once you help one, you have to help them all."

As they approached the edge of the camp, Fjona and Todie were able to follow the construction noise coming from the canal. Even this late into the evening, the labourers were evidently still working and the harsh clanging of metal on stone and the high-pitched squealing of cables as they pulled buckets out of the trench seemed to resonate across the desert.

They peeled away from the tents and trekked across towards the long, wide scar that disappeared over the horizon.

"It's bigger than the Racken," Todie said, peering into the far distance. "How can folk design something greater than nature?"

Fjona shrugged. "I suppose you can achieve anything if you have enough muscle."

They didn't get far on their approach to the trench before a soldier stormed towards them on a towering grey-brown horse. Astride the horse was an apparent summer elf, though her skin was paler than the rest of her kin.

Attached to her back was a bow and quiver stuffed with

arrows, and at her hip she carried a curved knife.

"What business have you here?" she asked sternly.

Her accent was strange, and certainly not like the other summer elves Fjona had met so far.

"We would like to speak with one of the guards here," Todie informed her.

"I am a guard here. Speak to me, then be gone."

Fjona chuckled. "You misunderstand my friend, here. We wish to speak with a specific guard. An Elian Sole."

The white-coated soldier studied Fjona for a moment through narrow eyes. "There is no one of that name here. Now return to the city. This is no place for visitors."

In a cloud of dust and sand, Perciville and Bosmar Fodd pulled up beside them.

The sage hopped off his camel and gave a polite dip of his head. "You will have to forgive my subordinates for their inadequate display of respect to a Noble Guard of the Sultan. I assure you, we mean to cause no harm or disruption to the works, only to speak with Elian Sole. We understand he is a ranger here?"

"You must have been misinformed. There is no such ranger among us."

"Could that corporal have lied to us?" Todie whispered to Fjona.

Before she could answer, they were interrupted by another soldier, who appeared on horseback. "Are they causing you trouble, Fayne?"

He was a brute of a man and, unlike Fayne, was most certainly a summer elf, with a thick beard like a black sponge and a strange rune tattooed on his cheek. His red-brown horse was bedecked with an ornate saddle and breastplate.

"Thank you, Captain Holden, but they were just leaving," Fayne replied.

Bosmar Fodd scoffed, revealing himself to the two guards. Evidently the frustration and humidity had boiled up to a point where he could no longer restrain his tongue.

"Yeah, bloody right!" he exclaimed, drawing each of their attention. "We haven't the time for your damned bureaucracy. We need to speak to Elian Sole."

Holden barely flinched as Bosmar appeared, merely acknowledging the Boglander with a look of repulsion. "What is this strange little creature?"

"Strange? Little?" Bosmar reached for his knife, but in the short time it had taken him to go from his reins to his hip, Fayne had equipped her bow and had an arrow nocked.

"Draw your weapon and your blood will be spilled," she stated.

"Now, now, now..." Perciville gestured for them all to calm. "There is no reason this need escalate. We come only with a simple request, to meet with one of your guards. Now, do you know of Elian Sole?"

Simultaneously, Captain Holden said, "Yes," while Fayne said, "No," at which they exchanged a bemused look.

The captain spoke. "Elian Sole is a Noble Guard here, but I cannot simply permit you to speak with him, especially since you have demonstrated a short temperament. What need have you with Ranger Sole?"

"We met Lais Stone in the desert—"

"We *saved* the life of Lais Stone *twice*," Fjona corrected the sage, "following an attack from a dalachite on our way south from Salamander. We are on our way to the city in search of a scholar who Lais Stone advised is a friend of Elian's. Apparently, he knows where we can find them..."

Holden looked carefully from Fjona to Fayne, then back to Fjona. "You met with Lais Stone, did you?"

Fjona smiled, finally sensing that they were making progress. "Yes, indeed! The formal corporal of the Fourth West Division."

The captain exchanged another look with Fayne.

Then, with a brief nod, Holden drew his sword. "You should have turned back when you had the chance."

He swiped at Fjona, but was intercepted by Todie's axe. Meanwhile, Fayne released an arrow at Bosmar Fodd, but he was too agile and slipped off his camel and easily away.

"This is all a misunderstanding," Perciville argued, casting a spell to hold the captain's sword from swinging at Todie.

"There is no misunderstanding," Holden growled as his muscles strained to fight the manipulation. "Lais Stone may have acted without thinking things through at times, but she was a ferocious soldier and damn fine leader. Her death has left a hole in the Fourth West that will never be replaced. For you outsiders to come here and throw her name around so callously is an insult to a great woman."

Todie pulled back his axe. "But we met Lais Stone only two days ago. She was alive and well."

"You lie!" Fayne cried, releasing an arrow in the direction of Todie.

"No!" Fjona screamed, drawing her wand and casting a pulse of energy, just in time to propel the arrow away from Todie.

For a moment, the Woven Wand appeared to radiate with a white glow, though it quickly faded away.

As Fayne prepared another arrow, Fjona manipulated the sand beneath the guard's horse, causing the animal to lose balance and topple onto its side.

Perciville, who had briefly been distracted by Fjona's spell, swiftly used his staff to raise the captain's cutlass up into the air, with the captain still clinging on. He dangled from the hilt, as if he were climbing an invisible rope.

"Now that I have your attention, Captain," Perciville said, "we would be much obliged if you could scurry on back to your trench and fetch Elian Sole for a quick word."

Holden nodded his heavy head from several feet in the air.

"I'm sorry, I didn't quite hear you," the sage provoked.

"We will send for him now," replied Holden as he tried to catch his breath.

"Excellent." Perciville smirked before dropping the captain ungracefully back into his saddle. "Oh, and Captain? No more games please. Send only Elian Sole and don't even think about calling for reinforcements. What you have experienced just now is a mere fraction of what I am capable of and, believe me, I can get nasty when I've been deceived."

With that, Fayne picked herself up off the sand, jumping onto her horse with a snarl, and she and Holden raced off towards a guard standing by one of the spoil heaps.

While they waited, Fjona caught Perciville staring up at Todie in his saddle. It wasn't a menacing look, or even one of disdain, but rather one of focused curiosity.

"You're making me feel uneasy," Todie said nervously, his face beginning to redden.

"Leave him alone, Harper, he hasn't done anything wrong," Fjona chided. "Harper? Are you even listening?"

The sage seemed to be completely oblivious to her and continued to stare intently. Then, slowly, and without glancing away for a moment, Perciville pointed his staff at Todie.

"Are you insane?" the cleric yelped, just as a pulse of dark purple energy erupted from the tip of the sage's staff and shot through the hot, stifling air.

CHAPTER 30

THE LONG WAND

Fjona wasn't even aware that she had been holding her own wand as she released a wave of energy that forced Perciville's manipulation away, nor was she aware that she was screaming as she did so.

Whatever the case, Fjona had intercepted the spell and spared Todie's life.

"What has got into you?" she yelled as she deflected yet another bout of energy from Perciville.

"He's mad!" Todie cried out, ducking down in his saddle as Fjona leaped from her camel and pointed her wand at Perciville.

Even Bosmar Fodd was taken aback by the sage's behaviour. "Why are you doing this now? He's kept his mouth shut since the corporal. Leave the kid alone!"

Fjona glared at the sage. "I swear Perciville, hurt him and I will kill you."

Perciville just smiled, wordlessly releasing another burst of manipulation at the cleric.

Wand glowing, Fjona cast the energy away, then released her own on Perciville. It wasn't much, just a shock of blue electricity, but it was enough to force the sage to stumble backwards and lower his staff.

When he looked up, Fjona expected to see an expression of anger or confusion, but instead, the sage wore a face of wild wonderment.

"What is wrong with you?" Fjona asked furiously, but it

quickly became apparent as to what Perciville was smiling at. Her Woven Wand was glowing bright white, like it had been dipped into the sun. Fjona gasped. "It's happening!"

The the seams between the woven wood appeared to tighten and seal, and the wand stretched out further to a rounded point. The wood felt smooth in her hand as the light began to fade.

The transition appeared to be over, but it wasn't. Suddenly, white light exploded out of the wand, so brightly that Fjona was forced to look away. She could feel the wand trying to expand and had to release her grip a little to allow it to breathe. As the initial radiance began to subside, Fjona looked back to see the wand grow further to a length about the same as her arm. This time, the white glow did fade away, leaving a new silverwood wand in Fjona's hand.

Perciville clapped his hands and started to howl with laughter.

Enraged, Fjona turned on the sage with the eyes of a predator and pointed her wand at his nose. "What is the meaning of all this?"

As if there wasn't a potential weapon held before him, Perciville grinned. "Relax, Miss Sarsen."

"Relax? You tried to kill me!" Todie complained as he rode over to the pair.

"Well... yes, granted, there was a minor risk of fatality, but look!" Perciville gestured to the new wand.

"Did you really engineer all that to force my wand to progress?" Fjona asked, her voice rising with scepticism.

"Twice! Which, admittedly, I hadn't foreseen. But look! Your wand has progressed twice!"

Fjona rolled the wand between her hands, admiring the smooth silverwood.

"I have never known of a demi-sage whose ability could surpass an instrumental grade... but, for whatever reason, you just did. You briefly held a Traditional Wand, but what you hold now is a

Long Wand. You are now just one step from achieving a Crook."

"But why?" Fjona asked, almost forgiving Perciville for his seemingly unnecessary act of aggression. "Why did it skip a grade?"

The sage shrugged. "The art of manipulation is complex and intrinsically powerful. For everything known about the way it works, there are a dozen yet to be discovered. It may be your historic bond with a childhood friend that summoned the strength to defend him, or it may be your love for him. Perhaps a fear for his life, or a sense of responsibility to protect him. Whatever the case, what you demonstrated superseded the capacity of a Traditional Wand. Marvellous!"

"Love?" Todie asked. "Like... platonic love?"

"Possibly," Perciville considered, "or sexual love, but it doesn't matter. The point is, we are closer than ever to what we need."

Closer to what you *need, maybe*, Fjona thought, but decided to keep it to herself.

It was then that Captain Callis Holden returned, accompanied by a white-coated Pentari Marrowborn.

"As promised," Holden said bitterly. "Ranger Elian Sole."

The ranger looked at each of them, as if trying to judge whether or not they were worth his time. "I thought you said there were four of them?" he said to Holden, seeing only Bosmar Fodd's camel and not the rider upon it.

The captain opened his mouth and was about to point out the Boglander to Elian when he saw Bosmar Fodd glaring at him angrily, shaking his head, and running his knife along his own throat as if to say 'speak and I will kill you'.

Holden cleared his throat. "I guess I was confused by the spare camel."

Elian mumbled in agreement, then addressed the three visible companions. "The captain tells me you met Lais Stone out in the desert. Is that correct?"

"Every word," Perciville assured the ranger.

"Well then, I'm afraid to say you may have been duped by an imposter," Elian replied.

"For what reason?" asked Fjona.

The ranger took a moment to consider. "To steal from you, or goad you into helping her?"

Todie looked to his companions. "Well she did persuade you to spare her life?"

"You were going to kill her!" Elian blurted out, then swiftly added, "Perhaps killing that imposter may have spared somebody else the trouble. Thank you, Captain, for seeking my attention. I'm sure you would like to get back to your command. You can leave them with me to escort them back to the camp."

"Very well," Holden said, his tattooed face motionless and dour. Then to the four travellers, he added, "Keep safe out there. The desert is a dangerous place, even for somebody with your..." He paused trying to find the right word. "Particular skillset." He looked begrudgingly at Perciville before steering his horse around and heading back towards the trench, leaving a plume of sand in his wake.

When Holden was out of earshot, Elian turned back to Perciville. "You tried to kill Corporal Stone?"

Fjona frowned. "I thought she was an imposter?"

"Oh, keep up, Fjona!" Todie replied in an uncharacteristically condescending tone, raising his eyebrows at her. He turned to the ranger. "My friends and I rescued her from the grips of a dalachite. I only told you that we'd spared her life because I could sense that you were withholding the truth..." His voice tailed off as his blatant lie lingered in the air between them.

The ranger nodded. "Very clever. So Lais Stone is alive?"

"Alive and well and heading towards Salamander, though she came close to being ripped apart. Had it not been for my companions and I, she may not have made it," Fjona explained.

"So then tell me, why exactly did Lais send you to me?"

This time, Fjona let Perciville do the talking. "We are researchers, of sorts, exploring the ancient Arvum and its inhabitants. Until meeting your former corporal, we were heading to the Archivus to procure a legendary and cryptic book that we believe was in the possession of renowned Proprietor of Intellect, Sialah Bouwer," he said, blending a sprinkling of truth within a heap of lies.

"Sialah Bouwer?" Elian repeated. "Has she not disappeared?"

Perciville nodded his head with false sombreness. "So we understand. However, Miss Stone seemed to recall seeing a book that fits the very description of Sialah's tome in the hands of another scholar. I can't say for certain whether it is the same book we seek, but it would be irresponsible, academically speaking, to pass up the opportunity to peruse. Your former corporal advised that we find you in the hopes you might introduce us to this esteemed scholar. Kaikura Kendi, if I recall correctly."

At the mere mention of Kaikura's name, Elian seemed to prick up his ears and his eyes appeared to twinkle. "I know her well, and I believe I know of the book you are referring to. San Kendi has taken it upon herself to decipher it."

"A monumental task, I should imagine," Perciville replied, "since it is said to have been written in a language unintelligible to man and elves alike."

Elian spoke with a note of pride. "Well, that's how it seemed to me, but Kaikura was able to read the cover and, from there, she has been slowly translating the rest."

The sage raised his eyebrows, as sceptical as he was intrigued.

"Tell me..." Elian began, raising the inflection in his voice, inviting the sage to introduce himself.

"Forgive my inexcusable act of rudeness! My name is Perciville Harper," he replied with cringeworthy politeness.

"Sun Harper, why exactly are you looking for this book?" the ranger asked.

Perciville smiled. "Let's just say, to satisfy my curiosities."

The ranger expelled a short breath through his nose. "Very well, I will show you to Kaikura's hovel, but know this... any trouble, any attempt to harm or deceive her, and I will ensure you don't leave Panamaya City in the same state in which you arrived. Do you understand?"

"Perfectly," Perciville replied, then gestured for the ranger to lead the way, before hopping back up onto his camel.

As the party ventured in the direction of the mountain, Fjona rode up alongside the ranger. "Are you not melting under that uniform?" she asked.

The ranger smiled warmly. "I'm a Pentari Marrowborn. We and the summer elves do not feel the heat as much as a northern Marrowborn such as yourself might." He looked Fjona up and down, from the cloth shawl wrapped around her head, down to the thin garments that hung loosely from her frame. "After the Arvum War, Havensend passed a legislation to permit all elven species admittance to each army in order to prevent further wars over race. Many rumour that the Sultan who ruled Panamaya following the Arvum War enforced the uniform to dissuade those other species from recruiting into his army. In my division, we are all Pentari except for Fayne, the island elf, though she has lived in the desert for so long that she is nearly as well adapted as the rest of us. Gods know she wouldn't complain even if the uniform did bother her."

Fjona nodded in acknowledgement. "What happened during the war? Who won?"

Elian looked at her strangely. "Where are you from?"

"Marrow Myre," she replied, unsure as to why he had asked. When Elian's odd expression didn't fade, Fjona added, "It's an island in the Near Sea. Have you really never heard of it?"

The ranger shook his head. "Never."

"Well, it's where your ancestors would have come from," Fjona said, recalling a conversation she'd had with Perciville not so long ago. "All the Marrowborns once came from Marrow Myre, although Todie and I are technically Myrish since we still live there. This is our first time visiting the mainland."

"Ah, well that explains why you know so little of what has happened here over the past few centuries. Unfortunately, you are asking the wrong person. My knowledge of history is minimal other than that the unified Arvum of old collapsed and the major cities fought one another to take claim of the continent. Havensend ultimately won, becoming the Free Capital, but allowing each city to maintain some degree of independence. That and enforcing military restrictions and trade. In truth, I tend to just keep my head down and follow my commands. Lately all I do is come down to the canal and patrol my segment of the desert. To be frank, I care little for politics and history."

"I grew up in a small village many miles from here," Fjona explained. "To learn of such conflicts and legislations is somewhat alien to me. Not to mention the scale of everything on the continent. I reckon Wychwold would fit in your city a thousand times with room to spare!"

"I know nothing of Wychwold, but Panamaya is quite the city. It's a shame that so many have been displaced by the tremors, especially since the canal is soon to be completed and, at this rate, there won't be anyone left to benefit from it," the ranger said.

Fjona gazed at the immense trench that disappeared far into the horizon. "How far does it go?"

"To the Precipitous Mountains on the west coast. It was originally intended to increase trade with Havensend, but Kaikura told me that the Sultan now intends to ship fresh water to the city."

"Is there something wrong with the spring?" asked Perciville in a near-accusatory tone.

Fjona was startled by the sage's voice, not realising that he had been riding so closely behind her.

"I don't know all the details," Elian replied, glancing back to face him, "but according to Kaikura, the spring was enchanted by a sage many years ago and it is soon to dry up."

"Huh…" Perciville said, counting his fingers. "I suppose it may only have another ten years or so left in it."

"What do you mean?" Elian asked, his eyebrows raised.

"My skills were only so good back then and to conjure a permanent spring was far beyond my ability. Had I realised the time, I would have visited sooner to restore it, although I'm not sure I'd be able to do much good for it at the moment."

"Wait, *you* enchanted the spring?"

"Enchanted? No, I conjured it entirely from nothing. Saved the Panamayan people from carrying water over from the mountains and gave the city a little more independence. It was a gift to the sultan at the time when my friend, another sage, and I visited the city. Daemund Fortuana, rest his soul. Let me tell you, he was brilliant! While I conjured the spring, Daemund transformed the courtyard to the Archivus. He'd become quite enamoured by the place and created an astonishing garden with trees and streams, if I remember correctly."

"Well, I fear all of your creations may crumble into rubble," Elian sighed. "The earthquakes are becoming more intense and nobody knows when they will stop."

The sage nodded. "So we have heard. These legends of the Sleeping Giant do seem to resonate more at times like these, but alas, I cannot advise you any more than your sultan at this moment. Perhaps some truth is buried in Kaikura's book, but until I can read it, there is little that can be done…"

He trailed off as they pulled up to a tall and wide iron gate at the base of the mountain. On either side sat a blue-coated guard atop a broad, black Pentari horse. The gate was open, revealing the base of a steep cobbled street that wound up and around the mountain. A little further up, Fjona could see a dense concentration of squalid shacks and shelters, no grander than those erected in the camp outside.

The guards acknowledged the travellers with only a cursory glance as Elian led them through the gate and they began the long ascent up the Sleeping Giant.

The road was narrow and bumpy at first and, although an effort had been made to hide the outer slums with wooden fences, tall cactuses and stone carvings, it did little to detract from the austerity with which the people here lived. A rancid smell of rotting meat hung in the stale air and it was enough to make Fjona wrinkle her nose up. Then there were the bedraggled children, clad only in rags or completely naked, begging for coin, food and water. The smell, Fjona could stand, but the starving children made her feel sick and even with her new wand she felt powerless to do anything about it.

Eventually, she noticed Perciville conjure a jug of water which he surreptitiously placed by the side of the road along with a smattering of coins. Nobody needed to know who had left it there, of course, and Fjona was relieved to see that the children found it first. They glanced around suspiciously at first before sharing the water between them and pocketing the coins. A small act of generosity, Fjona acknowledged, but it wasn't enough for her to forgive Perciville for his actions in the desert.

As the evening wore on and the street lanterns were lit, they passed through into what Elian referred to as the Lower Gate. Already they had ascended about half the mountain, following the winding, cobbled street up steep avenues and between cramped buildings. Had it not been for the accompaniment of a Noble Guard, it would have cost each of Fjona, Perciville, Todie and Bosmar Fodd three bassals to pass through the gate: the price of preventing the poor from mixing with the very poor.

"Once people can afford to pass into the Lower Gate, it is very rare that they should ever leave," Elian explained to Fjona, who was horrified at the tariff. "Those who have fled to the camp might never afford to return to their homes."

He spoke with a manner of acceptance as if the custom of segregating those by wealth was perfectly ordinary and not as heinous as it sounded to Fjona. Nonetheless, they passed through into the Lower Gate where hygiene and living standards were little better than below. The houses were proper sandstone rectangular blocks, but they were still squished into every nook and cranny. The cobbled road was somewhat wider, but it was still falling apart in places, causing the camels to stumble on occasion.

There was a faint breeze further up, however, so the fragrance of open sewage didn't linger for quite as long, and the only naked person Fjona saw was an inebriated summer elf who at least owned a pair of breeches, even if he had chosen to wear them around his head like a turban.

In addition, there was some evidence of commerce in the Lower Gate from the tiny stalls that had been propped up at the end of alleyways and between hovels. At this time of the evening, there were still one or two elves trying to sell their last cotton handkerchief or wooden toy to the final stragglers passing by. Fjona kept her head down ashamedly to avoid making eye contact and being pressured into purchasing a half-carved statuette of a horse, or a toy cart with only three wheels.

As they followed the road that skirted the edge of the mountain, they felt the earth quake with enough force to make their camels stumble, though not quite enough to topple them over.

"Heel!" Elian called, tugging on his reins. "Keep tight to the walls! We don't want anyone falling over the edge."

Fjona pulled her camel over, catching the pale, nervous face of Todie behind her as she did.

"It'll be okay," she assured him, but Todie could only offer an uncertain smile in reply.

Debris started raining down from above and Fjona was quick to extract her Long Wand and levitate a flat chunk of rock to stop it from cracking into Todie's head. She held it above him to catch smaller rubble before carefully placing the stone umbrella on the ground next to his camel.

"Are you sure it'll be okay?" Todie asked uncertainly.

"So long as I have this," Fjona replied, holding up her wand.

The tremor lasted no more than a few minutes and either the locals had become used to them, or there was nobody left around to scream or panic.

The party gathered themselves, then Elian kicked his heels and recommenced the trek up the mountain.

"I can see why so many folk have left this dump," Bosmar muttered to Fjona as they followed a rubble-strewn road up past a line of entirely collapsed hovels.

Many elves who had stayed behind poked their pointed noses out of their homes to view the damage.

"Be nice," Fjona admonished. "These were somebody's homes not so long ago."

The road continued to wind up the mountain, eventually straightening up into a long, steep avenue that stretched into a plateau.

"The forum," Elian said to Fjona, as they rode towards it. "A market during the day and a brawling spot for aggressive elves at night. Don't fret, Kaikura lives along a side street before we get there." He looked over to Fjona after she failed to reply. "You must be exhausted," the ranger commented with the bluntness typical of a soldier.

"It's been a long day," Fjona replied, suppressing a yawn. "In fact it's been a long few weeks..."

"Unfortunately, Kaikura is unlikely to have room for you to

sleep, but I can probably get you into an Upper Gate inn, so long as you've the coin to pay for it."

"That would be terrific," Fjona thanked him. "It would be nice to sleep in a proper bed again."

"I'll see what I can do."

The ranger led the weary travellers across the street, then through a labyrinth of indistinguishable narrow passageways. Here, they dismounted their camels for easier navigation as they squeezed through the tight crevices between the houses.

Eventually, they peeled out into a fractionally wider road, sided by block sandstone buildings with tall, thin wooden doors and ladders.

Elian proceeded to tie his horse to the bottom of one particular ladder, then instructed Fjona and her companions to tie on to his. It created a line of highly fatigued camels standing forlornly behind one another along the side of the road, blocking several doors and taking up half of the passageway.

"Hopefully we won't be too long," the ranger commented. He ascended the closest ladder to the top of the roof.

"Where is he taking us?" Todie whispered to Fjona.

Fjona just shrugged, then followed the ranger up.

"I have no desire to be seen by anyone else," Bosmar Fodd spat. "Think I'll stay down here and make sure no scummy elves come and steal our camels."

"As you wish," Perciville called from halfway up the ladder, "but don't go causing any trouble. I'd prefer you to not get us kicked out of here like you did in Salamander."

Bosmar raised his left hand then tapped it three times with his right fist towards the sage – a crude gesture he'd evidently picked up from an autumn elf.

On the roof, a faint candlelight glow spilled out of four low, flat windows that surrounded a central hatch.

"That's a good sign," Elian said in a hushed voice. "I wasn't sure if Kaikura would even be awake at this hour."

With Fjona, Perciville and Todie gathered around him, he tapped gently on the hatch door.

"San Kendi? It's me, Elian."

From beneath her, Fjona could hear the rustling of papers, the whistling of a kettle and the purring of what sounded like a cat.

Then it faded away and a quiet voice responded, "Come on down."

CHAPTER 31

KAIKURA KENDI

"I'm afraid I'm struggling to understand," Fjona heard Kaikura say to Elian, from down below. "How is it that these strangers even came to know of the book?"

"He's a sage," she heard Elian reply, "says he knew of Sialah Bouwer and that she was in possession of it."

There was silence as Kaikura pondered Elian's answer. "And why exactly does he wish to read it?"

"He claims to satisfy his curiosity," Elian replied.

"Do you trust him? Do you trust any of them?"

There was another pause before Elian answered. "I'm not sure. They seem legitimate. Two Myrish friends and a sage. Each with a camel plus a spare carrying a few extra belongings."

"Myrish?" Kaikura said. "Accompanying a sage? Perhaps it would be remiss of me to turn away such fascinating people from my home, so long as you remain for some support. Bobassa?" she shouted up the ladder. "Please permit them access."

On the roof, Fjona looked down at the copper and coal scaled creature with its long ears and dual tails. It growled threateningly at her, baring its pointed teeth before deftly slinking back through the hatch without a sound.

"Never been a fan of sandkats," Perciville said to Fjona, an irritated edge to his voice. "Loving and affable one moment, vicious and cruel the next." The sage leaned over the open door and poked his head inside. "Good evening," he announced with a comical grin, "allow me to introduce myself. I am Perciville Harper. You must be Kaikura Kendi? Mind if I come down?"

Fjona couldn't see the host, but she could only presume there was some form of nod or gesture as Perciville disappeared down into the hovel.

Before he had made it to the bottom, Fjona descended after him. It was a strange space inside. Boxy and confined, yet humble and lovingly decorated. Little more than a single room, but the sentimentality and particularness of Kaikura's belongings reminded Fjona of her own home.

Stacks of books occupied every surface, including much of the floor, and a sweet fragrance of tea hovered in the stuffy air, strong enough to sting Fjona's eyes.

Her feet had barely met the floor before she was subjected to a barrage of questions from the eager scholar.

"Are you a sage also? You appear to have a wand... and what is your name? You must be Myrish, correct? Here, let me make you some tea!"

"San Kendi," Elian said, spreading his hands out calmingly, "allow your guests some room to breathe! They are exhausted from a long journey."

"Exhausted, indeed," Perciville replied, then asked in as casual a voice as he could muster, "now, where is this book?"

Kaikura was far too excited to listen. She was hurriedly pouring tea into ceramic cups and thrusting them into the hands of her visitors.

"Forgive me," she said, so frantically that her own tea splashed over the rim of her cup, "I've had many a visitor over the past few weeks, but none have been so welcome as yourselves! I mean – an actual sage! In my hovel!" She was practically squealing with delight.

Perciville forced a smile. "It's quite a thrill, I'm sure. So, about this bo—"

"And what are your names?" the scholar interrupted, turning her attention to the others.

"My name is Fjona Sarsen, and this is Todie Farren."

"Oh such wonderful names!" Kaikura exclaimed, looking the pair up and down as if they were a work of art. "It really is such a pleasure to meet you, San Sarsen and Sun Farren! Or, perhaps I should say my *derine* and my *derin*?"

Fjona was impressed. It had been a long time since she had received such a greeting and it was strange to hear the expression from a summer elf so far away from home.

"You're familiar with our customs?" Todie asked, just as surprised as Fjona.

Kaikura nodded her head excitedly, then rummaged through her books beneath the table. "Oh yes, I am well read in the Myrish folk." She opened a dusty tome on the table to a page showing a map of Marrow Myre. "A fascinating species."

Fjona and Todie exchanged a confused look. Fjona had never considered the Myrish to be its own species before, and yet, to a summer elf, she supposed it was like comparing cats to dogs.

"This is simply charming, isn't it!" Perciville said, his lips still attempting to smile; his eyes making no such effort. "But what of the cryptic book we seek?"

Only Fjona seemed to detect the sarcasm in his tone, for Kaikura continued to ignore him as she busily ran her finger across the map.

"So enlighten me, where precisely are you from? Port Widow, perhaps? Or one of these hamlets in the Parish of Yore, the God of the elements?"

Fjona felt warm and squishy inside as she listened to the scholar discuss her home. To relate to something so familiar out here was unexpectedly comforting. She leaned over the table and pointed to her village.

"Actually Todie and I are from Wychwold over here, although we first met Perciville in Port Widow, isn't that right?" she said to the sage.

By now, the vestigial grain of patience with which Perciville had tried to endure had evidently burned away and instead of replying to Fjona with a morsel of etiquette, he slammed his staff angrily on the ground and cast a thundercloud above them. The dark cloud grumbled as if it were about to unleash a storm, and a heavy wind fluttered the pages of Kaikura's book and threw cups of tea about the place.

At first the scholar looked terrified as her eyes widened and she cowered away from the storm brewing above her head. Then her expression transformed into one of amazement as the reality of a sage casting manipulations in her hovel began to dawn. That look of wonderment lasted until she saw the angry face of Perciville, and her terror returned.

In the same instance, Elian had drawn his sword and was battling the wind, trying to edge the blade closer to the sage.

Meanwhile, Bobassa had extended his claws, but under the force of the wind, he was only just able to grind them into the floor and prevent himself from flying into the back wall.

"Perciville!" Fjona shouted above the roaring storm. "Stop this now!"

Satisfied that he had everyone's attention, Perciville ceased the manipulation, though he cast another quick spell to throw Elian's sword out of his hand. It clattered loudly to the floor, safely away from the sage's neck.

When peace resumed, Kaikura said between short breaths, "That's quite the spell..."

Fjona was quick to check on the scholar and she wrapped her arms tightly around Kaikura's shoulders.

"I'm so sorry about him," she said, glaring at Perciville. "He can get a little petulant when things don't go his way."

"Look," the sage replied firmly, "time is of the essence. I need to see that cryptic book now! Please, I need only to look at it briefly. After that you can keep the damned thing for all I care."

"And you'll promise to never return here again?" Elian asked sternly as he collected his sword.

"Believe me, that is my sole intention."

With that, Elian sheathed his sword and returned to Kaikura's side.

"You're very kind," Kaikura said quietly to Fjona. "Why do you travel with this man?"

"He can be brilliant," Fjona replied, "if you get him on a good day."

She smiled warmly at Kaikura then left the scholar to fish out the book from inside her satchel beside the table. It was barely out the satchel before Perciville snatched it out of her hands and examined the cover.

"The ranger said you can read this," he said, though he looked at Kaikura as if he were asking her a question.

"I can."

"Tell me, what does it say?" Perciville asked, twisting the book around so that Kaikura could see it.

He pushed it so close to her face that the scholar had to blink her eyes to focus on it.

"It has only the title, *The Compendium of Sages,*" she said, "with no mention of an author."

She had barely finished reading it aloud before Perciville was nodding in agreement.

"Fascinating that it should reveal itself to you."

"What do you mean?" asked Todie. "Only Kaikura can read it?"

"The cover at least," Kaikura replied, "though, with painstaking attention, I have been slowly making an effort to translate it. Here..."

Again, she reached into her satchel and extracted a wad of papers. They showed rough recreations of many of the pages, though replacing the ancient language with the common tongue.

She held them before Perciville expectantly, but the sage barely glanced at them. Instead, he started leafing through the original cryptic tome.

"Can *you* read it, then?" Elian asked as he peered over the sage's shoulder.

Perciville shook his head. "Not a word." Then he gave a deep sigh. "But language barriers have scarcely stood in my way. Ah-hah!" He turned the book to a particular double-page spread and placed it on the table.

"Unusual, is it not?" Kaikura proposed. "To have these blank pages. I couldn't fathom why."'

"Well, for one thing, they're not blank," Perciville informed her.

Fjona leaned in closer to the table then looked up at the sage, perplexed. "What are you talking about? They're clearly blank. There's not a so much as an ink spot or a smudge."

Perciville shook his head. "No, they're not blank. They're just concealed."

As he waved his staff over the empty pages, a fierce red light funnelled out of its tip and poured into book. The pages began to ripple gently like a pool of water and purple ink started to float to the surface. Slowly the ink waved into a sentence across the middle spine.

"*The Resting Place of Yilsommen*," Fjona read aloud. "The first sage?"

Perciville nodded, a look of contemplation on his face.

"Is that what you were hoping to find?" Todie asked, struggling to keep the disappointment out of his tone.

Perciville didn't reply. He was focused on holding his staff above the book, though to the untrained eye, he appeared not to be casting a manipulation. There was no bright light nor a wave of energy, just an invisible force binding the staff to the pages.

Then a single flake of paper drifted up from the book and hovered gently above it. It was soon joined by another flake that floated up to its side, followed by another and another. Gradually hundreds of paper flakes wafted up out of the book like ashes from a fire, congregating together to a form a pyramid.

Though it wasn't a pyramid, Fjona soon realised, but a scale model of Panamaya City and the Sleeping Giant. The detail was extraordinary. Although the city didn't seem quite as she had seen, covering a much smaller portion of the mountain than in reality, it was possible to pick out individual buildings and streets. The roof of the palace even appeared to sparkle as she had noticed from the desert.

"It looks different," Todie said, and Fjona suddenly understood why.

"This is Panamaya City from the time when the Sagedom collapsed, isn't it? I guess it must have expanded a lot during the last three centuries or so."

Kaikura stared in awe, walking around the model and viewing it from all angles. "It's remarkable..."

Perciville's manipulation wasn't finished, however. The perspective seemed to change and the model of the city quickly shrank to about half its size. It now stood on a bed of paper flakes that represented the desert immediately surrounding the mountain. Then the model zoomed in on a spot a short distance to the east of the Sleeping Giant, to a seemingly indistinct location. It was void of landmarks of any kind. Merely a stretch of sand like any other.

That was until the paper flakes began to glow faintly red and they started disintegrating back towards the pages of the book. The red light burned brighter and brighter until a bead of energy fired out of the paper and into the head of Perciville's staff. Once there, the staff shimmered with a red hue before the light faded into nothing.

Meanwhile the model had separated back into flakes that gently floated down towards the table. When it had entirely vanished, the words *The Resting Place of Yilsommen* in the book faded too and only the empty pages remained.

When the dust settled, Perciville turned to Kaikura. "Thank you sincerely for your hospitality. I promise to never bother you again." He attached his staff to his back and made for the ladder.

"Hold on!" Kaikura exclaimed. "That's it?"

Perciville paused. "Yes... that's it."

"Wait a moment, Sun Harper," Elian urged, placing a hand on the rungs to stop the sage from leaving, "aren't you going to explain what all that was?"

Perciville huffed petulantly. "I can't understand you people. You wanted us out of your hair the moment we could leave. Well, I've got what I was looking for and now we can go. What more do you want from me?"

"Harper," Fjona said firmly, "we all just want to know, in the name of the Four Good Gods, what just happened. Kaikura has been kind enough to let us into her home. The least we can do is tell her what's going on."

The sage pinched the bridge of his nose, then released a long, resigned sigh. "Very well. Without going into too much detail, Fjona and I are seeking an ancient relic, so to speak; the location of which was hidden in this very book. It transpires that the relic, a box of sorts, was buried in the tomb of Yilsommen, the very first sage from many thousands of years ago and whose final resting place had also been lost to knowledge. A few have attempted, and failed, to find it. Yilsommen was said to have fought for the summer elves, though whether she was one herself, an island elf or helven, nobody actually knows. Whatever the case, it stands to reason that she should have been buried in the desert and only a half day's ride from the mountain. I can now track her tomb down with my staff, which I intend to do first thing tomorrow."

"Tomorrow?" Fjona asked. "Why so soon? I thought I needed to be a demi-sage to access the tomb?"

Perciville nodded. "Indeed you do. It is likely that we will have to return when you are ready, but I think it wise to locate the box as soon as possible so that we can be certain of where it is. Any more questions?" he asked sarcastically as he looked about the group. "Excellent. Come now, let's find somewhere to sleep."

"May I come?" Kaikura asked timidly, as if she wasn't entirely sure that the words were hers.

All eyes, including Bobassa's, turned to her.

"Why can't you just sleep here?" Perciville replied, furrowing his brow.

Kaikura's shoulders slumped. "No, not now. Tomorrow. May I join you on your expedition tomorrow?"

Elian placed a hand on her arm. "Kaikura, this is not wise."

She brushed him aside. "My whole life has revolved around the study of the ancient past in every corner of the Arvum, yet never have I had the opportunity to leave the city. I feel intrinsically connected to Yilsommen having pored through this book, and to see her final resting place would enrich my entire educational sphere. Please, Sun Harper, San Sarsen, I won't cause any bother."

Perciville shook his head, but before he could reject the scholar, Fjona spoke up.

"Of course you may join us."

The sage shot her a dirty look. "This is not your decision to make."

"And why not?" Fjona replied. "This has been my journey as much as yours and I should have as much of a say as you."

"True, but—"

Fjona wasn't finished. "I know what it's like to feel excluded from the rest of the world and it is incredibly lonely. Besides, there may be more in that book that only Kaikura can help with."

Perciville considered Fjona's suggestion for a moment. "It could be dangerous."

"Panamaya City can be dangerous," Kaikura pointed out, "and I'll have Bobassa to keep an eye on me at least."

"San Kendi, please think wisely about what you are asking," Elain warned. "You do not know these people, you do not know the desert, and I am on duty tomorrow. I cannot accompany you."

Kaikura touched his arm softly. "I appreciate your concern, truly, but to miss the chance to visit an ancient tomb in the company of a sage would undermine decades of study. You must surely see that this is quite a unique opportunity?"

It was as if Fjona were watching herself pleading with a friend to permit her to travel. After all, it wasn't that long ago she had begged Perciville to allow her to accompany him and, despite many hardships along the way, she held not a single regret.

She stepped in between them and spoke to Elian. "Do not fear, I will personally stand between Kaikura and whatever dangers might be out there."

The ranger didn't say anything. He just breathed heavily and nodded.

"Oh grand!" Perciville exclaimed with as much derision as he had mustered all evening. "Then perhaps we can invite Kaikura's mother to join us? And maybe the ranger's cousins, and some of those beggars we met on the way up?"

Fjona rolled her eyes. "Give it up, Harper. It would do our group some good to have some intellect and decorum among us for a change."

"Fine. She may join us, but only for tomorrow. After that, we will drop her back here, and go on our merry way, understood?"

Fjona grinned. "Understood."

"And should anything ill befall her, then that is on you, Fjona, not me. I will protect her where I can, but if not, my conscience is clear."

"You do not need to babysit me, San Sarsen," Kaikura assured her. "I will be there just to observe and record a few notes."

"Well should you need any assistance, we will make sure that you are safe," Fjona replied.

The conversation was broken by a loud yawn from Todie, who had been quietly watching through drooping eyes in the corner.

"Forgive me, but it has been a most trying day and it would be nice to get some shut eye before the sun starts to come up."

Perciville nodded. "For once, I agree with the cleric. We have a big day ahead of us."

"Well then follow me," said Elian. "There is an inn just opposite here that will serve you fine for the night. I'm afraid you'll have to wait to see the Upper Gate on another occasion," he added, looking at Fjona.

"That suits me. The sooner I am in bed, the better. I will have to explore the Upper Gate when we return from our journey."

CHAPTER 32

THE TOMB

In truth, by the time they had got to bed, *tomorrow* turned out to mean *in a few hours,* yet with the Pentari sun burning through the open window, Fjona awoke with much vigour, as if she'd had more than just five hours' sleep.

She rubbed her eyes with the back of her hand and sat up in the bed. Todie lay topless beside her, the sheets barely covering his surprisingly muscular chest. Fjona had never noticed before just how strong her childhood friend had become. Clearly the days of Todie Toad were long behind him.

Tucked in the corner of the squalid room was Bosmar Fodd, peacefully dozing in a tub of, now-grimy, water. Perciville had been reluctant the night before to conjure the bath for him, but after much complaining and furious gesticulations by the Boglander, the sage had conceded. Needless to say, he was not in a good mood when Perciville had shared the fact that the scholar was now to be accompanying them. Especially since now Bosmar had to either reveal himself to Kaikura or submit his camel to her.

Fjona looked over to the spot where Perciville had been sleeping and realised that both the sage and the sheets that he had conjured for himself were now absent.

She could hear murmurings outside in the corridor before the door suddenly flung open and Perciville burst into the room, along with the intense morning heat. He was unusually buoyant with an unlikely spring in his step, and chuckling as if he were a child playing with his friends.

Kaikura followed him in, also giggling with the sage and clutching her satchel beneath her arm.

"You two seem cheery," Fjona said sceptically as she rose from the bed. Beside her, Todie began to stretch out and appeared to yawn himself awake.

"I decided to head into the forum to find some breakfast for us all and happened to run into Kaikura, who'd had the same idea," Perciville replied. "Granted, I tried to avoid her," he said with a grin, to which the scholar raised her eyebrows, "but with some tenacity, she persuaded me to accompany her to a particular stall, deep into the market. Can you imagine what they sold?"

"Caffeine probably..." Fjona heard Bosmar mutter to himself.

"Pentari spiced buns!" Perciville replied jovially. "I mean, Fjona, there is nothing in the Arvum like a Pentari spiced bun! They are soft and sweet, but also doughy and spicy all at once. Kaikura, please..." He gestured for the scholar to distribute them to Fjona and Todie.

"As you may surmise, they have rather a high sugar content," she said quietly, nodding towards Perciville as she handed out the buns.

The buns were wide, soft domes with a flat, slightly sticky base. They were a pale sandy brown on the top that faded gradually to a deep red at the bottom, and were coated in a dusting of sugar, cinnamon and flakes of salt.

Fjona was about to take a hearty bite out of her spiced bun when she froze in trepidation. Kaikura had stopped in the corner of the room and was staring curiously at Bosmar Fodd's bathtub.

"Huh," she said after a while. "What an unusual bathtub..."

There was a long, awkward pause as the Boglander stared eagle-eyed at Kaikura, and an uncomfortable glance was exchanged between Todie and Fjona.

Then Kaikura and Perciville burst into laughter.

"You must be Bosmar Fodd. Please, eat up!" Kaikura proffered a tantalizingly big Pentari spiced bun, but received only a moody scowl from the unashamedly naked elf.

"You can see me?" Bosmar asked, evidently annoyed as he splashed around in the water and reached for his loin cloth on the floor next to the bath.

"Relax, Bosmar," Perciville said. "She was bound to notice you eventually so I told her about you and how to spot you. The ruse about the bathtub was my idea."

"And don't worry," Kaikura added. "I've read a lot about Boglanders and I recognise how important your hidden appearance is. I won't break your concealment to anyone, I promise."

Bosmar just stared up at the scholar with beady, judging eyes.

"You really are quite a peculiar being, aren't you?" Kaikura continued, reaching out to touch his strange drooping ears.

"If you value your fingers you'll refrain from doing that," he hissed at her, causing Kaikura to stumble backwards.

"Wow, this is delicious!" Fjona exclaimed, breaking the tension between Bosmar Fodd and Kaikura as she tucked into her bun.

"Well, eat up," Perciville said, a seriousness returning to his voice. "We have a lot to do today."

Feeling nourished and energised, the companions were soon saddled up and on the road, commencing the long descent down the mountain. It appeared to Fjona that, despite the cautionary tales of earthquakes and a waking giant, few traders were deterred from venturing to the city and, as they made their way east across the Lower Gate, they passed a long stream of caravans.

Having Kaikura among them, her flint-tipped spear strapped to her back, was already paying off since she knew the quickest and least congested routes down to the east gate, despite never having been out that way before. She now led the way through the network of alleyways and streets, between hovels and gullies, and over wooden bridges.

Fjona spotted the strange feline, Bobassa, hopping along the rooftops and keeping his wide eyes on them. Somehow, had she or one of the others come to harm Kaikura, Fjona sensed that Bobassa might become very unpleasant. After all, he had made his sizeable teeth and claws very apparent back in Kaikura's home.

As they passed across a wooden bridge that spanned a wide avenue of houses, Fjona edged up to Kaikura. "Perciville was in a surprisingly good mood this morning. I can't remember the last time I saw him smile."

"Well, he wasn't when I ran into him, believe me. Perciville wasn't joking when he said he'd tried to avoid me, but I couldn't resist catching up with him. For one thing, it looked like he was going to purchase some pretty rancid meat for breakfast and it was only when I mentioned Pentari spiced buns that he came around to the idea of accompanying me."

"The bun certainly perked me up," Fjona agreed, before being dazzled by a bright light coming from her side. Squinting, she glanced over to the source and realised that the morning sun was reflecting from the golden dome of the Sultan's palace. "I can't believe how magnificent it is."

"Would you believe me if I told you the Sultan invited me to visit him not so long ago?"

"For what reason?"

"To counsel him on a recurring dream about the waking of the Sleeping Giant. Not exactly my expertise," Kaikura chuckled, "but I was recommended to his steward and she dragged me to the palace."

"What did you tell him?" Fjona asked.

"I waffled my way through what I knew of the mythology,

suggested it may be a premonition, unlikely as it may sound, and he duly rejected my ideas and decided that it was probably all over nothing. He has a conflicting character, so I understand. Cruel but fair, they say. Anyway, Proprietor Bouwer's book explains that the mountain is a burial mound for a species of ancient beast known as raithers which means no giant could possibly be sleeping beneath it. That's not to say that the tremors are completely harmless, but I don't doubt that they will pass before too long."

"Well I'd love to visit the palace myself. The grandest building I know of on Marrow Myre is the Paddolgolian Brothers' General Store and that pales by comparison."

"Perhaps, when we return from the tomb, I can show you around the Upper Gate and we can see the palace," Kaikura offered. "I doubt we'd be granted admittance, but we can at least view it from the outside."

Fjona's eyes sparkled with excitement. "I would truly relish the opportunity, and I could show you Swirleybucket!"

They followed a walkway around the rim of a steep drop that opened up into another bridge. This one crossed another wide avenue, beneath which a dense crowd of travellers funnelled and squeezed up the mountain in the direction of the forum.

Fjona paused to watch the flow of Marrowborns and elves, horses, camels and carts inch their way along the street. It was so compact among them that Fjona could only wonder how there was any room to move at all, yet gradually the clump of people pressed on between the houses.

Summer elves made up the vast majority of the traders, though not exclusively. At one point, Fjona noticed a startlingly beautiful spring elf wearing a stunning green dress. The elf had long pine-coloured hair and, surrounded by dust, sweat and animal faeces, her presence on this street was entirely incongruous. Her face was stern and preoccupied, though when she caught Fjona looking at her, the spring elf did return a sly smile.

The spring elf seemed to be in the company of a hooded figure and a tall, muscular summer elf. With the confusing mess of swathes of animals and folk heading up the mountain, for a moment, it looked as if the summer elf had a horse's leg. Fjona had to shake her head to restore some sense. An elf with a horse's leg would be quite impossible...

"Quit daydreaming," Perciville snapped. "We have a long way still to go."

Fjona pulled herself together and caught up with her companions. By late morning, they had crossed the threshold between the Lower and Outer Gates and were well on their way towards the east city entrance. There were two tremors as they passed through the slums, though both were relatively mild and caused little disruption, besides needing to wait for them to pass before continuing on.

As the sun slipped beyond the highest point of the day, they finally crossed the boundary between road and sand.

"Okay, Fjona, shuffle forwards. We are at the desert now," Todie said, having remained on foot for the mountainous portion of the journey so that Kaikura could have his camel.

Fjona sighed. "I suppose I did promise." She inched forward on the saddle and Todie hopped on behind her.

"Could be worse," he said, a little too closely to her ear. "It could be Shagwell."

As they adjusted themselves on the saddle, Perciville rode beside them with his staff raised forward. The familiar red glow burned at its tip and the sage, eyes firmly shut, waved the staff gently across the horizon in front of him. He then settled in a direction out across the blanket of sand.

"If you are quite finished fumbling about on your saddle,"

Perciville grumbled, "we should head on out. If we travel at a fair pace, we should arrive at the destination within a few hours."

"Lead the way," said Bosmar Fodd, his face underwhelmed, as though he cared no more for their expedition than he did about relieving his bowels.

After a relatively cool night, Fjona had almost forgotten just how excruciatingly hot the desert was during the day and she wrapped her shawl loosely around her head and shoulders.

Their camels were already showing signs of fatigue having been ridden relentlessly for several days in a row; though, being sturdy Pentari breeds, they remained strong and fast, and were able to cover a fair distance in a relatively short amount of time.

Before too long, Fjona looked back behind her to see the Sleeping Giant already shrinking into a vague silhouette, yet even out here she could see the shimmering of the Sultan's palace.

As they rode, the desert became more treacherous, with deep ripples in the sand and expansive dunes to surmount. It was rockier and drier out towards the east, occasionally decorated with crumbling pillars of ancient cliffs. Desert grasses and cacti started to appear, attracting black scorpions with pincers the size of Fjona's hand.

On they travelled beneath the wearying sun that sucked every bead of sweat off Fjona's skin before it had even the chance to cool her. When she licked her dry lips, there was no moisture. Only grainy, scratchy salt that reminded her of her burgeoning thirst.

They were forced to stop on several occasions to recuperate with some conjured water from Perciville's staff, but by now, everyone was too determined to reach their destination and the prospect of resting became less desirable.

Eventually, Perciville halted at a nondescript plane of open desert. It was entirely barren, but for a few scorpions, and stood out no more than a frog among toads.

At first, Fjona thought they had just stopped for another break, until the sage announced, "This is it."

For once, everyone, even Bosmar Fodd, was too tired to make wisecracks or sarcastic remarks.

Having come so far, Fjona inwardly prayed that Perciville was correct.

Perciville hopped down from his camel, conjured a wooden post into the sand, and tied the camel up by its reins. The others followed his lead, then gathered around the sage. He extended his staff to the sky and summoned his power.

The familiar red bead of light grew at its tip, then burst out of the staff in an arc away from him, piercing the sand and vanishing beneath the surface. A quiet rumbling ensued before the sand began to undulate and shift, folding away from the epicentre where the light had ensconced. Then the sand peeled away on either side and curved over a deep crater in the desert, forming a great archway above.

Right in front of Perciville's feet, a steep and dusty staircase descended into the crust of the Arvum towards a stone cavern at the bottom.

The sage attached his staff to his back, turned to face the others, shrugged, then proceeded to climb down into the crater.

"Here goes..." Fjona said quietly to Todie, whose face was a mixture of awe and trepidation.

Wordlessly, the companions, Bobassa included, followed the sage deep beneath the scorching surface and down into the cool, dark earth.

The entrance to the cave was a vertical mouth through the rock. There was no door or stone to block the way, though Fjona reasoned that the lake of sand above was a seal enough.

Inside, it was pitch black. It seemed that this was the only place in the Pentari Desert where the sun could not touch.

Perciville used his staff to conjure a light, just enough to illuminate a narrow corridor.

"It appears manipulations have been supressed down here," he said.

"How is that possible?" Kaikura whispered back in the gloom.

"Exceedingly skilled enchantments," Perciville replied, "like those of a sagen master."

They pushed through until the corridor opened up into a wide chamber, partially illuminated by candles along the walls, glowing with green fire. No sooner had they entered than Perciville's staff flickered out – his manipulations appeared to have been entirely restricted.

He halted abruptly to the sound of crumbling stone and pushed out his arms to stop the others from walking any further.

They stood at the edge of an abyss.

"Careful!" Perciville called. "We best not fall down there."

Fjona peered over the edge and stared into the darkness. The green candles lit the void well enough to see a fair distance down, though the bottom was far out of sight. On the opposite side, there was no visible ledge to stand on, even if they could get across.

"Where do we go?" she asked, turning to the sage.

He extended his staff and attempted to cast manipulations, but nothing showed for his efforts – it was futile. It really seemed they could go no further.

"What's that up there?" Todie asked, breaking the silence.

The cleric gestured to a shimmer of faint white, high up on a wall on the far side of the abyss.

Fjona strained her eyes to see what it was. "It looks like light around the edge of a door."

"Yes," Todie replied, "but an upside-down door."

There was silence again as the companions sought to make head or tail of the unusual flickering light high up near the ceiling.

"Oh!" Kaikura suddenly said excitedly. "I think I know what this is!"

All eyes turned on her.

"Care to elucidate?" Bosmar Fodd asked, bluntly.

"It's in here…" Kaikura replied, extracting both the cryptic book and her own translations. She peeled through the pages, then opened to one with an illustration loosely similar to the room they were in. She put her reconstruction beside it. "Yilsommen experimented with gravity later into her life, so it says here," Kaikura explained, but before she could go on, Perciville snatched the book out of her hands and held it in front of the chasm.

He glanced from the image before him to the void beyond.

"Umm, anyway," Kaikura continued, startled by the sage's poor manners, "Yilsommen discovered what is known as Gravity Warping Manipulation. Apparently she passed on the knowledge to bend gravity in such a way to her successors. Maybe they employed it here as a homage?"

"Or a deterrent," Todie added.

"Well, whatever the case," Kaikura said, "if this is what I think it is, by stepping into the void, you should actually fall upwards to the ceiling."

Todie scoffed. "And how do you suppose we do that?"

He had barely finished his sentence before two heavy hands pushed on his chest and the cleric stumbled back over the edge.

"Todie!" Fjona yelled, as the cleric's screams fell over the edge with him, then drifted back up along with the cleric.

She watched as Todie planted himself on the ceiling a short way ahead of her, brushed the dust off his breeches, and stood up.

"Surely there was a better way," Fjona snapped at Perciville.

"But not a more comical way," the sage replied. He grinned childishly and hopped backwards over the edge.

Just like Todie, Perciville fell a short way into the chasm before being caught in the reversed flow of gravity and being swept up to the ceiling. He made a slightly more elegant landing, somehow falling on his feet, and Fjona could see them gesticulating at one another. Most likely Todie sharing his disapproval with Perciville for pushing him into the abyss.

"Who's next, then?" Bosmar Fodd asked, his bulging eyes flitting between Fjona and Kaikura.

When nobody replied, he pointed to himself, nodded, and dived headfirst into the nothingness. Moments later, he too was on the ceiling.

When Fjona looked to Kaikura, the scholar's usually dark skin was suddenly washed out and several shades lighter. She was staring at the enormous gap and shaking her head.

"Here, take my hand," Fjona offered, but Kaikura was frozen by fear.

"Just leave her!" Perciville shouted from above, but Fjona waved the sage's comment away.

"You can't allow yourself to get so close to what lies in here and miss out because of fear. Please, Kaikura, take my hand."

"I-I c-can't..." Kaikura replied, her narrow shoulders trembling.

Bobassa, perhaps sensing his master's fear, purred warmly and brushed up beside her. Then, as if he truly recognised what needed to happen, the sandkat released her and charged towards the chasm in a blur of shimmering scales.

"Bobassa!" Kaikura cried as the sandkat leaped freely into gravitational pull and, whining happily, floated up to the ceiling.

"The only way is forward," Fjona said, "and besides, if things go wrong, I always have my wand."

What exactly she could do to rescue them with her wand, Fjona wasn't sure, but Kaikura didn't need to know that.

"Okay," the scholar agreed uncertainly.

Fjona grasped Kaikura's hand and could feel her fingers dig into her flesh. The scholar was still quite resistant as Fjona dragged her to the chasm's edge and, when she did, it took more than a little effort to tug Kaikura into the gravity.

There was a sudden lurching sensation as they fell a short way down before the gravity caught them. Fjona's stomach did a somersault. She felt completely disorientated, as if she'd consumed a pint of Myrish whiskey, as she fell back up out of the chasm.

They landed in a heap, looking up into the abyss and at four smiling faces.

Kaikura started to laugh first, but soon Fjona was giggling with relief as Todie helped her to her feet.

"That was the easy part," Perciville said, immediately souring the mood.

Somehow, though, Fjona knew the sage was right.

After regaining at least enough strength to stand, the sage led them to the curious sliver of silver light, stretched around the frame of an arched wooden door.

Erratic shrieks and screams echoed in the chamber beyond.

Fjona looked to Todie who returned her terrified expression.

"What is that?" Kaikura asked as Bobassa started to growl.

"Gaeya'San," Perciville replied, walking purposefully towards the door with Bosmar Fodd by his side.

"What's a Gaeya'San?" Kaikura asked Todie, but the cleric just shook his head.

"Believe me, you do not want to know."

At the door, Bosmar Fodd was rummaging in his satchel. For the first time since meeting him, Fjona saw that the Boglander actually looked nervous. His slimy hands were shivering faintly and he seemed to be avoiding all eye contact.

"You've got this," Perciville said to him as Bosmar Fodd extracted a small metal object, about the size of his palm.

It was as flat as a biscuit and in the rough shape of a bottle. In the middle it contained a glass prism that seemed to catch the light, even though there was hardly any. The Boglander turned to the companions, dipped his head astutely, then opened the door, inviting a cacophony of shrills and flashes.

"Remind me... how many have you got?" Perciville asked, anxiously.

Bosmar Fodd reached into his satchel again and extracted an additional four objects. One a triangle, two like a crescent moon, and the other a hexagon. All seemingly made of the same dark metal, and all containing a glass prism.

The sage glanced into the chamber then back at Bosmar Fodd. "Should be enough."

He patted the Boglander on the back who then duly slipped into the maelstrom of light, lurking in the shadows where the Gaeya'San seemed not to illuminate.

"What precisely is he doing?" Kaikura whispered to Perciville as he and Fjona peered through a crack in the door.

"Catching Gaeya'San," the sage replied. "Those trinkets, cast from the metal of a dalachite, are known as soulless vessels. Exceedingly skilled to make and very hard to come by, but Bosmar Fodd has his ways. Gaeya'San cannot be killed or destroyed. Once they exist, they exist. The only means to get around them are by capturing them in a soulless vessel."

Fjona watched as Bosmar Fodd gracefully floated towards a pulsing, erratic light and ducked behind it. He held his first soulless vessel up behind it, the one in the shape of a bottle, and waited as the glass prism turned a deep, cloudy grey. Then, gradually, the light of the Gaeya'San seemed to be pulled towards the glass, shrinking and fading away. When it was gone, its shrills subsided and the glass prism turned to a bright silvery light. Bosmar had managed to capture the first one.

"So you knew we would find Gaeya'San here?" Fjona asked.

Perciville nodded. "Sagen Master Herak Siadonis released them here as a deterrent before sealing the tomb away."

"And only a Boglander could get close enough to actually capture one?"

Again, the sage nodded his head as a second Gaeya'San, this one trapped inside the ripped and faded sagen robe of its former being, was successfully captured into a soulless vessel and the chaos within the chamber settled just a little bit more. It was like the mist dispersing in a storm, but the torrent of rain, thunder, and lightening remaining.

"The ability to be, not invisible, but completely unnoticeable," Perciville explained, "and although a sage might be able to enchant themselves, to reach a level comparable to a Boglander that is equally adept at evading Gaeya'San, it is incredibly difficult. In addition, Bosmar Fodd possesses a slyness and greed that provides him with somewhat more of an edge under these circumstances."

The Boglander floated deeper into the chamber between two Gaeya'San and, this time, he was able to capture them both in separate vessels simultaneously.

"What will he do with them when we are done?" asked Todie.

Perciville turned to him with a face of steel. "Trust me, it's best that you don't know." Todie opened his mouth to argue, but before he could, the sage added, "Seriously."

He turned back to the door.

On the other side, Bosmar Fodd was at the far end of the chamber, sneaking up on the final Gaeya'San. With shaking hands, he held the last of his soulless vessels upwards and waited as the prism turned grey. Like before, the silvery light sucked into the glass and disappeared. The chamber dipped into darkness. The job was done.

"Excellent work!" Perciville exclaimed, stepping into the

chamber with Fjona close on his heels.

The suppressing enchantment seemed to have been lifted in here and the sage was able to cast a light. As he did, however, the piercing shrieks and flashing silvery light returned and Fjona saw a sixth Gaeya'San emerge from a cavity in the wall nearest her.

Somebody yelled to her, but Fjona couldn't hear what was said over the screams. The piercing, unwavering screams. She became disorientated, petrified to her very core, but somehow blissfully comforted by the prospect of death. Like another had, this Gaeya'San was trapped beneath a thin grey sagen robe as if years of imprisonment had burned through the fibres from the inside.

Fjona was completely fixed to the floor as the Light That Kills drifted towards her, enveloping her in its deadly, chaotic energy.

She desperately wanted to avert her gaze, but she was forced to keep staring, bound without chains, trapped without bars. Her skin was a thin veil of icy sheets, marbled with goosepimples, yet her blood felt like lava coursing through her veins. Her brain pulsed and ached as the light burned her eyes and the shrieks burst her ears.

As a child Fjona had been terrified of the dark and the ghosts that hid in the shadows. Never would she have believed that the opposite – the total absence of darkness – could be so much worse. Yet here she was, her very soul being penetrated by a timeless, formless entity and, unlike a blanket or a candle to shield from the darkness, Fjona had nowhere to hide.

All perception of her surroundings had been stolen away from her and, in the presence of others, she had never felt so desperately alone. If Perciville were pulling her away, she could not feel it. If Todie were calling her name, she could not hear it. All she could allow was for her mind to collapse in on itself and to spiral into a bleak nothingness between her thoughts

Then somehow, somewhere, something awoke her from her stupor. An intense burning sensation against her skin. Against her leg. At first, Fjona thought that the Gaeya'San had reached her and that it was tearing her apart from her thigh up, yet the heat caused no pain. She realised it must be her wand trying to get her to cast some manipulation to save herself, but when she managed to take hold of her senses and dug a cold hand into her pocket, she revealed, not her wand, but the rose-shaped amulet Todie had given her at Aserae's Lip. The amulet that had belonged, most recently, to Todie's grandmother Lasmee, but that had been handed down his family for generations. The amulet that, Fjona only realised now, was cast from dark metal and contained a glass prism – one that had turned a cloudy grey colour.

As if the muscles of her hand were operating themselves, Fjona held the amulet up as Bosmar Fodd had done. Her arm ached under its weight, but she was resilient.

Sure enough, the Gaeya'San was slowly pulled into the vessel, the maelstrom of light and screams disappearing with it. Despite the power that now resonated inside the amulet, it felt no different than it had before. No heavier, nor any hotter. Just the very same amulet, only now with a prism that shone with a silvery hue.

Peace and silence ensued, and Fjona could hear muffled voices surrounding her and could feel a pair of strong hands under her arms.

Then she snapped back into focus, staring into the terrified eyes of Todie.

He was asking her how she was, but Fjona had only one question.

"Did you know what this was?" she asked dazedly, holding up the amulet.

The cleric just laughed and embraced her, his cheeks glistening with tears. "You're okay!"

"Yes, I'm okay." Fjona smiled. "Thanks to your grandmother."

"Remarkable," Kaikura whispered, staring at the amulet.

"Indeed," said Perciville. "To think you had a soulless vessel on you all this time."

"Oh yes, sage girl catches a single Gaeya'San and everyone sings a damn opera for her. Meanwhile, poor little Bosmar Fodd catches five and nobody bats a bloody eyelid," the Boglander complained.

"You weren't nearly killed by one," Fjona countered. "You were brilliant, though. For the first time since we met, you have actually impressed me."

Fjona wasn't sure for certain, but her endorsement of Bosmar Fodd did seem to make him smile, even if just a bit.

Once Fjona had rested with a jar of water and Perciville had made sure that there were definitely no more Gaeya'San about, Todie asked the next important question.

"What next?"

Fjona gazed around the chamber. Except for a tall, freestanding slab of marble at the far end, the room was completely empty.

Perciville stood before the marble, leaning on his staff. "So, Kaikura, have you come across one of these during your studies?"

The question was posed as if he were a teacher riddling his student.

"Actually, I have. I believe it to be a sagen altar."

"Bingo!" Perciville exclaimed. "Created during the Sagedom to temper the abilities of the sages, so that we wouldn't become too powerful too quickly. Each year, every sage would sacrifice a portion of their skill to a sagen altar somewhere across the Arvum, though I dare say those who remain do so very infrequently now."

Fjona walked over and pressed her hand against the marble. It was as smooth as silk and surprisingly warm despite being left deep underground.

"So what do we do?" she asked. "Do we need to make a sacrifice?"

Perciville nodded. "I believe we might in order to open it."

"Open it?" Todie asked.

Kaikura went on to explain. "Some sagen altars were enchanted to act as gateways between two locations, or so I understand. With no obvious way to continue through the burial chamber, one may only assume that this altar is indeed just that – a gateway."

Wordlessly, Perciville thumped his staff on the cold ground before him and focused his energy. The tip of his staff began to glow blue, but instead of emanating away from him, the light pulsed downwards and into his arm. Gradually, it spread up towards his chest where it seemed to linger for a moment before tracing back along his arm and into the staff. Once there, it flowed out again, but this time into the marble face of the altar.

When he'd finished, nothing seemed to have happened. No gateway had appeared, nor had the marble slab transformed, and yet Perciville turned back to his companions with a wide grin.

"I don't understand..." Kaikura said, speaking everyone's mind.

"The door will open only to the sage who wills it," Perciville explained. Then he appeared to walk straight through the marble as if it weren't there.

Fjona was the first to touch it, but it was just as it had felt before – smooth, warm, and very much in her way.

Then Perciville popped back out through the concealed gateway, making Fjona jump.

"Face the altar," he said to her, "and channel your soul. You need only to sacrifice a morsel of your strength to unlock it, barely enough to be noticeable."

"Would all sages really have sacrificed their power?" Fjona asked nervously as she raised her wand.

"Since the beginning," Perciville replied. "Many say that Yilsommen sacrificed all of her killing ability to an altar, thus mastering the skills of healing and conjuring."

"That can't be true," Kaikura interjected, attracting an inquisitive look from Perciville.

"Why do you say that?"

"Because Yilsommen killed all the raithers and buried them under, what is now, the Sleeping Giant."

Perciville raised his eyebrows. "Raithers?"

Kaikura nodded, reaching for her notes. "Yes, ancient beasts that once roamed the desert."

"Yes, I know what raithers are. I hardly see how this is relevant..."

Kaikura ignored him and hurriedly fumbled through the pages, until she reached one in particular, which she read aloud. "'*She fought them in the Pentari Desert and it was there that she laid them all to rest.*' See, she must have had the ability to kill them or how else could she have—" The scholar cut herself off as her brain whirled into overdrive. "She laid them to rest..." Kaikura said to herself. Her mouth suddenly dropped and her eyes widened as the terrifying reality finally dawned on her. "She laid them to *rest*! The raithers... the earthquakes..." She trailed off, staring into space.

"I think we broke the scholar," Bosmar Fodd murmured.

"We need to head back immediately," Kaikura snapped, her voice frantic. "We need to warn everyone and move the camp away before it's too late!"

Perciville stepped over to the scholar. "Whatever it is you are afraid of, I assure you, the worst is yet to come."

"The worst is yet to come..." Kaikura echoed, her face a platform of terror. "*Sil'yhab forlein.*"

"What has got into her?" Todie asked, but nobody replied.

"Kaikura," Fjona said, touching the scholar gently on the shoulder, but she agitatedly pulled away. "We need to move forward. Perciville and I are going to pass through the altar, but the others will stay here with you to make sure you're okay."

"Of course I'm okay," Kaikura replied sharply, "but the Sleeping Giant really is going to wake and I think it's far worse than anyone could have predicted. Fjona, go forth and find what it is you are looking for. I need to head back to the city before it's too late. I need at least to warn Elian…"

With that, Kaikura grabbed the book and her notes, stuffed them into her satchel and retreated back towards the exit with Bobassa close behind her, purring frantically.

When she had gone, Todie asked, "Do you think she'll be alright?"

Perciville shrugged. "She has the sandkat. She'll be fine." Then he turned to Fjona. "Remember, channel your soul and submit your power to the altar. Only then will it open up for you."

Perciville smiled warmly before stepping through the marble, leaving Fjona with her wand pointed forward.

She did as he had instructed. As she closed her eyes, she felt a sense of tranquillity wash over her. It made her feel perfectly in harmony with her soul and she could practically weigh her power inside of her. Fjona felt herself offering a portion of that power to the altar and she could almost feel the altar accepting it.

When she opened her eyes, the marble slab was still very much there, but now the front face had vanished and a candlelit corridor had opened up before her. Perciville was waiting on the other side.

CHAPTER 33

THROUGH THE ALTAR

Todie grabbed Fjona's arm and pulled her back.

"Don't go, I have a funny feeling about this..."

Fjona shrugged away his tight grasp. "Todie, don't do this again. I'll be back before you know it."

The cleric lowered his head, abashed. He looked so desolate, vulnerable. With everything that had happened since they'd left Wychwold, Fjona was only now just beginning to see the impact she, and their journey, had had on him.

She took his hands in her own and squeezed the amulet into Todie's palm, then planted a long, soft kiss on his lips.

"For good fortune," she said sweetly, then released him.

As she pulled away, Todie tried to hold on to her longer, but Fjona resisted.

"I'll wait for you," she heard him say as she passed through the invisible door.

When Fjona looked back, she saw Todie slump down against the face of the altar with his axe across his legs and his head hanging low.

"Let me know when you've finished pining over him and we can make a move," Perciville said with a tone of annoyance.

Fjona turned away from the entrance. "Lead the way." She forced a smile.

The sage nodded before turning on his heel and heading along the narrow corridor. The passage had been cut into the rock and the walls were adorned with lanterns burning with permanent green flames.

Fjona couldn't remove the terrified look on Kaikura's face from her mind. After all, the scholar appeared to have been highly logical and exceptionally academic. For her to have been suddenly shaken by an irrational fear spoke volumes about the threat that had sent her back out into the desert, alone but for Bobassa.

Shaking her head, Fjona tried to focus on the task in hand, following Perciville through a shallow corridor in the rock.

"What are raithers?" she asked after a while.

"Nobody actually knows."

"What do you mean?"

"Well, as Kaikura alluded to, raithers were an ancient, and arguably legendary, creature that once dominated the desert. They were around during a period known as The Age of Resurrection when disparate tribes of summer elves lived across the desert in isolated communities, much like the Kelner elves of today. For generations, swarms of raithers would rampage through the settlements, hunting for meat and flesh, bringing with them death and destruction wherever they went. It was only when the summer elves banded together and fought back that the raithers were defeated and the many tribes could meet, eventually settling on the Sleeping Giant and establishing Panamaya City. At least that's the story Santhé told me, sometime long before she dissolved the Sagedom and..."

Perciville trailed off and Fjona completed his sentence under her breath. "And died."

"It seems Kaikura has read a different account," the sage continued. "One in which the raithers were not defeated, but instead merely disabled by the hand of Yilsommen."

"And they are buried beneath the mountain?"

"From what Kaikura was jabbering on about, it sounds like

the raithers might actually be the mountain."

"But if 'waking the sleeping giant' actually refers to the raithers, then by sealing the Eight Afflictions away, we can prevent them from returning to the desert, right?"

Perciville didn't reply.

"Harper? Can we stop it?"

"Maybe..." he said, as light spilled into the corridor and they stepped out into another chamber. "It's our best shot."

The next chamber was a circular vault with polished timber walls, a ring of marble pillars and a stone floor. It was filled with a golden light as if the sun were bursting through a window, yet Fjona couldn't see a single window anywhere on the walls or high ceiling.

It was a surprisingly vast space that echoed with every step Fjona or Perciville took, and it was filled with a musty smell like the pages of an old book.

"Where are we?" Fjona asked as Perciville stepped into the centre of the room, his eyes transfixed to the floor.

When he didn't answer, Fjona joined him to see what he was looking at. It seemed to be an inscription, carved into the central stone slab, but it was written in a language Fjona did not recognise.

"Ancient Elvish," Perciville explained before Fjona could ask. "Which sadly I cannot read except for this here..." He pointed to the largest letters with his staff. "I've seen Yilsommen's name written hundreds of times in this script."

"So this is where the first sage is buried," Fjona said, imagining a soil-covered coffin beneath her feet.

Perciville looked around the chamber. "Not a bad place to spend the rest of eternity."

"It's magnificent." Fjona gazed around at the columns. "But where's the box? There's nowhere else to go and this seems like the safest place to keep it. Perhaps it's been concealed...?"

The sage shook his head. "An academic thought, but incorrect on this occasion. As it happens, we are not quite at our final destination."

Fjona looked around the room again, squinting through the dusty light.

"Then where next?"

"Ah, good question!" Perciville exclaimed. "There should be an entrance to a hidden passageway somewhere in this room. If we can find it, it will lead us to the box."

"Hidden how exactly?"

The sage shrugged. "I've no idea. The best bet is to feel around the chamber for a draft or a hollow part of a wall. Perhaps a fracture through a timber or a cunningly placed lever." When Fjona didn't react, Perciville added briskly, "I'm not pulling your leg here, Miss Sarsen. I've no manipulation that will reveal a hidden door."

With that, the sage stepped to the side of the crypt and proceeded to navigate the walls, tapping occasionally on the timbers with his staff and pressing gently against them with his fingers.

Despite his dismissal of the art of manipulation, Fjona did catch Perciville conjuring gentle streams of wind and rain to see if it might reveal a gap between the wood, but every effort he made was unsuccessful.

Fjona meanwhile inspected the floors in search of a trapdoor. She paced back and forth across the chamber, tapping lightly on each stone slab with the tip of her shoes in the hope of hearing a void beneath the surface, but every inch of the floor was solid.

"So," Fjona asked, trying to keep her voice casual, "what do you intend to do when we finish saving the Arvum?"

She looked over to Perciville, who seemed to be contemplating her question very seriously, with one ear pressed up against the wall.

"I'll probably head south," he said, relieving the wall of his ear then doing the same a pace further along. "Treat myself to a proper and well-deserved chalice of Autumn Elf Old Port. The real stuff – not just my conjuring. Likely spend the night in an unnecessarily ostentatious inn with a mattress the size of this room and have a decent night's sleep. After that, who knows? Maybe I'll return to the Rock of Caeznor and see if I can restore the Sagedom, now that the Tree of Birth has offered a new wand to a new sage. How about yourself? What will you do?"

Fjona was on her knees, tapping at a stone slab with her knuckles. Disappointed, she got back on her feet and carried on across the room.

"I'm heading straight back to Marrow Myre," she replied. "Firstly to see that my father is well." Her face turned pale and her eyes a little distant. "I really hope that he's well. Of course, I'll have to apologise to my mother for disappearing for so long, and Todie and I will have a lot to catch up Evelyn on. Will be nice to sleep in my own bed again and I am salivating already just thinking about my mother's cooking! You know, I think I'm actually looking forward to wearing a dress and sitting down with the villagers for breakfast. Aside from that, I'd like to keep honing the art of manipulation and see what may become of me. I've hardly used my wand since it progressed last and I can feel my strength simmering inside me. I know there's a lot to be sacrificed if I pursue becoming a sage, but I feel that I've come so far already."

"I agree," Perciville said sincerely. "I know you want to be rid of me as soon as possible, and believe me, I'd like my old company back, but if you were to come with me to the Rock of Caeznor, we may be able to restore the Sagedom together." He continued to tap methodically on the timber wall. "I mean, I know we haven't always seen eye to eye and I know I've got under your skin on more than a few occasions, but joining me would undoubtedly be your best hope at becoming a great sage."

"Hmm, that is true..."

"And who knows? Maybe I will become the new sagen master and you could be my marseiha."

Fjona turned her green eyes on Perciville with a look of incomprehension. "Your *marseiha*?"

"Yes, the heiress to the throne, essentially. Basically a princess, but with much more power."

"A princess?" Fjona asked uncertainly. "Fancy dresses and tiaras? I'm not sure that really suits me."

Perciville chuckled. "Don't worry, there is no obligation for a marseiha to wear fancy dresses. All you would have to do is study the art of manipulation, dedicate your life to the Sagedom, and prove yourself as a great sage."

"That's all? Perhaps we should just see how today goes."

Fjona's hands were feeling a little sweaty just thinking about the pressures of becoming the heiress to the Sagedom.

It was then she noticed scrape marks on the stone floor around one of the pillars.

"Hey, Harper, look at this..."

The sage glided over to Fjona and examined the pale white streak that stretched out from beneath the pillar.

"Curious..." He marched around the outer rim, gazing intently at the floor. "They all appear to have them."

Clutching his staff, Perciville stood again on Yilsommen's crypt. As he focused his energy, the tip of his staff burned green, then burst into each of the surrounding pillars like a firework. Slowly, they started to push outwards along the scrape marks, forcing Fjona to leap out of their path. Dust billowed up from the surface and the room filled with the screeching of stone abrasing stone. When the pillars reached the end, Fjona heard a loud clunk and watched as a floor slab, near the wall opposite, dropped down beneath the surface and moved to one side, revealing a staircase.

"Excellent work, Miss Sarsen. Just excellent! Come on!" Perciville exclaimed, practically running down the stairs with excitement before Fjona could even digest what had just happened.

She raced after him, calling his name, down through a cavernous stairwell with the faint figure of the sage disappearing into the depths below.

Ivy clung to the sides of the passageway, brushing Fjona's mess of hair as she descended into the bowels of the crypt.

At the bottom of the stairs, Fjona stepped out, not into another chamber, but into the unexpected tranquillity of a cherry tree grove. Pink blossom floated down from the trees in a gentle, cool breeze and landed in a stream of crystalline water. Here, iridescent fish poked their hopeful mouths above the surface to feed on critters that were carried down on the leaves, and splashed about near the edge of a waterfall that fed into a spring.

An arched wooden bridge with low sides crossed the spring to a small island in the middle. Above, the sky was entirely clear, but for the dazzling warmth of a golden sun.

Surrounding the grove was a dense forest and, when Fjona glanced behind her, she saw the staircase disappearing, not up through a cavernous passageway, but through the thicket of trees.

Perciville was standing at the entrance to the grove, staring intently at what lay in the middle of the island – the box.

It was made of grey stone, long and rectangular like a chest. The side was decorated with runes and letters, and there was no obvious lid. If Fjona didn't know better, she may have thought it was just a plinth or an altar, but in her soul she knew what she was looking at.

"Approach it," Perciville whispered, with a hint of urgency.

Fjona looked to the sage who feigned a smile; then, with a

sense of purpose, she proceeded to step towards the box.

She had barely made two paces when the grove was suddenly plunged into darkness and Fjona felt her stomach lurch. Instinctively she reached for her wand and looked behind her for Perciville, but even if he was there, he was shrouded by the blackness.

When she turned back around, she screamed – the decrepit ghoul from Willow's Brush stood before her. Its black eyes were sunken, its skin was taut around its bones and its sparse hair seemed as thin and grey as the being itself.

Its mouth opened and twisted into a grim, toothless smile. Then it raised its hand and beckoned Fjona with a long, crooked finger.

"What do you want?" Fjona yelled. "What are you?"

There was no reply from the ghoul. Instead, it just waggled its stiff, bony finger and tilted its head on a neck so sinewy and thin it was a wonder it could even hold it up.

"No!" Fjona screamed, pointing her wand at the ghoul, but she was powerless. Her energy seemed to have seeped from her fibres and she harnessed no morsel of strength.

The ghoul started to limp towards her, a frail, stiff arm outstretched. Fjona tried to inch away from it and, although there seemed to be space behind her, there was nowhere to go. The ghoul was edging towards her. Even at its slow, tired pace it came nearer and nearer until, had it any breath, Fjona would surely have felt it on her neck.

Its outstretched arm reached for Fjona's wand and she was too bound to resist. She could feel its weak weight as the ghoul gripped the wand's tip, like catching a fish on a line.

Then the ghoul's hand began to glow with a wild golden-orangey light that trailed into its fingers and leached into the silverwood of Fjona's wand. It continued to spread up through the wand until it was enveloped in radiance from tip to shaft.

When the ghoul let go, the Long Wand began to grow. It became longer, at least by a third, and much thicker, with a rounded knob at its tip, though it remained enveloped in the golden-orangey light. In Fjona's hand, it felt as if it were still composed of wood, yet there was no evidence of it.

She now possessed a staff, or Crook as Perciville had told her once, though it was still enshrouded in the glow delivered from the ghoul.

The darkness surrounding her began to lift; the ghoul simply vanished, and Fjona found herself standing over the box, with just Perciville behind her and the glowing crook in her hand.

"Impossible..." she heard the sage utter behind her, but Fjona was too distracted to reply.

Instinctively she held the crook over the box and summoned her strength. She felt that same familiar sensation of energy charge through her very being and tear down her arm. It burned at her hands and flared into the radiant Crook, from which a powerful, gold light erupted.

When it subsided, so too did the light of the Crook and it reverted back to the silverwood Long Wand of before. At the same time, Fjona watched as a seam of piercing white light appeared around the rim of the box and the lid began to slide off. It was so bright within that Fjona could not see inside and she was forced to avert her eyes.

She turned to face Perciville, but as she did, a shock of manipulation caught her under her ribs and threw her away from the box. Fjona landed beneath a tree in a heap, unable to move and barely able to breathe.

"Thank you, Miss Sarsen," Perciville commended, and not in a good way.

In that moment, a terrifying truth hit Fjona harder than the manipulation, and the harsh reality came crashing down upon her. She wanted to scream, to yell, to curse him and inflict pain on him, but she was completely disabled. He wore a grin of greed and anger, and his eyes were wild with power. It was only now that Fjona saw who the sage really was — it appeared that Todie had been right all along.

Perciville could not be trusted.

As she lay crumpled on the floor, staring up at the ghastly face of Perciville, she felt cold with fear as to what horrors this man was unleashing into the world. Bright, burning light enshrouded the sage as the lid slid away until it landed on the ground with a great thud.

CHAPTER 34

AWAKENING

Oolia had been pacing around her bedchamber all day, feverishly contemplating what to do. The Sultan's threat echoed around her head as clearly as if he were in the room with her.

That, coupled with the increase in earth tremors, was enough to make up the steward's mind. She must follow the example of Lais Stone and flee from the city.

Like there was no time left in the world, Oolia hurried around her chamber collecting what few belongings she may need to travel through the desert, though conscious that, should she be caught carrying a satchel stuffed with clothes by a guard, she might find herself being escorted back to the Sultan with her hands bound behind her back.

Fortunately, Oolia had very little in practical desert wear and her only cherished possession was a necklace given to her by her mother a very long time ago. It was composed of a sizeable ruby pendant, attached to a faded bronze chain. Modest but elegant and, crucially, valuable enough to fetch a few extra coins should she need them.

Besides the necklace, Oolia snatched her dwindling purse, wrapped a shawl around her shoulders and headed for the door.

Time was of the essence. Now was her only chance to slip away while the Sultan was indulging in supper at the rear of the palace.

Despite her nerves and the pounding in her chest, Oolia walked as casually as she could down to the entrance hall and towards the door where two Home Guards had been placed on the inside. She smiled at them as naturally as possible, but before she could pass, they lowered their lances across her, blocking her exit.

"Darazith," Oolia said to the Grugan guard, then turned to the muscular summer elf. "Terin, what is the meaning of this?"

"Sorry, boss," Terin replied, though Oolia didn't feel his apology carried any weight at all.

"You no pass," the Grugan added.

Oolia frowned and attempted to push through them, but the guards held her back with seemingly minimal effort. "Let me through this instant!" she demanded, but the guards were impassive.

Terin shook his head. "I'm afraid we can't permit that."

"What do you mean?" Oolia asked, clearly narked by the guard's unhelpful response. "I am your superior. You answer to me!"

"Higher!" the Grugan growled back, to which Oolia could only offer a look of bemusement. "Higher!" he said again, as if repeating the same word over may give clarity.

"What Darazith is trying to say is that although you are indeed superior to us, we answer to a higher power."

Oolia didn't need to ask to whom they were referring. "The Sultan commanded you to imprison me in the palace?"

"He didn't use the word 'imprison' as such, but yes, he asked us to restrict your movements."

The steward exhaled angrily from her flared nostrils.

"If you don't believe me," Terin continued, "go ask him yourself."

They had waited in a tavern inside the Upper Gate until the sun started to dip. Only when the long shadow of the palace was cast across the Panamayan spring did Lucinda, Feldin and Horse Leg take their leave and head back out into the quiet city.

Since the heightened fear from the earthquakes, fewer and fewer people seemed to mill about in the Upper Gate and only two guards awaited Lucinda at the entrance to the palace.

"The Sultan is not accepting any visitors at this time," one of the blue coats said through a mouth thinner than a piece of parchment.

Lucinda sighed. "It's really quite a shame. Since I've the ability to persuade you to let me through and there is nothing you could do to stop me, I would be able to spare your lives."

The two guards looked at one another anxiously.

"But regrettably, we cannot allow for any loose ends."

Before the guards could react, they were simultaneously caught in the throat by a throwing knife and they tumbled to the floor, blood gushing on their pristine blue coats.

From behind Lucinda, Horse Leg and Feldin emerged to retrieve their knives.

"Nicely done," Lucinda said as Horse Leg cleaned the blade against his tunic.

The doors suddenly swung open revealing two further Home Guards: one a Grugan, the other a summer elf.

"What the—" The summer elf extended his lance forward in one hand, drawing his short sword with the other.

The Grugan did the same and was about to take a swing at Lucinda's head, but Horse Leg reacted quickly. He removed the staff from his back and expelled a shock of chaotic white energy. It forced the two guards and their weapons aside, leaving them defenceless against Feldin's knife. The hooded bandit was upon them in a heartbeat, severing the tendons in their throats and beckoning a shower of blood to pool onto the marble floor.

Then Horse Leg and Feldin stepped inside the palace, gazing around the grand entrance hall for signs of more guards or servants, but the coast was clear.

"Impressive," Lucinda said to Horse Leg as she looked the staff up and down.

"It just came to me," he replied, a little surprised in himself, and strapped it again onto his back.

Feldin paused from dragging away the bodies. "You never mentioned guards on the inside."

"They must be a new addition," Lucinda replied. "I've never seen them there before." She shuddered as the ground began to tremble. "Hide the bodies somewhere, then head down to the well. I'll meet you down there shortly."

"Where are you going?" Feldin asked.

"I need to check something out first. I shan't be long," Lucinda replied as she headed for the stairs.

Oolia was loath to disturb the Sultan, but she was fresh out of options. As far as she knew, no steward had ever been confined to the palace and the Sultan had no right to deny her egress.

She pushed her way past the servants who were lined up outside the chamber, bearing platters of meats, breads and fruits, and threw open the doors.

"About time!" Ayermune said with a huff. "I am quite famished."

"Why have you trapped me in the palace?" Oolia asked directly.

The Sultan looked up from the table. He had been engrossed in a thickly bound book and was evidently surprised to see Oolia, particularly without her usual passive courtesy.

He stared at her with burning eyes of amber.

"How dare you speak to me in such a tone, steward!" he shouted, standing to his feet with a flurry of fine robes.

The days of quietly holding her ground and waiting for the Sultan's temper to cool were long behind Oolia. If execution might be her fate then at least she would go out knowing she'd spoken her mind.

"How dare you imprison me in your palace of corruption!"

The Sultan's jaw tightened and he swept the book off the table in fury. "I shall not be spoken to with such petulance!"

Oolia's heart was hammering against her ribs. "You have no right to restrict my movement."

The Sultan scoffed. "No right? No right! I am the Sultan of Panamaya City! I could trap you in a closet if I so pleased and nobody could stop me."

"Do you expect me to be grateful?" Oolia asked, clenching her fists with frustration. "For taking me on as your steward and *not* locking me up in a closet?"

"I expect you to show me some damned respect!" The Sultan stormed towards Oolia. "Did I not save you from a life of poverty? Have I not invited you into my home and shared with you my wealth, my food, my power? Now you betray me—"

"You betrayed yourself!" Oolia interrupted. "You are corrupt! You have compromised the reign of this city because of your own foolishness."

The Sultan slammed a fist on the table that echoed throughout the chamber. With convenient timing, the ground began to tremor and the Sultan and Oolia were pushed back from one another.

"You are the fool!" the Sultan replied with a dalachite's ferocity. "You have failed to take heed of my warning and now you insult me in my own palace! Tell me, Oolia, has your feeble mind perhaps been inflicted by an illness? Are you afflicted by disease to which you need help and guardianship? If you beg for your life, swear fealty to your sultan, and promise to never step out of place again, then I might just be able to forgive you..."

As the tremor subsided, Oolia looked at the Sultan with eyes of contempt. "I hope you rot in the desert."

"You are extraordinarily beautiful," the doorkeeper remarked, wide-eyed and standing up straight.

Lucinda's crystal eyes sparkled and she feigned embarrassment. "That is most kind of you to say."

"What brings such an exquisite spring elf to the Hall of Succession?" the doorkeeper asked. "You weren't sent by Pallec perchance? It wouldn't be the first time he's sent a lady of companionship to my post on the anniversary of birth."

Lucinda noticed the guard move a hand gently to the clasp on his belt and she quickly discouraged him. "No, no, I'm afraid I know nothing of Pallec and, had I been a lady of companionship, I dare say neither you nor he would be able to afford me."

The doorkeeper dipped his head in embarrassment. "Then why exactly are you here?" he asked.

"I seek the Font of Succession," Lucinda explained, to which the doorkeeper only laughed.

"Ha, you? Forgive my assumption, but you are clearly no sultan or soldier. Your admittance can't simply be awarded."

Lucinda frowned, feeling the heat of humiliation. However, since her initiation into the Covenant of Creation at the hands of her brother's staff, access to anywhere had never been an issue.

She gazed at him intently with her brilliant, mesmerising eyes. "I see no reason that I should not be allowed to pass."

The doorkeeper was transfixed to his post, entangled in the spring elf's persuasive charm. "While I cannot decide who may or may not enter," he said, stepping aside, "I insist that you try."

"Most kind of you," Lucinda replied with a glimmering smile. She reached out for the doorknob and, to the guard's amazement, twisted it open. "Thank you for your hospitality."

Lucinda wasted no time in heading straight to the suspended font in the centre of the chamber above a stone slab, engraved with an inscription.

"*Calis for'un eilech*?" Lucinda questioned aloud. "*Reveal thy face of merit.*"

Not understanding what it meant, she heard the sound of water sloshing around in the font. She looked inside to discover not water but a thick, transparent liquid, swirling around in the stone bowl.

Then a face began to appear from the shimmering depths. Her own face, but not mimicking her reflection.

"What does this mean?" she asked herself. "What—?" She ran back towards the door, swung it open and poked her finger into the doorkeeper's chest. "What is the Font of Succession? What does it show?"

The guard seemed confused. "Why were you so keen to see something without knowing what it means?"

"Just tell me."

"The Font of Succession bears the face of the next heir to the sultan's throne, in the event of his death," the doorkeeper explained. "The chosen successor will rule Panamaya City and the Pentari Desert without dispute or discrepancy from its people. To put it simply, whoever you saw in the font will be the next sultan."

Suddenly the words of the Contact resonated in Lucinda's head. She did indeed have a big decision to make and the prospect of dominion was not something she could willingly refuse.

Without a word, she raced back down the corridor, away from the Hall of Succession, her green dress sweeping the floor as she ran. Lucinda had already made up her mind.

"Get back here now!" came the Sultan's voice, practically shaking the walls of the palace as he chased Oolia through the winding corridors.

The steward knew that her outcome would be bleak, but her instincts told her just to run. Exactly where she was running to, she did not yet know, only that if the Sultan or his guards were to stop her, her fate would echo that of her predecessors.

Up ahead, she caught the flash of a green dress cross the doorway into the entrance hall, but when she got there, there was nobody to be seen. To her delight and immense relief, even Darazith and Terin had disappeared, and the Upper Gate beckoned her.

"I'm going to kill you!" she heard somewhere behind her, but she couldn't waste a moment looking back.

She raced across the marble floor to the great doors, noticing smears of blood on the tiles. She paused for a heartbeat, wondering what had happened here when, as she heaved open the doors, she felt the Sultan's cold hand on her shoulder.

"Death is the least you deserve," the Sultan said, his face a picture of fury. He shoved Oolia with enough force for her to tumble down the solid steps of the palace.

She tried to brace herself as she bounded from step to step, her slender frame bashing against the hard stone, but somehow she managed to protect her head. She landed, bruised and aching, in a heap at the bottom, her body stiff with pain.

The Sultan wasn't finished with her, however. He was

marching down the steps with a look of malice, ready to deliver her final punishment.

Oolia managed to push herself up off the ground with what little might she had left in her and hobbled away towards the spring, but the Sultan had caught up with her before she'd even made it to the bridge.

She turned, helpless, and spoke with as much courage as she could muster. "You can kill me now, but know this, what will become of you will be far more horrifying than you can possibly conceive. *Sil'yhab forlein*. The worst is yet to come."

Then she spat in the Sultan's face, antagonising him further. With little effort and no hint of remorse, he tried to throttle her, then dragged her to her knees and pushed her head beneath the surface of the spring.

Lucinda scurried down the spiralling staircase, deep below the palace. It was illuminated by green flames that flickered in their sconces along the wall, all the way down to a small chamber in the crust of the mountain. Here, Lucinda found an arched door that was wide open, with Feldin's key dangling in the lock.

She ran inside to another chamber, this one containing a well surrounded by a ring of pillars, where Feldin and Horse Leg stood either side in heated conversation.

"We must wait," Feldin insisted.

Horse Leg, on the opposite side, held the staff above the well. "The Contact told me what must be done when I first met him."

"Maybe so, but we should wait for Lucinda."

"Wait!" Lucinda called from the doorway. "We should not do this."

Feldin turned and croaked in a confused tone, "But this is

our calling, mistress. We have worked tirelessly to get here and we must not fall at the final hurdle."

Lucinda reached his side. "That was before I discovered that I am destined to be the next sultan."

Her eyes were wide with greed.

Feldin's cloaked head tilted to one side, utterly shocked by the news, but Horse Leg was unmoved.

"How is that even possible?" Feldin asked. "You are no summer elf. You have hardly even spent time in the city, let alone with the Sultan and his elites."

"I cannot say how, but it is true. I saw the Font of Succession myself and it revealed me to be the heir. If we are to wake the Sleeping Giant, we risk destroying the city, but if we walk away now, we can rule the desert ourselves and bring about real change."

Feldin was pensive for a moment. After a short while, he replied, "I shall do your will."

However, when Lucinda faced Horse Leg, his arm remained outstretched over the well, clutching the staff in his hand.

"Horse Leg? Lower the staff," Lucinda instructed, but the bandit just shook his head.

"I cannot do that. I must do right by the bigger picture."

Lucinda flashed her deep blue eyes at him. "We are the bigger picture. Please lower—"

Before she could finish her sentence, Horse Leg summoned an eruption of chaotic white light and dropped the staff into the well.

"No!" Lucinda cried, leaning over the edge to see an explosion of white, bursting up along the walls. Brilliant, horrifying whiteness. "You fool! We could have been so much more!"

Horse Leg was still unmoved. "No, Lady Denvillier, we could not."

The ground started to quake more violently than ever before

and rubble crumbled down from the ceilings. Deep in the well, animalistic cries spewed out and echoed around the collapsing chamber.

"Kill him," Lucinda demanded of Feldin, knife already brandished as stone and earth rained down from above and the scraping of claws crept up from the well below.

Horse Leg didn't allow Feldin the chance to attack. He stabbed Feldin in the arm with his own knife, pushed him aside, then ran for the door as the room filled with debris.

"Forgive me, Lady Denvillier," he said, slamming the door.

Even above the sound of falling rubble, Lucinda could hear the unmistakable clunk of the key twisting in the lock, as a scaly, clawed hand emerged from the well.

The Sleeping Giant was awake.

Oolia tried to scream, but her mouth immediately filled with water. Her legs kicked out frantically, but she could feel the Sultan pinning them down with ease as her strength drifted away from her.

Gently, her thoughts clouded before her and Oolia's body started to give up, too starved of oxygen to fight on. Death was a welcome prospect at her door.

As her stinging eyes stared down into the depths of the spring, she could a see a hand reaching up for her. Perhaps the Sleeping Giant really had awoken and was breaking through the crust of the mountain to bring destruction to the Arvum, or perhaps it was just here to take Oolia to the next life.

Whatever the case, Oolia didn't mind so long as it meant she was away from the captivity of the Sultan and his blood hound, Lahsilli.

The hand in the spring approached Oolia and was attached to a surprisingly muscular arm. Her vision must have been going blurry because there seemed to be several more hands breaking through the bed of the spring, all with long, sharp claws and thick, dense arms.

It amazed Oolia, even in that moment, how the reality of something other than a giant emerging from the mountain could be more terrifying. Yet when she saw the horned heads and sharp teeth of what she could only presume were demons, she was petrified all over again. Could it be that the scholar's book about the monsters beneath the mountain was true? Their hunger for flesh, their desire to kill.

Raithers.

Terror feeding her strength, she began to flail again as the raithers pushed past her and broke the surface of the water.

Suddenly, the weight of the Sultan lifted and she pushed herself up, gasping for air as she did.

When she came back onto land, she saw three of the enormous monsters tearing through the Sultan's flesh in a flurry of guts, chewing on his bones and ripping him apart.

There wasn't much meat on Oolia, at least not compared to the Sultan, but she knew she had to get away before they were finished.

Around her, the Upper Gate was crumbling as dozens upon dozens of raithers burst out of the mountain. Buildings were collapsing at an incredible rate, including the palace. Its columns had fallen into its golden dome and it was disintegrating into nothing, right before her eyes.

Instinct taking control of her, Oolia ran. She ran where the vibrations of the mountain pushed her. She ran where falling rubble didn't crush her, and she ran clear of emerging raithers as their screams drowned out the screams of their victims.

Never before had Oolia imagined chaos like this. An entire city and the rock on which it stood, collapsing into dust.

Smoke billowed into the air from across the Upper Gate as fires broke out and spread during its destruction, and Oolia's visibility became increasingly limited. She was desperate to escape to the Lower Gate and make her way down the mountain, but in all the confusion, she had no notion of where she was or whether the Lower Gate even still existed.

Eventually, she found herself sneaking past two raithers who were occupied picking the bones from a once portly elf. She raced along an alleyway behind them, feeling the ground beneath her sinking away into nothing as she stumbled through the gate into the surprisingly untouched, pruned and vibrant garden of the Archivus. Barely a moment later, the ground surrounding the square of the Archivus and its courtyard walls slumped away into a dusty, smoking heap, a long way below.

Oolia looked down at the rubble to see thousands of raithers spreading out through the debris, many heading towards what remained of the camp, the rest filtering out in all directions across the remnants of the city.

Although it was something of a relief to not be down on the surface to be preyed upon by this army of horrifying horned beasts, Oolia was aware that her release from captivity had been brief and she was trapped yet again, this time on a tower of rock, high above the desert.

The Sleeping Giant really was awake. Oolia just hadn't realised how many there would be.

EPILOGUE

The silvery light blinded and embraced her and, when it faded and Marseiha opened her eyes, she was no longer in the cabin. Instead, she was outside and could feel a softening, cool breeze kissing her forehead. She appeared to be lying down in some sort of stone casket, her wasted arms crossed over her bony chest, her hands clutching the ebony wood of her staff. She was no longer wearing the sand-coloured doublet and trousers, but instead a plain, though elegant, white dress.

As her eyes adjusted to the bright, cloudless sky above her, she became aware of a figure standing nearby.

Then a face loomed before her. A familiar face, yet it filled her with an icy dread. She remembered his name.

"Hello, Santhé," Perciville said, a hungry smile curling at his lips.

Then the sky went black and the ground began to shake.

Santhé, Marseiha of Caeznor, screamed, and not in a good way.

Acknowledgements

As before, it would be remiss of me to not offer my sincere appreciation to everyone who has helped shape the pages of this book.

To Niamh Batsman, forever inspiring me to keep writing and temper my craft.

To Lucas Abbott, who somehow found the time to read and critique an early draft of my manuscript. Thank you for the sage advice.

To Victoria Richards and the editing team at Cranthorpe Millner, without whom this book would live only as an unedited PDF on my laptop.

To Shannon Chapman, who can take the ramblings of a madman and manipulate them into beautiful cover art.

To Becca Stevenson, who brought the Sarsen Series to the world stage through the powers of marketing.

To Jenna Richards, for breathing more life into the ever-expanding maps of the Arvum.

The best is yet to come.

Simon

www.ingramcontent.com/pod-product-compliance
Ingram Content Group UK Ltd.
Pitfield, Milton Keynes, MK11 3LW, UK
UKHW030749190325
456461UK00002B/155

9 781803 782713